PENGUIN BOOKS

SENSING OTHER...

'Wicked humour . . . it is hard n...   ...thralled ... dark tale' *The Times*

'A darkly arresting debut from a gifted writer who approaches literature with the precision and coolness of a scientist . . . very readable' *Daily Telegraph*

'Frank Tallis's debut novel is distinguished by its author's sheer intelligence . . . Good reading' *Time Out*

'A very tight, thrillerish plot which unravels with the smooth elegance of film noir' *The Times*

'A funny and original novel' Robert Newman

'Like Ian McEwan rewritten by Robert Harris. Very unusual and entertaining' Toby Litt

'So bright you need sunglasses to read it' *Extracts*

ABOUT THE AUTHOR

Frank Tallis is a practising clinical psychologist and writer of fiction and non-fiction. He received an Arts Council Writers' Award in 1999 and won the New London Writers' Award in 2000. His first novel, *Killing Time*, is also published by Penguin, and his most recent work of non-fiction is *Hidden Minds: A History of the Unconscious*.

frank tallis
sensing others

PENGUIN BOOKS

PENGUIN BOOKS

Published by the Penguin Group
Penguin Books Ltd, 80 Strand, London WC2R 0RL, England
Penguin Putnam Inc., 375 Hudson Street, New York, New York 10014, USA
Penguin Books Australia Ltd, Ringwood, Victoria, Australia
Penguin Books Canada Ltd, 10 Alcorn Avenue, Toronto, Ontario, Canada M4V 3B2
Penguin Books India (P) Ltd, 11 Community Centre, Panchsheel Park,
New Delhi – 110 017, India
Penguin Books (NZ) Ltd, Cnr Rosedale and Airborne Roads,
Albany, Auckland, New Zealand
Penguin Books (South Africa) (Pty) Ltd, 24 Sturdee Avenue,
Rosebank 2196, South Africa

Penguin Books Ltd, Registered Offices: 80 Strand, London WC2R 0RL, England

www.penguin.com

First published by Hamish Hamilton 2000
Published in Penguin Books 2001
1

Set in Monotype Sabon
Printed in England by Clays Ltd, St Ives plc

'I feel more and more every day, as my imagination strengthens, that I do not live in this world alone but in a thousand worlds.'

— **John Keats,** from a letter to George and Georgiana Keats, completed on the poet's twenty-third birthday

contents

blue 1

It's difficult to get to sleep without a joint. I'm not allowed to do dope any more – not while I'm on the drug trial – and there's no point in trying to get away with it. The blood tests are every six to eight weeks and, just in case, all participants have been asked to sign a consent form agreeing to a random hair test. I can understand why all this is necessary. Dr McDougall explained very patiently how *concurrent substance abuse* might mess up the results. At that time I felt confident that dropping THC from my diet wouldn't be that big a deal; but it's turned out to be harder than I thought. I know it's not supposed to be addictive. I know it's a (so-called) soft drug. But if you give it up and you find that you're still missing it badly after three months then, shit, you must be addicted! I don't care what liberal-minded scientists and doctors have to say, my body clearly disagrees.

I find it so hard to sleep without a smoke. It doesn't matter how tired I am. When my head hits the pillow I'm wide awake – like a speeding epileptic. I jerk and convulse my way through the night while my nerves pop and snap. I've always been like this, even as a child. Subsequently, for me, sleep has acquired a kind of fabled poetic grandeur.

When I was about thirteen my mother played me Benjamin Britten's 'Serenade for Tenor, Horn and Strings'. Opus 31. I can still remember the number. I didn't like it very much and I thought that Peter Pears' wavering tenor (which so many people describe

1

as sweet), sounded as though he had employed some obscure form of genital torture to help him reach the high notes. Anyway, although I was singularly unimpressed by Britten and Pears, I was very impressed by John Keats, whose 'Sonnet to Sleep' is the final setting in the 'Serenade'. I read and re-read the poem, which had been reproduced in the CD booklet. Oh, how I wanted Keats' *soft embalmer* to visit me and *seal the hushed casket of my Soul*. A few years later, when I discovered THC, it seemed that my prayers had been answered.

Ever since childhood getting into bed has always jump-started my brain. I would find myself either going over the day's events or simply asking myself questions (many of which had no answers); however, all this mental activity would usually be channelled toward a single end-point, like water eddying down the slope of a funnel. Most nights I would finally revisit the same self-imposed challenge. I would attempt to identify the exact moment at which consciousness is exchanged for sleep. To do this is more or less equivalent to dropping whiz with your cocoa. You end up rapt, vigilant, watching your own mind, waiting for it to make a move, and, of course, it never does. It kind of stares you out.

I am not an insomniac. I simply became one through a combination of stupidity and self-indulgence.

Dope was a godsend. The *soft embalmer* closed my eyes like an undertaker, quietly turned the key and tiptoed out of the bedroom.

And now, of course, I can't fucking have any!

Since giving up dope I've explored a number of alternatives. Ovaltine does have a modest effect; however, drinking Ovaltine just doesn't go with the kind of rock 'n' roll jib I'm trying to cut. Camomile tea is a slightly more credible beverage but, frankly, it doesn't do a thing. Ambient sound is plain irritating and, as for whale-song, it gives me the fucking creeps. The exception is that tried and tested friend of all insomniacs, masturbation. On the whole *the big M* has a very good track record as far as I'm concerned; however, even for someone of my relatively tender years, masturbation can't be employed each and every evening.

Overindulgence does carry a subsequent performance penalty so I've got mixed feelings about love-handle sedation.

Recently, I've found Joni Mitchell helpful. Particularly the *Blue* album. She is a genius and I guess I should show her more respect. I mean, it's a peculiar compliment. You wouldn't find some art critic raving about Picasso on account of being laid out all afternoon by *Guernica*, would you? Yet it's true. I turn the lights off and hear that wonderful, mournful voice, making a description of a torn stocking sound like the most meaningful event in human history, and I seem to lose my fix on reality. As I listen to her climb, hover and swoop through a melody, I am melted by her intelligence and humanity. My brain becomes a sticky gloop that runs out of my ears and drips through the floorboards.

Sometimes, when I'm listening to Joni, I wonder what it would be like to have a relationship with her; however, before my fantasy gets very far, I have to remind myself that I was born several years after the *Blue* album was released so she must be getting on a bit now. In fact, Joni must be older than Cairo (and Cairo must surely define the upper limit) – the wrinkle barrier. If I go through that then I'll become the opposite of a paedophile. A Zimmerphile or something.

That night, I was quite late going to bed. Although I was feeling tired, my mind – as usual – began to race as soon as I closed my eyes. I seem to recall working my cock in a half-hearted way for a while but then giving up due to lack of interest. It had been a pretty boring day, and I was in a peculiar, listless mood. I couldn't even be bothered to come. I needed Joni's help. And I needed it badly.

I let my finger bounce down my stack of CDs and paused for a moment over *The Hissing of Summer Lawns*; however, the prospect of listening to 'Shades of Scarlet Conquering' wasn't quite enough to stop me from dropping three more trays to the *Blue* album. Once again, I was waiting for Joni to work her magic on me and, once again, she did. I don't think I was around for 'This Flight Tonight'. Her sorrowful wail had charmed me into a deep, peaceful sleep.

I opened my eyes and stared into the darkness. At first I had no idea why I was frightened. Then my brain started to work. I had the ghost of a sound in my mind. There had been a noise. I was sure of it. I had been woken up by a noise. Listening very hard, it was impossible to catch very much over the thumping of my heart and my violent, irregular breathing. I shut my mouth and placed a hand on my chest, a curiously feminine gesture, but the thumping couldn't be muffled. Outside, in the distance, a passing train clattered into the night. I looked at my digital alarm. It was ten minutes past three.

The noise of the train slowly subsided and again I strained my sense of hearing, tried to pick up something beyond the wild clamour of my heart and lungs, but there was nothing – or, at least, nothing detectable.

Even so, I knew that someone was in the flat. I just knew it. I swallowed, but my mouth was dry. For a moment I thought I was going to choke and cough. I sucked saliva from the inside of my cheeks and used it to help me swallow, once. It tasted like metal.

Perhaps I had been mistaken? I tried to calm myself down. Maybe there had been a noise outside. I had been disturbed by a cat or something. Surely that was more likely. But it didn't work. I remained unconvinced and horribly uneasy.

I shifted a little and raised my head. Then I heard it. A drawer, being slowly opened in the kitchen. All that I could think was *Oh fuck, Oh Jesus-fuck*. The drawer closed again, and whoever it was out there began filling the kettle with water. As I listened to the click made by depressing the kettle switch I couldn't help asking myself what kind of thief would stop to make a cup of tea? If he was after my stereo, why the fuck was he making tea?

What was I to do?

I couldn't think. I just lay there, trembling, and listening.

I don't know how long I remained in that state, paralysed by fear, but all of a sudden, I experienced the kind of juddering impact that sometimes shakes the mind as it crashes, unprepared, out of a bad trip, and at once I knew what to do. I silently told myself to open the bedroom door, run down the hallway and get out of the flat as quickly as possible. I added as an afterthought: *Don't try to fight him, just get out and run.*

In the kitchen the kettle came to the boil. I could hear someone opening a cupboard and the delicate chink of one mug colliding with another.

As I eased myself up into a sitting position, it occurred to me that I was totally naked. Totally exposed. Very quietly I would have to attempt getting dressed. It seemed implausible that I would be able to get past him without some protection, however rudimentary.

I gently pushed the duvet aside and started to roll off the bed. The mattress began to creak and I had to stop. I moved again, really slowly but, even then, the springs continued to announce and accompany every shift of position. *Jesus!* I felt so vulnerable.

Eventually my slow-motion turn was complete and I dropped to the floor – like a sack of gunshot. A heavy thud, followed by the snapping of knee joints. The rummaging outside stopped immediately. *Silence.* And then, footsteps, coming slowly toward the door. I took a deep breath and held the stale air in my aching, expanded lungs.

As the intruder approached, he kicked something by mistake, and I heard a distinct '*Shit!*' I crawled around on all fours, reaching out blindly for my underpants. They were nowhere to be found. The footsteps stopped. He was going to come in. My sense of his intention was overwhelming, and my terror ascended like a siren. It rose to a peak of almost unbearable intensity and took me to the very brink of screaming out loud.

The door handle began slowly to turn. I couldn't see it, but I could hear the handle rattling. My survival instinct suddenly engaged: I would have to jump him. I'm not sure that I was actually thinking this at the time. Not like you would think about switching the radio or the TV on, it was much more basic than that. I was thinking with my muscles and sinews, my body just seemed to take over. I adopted a crouching position, ready to leap. I had become the puppet of visceral, primitive instincts, and all the time my heart was pounding in my chest, a great leathery wing striking against the inside of my ribcage. As the door opened, a rectangle of orange-grey light appeared on the wall. A tall, shadowy figure was framed in the doorway. He stood absolutely still, like a reptile or a predatory insect. I continued to hold my breath and, as I did so, I had to remind myself that it was only me who could hear the winged creature thrashing around in my chest. Before his eyes had adapted to the deeper darkness of my bedroom I jumped up and threw myself at him.

It's difficult to describe what happened next. His reactions were so quick. Instead of making contact with flesh and blood I seemed to take off and float through the air. An instant later I found myself face down on the floor. A hand was clasped tightly over my mouth, one of my arms was trapped under my body and the other twisted half-way up my back. Two strong thighs were locked around my legs. The intruder held me perfectly still. I could just about breathe.

I tried to struggle, but it was hopeless. I let my body go limp and waited for his thumb and forefinger to close my nostrils and deprive me of air.

'Easy,' he said, and slowly uncovered my mouth. 'Easy now. It's only me, man.'

I recognized his voice immediately. 'Eric!' I let my head fall forward. My forehead came to rest on the carpet, and I felt the synthetic fibres tickle my lips as I asked, 'What the fuck are you doing?'

'What the fuck am I doing? That's beautiful, that is. What the fuck *are you* doing? Jumping around starkers at three in the morning?'

Eric stood up. My body was released from his machine-like grip and I rolled over in a curious mental state, a mixture of incomprehension and relief. I sighed and gazed up at the wiry, bedraggled-looking figure towering over me. Even in the half-light the deep creases of his well-worn face were clearly visible.

'Eric! What the . . .' I was speechless. I opened my mouth again,

6

raised my hand, but could find neither the words nor the gestures to express what I was feeling.

'You look really pissed off. Don't be like that. Stay cool, eh?'

'*Cool!*' I had shouted the word without realizing it.

Eric took a step back and shook his head. 'Yeah, cool. Do you want a cup of tea? The kettle's just boiled.' He shuffled off into the kitchen and turned the light on.

'I'm just going to get dressed,' I said in a tight, strained voice. It didn't sound like my own.

'Good idea,' he said, before opening a cupboard and reaching in for a box of tea bags. He only interrupted his tea-making to say, 'Look at the state of your tackle. That's only supposed to happen when you skinny-dip.'

I shook my head from side to side. 'You scared the living shit out of me! What's that supposed to do? Give me a fucking hard-on?'

'Only joking, Nick.'

I got up and stomped back into the bedroom to retrieve my underpants and a T-shirt. I found both articles hanging over the back of a chair looking sorry and threadbare. As I stepped into my underpants my toe got caught and I heard the material tear, but when I pulled them up there were no obvious signs of damage.

Eric called out, 'Have you got any real sugar or have you only got this processed shit?'

I quickly stuck my head around the door and hissed. He turned around.

'What?'

'Not so loud!'

'Why not?'

'Because of the neighbours!'

'Oh yeah.'

I sat down on my bed, closed my eyes and tried to relax. My hands were shaking, but at least my heart was beginning to slow down. Gradually, I managed to compose myself. I opened my eyes when Eric came in with the tea.

'There you go, Nick, old son.'

I took the mug and held it in both hands like a vagrant at a soup-kitchen. Eric sat on the floor, his back against the far wall.

'How did you get in?' I asked.

'Through the front door.'

'Oh fuck, you haven't broken it, have you?'

'No, of course not.'

'Then how did you get in?'

'With these . . .' He produced a curious-looking piece of metal with holes cut into it and a length of fine chain with a hook on the end. As he swung the chain like a pendulum he added, 'It was piece of piss, getting in here. You know, you should be more security-conscious. This isn't a safe area. I mean, there isn't much point in having a door like that. You might as well leave it open.'

'Thanks for the advice,' I replied.

Eric fiddled around inside his donkey jacket and produced the mandatory green Rizlas and a plastic film container. He detached the lid from the small black cylinder and tipped a rather manky piece of orange peel on to the floor.

'Got any oranges? My skin's dry.'

'No, I don't buy fruit.'

'Shame. You should buy fruit, Nick. Where are you going to get your vitamins from if you don't eat fruit, eh?'

Eric tipped some dope out of the film case on to his palm and began to lick and stick his Rizlas together in a vast mosaic that I knew would very soon be rolled into a prodigious joint. He had shown me how to do it several times, but I could never remember exactly how it was done. The skill was pitched somewhere between patchwork quilting and origami.

'Why did you break in, Eric?'

'I didn't want to wake you up. I thought I was being considerate.'

'You should have knocked.'

'Yeah, I suppose so. But I was so quiet . . .' There was a genuine note of perplexity in his voice. 'You know, I'm in and out of people's places all the time and most of them don't even know I've been. You must be a light sleeper, Nick.'

'I am. Very light.'

Eric nodded, 'Must be.'

For a moment, I considered how, on waking, I had been certain that someone was in the flat. I'd assumed that a noise had awakened me, but now I wasn't so sure. Maybe I had *sensed* him. Maybe his mere presence had been enough to disturb my sleep. I had been taking Naloxyl for three months, quite a long time . . .

'Come on, wake up!'

I suddenly realized Eric had been saying something. I looked at him.

'I said, are you pleased to see me?'

'Sure I am.'

'Good. I was beginning to wonder. So, how've you been?'

'All right.'

Eric was breaking up a herbal cigarette taken from a green packet that seemed to be made of blotting paper. I noticed the brand name – 'Contemplation' – printed in smudged, dark ink on the side.

'Seen much of Cairo, have you?' he asked.

'Yeah. You know . . .' He cut in before I could say *how it is*.

'Yeah, I know.'

The odd understanding that we shared required no further use of language. We both did the *man thing* of letting our lower jaws jut out while we nodded in silence. Women always bang on about how men don't talk, but we do – we do so by carefully punctuating silence (with a subtle repertoire of coded gestures and body movements).

We retracted our jaws, releasing the suspended moment, and allowed time to flow on.

Eric closed his eyes and recited the words of his pre-joint ritual. I could see his lips moving but could hear only a soft, sibilant whisper. The rite barely lasted a few seconds, but in those few seconds the room was transformed. I was in the presence of a holy man, an urban-ascetic. His tangled, grizzled beard and sunken eyes gave him the appearance of a yogi; but a yogi whose natural habitat might be the desolate wastelands of the inner city, and

whose cave might be made from the debris of motor collisions.
A spray-can brahmin.

He opened his eyes and lit what now looked like a king-sized
tampon with a pocket lighter that had the soul of a blowtorch.
He inhaled deeply, held it for a few moments and then released
two jets of smoke from his nostrils. His face, always only loosely
attached to his skull at the best of times, seemed to slacken further
and, for one perilous moment, seemed poised to slide down his
chest (*en route* to the floor). 'Oh, man,' he said, 'that *is*
good.'

He waved the joint at me, 'Djamba, my son?'

I reached over, and took the conical masterpiece from between
his fingers. 'Thanks, Eric.'

I inhaled and let that first, magical pollution of the bloodstream
cut the cords in every muscle of my body. It was good stuff. Gold,
I supposed. Sliced from some moist, scented brick, fresh from the
Lebanon. But then, Eric would only carry good stuff. It was his
altar bread, his sacrament. 'So, Eric,' I said, aware that I might be
prematurely raising a subject of reality with him, 'what brings
you to the leafy groves of Kilburn?'

'No, man' – he shook his head and waved a languid arm in the
air – 'let's chill out a bit, eh? I can tell you all that later. I've had
a long day.'

'Oh? Is that right?' I said, hoping to prompt an explanation,
however brief and inconsequential. But there was no point. Eric
needed to chill – and when Eric needed to chill, he really *needed*
to chill.

'Got any sounds?'

'Neighbours, Eric.'

'Oh yeah . . .'

And that was that. We sat, smoking, while Eric relaxed. I had
intended to continue our conversation again after the joint, but
somehow the conversation never got going again. It would have
needed leads and a very big battery to revive it. I can remember
thinking to myself: *Wasn't there something about cannabis you're
supposed to remember? Oh, that's it. You're not supposed to be*

smoking any. It was then that I must have lost consciousness. It was as effortless as breathing and as gentle as a kiss. Keats would have been proud of me.

2
the turtle tree

I awoke from a disturbing dream. I was walking down a hallway, a long, dim hallway in a house I didn't recognize. The floorboards were bare and the walls dirty. Large chunks of plaster had fallen from the ceiling, and rubble was strewn everywhere. I sensed that I was in a vast building, one that had been derelict for many, many years – perhaps even centuries. I stepped over a door that had fallen away from its hinges and into a room the far wall of which had completely collapsed. It was night, and the desolate landscape beyond was lit by a full moon; however, it was the wrong colour. Not white and silver but red. Although it shone with only a miserly light, this was just enough to show – across a blasted plain – a ruined city. One of the buildings looked a bit like the Millennium Dome, except fragments were missing, and it was cracked and dented like a broken eggshell. Next to it was what looked like the Canary Wharf tower but with a bite-shaped chunk taken out of the side. At the top a white light was flashing, irregularly.

I looked up at the moon again and couldn't see *the man's* face. It was featureless. And as I stared at it, I began to feel a weak heat on my face, like when you hold your hand a few inches away from your cheek. Then I realized it wasn't the moon at all but the sun. It wasn't night, it was day. And I can remember thinking: *Shit, it's daytime, what's wrong with the sun?*

Then, quite suddenly, the floor beneath me gave way. The boards weren't strong enough to support my weight, and I fell right through. It was like dropping through a trapdoor. I found myself lying on my bed, breathing heavily. 'What a weird dream,' I said to myself. Then, to my great horror, the floor gave way again, and the entire bed descended into a pit of darkness below.

I opened my eyes. I was looking up at the ceiling, although this time I was also aware of the damp bedsheets gripped tightly in my fists. For a short while I couldn't tell whether I was genuinely awake or simply dreaming I was awake. I released the sheets and swallowed. I then rocked from side to side to test how solid my reality was. It seemed fairly secure, and I sighed with relief.

My head felt full of glue. I could hear a curious rattling sound, like someone practising 'rolls' on a snare drum. Each roll decelerated and was separated by a few seconds' silence. In that curious state between being not quite asleep and not quite awake, I can remember wondering who it was that had brought a kit into my bedroom, but as I listened I was quickly able to identify the sound as a snore.

Eric!

Lying there, I tried to sense him. But the lines were dead; he was really out of it.

I sat up and let the mucus in my head redistribute itself along the vessels behind my nose and eyes. I could feel it reluctantly shifting through my clogged tubes, causing a band of pain to tighten around my forehead. A sound, not too dissimilar to cracking ice, seemed to emanate from inside my skull. Sharing a joint with Eric had been a bad idea, especially after such a lengthy period of abstinence.

As I rubbed the sleep from my eyes, Eric's body materialized at the end of the bed. He was still fully dressed and was exuding a slightly unpleasant sweaty smell. For a second I felt nauseous.

I got up, emptied my bladder but didn't pull the chain. I then made my way to the kitchen. I had left my wristwatch next to the kettle, and it did not surprise me to find that the time was 2 p.m. A very strong coffee made a promising start on the job of clearing my head. It tasted fantastic even though it was instant.

13

In the front room the answer-machine was blinking. I was reminded of the light on top of Canary Wharf in my dream. I dismissed the image and the bad feeling that came with it. The machine continued to blink. I had no recollection of being disturbed by the call tone. I must have slept through it. Reaching forward, I turned the volume down and hit the Play button.

'Err . . . Nick? You there?'

It was Andy. He always starts his messages like this. I tend to screen calls and pick up the telephone only if I know who it is. This has happened so many times now people who know me well have got into the habit of asking, *Are you there?* before leaving a message. I screen calls to avoid speaking to my mother. I have to be feeling quite good about myself to cope with a call from Mum.

After a longish pause Andy went on. 'No. Not there? OK. Listen. I've got some news. Scott and Phil ran into some producer last Friday. Anyway, they sent him the Watford demo and he's interested. Give us a call, yeah?'

At first I didn't take it in properly and wondered whether I had heard the message correctly. I hit Play again and concentrated hard. The tape rewound and Andy's voice crackled out of the box. Yes, *I had* heard it correctly the first time. Fuck! A producer? Interested? I felt a rush of excitement and my heart began to beat faster.

I punched in Andy's number. His phone rang for a long time. Finally, somebody bothered to pick it up.

'Hello. The Mitre.' Although Mr Cash (formerly Kaaszch) had been in England since the 1950s, he hadn't quite lost his East European burr.

'Oh hello, Mr Cash, it's Nick. Is Andy around?'

'Nicky, Nicky, how are you?'

'Fine thanks, and you?'

'So-so, you know? My leg is playing up a little, but there we are. Nicky, the boy isn't here. Out again.'

'Oh, will you tell him I called?'

'Of course.'

I doubted very much that Andy would receive my message, so I tried Scott and Phil; no reply.

After my second cup of coffee I munched through three bowls of Sugar Puffs and then prepared breakfast for Eric. He was already awake and appeared to be just lying on the floor, looking at the ceiling.

'Nick. All right?'

'Yeah, I've got you some Sugar Puffs.'

'Oh, cheers.' Eric sat up and took the tray on his lap. Before eating he closed his eyes for a moment and did some weird shit with his hands.

'I think I've just had some good news, Eric.'

'Oh yeah?'

'Andy left a message on the answerphone.'

Eric looked up and said, 'Who?'

'Andy. You know, the bassist? Apparently Phil and Scott have found a producer who's interested in our last demo.'

'Yeah? Who is he?'

'I don't know yet. I've tried calling back but everybody's out.'

Eric nodded. 'You'll have to play me some of the new stuff.'

'Oh, I will. I think you'll like it.'

After Eric had consumed his Sugar Puffs he went to the toilet. I pulled the curtains apart, but only a tired grey light filtered through the dirty, grime-smeared window. I looked around my bedroom and sighed; it was looking particularly wasted. I put the kettle on again and waited in the front room. Eric eventually reappeared and collapsed into his habitual half lotus on the floor. He offered me one of his herbal cigarettes, but I declined. 'No thanks, I'll have a Benson.'

I figured it was time to find out why Eric was paying me a visit. I hadn't seen him for about five months and I thought I deserved at least some explanation.

'Eric?'

'Yeah.'

'What are you doing here?'

'What do you think?'

15

'GLF work?'

'Of course.'

'I kind of figured that. But what GLF work?'

He didn't answer. He just sat, smoking and fiddling with his beard. Eventually he replied, 'Look I'm not being funny or anything, but it's probably best if I don't say. It's a sensitive job this one.'

'Who do you think I'm going to tell?'

'Nobody, I realize that.'

'Then why can't you say?'

'Policy. That's all. It's nothing personal, Nick, old son. I just can't say.'

Eric, was always on some kind of mission or other; however, he was generally quite open about the nature of his GLF activities. The Gaia Liberation Front (formerly Free Earth) was a small cadre of militant 'greens' – although to call them militant is something of an understatement. They were not only disapproved of by the establishment but also by Greenpeace, Friends of the Earth and just about everyone except the most deranged eco-freaks. Nevertheless, for those whose New Age philosophy had taken them to the edge of mental illness, the GLF were folk heroes, and Eric Wright was their big enchilada. Their very own Che Guevara.

'Now the thing is, Nick,' he went on, 'this business might take a bit of time, yeah?'

'So?'

'So I was hoping you would be able to put me up?'

'For how long?'

'Until we do the business.'

'Yeah, but how long is that going to take?'

He thought for a few moments before replying, 'Not longer than a month.'

'A month!'

'Well, maybe. But then again. Maybe not. I could be off by next week for all I know.'

'Eric, it isn't that easy at the moment. I'm still having a lot of problems with my landlord. I think he's trying to get me out. He keeps on dropping in unexpectedly, looking for problems. Looking for things he can make something of. You know?'

'Yeah, but I'll hardly be here, Nick.'

I could see that Eric had little if any sympathy for my supposed predicament. My excuse was half-baked and he knew it, and I simply couldn't be bothered to expend the energy required to invent a really good excuse.

'All right. Let's say a couple of weeks, and we'll review the situation then. OK?' As I said these words I knew that I would very probably live to regret them.

'Oh, you're a fucking star, Nick.'

'Thanks,' I replied.

The phone suddenly started ringing, and I jumped.

'Easy,' said Eric, stubbing his cigarette out.

I got up and lifted the receiver. 'Hello?'

'Nick, it's Andy.'

'You got my message?'

'Yeah.'

'So what's happening?'

'There's a producer who's interested.'

'Yeah?'

'A Swedish bloke. Wants us to meet him down his office. Somewhere in Notting Hill.'

'Amazing.'

'Yeah. He thought the demo was really good. Sounds like he's serious.'

'Who is he?'

'I don't know. Phil just said he was a producer. He had money in ABBA once.'

'ABBA?'

'You know ABBA.'

'Of course I do, but . . .'

'What?'

'Well, what's he done since then? That was twenty-five years ago.'

'I don't know.' There was a rather uncomfortable pause before

Andy continued, 'Look, don't go all moody. It's a break for fuck's sake.'

'Sorry, Andy. It sounds all right, really. I got a bit stoned last night, that's all.'

'I thought you'd given up.'

'I forgot.'

'What?'

'That I'd given up. Eric broke into my flat in the middle of the night.'

'What, Turtle Tree Eric?'

'Yeah. So, I was kind of disorientated.'

'Jesus.'

I suspected that Andy was picturing Eric, flying through the window, wielding a machete, having finally lost his famously weak purchase on reality. 'No, it's not like that. He just thought he'd break in so as not to wake me up.'

'I don't quite follow that.'

'Well, that's Eric, isn't it?' I looked over at the man himself, who seemed to be only vaguely aware that I was talking about him. He had produced a grubby-looking paperback, which he was casually flicking through. I bent down to read the title, which was *New Developments in Fertilizer Research*.

'Do you want me to call back?' asked Andy.

'No, it's OK, really. Go on . . .'

Actually, Andy didn't have that much more to say, and the conversation soon came to an end; nevertheless, what he had said seemed very encouraging. We had had interest in the past, although it routinely amounted to nothing. The music biz is full of jerks who seem to 'get off' on bullshitting. You could waste a lifetime waiting for their promises to materialize. The fact that this producer had an office and was already talking about a date in the diary sounded good.

When I had finished talking to Andy I felt really high. Maybe things were going to happen after all? My nose had cleared and my headache had become only a dull pain behind my eyes.

'Everything all right, is it?' asked Eric. He turned over the corner of a page and placed his book on the floor.

'Yeah, seems so,' I replied. 'Apparently, this producer used to have money in ABBA.'

Eric assented with a sniff before asking, 'What's his name?'

'I don't know. I didn't ask. But he's a Swede.'

Eric repeated '*a Swede*' as though the term had some special significance.

As I looked at Eric, I had to ask myself a few searching questions. Why had I allowed him to gatecrash my life? He was looking quite rough. I noticed that his collapsed cheeks had acquired deep, parallel seams. It was as though time had decided to cut him, two razor slashes inflicted by his own mortality.

Of course, maintaining my cred with Cairo was an important consideration. She retained a soft spot for Eric. I didn't want her to hear that I had turfed him out for no good reason. That would be so *uncool*. But there was more to it than that. A lot more . . .

I have all of Eric's albums. It took me two years. Two years of attending record fairs and scanning collector's magazines. It was a labour of love. I also have them remixed and cleaned up on CD. But handling the CDs doesn't give me quite the same thrill as handling the originals, with their Roger Dean-style Gemini logo in the middle: two naked hippy chicks staring at a crescent moon, a star suspended between the lunar horns. I never fail to get a sense of satisfaction watching their tight identical arses orbiting my deck at thirty-three and a third revolutions.

The Turtle Tree formed in 1970. Not many people have heard of them now, but they had a following in their day. The first album, *Tortoise*, was a fine collection of what Eric calls 'heavy' numbers; his dialect doesn't seem to have changed much since his adolescence. By 'heavy' he means the good old riff-based rock'n'roll that eventually became metal. One of the tracks, 'Vigil', is, in my modest opinion, a highly underrated song. And, if there was any justice in the world, bands like Led Zep would have been more forthcoming in citing the Tree as an influence. The second album, *Firebird* (the name was nicked from

Stravinsky), marked the beginning of the Tree's transformation into a proper early seventies prog-rock band. They were joined by David Veale, a keyboard player who had abandoned his classical education after studying for two years at the Royal Academy of Music. Veale had begun to earn a fair whack as a session musician, and the prospect of yet more scales, in thirds (contrary motion), had begun to lose its appeal. Besides, he had always been something of an extrovert, and the rock circus afforded him an ideal excuse for expanding his wardrobe and developing a dress sense that would embarrass a character from *The Lord of the Rings*.

The combination of Eric's thrashy guitar and Veale's big block chords on the Mellotron was arresting stuff; however, the real jewel in the *Firebird* crown was a track called 'Rain', a fantastic slow ballad that gradually built up into a tremendous, pounding metal anthem. Again, it's difficult not to make a comparison with Zep's 'Stairway to Heaven'. Of course, 'Stairway to Heaven' is a superior song, but nevertheless . . .

The Turtle Tree then went quiet for a bit, causing rumours to spread about a split (because of a woman), mental illness (due to drug abuse) or contractual difficulties (with their manager) – the usual suspects. In fact, the Tree had locked themselves away in The Manor, a converted pile in the heart of Buckinghamshire, and were producing what old prog-rock *aficionados* would unanimously hail as their classic, *Eugene's Moment of Truth*. This was, dare I say it, a *concept album*, typically panned by the critics when it was released in 1973. One of the problems with the 'concept' was that none of the band seemed too clear about what the concept was. Furthermore, when they were interviewed by the music press, none of them seemed that eager to explain. Nevertheless, the album contained some impressive material. It only has two tracks, 'Eugene' and 'The Moment', and both are continuous, occupying the whole of sides one and two. The Turtle Tree had started to work with a talented recording engineer called Aloysius Jakoby, and although in places the album was undoubtedly overproduced, together they were certainly pushing the equipment they had to its limits.

So there they were, in 1973, showing considerable promise, a controversial album in the charts and a US tour planned for the autumn when – all of a sudden – Eric split. Just like that. Without any explanation. He chucked the whole thing in.

The band had taken the summer off, and Eric had been chilling out in North Africa and the Middle East (of all places). When he came back, he refused to fulfil any of his contractual obligations.

There are many versions of what happened, but none of them stand up to close inspection. The fact of the matter is Eric won't talk about it. He never has.

I had tried, on several occasions, to get Eric to talk, but whenever I did he always chose to peddle the same empty clichés: *You know, man, it just wasn't the same; there were too many suits in the studio; we went as far as we could go* . . . And, if I persisted with my questioning, he would start to get impatient (prior to becoming thoroughly pissed off): *Fucking 'ell man, what is this? The Spanish Inquisition!*

I mean, really. *Monty Python*. Figures of speech from the early seventies have become fossilized in Eric's English. In the autumn of 1973, the Tree found a new lead guitarist and released a follow-up to *Eugene* (which didn't do so well). Without Eric's distinctive sound and, more importantly, without his material, the Tree just weren't the same. By the time they released their final album, *Museum*, punk had started to happen and the critics had a field day with the title (not to mention the eight-minute drum solo on side two).

And that was it for the Turtle Tree. They folded.

Not a lot is known about what Eric got up to in those wilderness years. I've spoken to Cairo about it, and even she doesn't know. He simply vanished; just burrowed under the topsoil of existence and went into hiding. He finally resurfaced in an old hippie commune somewhere in north-east Scotland. One of those places where they chant to root vegetables and *come on strong* with cabbages. Achieving complete self-sufficiency was high on their agenda and, with this in mind, Eric started to attend agricultural college. After a few months he got kind of side-tracked. Learning about fertilizers and crop cycles had introduced him to chemistry, a subject which – to the amazement of all – he found endlessly fascinating. Eric jacked in agricultural college and signed up for an Open University foundation course. He carried on studying for another few years but never took his degree. It wasn't that Eric couldn't apply himself or wasn't bright enough. Far from it. He just found the idea of being awarded (what he called) *a piece of paper* entirely meaningless.

In the late seventies the commune was evicted. The tenancy agreement they had signed with the old laird was exhumed when his rakish son inherited the estate. It didn't amount to much, and I guess *laird junior* was the kind of guy who took a dim view of layabouts talking to turnips.

The commune didn't go down without a fight, and it took months to round them all up. Once they were evicted the new laird was free to flog a huge chunk of his land to the MOD, which subsequently converted some of the coastal inlets into nuclear-submarine berths. Maybe it was during this period that Eric developed his taste for agitation. He orchestrated a negative publicity campaign and managed to arouse a good deal of local hostility. Eventually, the demise of the commune and the arrival of nuclear subs in north-east Scotland attracted the national broadsheets.

Eric became more and more involved with ecological groups. It must have been about 1978 that he joined Free Earth, and in no time he became their most venerated activist. He acquired a reputation for being something of a desperado. Indeed, the Free Earthers claimed to have footage of kamikaze pilots with a more highly developed instinct for self-preservation. Eric chained himself to the Rona-Alpha rig in the North Sea minutes before it was supposed to go down and, legend has it, boarded and then took out a Norwegian whaling boat. Eventually, Eric's exploits became so extreme that even some of the Free Earthers began to express reservations. The organization split and, subsequently, Eric became the linchpin of the newly formed GLF. He holds some ridiculous title like First Juggler of the Supreme Council.

Which is overstating the case, as I think the Supreme Council only has about four members (or *conjurers*, as they like to be known). He's quite secretive about the identity of the others but I know that one is a Greenham veteran.

Eric has been a GLF man since 1979. As far as I know, he doesn't even own a guitar now. I've certainly never seen him play one. And as for the Turtle Tree it's as though the band never existed.

How could I refuse Eric a place on my floor? Really? He played the original Marquee. He played the Roundhouse. He played the Rainbow, for fuck's sake. Eric wrote a *concept album*! In 1966 he gave Hendrix a couple of spare E strings before Jimi went on stage at the Hillside Social Club in Folkestone. How could I refuse this man a place on my floor? Really? *Impossible, n'est-ce pas?*

naloxyl

A few days later I had to go down to the Maudsley to see Dr McDougall. I took the Tube down to south London and, to pass the time on this long and tiresome journey, practised my new skill. I say 'new' but what I really mean is *recently improved*. It must have been about a year ago when I first started sensing others; that was after hearing a programme about it on the radio. One of those really late phone-in programmes, cherished by insomniacs. This scientist guy was on, taking calls and inviting people to participate in some experiments that he was running. I can remember thinking that it was probably a load of crap, but what he said somehow stayed with me – just got lodged in my head. Subsequently, I found myself taking advantage of various practice opportunities. I quickly learned that Tube travel is pretty good in this respect. I don't know why, but it really encourages staring. On the Tube, people are always trying to give each other *the once-over*; particularly so if they think they can get away with it.

What started off as a game became a kind of habit. But recently it's become more like a compulsion, something I just have to do.

My technique is a very simple one. I close my eyes and let the Tube rock me from side to side. I then try to sense the stare. I usually get *the wave* very quickly. The direction is less easy and usually takes more concentration. In books, writers always describe the sense of being stared at by using phrases like *She could feel his eyes boring into the back of her neck*, but it's not like that at all, for me. It's far more subtle. In fact, it's almost impossible to describe. I suppose I call it *the wave* because it brings to mind the idea of fluidity. A wash of sensation. Sometimes it's warmish but not always. A more appropriate way of describing it would be *the change*: I register that something is different – but *the change* suggests a load of stuff to do with middle-aged women behaving badly, so I think I'll stick with *the wave*. Sometimes, although not always, I also get a strong idea of gender. Again, it's almost impossible to describe how I know, although it has something to do with position or posture. When it's a woman I want to change the way I'm sitting. I know this isn't possible, but my spine seems to shift.

Lately, in addition to direction and gender, I've also begun to get – and I'm not sure whether this is really justified – something that might be emotion. It's really, really subtle, like the hint of aftershave on an old jumper that hasn't been worn for a long time. Or maybe the sour, metallic aftertaste of milk as it nears its *sell-by date*. The wave, too, is sometimes seasoned or spoiled. It can be spritzed up with joy or sharpened by a touch of malice, but these shades of emotion are barely detectable – almost subliminal, in fact.

I usually sit, with eyes closed, sensing the target. First, I establish location, and then – if I'm on form – gender. Every now and again what I think is emotion will follow. Suddenly, without any prior sign or warning, I open my eyes and catch them at it. Catch them, mid-take. They look away immediately or pretend they're reading an advert displayed above my head, but I know what they've been up to. *Un point*.

Since the trial began my hit rate has really improved. I can't help wondering whether there's some connection. Maybe the Naloxyl is giving my brain the equivalent of a service? Maybe it's upgrading the hardware. Who knows? Of course, I still make mistakes, but on a good day I can turn in an impressive performance. For example, on the Kilburn to Oval run I can notch up an 80 per cent hit rate. I've thought about discussing this with Dr McDougall, but I can't think of how to put it. Every time I rehearse this imaginary conversation in my mind I see McDougall's expression turn from interest to concern. It just wouldn't be worth it. So, for the moment at least, I'm going to keep quiet. When the trial's over I might just mention it to McDougall. But then again, maybe not.

Naloxyl is now my only reliable source of income; I make a little from gigging but certainly not enough to live on.

I had volunteered to take part in the Naloxyl trial six months earlier in response to an ad in the press. After calling I was summoned to the out-patient department of the Maudsley hospital, given a medical (including a blood test), and asked to sign a form that allowed Dr McDougall and his colleagues to take a look at my GP notes. After about six weeks I was given another appointment, a second blood test and sent off with a blister pack of ten Naloxyl. I had to go back once after ten days, then again after two weeks. Thereafter, I only had to put in an appearance once every six to eight weeks. It paid well – very well, considering that I didn't have to do anything. Letting Dr McDougall experiment with my brain chemistry was worth £200 a week, which seemed to me to be money for nothing. A free lunch. Well, more than that really. A free lunch with coffee, sweet and an optional blow-job from the waitress. After all, I had been experimenting with my brain chemistry in an informal capacity for years.

Naloxyl, so Dr McDougall tells me, is a new, experimental anxiolytic. He said that it hasn't been licensed yet – whatever that means. DEMA-Pharmaceuticals (DEMA-Pharm), the manufacturers, were funding our trial to monitor the long-term side-effects of Naloxyl in a normal population. It was comforting to know that I was considered part of the normal population.

The trial was a gift. Apart from some minor symptoms, which I developed during the first ten days, there had been hardly any problems at all. I felt fine.

I caught a bus from Oval Tube to Camberwell Green and then walked up Denmark Hill. It was very busy. The road channelled a continuous stream of slow-moving heavy traffic. The air tasted of oil and shook with the sound of massive, idling diesel engines. Cars, stuck between vertical cliffs of tarpaulin and metal, became indistinct as exhaust fumes settled around them.

Just ahead of me two cars, bumper to bumper, were sounding their horns. They were pitched at an unpleasant discord that produced an effect not too dissimilar to chalk scratching on a blackboard. It seemed to dislodge each of my vertebrae and made me hunch my shoulders. I twisted with pain and irritation. The driver in the rear vehicle was slamming his hand against the steering-wheel. His face was red and veins were showing down the side of his face. He was shouting but his cries were drowned by his own hooter.

Suddenly, he got out of his car and marched up to the one in front. The air began to sizzle with the prospect of violence. He kicked the door and smashed his fist on the roof while shouting, 'Get out, you cunt!' He managed to pronounce 'cunt' with two syllables.

There was something curiously canine about his appearance. He reminded me of a pitbull. His face was too far removed from the back of his cropped head. Moreover, he was short and stocky, giving the impression of a body wrapped in solid, compressed muscle. *Another hammerblow on the roof.* 'I said "out", you cunt!'

He pulled the door open. I had a sense of the other driver cowering inside. He had stopped sounding his shrill horn. The pitbull thrust his head into the shadow, but I could still hear his muffled barking. I half-expected to see blood splattering across the windscreen. This was a terminal case of road rage. I couldn't understand how the 'situation' had developed. They were just drivers, next to each other in a traffic jam (for Christ's sake).

I quickened my pace; however, the violence was exerting its magnetic influence. My head was being pulled around like the needle in a compass. Even though I really didn't want to see how things were turning out, I couldn't stop myself from looking over my shoulder.

Fortunately the pitbull had removed himself from the other man's car. He slammed the door shut and smashed his clenched fist on the roof one more time. I sighed with relief and turned away, barely able to watch the extremity of his senseless ferocity.

The arbitrary roar of lorries and double-decker buses diminished as I veered towards the hospital. I tried to squeeze the violence out of my head, but the image of blood splashing across glass was persistent.

The red brick edifice of the Maudsley is quite impressive. A rather grand-looking building that seems somehow out of place. It would have looked more properly positioned in front of a landscaped garden or ornamental lake. Instead, it faces the equally imposing King's College hospital and several very ugly tower blocks.

I stepped into the foyer and felt glad to have a brick wall between myself and the madness outside – ironic given that I had just stepped into a big-league lunatic asylum.

After notifying an indifferent receptionist of my arrival, I waited in Out-patients with a motley group of depressed, psychotic and anxious individuals. I had no desire to test out my sensing ability with these people and instead passed the time by flicking through a pile of crumpled *Hello* magazines. Some had been horribly defaced (although often to comic effect). I particularly enjoyed a picture of a pompous Hollywood star *at home* with his young family. They were all saying grace before a meal, but a salt-cellar at the centre of the table had been turned into a magnificent nine-inch dildo. The drawing was not without artistic merit. Unfortunately, a lot of the other entries were crazy, just biro scrawled across the page: *And ye shall suffer, God is love*, and so on.

I began to deliberate about the dope. Should I tell McDougall? Could I get away with it? Should I take a chance? But then I caved in. What was the point? If I got found out I'd only end up in deeper shit. I decided it was only right that I should be honest. If I lost my income now, then it wouldn't be *so* bad, not with a possible deal in the pipeline. Although, I still needed the money; I hadn't finished paying the instalments on my amp.

Eventually, the indifferent receptionist called out my name, and I walked up the stairs to Dr McDougall's office. I knocked on his door and he welcomed me in with a hearty Caledonian handshake that almost dislocated my shoulder. He was dressed in the same shabby old suit he always wore, the grey hues of which matched the colour of his rather wild-looking beard. McDougall looked like a traditional Highland Scot. You could easily imagine him, striding over the heather, his sporran swinging from side to side, and the network of fine, reddish lines (which latticed his protuberant and well-developed nose) betrayed his inevitable fondness for fine single malts. I had him down as a Laphroaig man.

In spite of his appearance, which was somewhat daunting, Dr McDougall was a really nice bloke. He smiled easily and had a deep, resonant voice that sounded sincere and reassuring. 'Nick, laddie,' he cried, 'please, do sit down.'

I was feeling seriously guilty. I had trouble maintaining eye contact because I knew that I'd really let him down. First of all we did the symptom checklist. This happened at the beginning of every visit. Dr McDougall would produce his extensive list, and we would begin to work through it.

'Headaches?'

'A few . . .'

'How many?'

'Not more than four?'

'Anything remarkable about them? More severe than usual?'

'No.'

' . . . And where did you experience the pain?'

'Here, across my forehead.'

'Nothing at the back of the head?'

'No.'

'I see. Any nausea?'

'No.'

'Dizziness?'

'No.'

'Regular stools?

'I had diarrhoea, but that was only after I had eaten a dodgy take-away.'

'I see. Nothing remarkable in that, then, eh?'

'No, not really.'

This usually took about fifteen minutes. Sometimes McDougall would ask me more detailed questions if I volunteered an interesting symptom, but it was all quite superficial really. He then took my blood pressure.

'How is it?' I asked.

'Fine.'

And then, he took a blood sample. He seemed in a pretty good mood, so I thought, what the hell. Get it over with.

'Dr McDougall?'

'Yes, Nick.'

'I'm really sorry, but I've got a confession to make.'

'Oh, yes.'

He looked over his half-moon glasses, and I had to look away. 'Dr McDougall' – I forced myself to look back at him – 'I really am sorry about this, but I've had some dope.'

'Oh, Nick!' he said, tossing his pen on to the table.

'Look, I'm really sorry. I won't bore you with any excuses. But the circumstances were unusual and . . .'

He was shaking his head. 'We had an agreement, Nick. You signed it! You promised me!'

'Yes, I know. And I'm really sorry.'

'How much? How much have you taken?'

I paused, and McDougall added, 'The truth now. There's no point in fibbing.'

I looked at my feet. 'A joint, that's all.'

'I see.' McDougall started to write on what I guessed to be my form.

I looked up again. 'Does that mean I'm off the trial?'

He paused for a few moments and returned my gaze. I couldn't help noticing how bushy his eyebrows were. They had long hairs that curled upwards at either extremity. For some reason, my mind wandered way off the plot and I began to wonder what manner of creature Mrs McDougall was. What kind of woman would take a fancy to this mass of Caledonian heft and willingly accommodate his heaving bulk between her thighs?

'You're an intelligent boy Nick . . .' His voice called me back and I let the image dissolve. 'I really didn't expect this of you. You must understand, the trial is important medical research. These results will affect whether or not Naloxyl is made available to the general public. If you take cannabis, this will affect your brain chemistry. It will also affect the symptoms you describe.'

'I know.'

'You're getting paid for this, eh?'

I nodded.

'So, you have to treat it like a job, laddie. There's a responsibility here. But it's more than that. It's not just any old job, is it? You're also taking part in a very worthwhile project. A piece of medical research . . .'

Dr McDougall said the words *medical research* as though they were holy. He might have been describing a splinter taken from the crucifix or a thread from the Turin shroud. I was entirely convinced.

'I know, and I'm sorry.'

McDougall looked so sincere, so much the *caring doctor*, I felt like a total arsehole. 'Now, you have been honest here, about the amount?'

'Of course. I really wouldn't lie to you about this, Dr McDougall.'

'You've only had one joint?'

The use of the word *only* sounded promising. 'Only one.' I repeated.

' . . . And you give me your solemn promise that you will take no more cannabis – none at all – until the trial is completed?'

'Absolutely. You have my word.'

'Very well, then, you can stay on the trial. You're so far in now it would be very costly for us to lose your data set.'

I smiled and, keen to provide further reassurance, said, 'I won't do it again. I promise.'

'Good lad,' he said, and then proceeded to make a few more notes on my form.

It was a relief to get it off of my chest, and McDougall seemed to recover his avuncular mien and benevolent attitude with remarkable speed. Within a few minutes, it was as though I had never even mentioned the dope. I liked that in McDougall. He wasn't a man to harbour grudges or bad feeling.

We usually had a little chat before I went. I quite looked forward to it, really.

'So, how's your music? Are you a star yet, laddie?'

'Nearly.'

'Oh?'

'It looks like my band might be offered some sort of record deal.'

'Congratulations.' McDougall then looked out of the window, over the horrible, disorganized pile of boxes that made up the architectural deadzone hidden behind the Maudsley façade. 'Did I ever tell you I was a bit of a musician myself once?'

'No.'

'Oh, aye. When I was a medical student I was part of a trio. We got a residency in a club in Aviemore in 1958. During the summer.'

'Oh? What did you play?'

'Rhythm guitar.' I didn't feel inclined to probe for further details, but McDougall proceeded to tell me that his trio performed a very rousing version of 'Bye-bye, Blackbird'. Or 'B'bi Blackbur'ud', as he would have it.

We both made small talk for a while and soon it was time for me to leave. I got up and went to the door; however, I couldn't open it without asking a question first. 'Dr McDougall?'

'Yes, Nick?'

'What kind of symptoms have people been getting on Naloxyl?'

'Well, you know I can't tell you, Nick. I think I made that clear, at the original assessment? You see, people tend to be quite suggestible, and if you tell them that they might expect a certain symptom then they're very likely to get it! It's the power of the mind, you see, so I can't tell you.'

I still couldn't leave. 'But . . . if something weird were to happen. You know, if one of your people started getting odd symptoms. I don't know . . . started picking up radio waves or . . . I don't know, something really mad. You'd let the rest of us know, wouldn't you?'

'Nick. If someone started picking up radio waves, then that would have nothing to do with the Naloxyl.'

'What would it be then?'

'In all probability, a serious psychiatric illness.'

'But what if Naloxyl made someone go crazy, on the trial? Something serious like that. You would tell the rest of us, wouldn't you?'

'Nick. That's impossible. It just isn't *that* sort of drug. If someone did go mad on the trial, then that would have nothing to do with Naloxyl; however, if someone started to report significant symptoms that were theoretically related to the chemicals in the brain that Naloxyl affects (and as I've already said, I can't really say what those might be), then of course we would alert everyone to the danger. It's very likely that all trial members would be contacted and the trial might well be abandoned.' He smiled. 'Don't worry,' he continued, 'we know what we're doing here.' He reached out and shook my hand. 'And Nick . . .'

'I know,' I said, 'no more cannabis.'

I closed the door and walked down the stairs, beguiled by his Caledonian charm and with the faint drone of distant pipes teasing the echo of my footsteps in the corridor.

When I stepped out into the open I saw a woman running down Denmark Hill pursued by two nurses. The traffic had become gridlocked, but there was no sign of the pitbull and his victim.

Getting the Tube back to Kilburn was uneventful. I closed my eyes and let the train rock me into a state of deep relaxation very close to sleep; ironic that the Tube can do this to me with its anvil chorus of metal and steel, its rush, joggle and bump. Hurtling through tunnels, deep under London's concrete skin, the big rattler sealed *the hushed casket of my soul.* I drifted in and out of existence. And every time I came to, the metal and steel hammerblows beat me back into a state of welcome insensibility. I guess there was still a significant amount of THC in my bloodstream, too. Which always helps. Fortunately, I was awake at Charing Cross and didn't miss my change for the Jubilee line.

Sometimes, when I'm on the Tube listening to its hypnotic beat, I start humming very quietly. Quiet enough so that no one else hears. When the Tube brakes and the screeching starts it's like I've been joined by a machine-Hendrix; a mournful, free-form wail. These are my private compositions. My pieces, scored for Tube train and disaffected youth.

I emerged from the bowels of the earth, blinking, into a dismal Kilburn afternoon.

Kilburn's a shit place to live. I wouldn't choose to live in Kilburn; but if you haven't got any money then Kilburn's one of those places in London where you just end up. A squalid little neighbourhood, distinguished only by a conspicuous superabundance of pubs and bars. Kilburn must be the piss-head capital of Europe. Almost everyone in Kilburn is pissed. The hour of the day is irrelevant. Whether it's eight in the morning or eight at night, walking down Kilburn High Street is like getting through a human obstacle course. No one can walk in a straight line.

Any benefits arising from my dreamy ride home on the Tube swiftly disappeared when, as I paused to look in the music shop, a drunk bumped into my back (and my nose banged into the window). The initial collision had forced a blast of air from his lungs, the smell of which betrayed the presence of interstellar levels of alcohol. I turned around to shout at him but had to hold back when I saw that he possessed only one leg. For a moment, I confronted him with a mute, angry gape. He didn't respond. There wasn't anything properly conscious staring out from behind those red and yellow weeping eyes. A noise – not quite human – accompanied a thread of spittle over his cracked lower lip and down his puss-encrusted chin before he made his haphazard

34

way down the main drag, past a gaudy neon bar sign, flapping promo posters and boarded-up shopfronts, furiously stabbing the pavement with his crutch like a demented ancient king.

I rubbed my head, quashed a residual shred of pity and continued my journey.

About a year ago I read this huge book on Keats. It was mostly boring, but I made myself finish it. I suppose I read it because of the 'Sonnet to Sleep'. I felt that, as I liked the poem so much, I should know more about the man who wrote it (*Yo, respect!*) But I also read it because, every now and again, it would refer to somewhere I knew, somewhere I was familiar with, and of all those places mentioned, it was *Kilburn Meadows* that really blew my mind. Keats and his mates would go for walks in *Kilburn Meadows*. And here I was, probably walking in the exact same place.

Looking down the highroad, it was difficult to imagine fields and farmyards, duckponds and dairymaids; the gently flowing Bayswater river; rustics leaning on gates, looking south towards the city. Who would have thought that London would spread this far (and beyond), burying Kilburn's sweet meadows and destroying its rural peace?

Within a few minutes, I was drawn back into the twentieth century by Kilburn's matchless temple of kitsch – the *Catholic shop*. This place reliably stops me in my tracks. It fascinates me. I have to look, while my lower jaw slowly descends, like the cassette door on an expensive hi-fi.

The windows of the Catholic shop are crammed with religious paraphernalia, most notably plastic effigies of the Virgin Mary and a range of tormented 'Christs' (on crucifixes of varying sizes). I really can't think what kind of psychological state you have to be in suddenly to decide that an empty space in the corner of your lounge might be nicely filled with a three-foot-high plastercast of the Virgin Mary. And how do you decide which size of tormented Christ to put over your bed?

At Easter the Catholic shop manages to obtain and display some truly disturbing stock. The kind of effigy that graces the

bedroom of every Bible-thumping serial killer. My favourite
Catholic shop offering was a Christ whose body had been flayed
to the bone. The exposed muscle tissue had been carefully moulded
and then hand-painted in reds and purples; however, the
distinctive feature of this particular figure was Jesus's eyes, which
glowed in the dark. Two predatory pulsing embers. There was
no electricity cable visible, so I assumed that the crucifix was loaded
with Walkman batteries. It was an absolute *must have* for any
aspirant religio-maniacal murderer this side of Memphis.

I managed – with difficulty – to pull myself away from the
Catholic shop and headed off into the backstreets.

4
light and two slits

When I got back home Eric was in the middle of one of his tai chi routines. He was remarkably well disciplined and performed his exercises every day, without exception, which was rather surprising, given Eric's general laxity. He was dressed in dark-green combat trousers, and his long grey hair was contained under a red bandanna. Although painfully thin, the muscles on his torso were sharply defined. I recalled the speed with which he had overcome me when I attempted to escape. Even though Eric was past fifty, you wouldn't want to fuck with him. I wondered how many policemen and security guards had ended up face down in shit before finishing the sentence: *I'll have him*. Quite a few, I guessed. He was, after all, the GLF's number-one tactical.

'All right, Eric?'

'Yeah. You all right, Nick, old son?'

I stepped into the front room. Eric was raising and turning his right arm, very slowly. I immediately noticed the tattoo on his bicep. Eric clocked my expression and stopped moving. 'Yeah?' he said.

I stood gaping for a while, before lifting my finger and pointing at it. 'What the fuck's this?'

'What does it look like?'

'A swastika.'

'Spot on.'

It took me a moment to recover my sense of balance. 'What? I mean . . . Have you joined the League of St George or something?'

'No.'

'Then why the fuck did you have this done?'

Eric grinned.

'Forgive me,' I continued, 'but I don't see the funny side of this.'

He sighed and let his shoulders drop. 'Nick, old son, sometimes, you don't know your arse from your knob-end, do you?'

'I think you'll find that I do,' I responded, with just a touch too much pique.

Eric shook his head and stabbed the swastika with his left index finger. 'This here is one of the most ancient and powerful of all symbols. Its origins are shrouded in the mists of antiquity. It is the Buddha's footprint, Thor's hammer, the *crux gammata* . . .'

'Looks suspiciously like a swastika to me.'

Eric nodded, adopting an expression of infinite patience. The kind of expression that would be useful if prevailed upon to explain the concept of monetary inflation to a cute but dim child. ' . . . And what language is the word "swastika" taken from?'

'Err . . . German.'

'No, Sanskrit. It's Sanskrit for well-being. The swastika is the supreme symbol of good fortune and well-being. The early Christians used it, the Mayans used it, the Navajo . . .'

' . . . And the Nazis. You don't want to leave those boys out.'

Eric rested a hand on my shoulder. 'That's the point, though.'

I blinked and tilted my head to one side. 'No. You've lost me again.'

'I'm reclaiming it.'

'How do you mean, "reclaiming it"?'

'Repossessing it. It's about time we started putting the swastika back into operation. Putting it back in its proper place.'

'What, on New Labour stationery?'

Eric shoved me so hard I fell back on to the sofa. 'I don't know why I bother,' he said. I was – of course – much relieved by Eric's explanation. The thought of Eric going over to the dark side was just too dreadful to contemplate.

It was quite late and I was beginning to feel hungry. 'Have you eaten yet?'

'Eaten?' he responded, as though I were introducing an unusual topic of conversation, a radical new concept.

'Yeah, you know. Food?'

Eric considered my question for a few moments, before saying, 'Well, now that you mention it. No.'

'Do you want something?'

He paused again, almost wary. 'What have you got?'

'I could do a stir-fry. It'll only take a few minutes.'

'No meat, yeah?'

'What?' I said in mock surprise. 'You're *still* a vegetarian?'

Eric didn't smile, but raised his hand to his chin and peered at me through half-closed eyes. 'Have you been using those paprika suppositories again?'

I suppressed the urge to laugh and turned my back on Eric to conceal any emotional leakage. He followed me into the kitchen and watched me very, very closely. I picked up a bottle from inside the cupboard, and Eric immediately asked, 'What's that?'

'Black-bean sauce, Eric.'

He extended his right arm and opened his fist. I placed the bottle in his palm. Eric lifted it up to his face and began reading every word on the label while making various disapproving noises, the culinary equivalent of a back-seat driver. Eventually my patience was exhausted. 'Look, Eric. It hasn't got any meat in, all right!'

'Yeah, but look how much other shit they've put in here.'

'How can you say that! What about all the grass you smoke?'

'Leave it out, Nick. It's natural, it's weed, it soothes the mind. This'll have you up all night. Look at this, E155 . . . that's an azo dye, see . . . it gives the sauce its rich, dark colouring. But it'll also turbo-charge your brain stem. This would send a hyperactive kid through the wall at warp 10, Mr Sulu.'

'I think Mr Data now.'

'What?'

'Never mind.'

Eric pulled another couple of jars out of my cupboard.

'E102 . . . that's tartrazine, E110 . . .' Eric shook his head again.

I had had enough. 'Look, do you want to eat? Yes or no! If you do, choose a fucking bottle.'

'They're all as bad as each other, Nick.'

'All right, we'll have this one,' I said, assertively returning to Plan A and the black-bean sauce.

All this talk of dodgy ingredients seemed to evoke a fond memory for Eric. 'I decommissioned a McBastard's once, you know?' he said, proudly.

'Did you?'

'Yeah. They had planning permission and everything. But we caused them so much grief, they just gave up on it. Never opened the place.'

'Well done,' I said, thinking of how I could kill a quarterpounder.

'You know, I heard a really freaky thing the other day,' Eric continued. 'I don't know whether it's true or not, but it wouldn't surprise me if it *was* true. McBastard's are planning to put their logo into orbit. A fucking great McBastard's *M*. Not content with sticking them in every corner of God's good earth, they now want to stick them up in the sky.'

'That's got to be bullshit. Even McBastard's wouldn't be allowed to pull a stunt like that.'

'I dunno,' said Eric, 'McBastard's donations have proved to be very persuasive in the past.'

I tossed some pre-packed vegetables into the wok. Eric watched them sizzle before saying, 'Did you know that 20 per cent of people in the industrial world can't shit properly any more?'

'No, I can't say I did.'

'Irritable Bowel Syndrome. They've fucked up everything. Even shitting.'

'Is that so?'

'Yep. We eat so much crap, we can't crap.'

'Well, there's a thought.'

I pushed the vegetables around and covered them in black-bean sauce. Eric was gratified to find that my soba noodles contained 30 per cent buckwheat flour and were a reassuring brown colour.

In spite of Eric's general dissatisfaction with the chemical contents of the black-bean sauce bottle, his interest in eating was clearly aroused as the vegetables hissed and a rather pleasant aroma filled the tiny enclosure of my kitchen. After soaking and straining the noodles I produced two mountains of steaming food, which we carried into the front room.

Eric sat on the floor and closed his eyes before performing his equivalent of grace before meals.

'Do you want to hear the new Watford demo?' I asked, a little nervously perhaps.

'Yeah, all right,' he replied.

I slotted the cassette into my old blaster, which was perched on top of the Rhodes, and pressed Play. Within moments the first chords of 'Trade' crashed out, and Eric was nodding away as he expertly manipulated the stir-fry with his chopsticks.

He was suitably impressed and said things like *Yeah, nice feel* between tracks. Or 'I like that shuffle on the skins.' Because he was my guest I'm sure he felt obliged to compliment the Rhodes solo on 'Forever Young', but I guess he might have meant it. Whatever, I couldn't stop myself from feeling warm inside. Eric Wright thought my Rhodes solo was cool! What more could a boy want?

In spite of this, I was always aware that the subject of music had to be treated very carefully with Eric. You had constantly to gauge his feelings and keep an eye trained on his expression. If you kept talking about music for too long he would kind of switch off. He would become withdrawn and a bit tetchy. So, once the demo was finished, I removed it from the blaster and dropped the subject; however, I did put on some Miles Davis, *Kind of Blue*, which is – of course – almost impossible to dislike.

After dinner Eric rolled the usual, compulsory joint.

'None for me, Eric,' I said.

He looked up, bemused.

'It's this drug trial,' I said by way of an explanation, 'I'm not allowed to take any.'

'Oh yeah . . .' he said, before closing his eyes, chanting and lighting the first joint. The smell of dope filled the room. A wonderful, heavy, intoxicating perfume. Eric sighed and settled into a more comfortable position.

'*All right* . . .' he said to himself, smiling.

I inhaled deeply and tried to draw the outer edges of the expanding cloud in my direction.

'Are you sure you don't want some of this?' Eric leaned towards me and offered the joint. The smoke spiralled upwards. A rotating column that took on the appearance of a beckoning hand. I thought of Dr McDougall, my solemn promise, the sanctity of medical research, and said firmly, 'Oh all right.' I brought the spliff to my lips and kissed the essence of pleasure.

'A few tokes won't hurt,' said Eric.

'No, I suppose not. But this has got to be the last time, OK?'

'Why?'

'Because I'm not supposed to. It's wrong.'

'No, mate. Paying kids who don't have any money to take part in experiments, that's wrong.'

'*Yeah* . . .' I said, and sucked again on the cardboard filter. I wasn't really listening. *Beautiful.*

'It's all about profit, nothing else.'

'What is?'

'Pharmaceuticals. So-called medical research. And particularly the brain-fuck market. Psychotropics.'

I handed the joint back to Eric, who I suddenly felt was just about the most amazing bloke in the entire galaxy. He took a long toke and said, 'They promote drugs like popstars now. Celebrities. I mean, Prozac made the cover of *Newsweek*. Would you credit it? A capsule, on the cover, instead of a person.'

'But loads of people take it . . .'

Eric cut in. 'A load of people take it because of spin and hype. They were told it was a thymoleptic.'

'A what?'

'A drug that changes personality. A personality enhancer.'

'And does it? Does it change personality?'

'Of course not. But that's what people were told. DISTA pitched it like a fashion accessory. A designer drug. *Drink Coke; Wear Armani; Take Prozac.* Of course, they underplayed the side-effects. Rashes, drowsiness, heart failure, epileptic fits, nausea, headaches. It kills interest in sex, too . . . Be a *Prozac babe*, cool, eh?'

'Prozac does all that?'

'Can do.'

'Fuck.'

'So you enjoy this,' he said, handing me the joint back, 'this won't do any of that shit.'

'Thanks.'

'Anyway,' he continued, 'they're all in bed together.'

Had Eric changed channel? 'Who are?'

'The drug companies, agribiz, the food industry. You put chemicals in food to speed people up . . . and then offer them drugs to slow them down. Hoffman-LaRoche made over $10,000 million from Valium alone last year. And it's about a billion times more addictive than weed.'

I suddenly had a flashback. Mum, a few weeks after Dad split. Tipping the pale-blue tablets into her palm and gulping them down like Smarties. I was just a kid. I found one behind a cushion on the sofa once. Roche 10. I threw it down the toilet.

Eric was still talking, 'You see, most big drug companies are owned by huge multinationals. So the manoeuvre is quite straightforward. You slip uppers into the food-chain with one hand while you dish out downers with the other. You create your market to ensure profit.'

'What? So you reckon these doctors I see, at the Maudsley, are in cahoots with, what, General Motors or something?'

'No. Those cunts don't know what day of the week it is. They think they're doing *bona* medical research. It's only the honchos on floor 100 who know what's really going on.'

I offered the joint to Eric.

'You finish it,' he said. There wasn't much left, so he started to roll another.

I thought for a few moments before saying, 'I don't know. Sounds a bit far-fetched to me.'

'Oh, no, my son. We're talking about serious dough here. And when the stakes are high, anything goes. Anything is possible. Look, the big multinationals are worth more than almost every economy in the developing world. We're talking hundreds of billions . . . hundreds of billions. You'll do anything to hang on to that sort of wealth and power. Anything.'

The dope had clearly unstitched a few seams in my head. There was a pause in the conversation that might have lasted anything from ten seconds to ten minutes. My brain seemed just to shut down for a while. When it started up again I asked Eric, 'So, what have you been up to?' We hadn't really had a chance to speak properly since Eric's arrival. Clearly, he had meant what he had said about not being around much. He took a toke on the second joint and replied, 'This and that . . .'

'It's not all a secret, is it?'

'No. Of course not.'

'So? Where have you been?'

'Well, I've spent a lot of time in Luton.'

'Doing what?'

'Fuck, don't you watch the news?'

'No, not really.'

'They want to build a new runway there. So GLF got involved. We helped with the tunnelling.'

Eric and his associates had occupied the ground under which the new runway was to be built. They had burrowed deep, creating a subterranean maze. His troop of activists were virtually invulnerable. It had taken the authorities four months to flush them out. Most of them escaped and evaded prosecution, which Eric viewed as a monumental victory for the GLF. He had also spent several months decommissioning plant vehicles hired out to contractors working on major road projects. Eric's activities had delayed the completion of at least three new bypasses and had halted a lane extension on the M25. He was well pleased. I wondered how much Eric and his friends cost the average British taxpayer each year. The GLF was probably worth a penny in every pound!

Eric's own finances were something of a mystery. Although he lead an itinerant life, he clearly had some source of income. For example, he always carried dope, and I was pretty sure that his inexhaustible supply was not donated by various green organizations (as a token of appreciation). He had to be buying it and, if he was, then money was surely changing hands. Moreover, unlike many of his kind, Eric didn't make use of the social security system. He condemned the social security system – with the National Health Service – as an instrument of social oppression. He believed that both were sops, thrown from the high table of capitalism to pacify the proletariat.

Although Eric would have been heartily embarrassed to admit it, I strongly suspected that he was still in receipt of royalty payments. The Tree were probably still played on a few special-interest radio stations, and you could still pick up the *Best of* compilation CD in some of the bigger stores. The idea of Eric going to a bank to withdraw a little cash seemed to go against the natural order of things, yet I was convinced that this was the case. His single concession to *the system*.

Nevertheless, Eric's existence was hardly lavish. He seemed to tread a path between unorthodox religious retreats, old hippie communes, GLF safe houses and the homes of a diminishing group of individuals he could call his friends. And when he wasn't with any of these people he seemed to be off on expeditions with New Age travellers or helping druids to get through the perimeter fence around Stonehenge.

As I looked at Eric through a thick cloud of smoke which hung suspended in the air around his head, his grizzled beard, sunken eyes and deeply lined face, I couldn't help wondering how many more years he had left to follow the way of the ecowarrior. Surely time was taking its toll. He had passed his half-century and, even if he had been blessed with a remarkably sturdy constitution, Eric's days on the front line must be numbered.

He handed me the second spliff, and I took a deep, overenthusiastic toke. My throat burned and I experienced a sensation in my chest like a haemorrhage. I coughed, felt a not unpleasant disjunction between my sense of self and my body and had then to concentrate really hard to recover my previous line of thinking. 'Do you ever consider retiring, Eric?'

'Retiring? What do you mean, retiring?'

'From the GLF.'

'I'll see how I feel.'

He paused before continuing. 'Look, I know I can't go on for ever, Nick, old son. I realize that. But the thing is, as I get older, I seem to get stronger and stronger. I'm in much better shape now than I was when I was your age. Much better shape.'

This was true, despite his misleading appearance. 'But, when you have to give up. What will you do?'

'Fuck knows . . .'

'Doesn't that bother you?'

'No.'

'Why not?'

'Because it's too far ahead, man.'

And it was. Eric lived the clichés. He could 'go with the flow', 'be here now' and do all those other things that captured the spirit of a long-gone age when to be hopeful and spontaneous were virtues rather than signs of hopeless naïveté.

After some more disconnected conversation, Eric asked after Cairo.

'She's fine.'

'Do you think I should go and see her?'

I wasn't quite sure how to answer this. 'Mmm . . . That's up to you, isn't it? I'm sure that she would be happy to see you, Eric.'

'Yeah?'

'Of course.'

'Maybe I will. The last few times I've been in town I haven't got around to dropping in. You don't think she's pissed off with me, do you?'

'No. What makes you say that?'

'Oh, nothing.'

Then Eric made one of his rare references to the past. 'Does she ever mention the old days?'

'What, when you were with the Tree?'

'Yeah. The old days.'

I thought for a moment.

'Only in passing, Eric.' He was neutral, showing neither approval nor disappointment. I added, 'She's really into her art now.'

'Yeah . . .'

' . . . And the cats of course'

'Yeah, the cats.'

I had hoped that Eric would pick up the theme of the past and regale me with some vignette of rock history, a rare disclosure that I would be able to share with the boys, but he simply clammed up. He became still and contemplative, inhaling and relaxing until his presence was negligible.

We listened to some more Miles Davis – *In a Silent Way* – and after a time Eric began to revive. He discussed some of his beliefs – most of which I failed to grasp – and he was clearly feeling in a philosophical frame of mind. He had slowly shifted down a few gears, from eco-prophet to guru. It was as though I were eavesdropping on a conversation taking place around 1972. I started hearing words like 'hollow bamboo' and 'bhakti' and 'the ocean of existence'. It was 'far out', man . . .

We were both very stoned. I wasn't too far gone, though. I can tell when I'm seriously gone because when that happens Eric's spiritual ideas start making absolute sense.

I was lying on the sofa, and Eric was sprawled out on the floor. Miles was redefining *cool* with a long, overarching phrase of gold which hung over a glittering river of turns and touches on Rhodes and Hammond. I retuned to Radio Eric.

'It's like . . .' said Eric, 'we just think we know. But we don't. We know fuck all. You know, you get these scientists, and they think they're getting a handle on it all, but it just blows their minds. It just blows them away, man. Even they're getting to see that now. It's, like, the closer you look, the weirder things get.'

'Right.' I closed my eyes and enjoyed the sensation of the room slowly turning.

'See, there are these experiments. One of the GLF guys – Dutchy – he was a physicist, before it blew his mind and he jacked it all in. He spent some time out at that big place in Switzerland – Cerne. They smash up atoms there. He couldn't stop thinking about the meaning of some of these experiments. And they are fucking amazing . . . they prove that there are an infinite number of universes.'

'Infinite number of universes?'

'Yeah.'

'How's that then?'

'OK. You gotta listen carefully to follow this. OK?'

'Sure.'

I turned my head slowly to look at Eric, who was addressing the ceiling in an animated fashion. 'Imagine a screen, with a panel in front of it.'

'Got it.'

'And in the panel are two slits that can be open or closed.'

'Yep, got it.'

'If you shine a light at the panel with one slit open, you get a bar of light on the screen behind.'

'OK.'

'If you shine a light at the panel with two slits open, you get a zebra-crossing pattern of light and shadow on the screen behind. The reason for this is that the two beams of light interfere with each other. The zebra-crossing effect is an interference pattern. Are you following?'

'Yep.'

'Interference patterns happen when photons – tiny light particles – smack into each other. So with both slits open photons come through both slits and crash. They kind of decommission each other. That causes the dark stripes on the zebra crossing. No light gets through, see?'

'Crash. Dark stripes. Zebra crossing. Yep.'

'Now, if you leave the two slits open and shoot photons at the screen, but only one at a time, and then clock where each one has landed, what kind of pattern would you get?'

'Hang on. One at a time, you say? One tiny particle of light at a time. Look at where each one has landed. Then look at all the landing sites together?'

'Yeah.'

' . . . And interference patterns happen when the photons going through one slit bash into photons going through the other slit?'

'That's right.'

'Well, if the photons are only being released one at a time, you'll get a sort of random pattern?'

'No. You won't.'

'Err . . .'

'You get an interference pattern. A zebra crossing.'

I thought for a moment. 'But if there was only one photon going through at a time what was interfering with it?'

'Exactly, my son. The only explanation is that each photon has been interfered with by a counterpart, or counterparts, in other parallel universes. *Something* is interfering with its course. And if that *thing* isn't detectable in this universe, it must be located in another one . . .'

'And this is for real, this stuff?'

'Sure it is.' Eric turned to look at me and we both stared at each other for a while. 'But, that's not all,' he continued, 'what blew Dutchy's head right off was the deeper meaning of all this shit. The fact is every time one thing can happen rather than another, the universe sort of divides. So, like, now, I'm going to lift up this ashtray.' Eric reached out and picked up the ashtray. 'Now, I had to decide to do that. But, at that point in time, where I could have picked up the ashtray, or not, the universe splits. In one universe, *this one*, I pick it up, but in *the other* universe, I don't. I just leave it on the floor.'

'Is that a fact?'

'Yeah.'

I was only half-listening now. But even so, I could see that his thesis wasn't entirely plausible. 'But we're doing things like that all the time, Eric. You know? I'm going to lift my leg up now.' I lifted my right leg up but I had to let it drop again really quickly.

49

It was much more difficult than I thought. 'Are you saying that I just created another universe?'

'Sure you did. There's this one, in which you lifted your leg. And there's another one now, in which you didn't.'

'But that's stupid. That would mean that there were zillions of universes.'

'That's right, man. There are zillions and zillions of universes. And they're all different. There are some that are really just like ours, but there are others that are completely different. Like, there's a universe in which Pete Best didn't die and stayed with the Beatles. A universe in which the Germans won the war. A universe in which the earth was never formed, and a universe that's just like this one, except you didn't move your leg . . .'

I thought about this for a moment. Well, let's say I tried to think about it for a moment. 'That's just got to be bollocks, Eric.'

'Why?'

'It just doesn't make sense.'

'Why not?'

'Well, it seems a bit extravagant, that's all.'

'Nick, old son. It's all relative. Here we are, sitting on a rock that's whizzing round the sun, which, in turn, is shooting round the galaxy at about 150 miles a second. Astronomers have detected objects over ten billion light years away. The universe is huge, but once it was smaller than a turnip. And you say: *No that's all right. I can buy that. No beef there.* But imagine if we could talk to some medieval bloke. Imagine if we got some monk here and said: *Listen up. This is the way it is. We're spinning around the sun, and the sun is shooting through space. And space just goes on and on . . . but once the universe was smaller than a turnip.* What would he say? I'll tell you what he'd say. He'd say: *Leave it out, son. Sounds bloody extravagant to me. You're talking shite.* It's all relative, see?'

I reached out for the third joint, which Eric had rolled while we'd been talking. I took a toke and said, 'Yeah, but all that's been proved, hasn't it, the sun, the earth, the expanding universe?

But the existence of zillions of universes, that hasn't been proved. Not really.'

'Yes it has. It has been proved. The two slits experiment. That's what I'm saying. There's no other way of explaining these results. But people can't accept it. They don't want to know.'

'Well, it is difficult to believe, isn't it?'

Eric was looking at the ceiling again. 'There's a book, Nick, about all this. Came out recently. You should read it. I've forgotten what it's called now. It was written by some famous scientist. One of those guys who's decided to explain everything to everyone. And you could see that this stuff had blown his mind, too. The only way you can explain the results of these experiments is by accepting what he called the *Multiverse*.'

'The multiverse . . .' I repeated.

'Yeah. The multiverse.'

I handed the joint back to Eric. I could hear him laughing to himself. 'Ahhh . . . He's a cool bloke, Dutchy.'

'Why's he called Dutchy?'

'Because he's Dutch.'

'What would you have called him if he was from Scotland?'

'Scottie . . .'

'Beam me up . . .'

' . . . Scottie'

I let my hand drop but, unfortunately, it landed in a plate of noodles. I have no further recollections of the rest of that evening.

As a band, we were very lucky. Andy's dad was a friend of an eccentric and rather wealthy Essex solicitor, Vincenzo Castiglione. Uncle Vince had a thriving practice on the Romford Road, the sole aim of which seemed to be to pervert the course of justice. He had established conspicuously cordial relationships with a number of old-style East End barons. Indeed, it was common knowledge, beyond Buckhurst Hill, that the underworld was rather fond of Vince. Gratitude would frequently be expressed in the form of an extravagant gift, the value of which might well exceed Vince's original and quite substantial fee.

Perhaps it was Vince's Sicilian origins that enabled him to operate so comfortably in the presence of villains. Italians do seem to have an inborn and naturally ambivalent attitude to crime. I gather that Vince's immigrant father, who owned a barber-shop on the Mile End Road, fondly recollected the patronage of the Krays in the 1950s. He described them as gentlemen. Indeed, over a period of five years, they only 'troubled' him once to hide a bloodless stiff among the towels in the basement. Apart from this trivial imposition the Kray brothers' behaviour had been exemplary.

With his largely ill-gotten gains Vince had purchased what was once the east wing of a crumbling mansion on the edge of Epping Forest. The restoration work, which had taken several years, was almost complete. The central and most impressive feature of the east wing was a grand hall (or ballroom) where Vince let us rehearse during the day.

He was, I suppose, a flamboyant character. (My mother would have described him as 'vulgar', the thought of which almost immediately disposed me to view him favourably.) The legal world – and criminal law – wasn't that glamorous. Subsequently, Vince was attracted to anything that brought him into the orbit of popular culture. His generous donations to Leyton Orient football club had already secured him some influence in the world of sport (and not infrequent invitations to parties attended by minor television celebrities). Vince saw our band as his entrée into the music biz. He referred to us as *his* rock hand, a further accessory to go with *his* football team and *his* Roller.

Nevertheless, we were far from being exploited. Indeed, our arrangement was mutually beneficial and entirely satisfactory. Vince got to play the big-shot lawyer, while we got rehearsal space and the offer of free legal advice (should the need arise).

Going to rehearsals was always a bit of a hassle. I could just about get the Rhodes (with its legs off) into my Honda with all the seats folded back. Phil and Scott transported the kit and the amps over to Vince's place in the van, a rusty Bedford that we prayed day and night would not let us down and, by some curious dispensation from God, the thing never did. Andy usually made his own way to Vince's place, from The Mitre, which was just up the road.

The drive through Epping was not unpleasant. I pulled off the main road and crunched up the gravel drive that led to Vince's residence. I parked by a fountain that had probably been dry since 1810 and admired Vince's small but impressive fleet of motor vehicles. I could see that the boys had already arrived. The Bedford was squatting between a Merc and an old Bentley.

Before we even started to set up the gear we had to have a band meeting, so we sat on two white leather sofas which faced each other across an expanse of floor. Vince had placed a tiger-skin in the middle. A real one, with the beast's head still intact. Huge, yellowing incisors projected from its permanently opened jaws, and its two glass eyes stared impassively up at the ceiling.

The first and only item on our agenda was *the Swede*. 'So, who is he?' I asked.

'His name's Jarl,' replied Scott.

'Jarl?'

'Yeah.' He then began to laugh. Scott has a habit of spontaneously giggling if he finds something even remotely funny.

'And where did you meet him?'

Scott managed to recover his composure, although only just. 'Bliss. But he's not gay.'

'Then what was he doing there?'

'A lot of straights do Bliss.'

'Yeah, right,' said Andy, assuming an expression of total disbelief.

'Look, he's not gay. He was with another bloke and two women. Anyway, he's married.'

It was my turn to catch Andy's eye and assume an expression that could silently communicate concepts such as *closet homosexuality* and *denial* which, to my surprise, was accomplished with remarkable ease. Scott ignored us and went on. 'We got talking to him and told him about the demo and, well, he seemed a nice bloke. Said that we should send him a copy. So Phil drove over to his office and put it through the letter-box on Sunday morning. Then Monday we got this call. He said he thought it was great and he wanted to meet you and Andy, too. He's involved with an indie label called Retro and said that he might be able to sort something out.'

'What, does he think they might sign us?'

'Yeah. He really liked the sound. He said that the guys at Retro really like bands with a late sixties, early seventies feel. I think he wants to lift a single from the Watford master.'

'He can't do that, it's too rough.'

'No. That's the point,' said Phil, helping himself to a tumbler of Vince's Oban on the other side of the pink-quilted bar front. 'He wants it rough.'

'Which track does he want to release?'

' "Trade", I think. Either that or "Smart Peroxide".'

We all looked at each other, unable to suppress smirking.

'Fuck,' I said.

'So,' said Scott, 'he wants us down the office on Friday night.'

Phil poured another three tumblers of Oban. There was good reason to celebrate (and Vince wouldn't notice anyway).

We rehearsed a few covers to warm up ('Light My Fire', 'Foxy Lady'), and then went through *our* set. Because we were feeling good we played really well. Scott improvised a really amazing solo in the middle of 'Luminous Juice', giving it plenty of fuzz on the lower strings and, in response, I improvised some very funky stuff towards the end of the number. The kind of thing you might hear as the credits roll at the end of a blaxploitation pic.

When we took a break I went outside for a smoke with Andy. Scott had started to give Phil the eye, so we thought we had better leave them to it. The good news had made them frisky. They didn't even notice us leaving.

Andy sat on the fountain, lit up and started to cough. He always looks unwell. Black hair, anaemic complexion, a few days' stubble. Sort of heroin or (more accurately) mortuary chic. Although, to be fair, he would never do H, of course. He's a good Essex boy, keeping his brain in a holding position, with copious amounts of whiz and booze. 'You know, I don't know what Scott sees in Phil,' he said.

I didn't reply.

'I mean, Scott's such a star. And Phil can be such a plonker. When we were doing that shit tour of Norway, years ago, I walked in on them while Scott was giving Phil a blow-job. It just didn't seem right . . .'

'Well,' I said, 'as the old Yorkshire saying goes: *There's nowt s'queer as queers.*'

Andy started to laugh and said, 'Fook off.'

'So what accent's that then?'

'Somewhere fooking North of Buckhurst Hill.' He started to laugh again, but his laugh began to break up because of phlegmy radio-interference. It finally broke down completely and became a hacking cough.

'You sound really rough,' I said.

'Yeah, I feel like shit,' he replied. 'I was out with Zorba last night.'

'The Greek?'

'Yeah, you don't know him, do you?'

'No, it was just an educated guess.'

'He's always down the Mitre. Bit of a case. Anyway, after closing time we went down Xara's – a really shit nightclub in Romford – it's owned by one of Zorb's cousins. You should check it out with us. I mean, packed to the strobes with prime Essex snatch. I tell you, those girls are doing it for Oxfam or something . . . So, I picked up this tart and went back to her place. And, little did I know, but she had this skin disease . . . alo-something?'

'Alopecia.'

'Yeah, that's the one. Sounds like a Greek island.'

'Hair loss?'

'Yeah. She'd been wearing a rug at the club. Really, she was as bald as . . . as . . .'

'A bald person?'

'Only more so.'

Andy shook his head and took a drag from his cigarette,

55

wheezing a little. 'She wanted to do it with the light off – shy, I suppose – but once we got going I turned the light back on again. It was quite a turn-on, really. No pubes either . . .' He dropped his dog-end into the dry bowl of the fountain, sniffed and rubbed his nose with the back of his hands. 'So,' he continued, 'I didn't get back to the Mitre until – fuck knows – I'm surprised I got here today, to be honest. I'm well shagged.'

'Are you going to see her again then?' I asked.

Andy raised his eyes to the sky and didn't even bother to articulate an answer. 'I tell you what,' he said, in a way that suggested he was taking me into some great confidence. 'If we make it . . . if this Swede delivers the goods . . . I'm going to fuck every tart in Essex.'

Yes, I thought, *you probably will*. '*Who are these coming to the sacrifice? To what green altar, O mysterious priest . . .*'

'What?'

'Nothing. Shall we go back inside?'

red5

Cairo has a big house on Highgate Avenue. It's just opposite the Tube and a stone's throw away from Highgate Wood. It's an odd area, Highgate. A kind of lesser Hampstead. It's populated – in the main – by the same kind of people who live in Hampstead, although they seem more subdued. It's as though their egos are wearing silencers.

There weren't any parking spaces on Highgate Avenue. So I drove up the hill towards 'the village'. I still couldn't find anywhere to park. Subsequently, I turned around and took off towards Muswell Hill. Eventually I found a place off the main road, about half a mile away from Cairo's house. London has so many cars. One day the whole capital will just seize up, its arteries blocked with metal and chrome.

I made my way down towards the Archway road and eventually made it across to Cairo's door. I lifted her heavy, black lion-face knocker and struck three times.

After a short wait, Cairo appeared. 'There you are! What took you so long?' She threw her arms around me and gave me a hug. I smelt her familiar fragrance, the smell of patchouli.

'I couldn't find a parking place.'

'I know, its getting terrible, isn't it?'

She rubbed my back gently, as she always did. A curious, automatic gesture. It was as though she were soothing me, or consoling me, but without reason. It was just one of her *touchy-feely* mannerisms. She finally released me from her embrace and closed the door.

We went down a short flight of stairs, into the kitchen, but there was nowhere to sit. Every available chair was occupied by a cat and I knew that Cairo didn't like them to be disturbed. So I just stood there while she made the coffee and the cats slept on.

'So, how have you been?' she said, smiling at me.

'All right. I've had some good news. There's a producer who's interested in the demo. Looks like there might be a release.'

'Oh, congratulations.' She came over to me and kissed me on the lips and then rubbed my arm. 'I'm so glad for you, Nick. What track do they want to release?'

'Well, we're not really that far along the line yet. It's early days. As usual, the whole thing may fall through. But Andy and Scott think that this guy's genuine.'

I told her about Jarl and his involvement with ABBA, and she nodded and smiled, occasionally reaching out to rub my arm or touch my cheek. Sometimes, she seemed to treat me like one of the cats. 'I've got some new Columbian? Would you like to try some?'

'Coffee?'

'Yes.'

'Sure.'

Cairo's kitchen was full of chunky pine furniture and bulging earthenware pots. The shelves were full of large glass jars, which contained lentils, chickpeas and a range of other more exotic pulses which I couldn't recognize. Pans and cooking utensils hung from the ceiling, and a colossal spice rack displayed over a hundred bottles with handwritten labels. The lettering was bold and italicized, in turquoise ink. The kitchen had a comfortable, well-lived-in feel, which I guess is uncommon among those who live on their own. Cairo handed me a mug of coffee.

'And the other news is that Eric's in town.'

'Oh, really, where's he staying?'

'With me.' I then told her about Eric's unorthodox arrival. I must say, I did lay it on a bit thick, for dramatic effect. Cairo likes a good story. All the way through she pulled faces that reflected the full gamut of human emotional experience. Each of her gestures had a studied, almost theatrical quality. She would raise the back of her right hand to her forehead and say *Oh my God* or press both hands against her cheeks and cry *Oh no*. It was a joy to watch.

When I reached the conclusion of my tale, Cairo shook her head and tutted. 'Eric!' she said. As though merely saying his name was sufficient comment. Which of course it was. 'What's he in town for this time?' she added.

'I'm not sure really. He wouldn't say.'

'Why not?'

'I think he's on some sort of secret GLF mission.'

'Come on,' she added, 'let's go upstairs and chat.'

We walked back up the stairs and into Cairo's lounge. There were two monstrous sofas, covered in swathes of red velvet but no other furniture – well, with the exception of a couple of lamps (draped with coloured scarves) and about four hundred cushions (mostly of Indian design and encrusted with tiny mirrors). Cairo was the archetypal *old hippie bird*. There was no doubting that. She was the queen. Every single cliché imaginable applied to Cairo. She was classic. Top drawer.

She slowly lowered herself on to an enormous cushion (like a ballerina), coming to rest with her legs partially crossed, and her back as straight as a ruler. I slumped back on the larger sofa and almost spilt my coffee. I had miscalculated the sofa's 'give' and sank further than I meant to go. It nearly swallowed me.

Cairo took a micro-sip of her coffee. 'So, did Eric say what he'd been up to?'

'Well, yes. He said that he had done some tunnelling at Luton. You know, occupying the new runway site. Apparently the GLF held the work up there for months. And he's been sabotaging equipment. Stopping bypasses being built, that sort of thing.'

'So I expect he's quite pleased with himself.'

'Sure. He's on form.'

Cairo offered me a cigarette. A healthy Marlborough Light.

I took one.

'You're still not smoking?'

'Dope? No, I can't.' I lifted my palms up and shrugged. Cairo always had a large stash. We usually shared a joint while chatting. 'But you go ahead and have one if you want.'

'No, it's OK.'

She did me the kindness of keeping me from temptation. She was good like that, Cairo. 'You see, I've already fucked up badly,' I went on. 'I promised the doctor at the Maudsley, Dr McDougall, that I wouldn't touch the stuff. But since Eric turned up it's been impossible. You know what he's like . . .' I had started to feel really guilty again.

We talked some more about Eric, but gradually the conversation moved on. 'So what have you been up to?' I asked.

'Quite a lot. Nothing *outer* . . . mostly *inner*.'

'Painting?'

Cairo nodded, shifting her voluminous dress. She was wearing a standard Indian cotton number, with loads of tassels and bells. When she moved, it was like listening to wind chimes.

'So, can I see some?'

She paused for a moment, a little uncertain, before replying. 'Oh, all right. Why not?'

We marched right up to the top of the house, making sure not to step on various Persians and Siameses that had placed themselves strategically to make our ascent a near-impossibility. When we reached the final landing we climbed a ladder into Cairo's converted loft. She had had two massive windows put in the roof, so the place was flooded with light. There were various sculptures and wire frames littering the floor. There was also a canvas on an easel right in the middle.

The canvas was about three foot square. It was red all over. The same red. A uniform monochrome. The paint applied thickly, almost crudely, as though spread on with a spoon. When you got close up it was like a harrowed field of coagulated blood.

'What's it called?' I asked Cairo.

'Well,' she replied, 'I'm not sure yet. First of all I was thinking of calling it "Cycle" . . . but the more I worked on it the more I felt comfortable with "Red".'

'Mmmm . . .' I said, trying to affect an appreciative expression, 'very appropriate.'

She suddenly turned, almost anxious, 'Do you think so, Nick? Really?'

'Yes, I do. It's a very direct one this . . . and' – I was floundering, but I still had my eye on the ball and I could tell up from down – 'you need a direct title. "Cycle" is too weak . . . but "Red" . . . that's bold. I like it.'

'Yes,' nodded Cairo, deep in thought.

As she looked at her work the sun came out and pillars of light crashed through the ceiling. The sunlight ignited Cairo's blonde hair, but for a moment I almost had to turn my eyes away – it wasn't flattering. The light illuminated each crevice, each wrinkle and emphasized the puffy, slightly bruised-looking skin under her eyes. She was getting on, there was no doubt about that.

'But do you like it, Nick?'

'Yeah.' I did actually. I could say I liked it with absolute sincerity. There's something about a really strong colour that moves me. 'Yeah, it's great.'

Cairo rested a hand on my shoulder. 'But what does it say to you?'

And this was where I became unstuck. I don't know that much about art, even though Cairo has been heroic in her attempts to teach me. I guess I'm happy to look at art, but I'm not really that motivated when it comes to understanding it. It was necessary at this point to bullshit. I don't like bullshitting Cairo. I don't like bullshitting anyone, actually. It's just that, if I didn't say something, then Cairo would be disappointed. So, knowing Cairo, and taking my lead from her abortive 'Cycle' title, I said, cryptically, 'For me, it's very lunar . . . yes. Very lunar.' And that did the trick.

Cairo smiled and gave me a kiss. She let her tongue slip into my mouth – for the briefest moment – before withdrawing and walking over to the far wall. 'Take a look at these,' she said, swinging her hand in a wide arc, like a stage magician. On the floor, where she had gestured, were three almost identical small canvasses painted entirely in purple.

'Oh, yes,' I said, hoping that I would not have to justify my appreciation.

'It's a small triptych I've just completed.'

'Beautiful.'

They were less striking than 'Red' but OK, I guess. I thought I shouldn't be entirely dishonest so made a valiant and risky effort to secure my cred. 'Cairo, these are really beautiful. But, you know . . . Well, I'm sure you know this already. They're not in the same class as "Red". I think you've really got something there.'

Cairo closed her eyes – paused, and then opened them again. 'I think you're right, Nick. It's been really exciting, watching it develop.' She turned back toward the red canvas. For a moment I thought she was going to retreat into herself, commune with her muse or something but, instead, her expression suddenly changed.

'Nick!'

'Yes?'

'Nick, I've had a wonderful idea. Let me take you to see the new Brunelleschi installation. I used to know the artist quite well, back in the sixties. I've lost touch now, but I still keep up with his work. I'm sure you'd appreciate it.'

'Yeah. OK, sounds great.'

We went downstairs and, immediately, Cairo went into *educate-Nick-about-art* mode.

Bruno Brunelleschi had first come to the attention of art critics in the 1960s and was one of many avant-garde Italians who came to prominence at about the same as time as those tedious 'trendy' films, the ones about young blokes on scooters – with big shades – tearing around Rome, shagging and talking to priests. Apparently, in those days, Brunelleschi was still producing canvasses, however, he was very conceptual, right from the beginning. Cairo produced an enormous art book and showed me a photograph of one of his characteristic early works. It was a large picture of a spiral galaxy, but it was painted using a mixture of gum and beluga caviare. The materials alone cost something like the current equivalent of £30,000.

Brunelleschi began to get into 'happenings' and became more and more conceptual, to the point where he eventually made no distinction between life and art. Indeed, in his notorious *realismo* phase, he actually charged people to talk to him. He maintained that simply being in the presence of an artist was an edifying experience worth hard cash. And, rather curiously, people were prepared to do this; however, I guess in the late sixties people thought differently about things.

In the 1970s Brunelleschi became involved in a number of small arts festivals in Northern Italy. These were largely engineered by the socialist intelligentsia. A small out-of-the-way northern village would be chosen, and then the most significant avant-garde figures of the day would converge there and, presumably, bore the natives senseless with unlistenable music and incomprehensible mime shows.

It was in the summer of 1975 that Brunelleschi was involved in the Tivoli Arts Festival. He had organized an exhibition of 'sculptures' at the local town hall. These were not so much sculptures but rather a collection of curious objects, all displayed on plinths in the classical style. These objects included a cabbage, which over time slowly decomposed and was entitled 'Decomposition', and a glass of water, entitled 'Evaporation'. The series concluded with a hand grenade titled 'Sudden Death'.

On 3 July the town hall exploded, killing all twelve people inside. Brunelleschi denied that the grenade was live and said that any such suggestion was entirely ridiculous. He blamed an extreme right-wing group called I Pippi or, alternatively, a defective boiler. Unfortunately, the Italian forensic team was so disorganized that no hard evidence was ever produced, and Brunelleschi was never able to emerge from under a dark cloud of suspicion.

'Oh, it was all so stupid,' said Cairo. 'Bruno would never have done such a thing.'

'Are you sure?'

'Of course! The papers were out to get him. They were so jealous. He had such a reputation with women.'

I was unconvinced. 'What's his new exhibition called then?'

'Brain Damage.'

'Look, Cairo, are you sure I'm going to like this?'

'You'll love it!'

By seven-thirty I realized that we weren't going to have sex. Sometimes it happens, and sometimes it doesn't. Usually I can tell when, and tonight was definitely a non-starter. Cairo was far too preoccupied with her art and didn't want to be distracted by sex. So she gave me a hug, put her tongue in my mouth (which is Cairo's version of a peck on the cheek) and pointed me in the direction of Muswell Hill.

I wasn't that disappointed. Seeing Cairo illuminated in the unforgiving rays of the sun had somehow made me less keen anyway, as that sort of thing does.

When I arrived back in Kilburn the light had started to fade. The sky had clouded over and the first heavy drops of rain had begun to fall, giving the pavement a mottled appearance. Each glob fell vertically and hit the concrete with a distinctly audible smack, bursting at the point of impact. The sound was quite satisfying. I stood and looked at my feet. Around them, blotches of darkness were exploding. The pavement had become the canvas of an enraged artist whose anger could no longer be checked and directed by skill. Splodges of ink were appearing swiftly and indiscriminately, fusing and superimposing until the dappled surface was transformed into a slab of uniform darkness. I could also feel rain dripping down the back of my neck. It brought me to my senses and I ran for it.

I stomped down the concrete stairs to the basement door. The lock accepted my key after a few stabs and turned easily. It seemed to be working well enough (although Eric's warning was still fresh in my memory). I shouldered the chipped, flaking paintwork, and the door gave after a moment of sticky resistance. It opened into a lightless, narrow space, which I laughably call the hall. As I stepped out of the rain, a dank, musty smell filled my nostrils. I'm used to it now. So much so that it's no longer unpleasant. It is the smell of home.

I think the smell emanates from the toilet. The walls of the toilet would be of considerable interest to the Royal Botanical Society. I am convinced that I have more species of fungus growing in there than can be found on the South American subcontinent. You hear about these guys going off down the Amazon looking for plants that might contain a cure for cancer; to me, this seems to be premature – they should take a look in my bog first. I remember, not so long ago, I went to bed pissed and had to get up in the middle of the night for a slash. I opened the toilet door and was shocked to see that the wall in front of me was covered in what looked like a luminous green map of the Polynesian archipelago. And, as I stared at it, I saw tiny red lights, winking, like cities seen from orbit. I guess I could have been out of my head, but I don't think I was. I'm sure it actually happened.

There isn't much furniture in my lounge, a battered two-seater sofa and a beanbag, that's all. The lounge is really the music room. It's where I keep my Rhodes, a real, 1973 Fender Rhodes electric piano. It looks a bit distressed (and a few of the keys are scorched by cigarette burns) but who cares? It's *the goods* and wired up to a small but very poky Marshall Amp. I also have an original – and now quite rare – ARP Odyssey synthesizer (probably 1975). Its raked silver patchboard looks like something out of a 1950s science-fiction B-movie. The numerous slide controls are topped with little coloured plastic beads. Unfortunately, a few have fallen off, and I've had to replace them with shirt buttons. It is a wonderfully primitive machine, with its white-noise generator and ring modulator. A real antique. It's too temperamental to take out gigging. Sometimes it just refuses to co-operate so I only use it in the studio now, to get an authentic 'low tech' sound.

'Eric?' I called out. Nothing. 'Eric?' Still no reply, only the splash of rain falling from a faulty gutter and the gurgle of a distant, hungry drain. I stepped into the kitchen, made a cup of coffee and smoked a few Bensons. I noticed that Eric had left some bottles of spring water in the fridge. Apart from these, there were no other traces of his occupation.

I thought about writing some new material.

After switching on the Rhodes, I tried to improvise a few interesting chord sequences. But nothing really came. I just ended up going through old sequences that I tend to play again and again when nothing interesting develops. I then resorted to plagiarism. I should be embarrassed about this, but I'm not. I get Part One of Bach's 48 *Preludes and Fugues* and just randomly pick out chords. Just one or two, here and there. Or, I get an arpeggiated section and block it, to see what it sounds like. There are loads of really juicy chord changes embedded in Part One of the 48. Scott is always remarking on how original some of my changes are; I daren't tell him how I do it.

I suppose I have an advantage when compared to the other members of the band. I have been classically trained. Not to a very high standard, but I could have got into the Royal Academy (if I hadn't dropped out). My technique isn't so good now, but if I put my mind to it, I think I could get up to speed again.

To say that I have been a disappointment to my mother would be a dramatic understatement. She has a passion for classical music. Indeed, she's a pretty good pianist herself. And, by all accounts, she was even better when she was younger. She was overjoyed when I first started messing about at the keyboard. Being one of these non-pushy, liberal parents, she never forced me to play or practise. She just waited for me to start experimenting, then asked me if I wanted to learn.

My mother didn't have a great deal of money then. My father, who I can barely remember, had run off with his secretary when I was still very young. I think they emigrated to South Africa (where I guess they must have settled and started a family or something). Whatever, he kind of disappeared from our lives, and Mum had to support me on her own. She got some help from her parents, who were reasonably well off, but not a huge amount. I gather they never really approved of my father, and Mum must have felt bad about asking them for financial help. Maybe she thought she was getting her *just desserts*. I don't really know. But in spite of this early financial hardship, Mum managed to make her librarian's salary stretch to piano lessons.

My piano teacher was an extraordinary bloke. A lanky old Pole – a widower – called Mr Szczecin. It was Mr Szczecin who taught me how to plagiarize Bach. Of course, he didn't intend to teach me how do that. It was just, one day, he started to block-chord the first prelude in C, just to make the harmonic progression clear. Well, I saw the potential immediately.

My mother was delighted with my progress. We went to concerts together, discussed composers, and even played the odd duet. We did a particularly rousing arrangement of Schubert's *Marche Militaire*. But the girls at school didn't seem to be interested in *Marche Militaire*. In fact, nobody seemed to give a fuck about *Marche Militaire*.

I did get my music A-level – no sweat – and a very poor English pass as well. I could have done better on the latter, but I wasn't really trying, my mind was on other things. The English syllabus didn't interest me much (although I did pay a bit more attention when we covered Keats).

When I didn't go to university or music college my mother was deeply hurt. Almost every time she calls she reminds me of how talented I am, how it's not too late, how I could still go to university if I put my mind to it. Christ, it makes me feel so bad. It's strange, too, because she was never like that at the beginning.

When I was sixteen I wrote the first movement of a string quartet. There are some sketches for an adagio, too, but nothing very developed. I still have it somewhere. Perhaps one day I'll complete it.

The chord sequence wasn't coming together, even with Bach's help. So I switched off the Rhodes, walked to the window and listened to the rain. In my condensed breath, I drew a crude, glum face. It sort of reflected how I was feeling. I wanted Eric to come back. I wanted to talk to someone.

6
dinosaur in a snowstorm

It must have been about one in the morning when Eric came back.

'All right, Nick, old son?'

'Yeah. Busy day?'

'So-so . . .'

'Do you want a tea or something?'

'Yeah, if you're making one. But use the spring water, yeah?'

I went to the kitchen and left Eric in the lounge. When I returned he was sitting cross-legged on the beanbag, eating what looked like a take-away salad kebab.

'Where did you get that from?'

'There's a Greek place on the highroad that stays open late. Do you want a bit?'

I looked at the soggy pitta bread and the grotty-looking tuft of vegetable matter that hung from its open end. 'No thanks, I've already eaten.'

'Fair enough.'

I handed him the mug of tea.

'Thanks. So what have you been up to?'

'I went to see Cairo this afternoon.'

'Yeah?'

He looked up, chewing hard. A hank of shredded lettuce was hanging from his lower lip. Thankfully, he sucked it back into his mouth.

'I told her that you were around. You *should* go . . .'

Eric took another bite, before saying, 'I will. Really. It's just I haven't got that much time at the moment. A few other things have cropped up.' He didn't elaborate. Instead, he washed another mouthful of food down his gullet with a slurp of tea.

I put on some music very quietly and we sat smoking and talking (about nothing in particular) until half-past two. Eric got up and walked over to the window. 'Stopped raining,' he said.

'Yeah.'

I thought he was about to announce that he was ready to hit the sack. Instead he said, 'I'm going out for a stroll? Coming?'

Outside, the road was still wet. The clouds were low enough to reflect the city lights and subsequently seemed to glow from within, an eerie, red luminescence. They were drifting across the sky like a fleet of massive airships.

We started off in the direction of the highroad and soon came to the corner shop. The security grille was down, but you could still see the window display. It didn't seem to have much of a theme. The only factor that seemed to have influenced inclusion was price. Everything was really, really cheap.

'Look at that,' said Eric, shaking his head. I crouched down and inspected one of those little glass domes that you shake to create a snowstorm. Sitting in a pile of synthetic dandruff and beneath an air bubble was a bright orange dinosaur. But it wasn't a real dinosaur, it was a sort of composite. A sort of T-Rex with a neck ruff and body armour. 'I mean, somebody had to think of that,' said Eric. 'Somewhere, someone in a office said, "Tell you what . . . let's produce a dinosaur in a snowstorm." And someone else must have said, "Yeah, all right.'"

'It's probably made in Taiwan, Eric. So the conversation probably went, "Aahh . . . dinosawr in snowstowm . . . velly good fouwr Blitish market.'"

Eric didn't smile, he just stood staring at the dinosaur. 'It's crazy what people are willing to buy now,' he said.

'Well, the people around here can't afford much, can they?'

'All the more reason not to buy this shit, eh?'

'Maybe.'

Across the road a bunch of piss-heads were coming out of the kebab shop. One of them threw a can like a grenade, which landed on a car roof and clattered, noisily, into the road. Another car crunched over the can before it stopped rolling.

'Quite lively down here, innit?' said Eric.

'I'm not usually out and about to see all this.'

'See. No one sleeps . . .'

Eric said this more to himself than to me. But I felt it was necessary to respond. '*Nessun dorma*.'

'You what?'

'You know. *Nessun dorma*. No one sleeps . . . The big tune from *Turandot*. The opera?' I hummed a few bars.

'Oh yeah, that one. No one sleeps, eh?'

One of the piss-heads across the road – the biggest one – spotted us and raised a hand to his forehead (as though trying to block out sunlight). He bent forward a little, then grabbed the arm of one of his mates and pointed at us.

'Eric . . .' I said, uncertain and nervous.

'Stay cool, eh? I'll take the big cunt and his mate, you take the other three.'

'Eric!' I could feel my bowels loosening.

'Only joking. No problem. No problem at all, old son.' He showed no sign of fear, only mild amusement.

The sound of a police siren suddenly made the piss-heads stand erect and swivel around in the same direction, like a pack of meerkats. While they were bobbing up and down, shielding their eyes and pointing, Eric placed a hand on my shoulder and said, 'This way.' We turned on our heels and slipped into the shadows like a couple of ghosts.

'They were going to *do* us, weren't they?' I said, still shaking a little.

'Well, let's say they were going to have a fucking good try.'

'Cunts.'

'That's the word.'

'It's so fucking senseless. All this violence. It's really pissing me off. Last time I went to the Maudsley I saw this guy nearly kick the shit out of this other guy in a traffic jam. I couldn't work out what it was all about.'

'Maybe it wasn't about anything.'

'Well, it must have been about something.'

'Not necessarily . . .'

The backstreets were relatively quiet but never so quiet that you could forget the presence of London. No matter how far you strayed into this residential wilderness, you could always hear the rumble of distant traffic and the crackle and buzz of electricity.

'Let me show you something,' said Eric.

'What?'

On the next corner was a tiny old pub, long since closed. The windows were boarded up and the doorway blocked with sheets of corrugated iron covered with graffiti. Under *Black Wogs Out* someone had scratched *This is a tautology.*

Eric looked closely at the stone moulding around one of the windows. He stroked a circular, patterned outgrowth – it might have been a rosette once but most of its detail had been worn away. 'Watch this,' he said. Eric gripped the rosette and squeezed. It shattered. A small fragment of stonework landed in Eric's beard, but he didn't notice. Eric clapped his hands together, brushing away the dust and powder.

'All right, you're a real tough guy, Eric. And I'll do whatever you want.'

He smiled. 'You could do that.'

'No, I couldn't.'

'Oh, yes you could.'

'So? What if I could?'

'Do you know what does that to stonework?'

I suddenly caught on. I was being educated. 'No, I don't.'

'Acid rain. Know what that is?'

'Of course I do.'

'What is it then?'

'It's rain . . . rain that's become acidy.' *Genius!*

'Caused by?'

'I don't know.'

'Sulphur and nitrogen oxide emissions. From fossil fuels, yeah?'

'If you say so.'

Eric wasn't smiling now, or messing about. He pointed at the ground. 'Dig down here, and you'll find water pipes. Old pipes, made of lead and copper. Acid rain is part of the water cycle now. When it goes through these old pipes, it releases lead and copper into drinking water. This shit builds up in the nervous system.'

He raised his finger and banged it on my head. Harder than I was actually happy with, but I refrained from saying *Ouch!* 'And what do you think that does to your block?' he asked me.

'Fucks it up?'

'Sure. But first you get stupid. You get irritable. And you get angry . . . yeah?'

He looked at me, as though waiting for a response. I understood, and nodded. 'I see.'

He slapped me on the shoulder. 'Come on then.'

We set off into the Kilburn heartland. In my mind, I kept on thinking: *Kilburn Meadows, Kilburn Meadows.* The houses we passed were almost identical. Each had only a ground and first floor. They seemed cramped, compressed together. Most of them were in darkness, although an occasional upstairs curtain showed a crack of lamplight. There was one exception. Eric didn't look in, but I couldn't resist it. The room was empty, and a shadeless bulb hung from a long cord. A man was standing under it, staring at a featureless wall. He was wearing thick, heavy-framed glasses. His hair was short but very untidy, bunched together in matted, sticky clumps. His expression was intense, concentrated, as though he was expecting something to appear. It really unsettled me. I felt a genuine shiver run down my spine. 'Weird,' I said.

'What is?' asked Eric.

'That guy in there, looking at the wall.'

Eric turned, but we had already passed the house. He just shrugged and walked on. It occurred to me that in a city as vast as London there must be thousands of isolated, alienated individuals, stranded in cell-like rooms, trapped in hallucinogenic, nightmare worlds. Schizophrenics and junkies, waiting for imaginary predators to squeeze through the central-heating pipes or to seep out of the walls with the damp. I thought about the out-patients at the Maudsley, expelled into the big city with a pocket full of pills and a head full of horror. Strangely, I had never considered what kind of lives they might lead in the dead hours of the night and early morning.

We didn't talk much, Eric and I, that night, and when we did, it was in a subdued way. It was almost as though we didn't want to disturb the uneasy stillness.

Eventually, we came to a bridge overlooking West End Sidings. An expanse of railway lines disappeared in the distance, toward the West Hampstead Thameslink. In the other direction, the line cut back to the massive railway junction at Cricklewood.

The bridge we were on was cluttered with litter. Coke cans, polystyrene junk-food containers and the odd smashed bottle. Eric stopped and leaned against the parapet. He lit up a herbal, and I had one of my Bensons, then, we both looked out across the tangle of railway lines, toward the dirty orange horizon broken by a monolithic tower block. We stood there, smoking and thinking, thinking and smoking. I noticed that a few empty carriages were lined up on the sidings to the right. They looked as though they hadn't been in service for years. 'It'll be along soon,' said Eric, flicking the glowing dog-end into space. He'd been quiet for a long time, and these words were spoken as he cleared his throat and coughed.

'Sorry?'

'The Fall-out Express.'

I turned to face him. Eric continued looking out, far into the distance, like a mariner scanning the horizon for the first sign of land or a sail. 'What?'

Eric didn't look at me. 'The waste train. It comes through here.'

'No, it doesn't.'

Eric turned around, looking surprised. 'I'm sorry?' he said.

'The waste train. It doesn't come through here. It's the Willesden line.' By chance, I had read a protest poster at Wembley Central earlier in the year.

'No, my son. That's what everybody thinks. But, I can assure you, the bastard comes through here.' He said this with absolute certainty. 'It's loaded,' he continued, 'with containers filled with nuclear waste from Russia. They pay a company called *Z R B-Tech* to process it for them. Once it's been processed it's dumped in an underground site near the Suffolk coast.'

'How do you know that?'

Eric didn't reply to my question but continued in a neutral tone, 'There's a GLF sympathizer who does epidemiology at St Mary's, know what that is?'

'No.'

'It's to do with diseases – how common they are, that sort of thing. Anyway, they'd noticed an increase in the incidence of rare genetic diseases. You know, really horrible shit. Kids born with serious birth defects . . . The thing is, if you look at where their parents live, they sort of follow a line on the map. This one. The West London mutant line.'

'Shouldn't you let people know about this?'

'All in good time.'

There was obviously some kind of GLF agenda here that was going way over my head. He paused and looked at me. I didn't know what to say.

'Do you know what a half-life is?'

I nodded, but Eric went on to explain anyway. 'Half the time it takes for a radioactive substance to lose its poke. The half-life of uranium can be up to four or five million years – humans have only been using their legs properly for about a million.' He lit another herbal and turned to look at the horizon again.

I guess we waited there for about twenty minutes, in silence. I heard it before Eric: the clatter of metal wheels. 'I can hear something,' I said. Eric tilted his head and listened. Then he nodded. As the volume increased, I thought I could see something approaching. 'Here it is,' I said. It was definitely a train.

'No, that isn't it. That's the escort.'

A small engine came down the central track, moving very, very slowly. It passed beneath us and rattled off towards Cricklewood. But almost immediately the air filled with a louder sound, that of a much bigger mass of iron. Out of the murky meeting-place that marked the distant convergence of rail lines, the ominous bulk of the Fall-out Express appeared. It had a certain terrible majesty. The grinding of its weighty metal parts produced a chilling screech, and its funereal pace evoked images of burial and the grave. The train was black, like a hearse; but unlike a hearse, it was delivering death, not taking it away.

Eric leaned over the parapet like a maniac, shook his fist and screamed, 'You cunt!', at the top of his voice. I could barely hear him; the bridge beneath us was vibrating, as though its frame and girders were being shaken by an earthquake.

After the train had passed I turned towards Eric and said, 'Is this why you're in London? Are you going to take it out or something?'

Eric smiled. 'No. Not this time.' But his eyes were shining.

7
notting hill

We met in a Notting Hill pub at about seven-thirty and were due to arrive at Jarl's office at eight. Not surprisingly, we were all in pretty high spirits. This was our biggest break to date.

Even though it was early, the pub was quite full. A typical Notting Hill crowd: young intellectuals, mostly, talking about film and publishing, overusing words like *jejune*. I hoped that none of them were eavesdropping, especially some of the quite tasty stick-women. Our conversation was seriously underpowered.

Andy leaned across the table, his elbow sliding through a small puddle of lager. 'I had this really weird dream last night. It was like a film.' His eyes were a bit glazed, and his fingers restless. We looked at him, none of us saying anything. Scott – of course – couldn't keep it up, and started to giggle. 'No, really,' he continued. 'It was like one of those trippy sixties progs. You know, like *The Prisoner* or *The Avengers* or something. There was this title sequence. A silhouette of this bloke, doing karate moves and stuff. Then the last shot was kind of big and grainy, but you could see that he was wearing a dog-collar. Then, across the screen, it says, in big letters, THE VICAR.' Scott was beginning to shake uncontrollably. 'No, really,' Andy went on, 'straight up. THE VICAR. He was like a spy, or James Bond. And he had this sort of adventure and, at the end, there was this scene where this master criminal – who was (get this!) a Swede – has got the Vicar tied up. And this master criminal says – *More tea, vicar* – and in walks

Ice-T. It was fucking weird, man.' Andy's face was entirely earnest.

Scott's laughter petered out, 'I wonder if it means anything?' he mused.

'It means that he's fucked in the head,' said Phil.

There was always a curious tension between Andy and Phil. I could never really work it out. I suppose they just didn't like each other. A clash of personalities, as they say. Although – to be fair – they never had any serious arguments. They just exchanged the odd bitchy remark and tired expression. Nevertheless, enough of this went on to create an uncomfortable atmosphere now and again.

'Well, what do you dream about?' Andy asked Phil.

'George Michael.'

'George Michael?' said Scott, aghast.

'Yeah,' continued Phil, 'George Michael, over a barrel.'

'You dirty bastard!' said Andy.

One of the intellectuals turned and gave us a sneer. Thankfully, the boys didn't notice. If they had, they might have misbehaved.

Like Andy, I often reflected on Phil and Scott's relationship. They were so different. But maybe it was the very fact that they were so different that made the relationship work. Scott looks like a regular bloke, but underneath he's as camp as Christmas. I gather that, when entertaining at home, one bottle of Riesling is all it takes to make him dress up as Liza Minnelli and perform a medley from *Cabaret* – which, apparently, he does rather well. But Phil? Phil is anything but camp. He looks a bit like a squaddie on leave – number-one crop, heavy, muscular build. In addition, his right eyebrow is broken by white scar tissue, dating back to an incident which nearly put him in remand school when younger. If you didn't know him, you'd probably cross the road to get out of his way.

'Do you reckon George Michael used to slip that Andrew Ridgeley a length when they were together in Wham?' asked Andy.

'How the fuck should I know?' replied Phil.

'You're gay.'

'So?'

'So, you must know.'

'*What* . . .' said Phil, shaking his head in disbelief. Although I think he had sussed that it was a wind-up.

Our Phil has an interesting personal history. He told me that, when he was a kid – which, let's face it, wasn't that long ago – he used to hang out with a gang from Tower Hamlets (probably League of St George) and go queer-bashing. I suppose a shrink would be able to make quite a lot out of that. When Phil told me this, I tried to get him to talk about it – properly – but being Phil, he didn't elaborate. It was just a statement of fact. Before he came out, he used to queer-bash. End of story. *Nuff said*.

It struck me as rather sad. He must have been like one of those doomed characters in mythology; fated to look and not to have, to see and not to hold. Fated to seek out people whom he might love only to give them a *good going-over*. A young man cursed to ruin what he perceived as beautiful.

'I had a weird dream, earlier this week,' I chipped in.

'George Michael again?' asked Andy.

'No. Not my type. I dreamt . . . Oh, it doesn't matter. It was a load of bollocks, anyway.' I realized, almost immediately, that I had misjudged the moment.

'No, go on, tell us,' said Scott.

What the hell!

'Oh, all right. I was standing in this ruin, looking out towards East London. And there was the Dome, and Canary Wharf, but they were falling apart. And there was something badly wrong with the sun . . . it was like the end of the world.' I tailed off. They were looking at me as though my eyes had slipped out of their sockets.

'So, this George Michael dream . . .' said Andy, to Phil.

After a few more drinks we made our way to the office. It wasn't in a block or anything like that but in a flat, a regular – albeit classy – flat, down a smallish side-street. A discreet brass plaque next to the bell read 'Haarle-Legge Associates'. To tell the truth, we were quite overwhelmed when we got inside. As we made our way up the stairs we passed two or three gold discs and some big posters of German bands like *Neue Dimension* and *Haus*. I heard Andy say 'fuck' under his breath.

Jarl was a thin, middle-aged man. He had begun to go bald; however, this hadn't prompted him to opt for a fashionable crop – instead, he sported a mane of wispy blond hair that owed much of its body to either mousse or hair lacquer. If he stood too near a naked flame I suspected that he would go up like a torch. A high forehead projected from his fibreglass coiffure, and his face had the traditional, well-worn rock'n'roll look.

'Phil, Scott, come in. And boys, good to see you. Glad you could make it.'

He ushered us into a flashy-looking lounge. Impressive antique furniture, curry-house wallpaper and heavy brocade curtains. He introduced us to a colleague of his called Bo. I assumed that Bo was also Swedish because Jarl said that he and Bo had enjoyed a long working relationship, going back to his days with ABBA; however, I couldn't really tell. He had one of those Euro-accents that are difficult to place.

The only other person present was a youngish girl, about eighteen, who was introduced to us as Emma (without further explanation). She was – I suppose the term is – horny. I was glad to see that she was eyeing me up. I smiled at her, but she didn't smile back. She just sat there being cool and moody.

Jarl grabbed a bottle of champagne (from one of several) in a large ice bucket, filled our glasses and proposed a toast to 'friend-ship, success and prosperity'. We all joined in and then sat down.

He put on our demo, and we listened to it through a few times. Bo occasionally volunteered a comment like 'That is very cool' or 'Jarl, you know, that would make an excellent choice for the German market.' It was a real ego-trip, to be sitting there in this smart office, being told that our work was fuckin' A.

After we had discussed which track would make the best single, Jarl asked us, 'So where has this sound come from? It's very distinctive, and I like it very much. What are your influences?'

The other guys looked at me, as they often did when anyone

asked us a direct question. The assumption was – and quite correctly – that I would provide the most articulate answer. 'Well, Jarl, we're all very keen on early seventies music. Not so much the commercial stuff – more the underground. A few of the fusion bands and some of the old prog-rockers.'

'Yes, but why? You know, you're all so young.'

'Well, I got turned on to it through friends. I know a few people who were involved in the biz in the early seventies.'

'Would I know them?'

'Eric Wright? Played lead and wrote for the Turtle Tree?'

'Yes, I remember the Tree. I think I may have caught them at the Rainbow . . . must have been about 1971 or 1972.'

'Really?'

'Oh yes. Although, I must be honest with you, Nick, the music they began to produce toward the end wasn't my cup of tea.'

'Sure, it was a bit excessive.'

'And you, Scott . . . Why this sound?'

Scott wasn't terribly good at explaining himself: 'Well, my mum used to play me a lot of early seventies . . . I used to like some of it. You know, Bowie . . . but I didn't really listen to the other stuff. The other stuff that was going on at the time. Then, when we got together with Nick . . . he had some ideas. And it just came together.'

Jarl nodded like an MTV interviewer, listening intently to Scott's mumbling as though he had incisively laid bare some fundamental truth. 'You see, what I like about your sound,' continued Jarl, 'is its simplicity. You have this simple line-up: drums, bass, electric piano and lead. It's raw, but the music is . . . sophisticated. I like the contrast. I also like the way you do new things with an old sound. You know, you use things like wah-wah pedal and a fuzz box . . . but, it sounds fresh.'

We agreed with him.

'And the drums and bass . . . very solid. Very solid. What guitar do you have, Andy?'

'An old Rickenbacker.'

'Fine instrument.'

'Yeah, cost me a fucking arm and a leg.'

'I bet.'

' . . . And I use rotosound, roundwound strings . . . to get that ring? That metally ring?'

'Sure . . .' Jarl took a sip from his glass. 'You know. This sound is really very commercial . . . I think you could be big.'

Those words sent a perceptible shiver around the room. I looked over to Emma, who remained unimpressed, her legs curled up under her arse and her whole body cupped in an enormous, cushiony sofa.

Bo was nodding.

'Wow,' said Scott.

' . . . And I like the name of your band,' Jarl went on, 'The Free Radicals, I like it.' He started speaking to Bo, in German, not Swedish, and Bo smirked. A small, effortful change of expression.

'Who writes the material?'

'Well, sometimes we all collaborate, but Scott and Andy tend to work together, Andy doing the lyrics, and I tend to work on my own . . .'

'That's interesting. Is the material different?'

'I guess my stuff tends to be more jazzy. But jazzy in the way that, say, Portishead are jazzy.'

Jarl nodded.

'Our stuff tends to be more boppy,' said Scott. Andy winced slightly at Scott's use of the word 'boppy', but he didn't say anything.

'So let me see . . .' said Jarl. He picked up the cassette box and looked at our track list (scrawled on the side in Phil's almost indecipherable script). Jarl looked at me.

'You must have written "Forever Young"?'

'Yeah, that's right.'

'And you two,' he continued, looking at Scott and Andy, 'must have written "Trade"?'

Scott and Andy said 'Yeah' together, then looked at each other and smiled.

Jarl emptied another bottle of champagne into our glasses and then caught Emma's eye. She got up, assuming what can only be described as a petulant expression, and left the room. She returned shortly after with another two bottles.

'Look. I'm going to be honest with you,' said Jarl, 'I'm keen to be involved. I think you've got a great sound and I think your material is strong. Now, I have close contacts with an indie label – you may have heard of them – Retro, and I'm pretty sure I can swing something there for you. But the thing is, they are almost certainly going to want to see you live. Are you gigging at the moment?'

There was an embarrassed silence. The truth of the matter was that we weren't gigging that much. And, as Sod's Law would have it, we didn't have any dates in the diary.

'Err . . .' I started, 'you see, we've been trying to tighten up our set, Jarl. And, recently, we haven't gigged as much as we could. But that could be arranged . . . if someone was keen to see us. Sure . . .'

'OK. Where?'

'We do quite a few of the pubs around Essex. Would your contact be willing to come out there?' I was hoping he would say no.

'Of course. When do you think you could set something up?'

It was Phil who generally sorted out our gigging arrangements. So we all looked at him. 'Oh . . .' he replied, 'soon.'

'How soon?'

'Fairly . . . can I get back to you on this?'

'Of course you can.'

Bo said something in German. Jarl didn't even look around, but just continued, 'Now, I want to move quite quickly on this. You see, I think the time is right, and I don't want to hang around. I have some contracts here, which I'd like you to take away. They're pretty standard . . . Do you have someone who could take a look at them?'

I guess that we would have signed them there and then if we had been asked. And I'm pretty sure Jarl realized that, so it seemed quite a good omen that he wanted us to get an outside opinion.

'Yes,' said Andy, 'we know a solicitor very well.'

'Great, that's really good.'

He turned to look at Bo, who shrugged. He then continued, 'I know that contracts and stuff probably don't interest you, but it's very important. You know, in this business, you have to do things properly. So, I want you to take them away, discuss the terms with your solicitor, and really understand what you're signing, OK?'

We all agreed.

After the contracts had been laid aside Jarl began to tell us a little about himself. He had been a singer back in the 1960s, promoted as Sweden's answer to Elvis Presley. After a few European tours it became apparent that the distance between Stockholm and Graceland could not be bridged, even with the best intentions. Jarl's tours weren't very successful and, with the money he had managed to save, he began to invest in what he considered to be promising bands. Being Swedish, he was in a position to invest in ABBA, and he made enough money in the seventies to see him through the next fifteen years. Even so, he kept his finger in a few pies and was lucky enough to have backed a few one-off novelty records, several of which did very well in Europe, in particular, in France, Germany and Italy. I hadn't heard of any of them. But then again, why should I have?

As the evening drew on, we got more and more pissed. The original tensions had completely dissipated. I think this was helped by the disappearance of Bo. He was a rather stony-faced and humourless bloke. Once he had gone, Jarl said that he had a treat for us and produced several lines of nose candy. Everybody had a snort except me.

'What's your problem?' asked Jarl.

'I'm helping with some medical research. I'm on a drug trial; and I'm not supposed to take anything like this. I've already blown it a few times and . . . much as I'd like to . . . I just can't.'

'Come, now, Nick, just one line will be all right.'

'No, really, Jarl, I don't want to seem ungrateful, but I can't.'

'Oh very well. Some other time perhaps?'

I must say, I astonished myself. Dr McDougall would have been proud of me.

After the coke things got a bit boisterous, and we started telling Jarl a few anecdotes about Andy's bad behaviour. For example, about the time when Andy went into a corner shop to buy some fags with his cock hanging out of his trousers; about the time when Andy mooned at a coachload of pensioners on the M11 and later got pulled over by the police; about the time when he threatened to bottle a heckler at the Docker's and had to leg it off stage to escape; and so on. Of course, if we had had any sense we would have kept quiet about all this, but we were all annihilated, ego-tripping or both, and caution went down the chute. It was a real circle-jerk.

All of a sudden, Jarl looked at Andy and said, 'Andy, you know, with all this talk, it gets one thinking. I'm sure Emma would like to see this cock of yours.'

Andy was way out of his head and fell back laughing.

'No, really, Andy' – Jarl fixed him with a very serious stare – 'I think you have a reputation to consider. You can't just tell us these stories and disappoint us. And, really, Emma is very interested in this sort of thing.'

There was only the hint of a smile on Jarl's face.

'Go on, Andy,' said Scott. 'Show them.' He then burst out into a fit of girlie giggles.

'All right,' said Andy. 'All right.'

Oh by Christ, I thought. How the fuck did we get to this point so quickly?

He stood up, undid his jeans, let them drop and pulled out his quite impressive cock, which hung out of his boxers like an elephant's trunk.

'Very good,' said Jarl, while Scott and Phil bent up double laughing. Not being quite so gone, I was able to watch these events with some detachment.

Emma had begun to smile for the first time. Jarl looked at her and then at Andy's dangling cock. Andy is – to say the least – rather well endowed. Jarl nodded once and, in response, Emma uncurled herself from the sofa, with a graceful unravelling that reminded me of a snake and slid across the floor. Andy drew back, surprised.

'Ahh . . . I see,' said Jarl, 'shy, really, are you?'

'What?' Andy was momentarily confused. He looked at Jarl, then at Emma, who was kneeling in front of him. She reached out and began to stroke his flaccid penis. She edged a little closer, opened her mouth and took the swollen helmet between her lips.

Fuck was all Andy could say. To his enormous credit, he was able swiftly to produce a mighty erection.

Emma stood up, grabbed Andy's cock with her right hand and led him towards the door. She looked at me, rather scornfully, as she led him out. I was horribly jealous.

When I got back home it must have been about four in the morning. I was really wired. I was too excited to sleep, and I guess I must have made a lot of noise. While I was making myself a cup of tea, Eric appeared in the hall and came into the kitchen.

'Oh, sorry, Eric, you're back. Did I wake you up?'

'It's all right, Nick, old son. I've got to be off early this morning anyway – doing a bit more surveillance work.'

'Tea?'

I could see he wasn't sure. There was obviously an issue lurking behind his indecision. Whatever, the issue suddenly resolved. 'Oh, go on, then.'

I made a couple of mugs, using the spring water in the fridge, and sat down with Eric. I told him about Jarl and gave him a rundown of the evening's highlights. He smiled. 'Sounds all right. But be careful, eh? Get the contract looked at, yeah?'

'Sure we will.'

There was a lull in the conversation. Eric lit up a herbal and I lit up a Benson.

'Eric?'

'Yeah?'

'Do you ever miss the biz?'

He thought for a few moments, then said, 'No.'

'Not at all?'

'Not at all, mate.'

'What about playing then?'

'No. Not really.'

'Well, what ab—'

'Gi's a break, eh?' he cut in. I had overstepped the mark, and dropped the subject immediately. We chatted about nothing in particular for a while, then Eric said, 'So, is this what I think it is?', pointing at my black dustbin bag, half full of magazines and bits of paper.

I was a little embarrassed. Earlier in the week, Eric had told me that if we didn't save our trees, then carbon dioxide would build up in the atmosphere so quickly we would all be fucked by the time he was celebrating his hundredth birthday. I kind of knew that already, but I hadn't thought about the whole follow-through. I hadn't thought about the detail: the ice-caps melting, the sea-level rising and coastal cities going under. I hadn't thought about refugees, flooding, starvation and disease; politicians panicking, fingers over buttons. Eric had also spoken about the release of vast stores of frozen methane in the ice-caps, fast-tracking the whole process — a sort of oblivion overdrive. If stuffing a few mags into a refuse sack helped prevent all this, it seemed a bit dumb not to.

Some of Eric's comments about global warming had begun to resonate with my personal experience. When I was a kid I can remember we had proper seasons. It was hot in the summer and cold in the winter. I can remember snow. I can remember it being so cold it hurt. I can remember my dad always scraping the ice off his windscreen in the winter. It's always wet and warm in London now. I don't even own a scraper.

I looked up from my tea but didn't make proper eye contact with Eric. 'Yeah. *It is* what you think it is,' I said, sheepishly.

The crow's feet around Eric's eyes deepened as his face made room for a broad, beaming smile. He looked so happy I thought he was going to cry. 'Appreciated,' he said. 'Much appreciated, Nick, old son.' It made him so deliriously happy that I resolved, there and then, to start saving bottles for the bottle bank the next day.

Eric drained his mug, gave me a playful punch on the shoulder that almost put me through the wall, then said, 'I'm off.'

I heard the door close quietly and then went into my bedroom. I lay on the bed and tried to get to sleep, but it was hopeless: I couldn't get the images of the evening out of my mind; they came in quick succession. Jarl, Bo, Andy being led out of the room by Emma. The contract, the heavy curtains, the gold discs . . . and Eric. Eric, heading out into the night; Eric – foot-soldier of the Aquarian age – doing his tour of duty in the badlands that were once *Kilburn Meadows. I wonder what happened?* I thought. *I wonder why he left the Tree so suddenly, all those years ago.*

I reached out for Joni but – on impulse – changed my mind. I slipped some Puccini into the deck. *Nessun dorma. No one sleeps . . . No one sleeps . . .* It seemed more appropriate. There was no way the *soft embalmer* was going to peddle me any shut-eye. Not tonight.

8
the falling sperm count

The following day I really needed to clear my head. I popped a Naloxyl, ate two bowls of Sugar Puffs and drove out to Hampstead. I started off thinking that I would walk over the heath, but somehow I ended up in the village and eventually in Our Price. I picked up a reduced John Coltrane for £6.99 and bought it like a robot. Almost all of my trial money goes on CDs. It's like a compulsion. I have no self-control. In order to prevent myself from buying a second CD I knew that I should physically remove myself from the shop, so I forced one leg in front of the other until I was through the door and in the street.

With nothing better to do, I turned around and walked straight into Waterstones. I didn't really intend to buy anything, I just thought I'd browse. First I looked at the music books. I flicked through some of the big glossies on contemporary girlie bands, just for the cheap thrill. This gave me the idea of checking out the art section, so I found a few semi-pornographic art books and tried to look sophisticated as I flicked through various photographic studies of nipples and pudenda, all very tastefully lit. Fortunately, there weren't that many people around so I was able to appreciate these examples of high art at leisure. I then tried to find a book on Brunelleschi but only found one on another Brunelleschi. Well, I assume another Brunelleschi, unless Cairo's one was pushing 500.

Eventually, I got bored of the art books and went upstairs. For some reason, I don't know why, I remembered my conversation with Eric about the multiverse. So I inspected the science books and came across one titled *Many Worlds* (which seemed close enough) and, to my great surprise, I found a diagram in it that corresponded with Eric's description of the experiment with slits and light. I wasn't sure whether it was the exact book that Eric had suggested I should read but, if it wasn't, it was certainly a close cousin.

A light source was shown, and two slits, letting two beams through to make a zebra-crossing pattern on a screen. The passage underneath read:

In the two-slits experiment, it is as though some magic influence affects the course of the photon. The single photon is seemingly discouraged from entering the dark areas. But what does the discouraging? Physicists suggest that the photon is – as it were – interfering with itself.

Because I have a mental age of twelve, this, of course, made me laugh.

Potential paths through both slits influence the actual path. Another way of understanding this phenomenon is to invoke the concept of multiple universes . . .

I tried to understand more of it, but I was unfamiliar with the terms. The book was supposed to be for 'the general reader', but I think the author's idea of 'the general reader' was very different from mine. Is the general reader really familiar with Heisenberg's Uncertainty Principle or the Einstein-Rosen-Podolsky Paradox? I doubt it. I loved the terms, though. They struck me as bloody good names for bands I might form in the future. I was standing there, trying to make sense of these diagrams, when I felt a *wave*: someone was looking at me. It was amazingly strong. I closed my eyes, and something really odd happened. I got female gender, and then what I can only describe as sexual interest. It was quite specific. I was getting the feeling of being stared at, accompanied by strong sexual feelings. I turned around quickly and, sure enough, on the other side of the shop, was a woman, about nineteen, looking directly at me. As usual, she turned away as soon as our eyes met. She bent her head down and looked at the book she held in her hands. For a moment I was stunned. Had it really happened? Or had I just imagined it? It was so powerful.

The experience had left me a little disorientated. It was almost as though, for a moment, one fleeting, insubstantial moment, I had been inside her head. It was really, really weird.

I put *Many Worlds* back on the shelf and left the shop in a hurry, aware that the woman's gaze was following me again as I trotted down the stairs. When I got outside I took a deep breath of warm, damp air. I shook my head, swung the Our Price bag around my wrist and walked briskly back to the car.

At our next rehearsal the gig problem was high on the agenda. Phil stood at the bar, redistributing the contents of various bottles so as to disguise the enormity of our now routine, almost slovenly abuse of Vince's generosity.

'I'm not happy about inviting them to our next gig,' said Andy. 'We haven't played in front of an audience for a while, and it's not like rehearsing, is it?'

'No,' I said, unhelpfully.

'It's a shame we can't do a few warm-ups,' added Andy.

'No chance,' said Phil. 'The Cranbrook was the only pub I could get before the end of the month.'

'I don't know,' continued Andy, shaking his head. 'The Cranbrook. It's a bit of a shit-hole. I'd feel better if they came to see us at the Greyhound, or the Three Rabbits.'

'Yeah, but we haven't got the Greyhound or the Three Rabbits. We've got the Cranbrook,' said Scott. 'If Jarl wants to get things sorted quickly, then we shouldn't piss about. We should get him and his mates down the Cranbrook pronto.'

'Yeah, but we could blow it,' said Andy. 'We haven't been gigging regularly and the Cranbrook audience is shit.'

'I don't know,' I cut in, 'we get a few familiar faces there.'

'Yeah, a few,' replied Andy, 'like three or four. That's hardly going to lift us, is it?'

'Look,' replied Scott, with uncharacteristic assertion, 'we won't blow it.' He never seemed to have any self-doubt when it came to performing.

Scott had never wanted to be anything other than a rock star. From the age of eleven he used to dress up – in his mother, Irene's, clothes – and strut around his bedroom throttling a cheap acoustic that his uncle bought him for his birthday. He would experiment with Irene's make-up and felt quite comfortable in a pair of coloured tights, thigh-length boots and a body that she used to wear for aerobics. His role model, without doubt, was *Ziggy Stardust* (which he had discovered in Irene's extensive Bowie collection).

Ziggy was, of course, somewhat unfashionable in 1986, but this didn't bother Scott. It did, however, bother Ron, Scott's dad. Irene – although having serious doubts about the nature of the creature she had brought into the world, was astute enough to realize that if the boy *did good* he might provide them all with a way out of their squalid little council flat in Hackney. She did not, therefore, discourage him. And, when the family went to Butlins for a holiday and Scott insisted on entering a talent competition, which he won by doing a *Ziggy* impersonation, Irene was already fantasizing about moving east into a big house in Buckhurst Hill. Ron, acutely embarrassed, spent that evening playing darts.

Out of all of us, I guess Scott is the one who has real star potential. He was born to strut in front of an audience. When Scott gets up on stage, he is transformed. He becomes more substantial, commanding even. It's such a contrast to his off-stage personality. Maybe it's all down to the fact that he looks good. Lean and gaunt, with a very distinctive, lantern-jawed face. He's not so much attractive as arresting. He also has the advantage of being lead vocal and guitar. A rare and devastating combination. But there's more to it than just appearance, more to it than competence. When Scott gets up on stage, it reminds me of the sudden grace displayed by a bird taking flight; something awkward suddenly becomes elegant and poetic. When Scott is warmed by a spotlight he is clearly basking in his natural element.

'I don't know,' continued Andy, still shaking his worried head, 'I'd feel a lot happier if we could do a dry run. Any audience would do. Just bodies in front of the stage.'

Phil distributed a set of tumblers, although only two contained whiskey. The others contained advocaat and white wine respectively. Scott fazed us all by actually choosing the advocaat. Phil took a swig of his whiskey and slooshed it around his mouth as though it was mouthwash. For a moment I thought he was going to spit it out.

'Don't do that,' said Scott.

Phil stopped. 'You know,' he said, after finally swallowing. 'I just might . . . just might be able to arrange something.'

'Where?' asked Andy.

Phil kept us in suspense for a few more moments. He moved his jaw from side to side, making clicking sounds, the purpose of which seemed just to annoy Scott. I guessed that maybe they'd had a bit of a lovers' tiff. 'If it's a gig that doesn't matter. Then . . .' He paused before carrying on, 'You see. There's this club . . .'

Scott began to shake his head. 'No way, not the Prince Albert! No one wants to play the Prince Albert, for fuck's sake!'

'That's not the point, is it?' replied Phil. 'We don't *want* to play the Prince Albert, but it *would* be a warm-up gig. That's what Andy's on about.'

'No,' said Scott, 'we can't. And besides, what about these two?' Andy and I looked at each other.

'They'd enjoy it!'

'There's a no-straights rule.'

'Well, we'll tell them they're queer.'

'But we're not!' said Andy and I together (just that little bit too quickly).

'You won't get any hassle . . .' Phil was about to continue when Scott waved his hand up and down in front of Phil's face.

'Is anybody in? Are you there?' He then knocked on Phil's head really hard. 'Phil, we're talking about the *Prince Albert* club. Yeah?'

Phil shrugged and rubbed his head. 'Just a suggestion.'

'Hang on!' I said. 'We've played gay bars before. What's the problem?' I was puzzled by their reticence.

'It's a private club, yeah?' said Scott.

'So?'

'Special interest!'

'What?'

'S&M, that sort of thing. But the punters are really serious.'

'So?'

'It gets heavy in there.'

'What, watching a couple of queers smack each other about bit!' said Andy, 'Are you really calling that heavy?' He then put on a camp voice, 'Oooh, slap your cock!', stood up and minced around the room, gesticulating in the most politically incorrect manner conceivable.

Scott and Phil looked at each other knowingly.

'All right!' said Scott. 'You fuck-wits! If you want to do it, we'll do it!'

'But you two will have to pretend to be an item. And you'll have to stick very close together all night,' added Phil.

Andy grabbed my hand, and I looked into his shadowy eyes, fluttering my eyelids.

After the rehearsal we waited around for Vince, as he had promised to look at the contracts for us. We packed our stuff away and just hung around, playing pool upstairs. All four TV sets were on at the same time, so that you could follow a programme while playing. That sort of stunt was *very Vince*. He was the kind of guy who had to be doing nine things at once to save himself from self-awareness.

We had the ten o'clock news on, and there was a feature on rising levels of female hormones – from the contraceptive pill – getting into lakes and rivers. It opened with a shot of some guy scooping fish out of a river and pointing out that they were all hermaphrodite. He then made a link between this and the falling sperm count.

'Are we going to grow tits then?' asked Andy.

'Shut up, I'm listening.' I waved him down.

'If I grow tits I'll play with them all day.'

'For fuck's sake, shut up.'

'I can lick my nipples already . . .'

'Yeah, but can you lick your own cock?' asked Scott.

'If I lie on the floor with my legs back over my head, just about.'

'You liar,' said Scott, already beginning to crack up.

'I fucking can!' said Andy.

'Oh, for fuck's sake!' I shouted. 'I'm trying to listen!'

'Oooh . . .' Andy wailed, mimicking the rise and fall of a police siren to express indignation. He pulled a face, half amused, half surprised.

When I looked back at the screen it had cut to a boffin, complete with white coat and receding hairline, who assured the interviewer that the build-up of non-degradable, artificially engineered oestrogens in the water supply posed no serious threat to male sexuality. I couldn't help noticing the DEMA-Pharm logo on his breast pocket. As I bent over to take my next shot, Andy grabbed my hips from behind and started simulating rectal intercourse.

'Nothing wrong with my sexuality,' he said.

Against my better judgement, I had to laugh. Scott was creasing up, too, while Phil looked on, slightly bemused.

The screens all blinked to the Middle East, where some flag-burning was going on. I had seen this scene so many times I lost interest automatically. My attention returned to pool.

We had a queers versus straights game, which Andy and I won but only just. Then a mixed doubles game, with Andy and Phil playing Scott and me. Predictably, Scott and me got absolutely smeared. We were just starting the alternative mixed doubles combination, when Vince arrived.

As we made our way downstairs we saw that he was accompanied by a youngish woman and three large men. He introduced them in turn, as 'Deb from the office', 'Brian' and 'the two Bills'.

Deb was the most spectacular example of Essex womanhood, every inch of her, from the top of her stacked, spot-welded hair down to the four-inch white heels that supported her short (though very shapely) bare legs. The men were clearly serious muscle – not to be messed with. They had grotesquely enlarged chests and narrow eyes that, when looking at you, inspired consideration of the fragility of human life. As Eric would say, these guys had a *bad vibe*.

After Vince had introduced us, he asked Deb to entertain the boys at the bar and then took us around to his 'office'. He slung his jacket on to a small coat-stand, revealing a pair of bright red braces. Undoing the top button of his shirt, he loosened his tie and tugged on the knot until it was half-way down his chest. He looked quite sweaty, and his chin had become darkened with stubble which he had a habit of rubbing, thus punctuating our conversation with sounds reminiscent of someone doing a bit of sandpapering next door.

Vince sat behind his large oak desk, with its rich leather inlay, and smiled at us. There were only three chairs in front of the desk, so Phil stood by the window.

'Andy? Nicky? What do you think of that Deb, then?'

'All right, Vince,' said Andy, and I nodded appreciatively.

'See the arse on it? What a piece! Seventeen, she is, and fucking gagging for it. If I don't get my end away tonight then I must be John Cunt!' He then took in Phil and Scott. 'D'you two have any idea what you're missing? Do you?' Scott and Phil shrugged. Vince shook his head, without malice, but rich in pity. 'I mean,' he continued, 'I'm not totally impartial to a bit of shit-stabbing myself – with the right girl of course – but, for fuck's sake, it's no substitute. Believe you me.' We all took a quiet moment to reflect on Vince's wise and perceptive observations. 'So,' he continued, 'Where's the deal?'

We gave him one of Jarl's contracts. He flicked open a box of cigarettes and lit one, saying, 'Help yourselves.'

We all did. And then we sat, listening to Vince coughing and rubbing his stubble. His eyes were going from side to side at high speed, and I wondered whether he was taking it all in. After a few moments he looked up and said, 'I think I'll get her into the jacuzzi first.' His comment was met with a wall of blank and impatient faces. 'Sorry, boys,' he said, 'I've had a busy day.'

He returned his attention to the contract, and again his eyes shifted from side to side like the mechanism of a scanner or a bubble-jet printer. In under a minute he said, 'It's a contract.'

'But is it a good one?' I asked.

'It's the only one you got!'

'Yeah, but should we sign it?'

'Do you want to release a single?'

'Of course.'

'Then, if it's the only one you got, and you want to release a single, seems to me you haven't got much choice.'

'But is there anything in there that you don't like?'

'You could quibble with the percentage here. Your Swede gets 50 per cent of overseas sales, which is fucking high. But, if that's what he wants, then that's what he wants. It's a two-album deal – and any singles from those albums – but after you've done your two albums you can walk away. There are no strings attached here.'

'So we should sign?'

'As I said, this Swede's cut looks pretty high to me but, then again, that's not always a bad thing. I mean, this guy must have other interests. So, if it's really worth his while to push you, then he's more likely to do so. If you smart-arse him down to 10 per cent and his other acts give him a better return, who do you think he's going to push?'

Vince looked at us, and we nodded. It seemed to make sense.

Scott said, 'So we should sign . . .'

'Look,' explained Vince, '50 per cent of something is better than 90 per cent of nothing, right? If you think you can work with this guy and he knows the biz, then what the fuck, eh? Where's the competing offer? Show me the better deal!'

He was right. There were no other options. We signed the

contracts, and Vince was our witness. Jarl had already signed his bit.

'Congratulations,' said Vince. 'You're on the way at last. And, when you go platinum I'll expect to be top of the guest list, right?'

We all smiled and agreed that he had been an enormous help to us. He had.

'Look,' he continued, 'I've got to finish some business with the boys outside, so I'm going to have to be rude and ask you to leave. OK?'

When we stepped out of the office, the three men were sitting on bar stools, while Deb stood behind pouring the drinks. I couldn't help noticing that one of them was now supporting a rifle between his legs. A fucking great huge thing. Vince looked over to the bar and called, 'Be with you in a sec . . . hope you've been taking care of the boys, Deb?'

The young woman let out a hysterical and explosive laugh. I had no idea what was so funny.

When we stepped outside into a warm, sticky night, Vince stopped us and said, 'See anything unusual then?'

We all shook our heads.

'Well done, boys.'

He pulled my cheek between his thumb and forefinger, and shook it, like he thought he was Robert de Niro or some character in *The Godfather*.

9
the prince albert

The Edward II was a really seedy gay pub situated somewhere behind King's Cross station. We arrived early and parked the van and my Honda in an adjacent alley which served as a kind of unofficial car park; however, you couldn't get more than three or four vehicles in there. It was just a gap between the pub and a disused warehouse. The alley was cold, dark, and damp. Although its walls were – unusually for London – entirely clear of graffiti, the cobbled ground was littered with used condoms and syringes. The whole area should have been cordoned off and designated a bio-hazard.

The manager of the Eddie, Pete, greeted us warmly. He seemed OK, and apparently knew Scott and Phil quite well. Maybe I was being oversensitive, but I thought he viewed Andy and me with some suspicion. We weren't *faces*. He hadn't seen us around. I felt like we were being interrogated. Scott and Phil were quick off the mark. They butted in and prompted Pete to tell us about his recent holiday in San Francisco – which he did at some length so we survived the small talk.

We then set about the tedious business of unloading the gear.

The Eddie was a pretty small pub, with a surprisingly large toilet, and a fuck room. I'd never seen a fuck room before and asked Scott if I could take a look.

'Sure,' he said, 'but let me come with you. You see, Pete's a bit of a slag. If he catches you hanging round there, a situation might develop, yeah?'

'Thanks.'

Fortunately, Pete wasn't around, so we were able to take our time. It wasn't how I expected it to be. I thought it might be sensuous and decadent, like Cairo's bedroom. But, instead, it was cold and clinical. I opened the door and stepped into what seemed to me to be an oversized cubicle. A kind of large, converted shower. The floor and walls were tiled, and in the corner was a small stainless-steel grille. Obviously some kind of drainage system. Scott followed me in.

I closed the door and, as I did so, it became pitch dark. There was no light or light switch. It was like being buried alive, trapped in a tomb. 'Scott?' I called, feeling a sense of rising panic as the darkness pressed in on me.

'Yeah?' he replied, puzzled at the pitch and volume of my voice.

I felt really stupid. He was standing right next to me, but for a moment I had felt totally isolated. In order to cover my embarrassment, I asked a question. A feeble attempt to create some illusion of casual conversation. 'Have you used one of these?'

'Yeah.'

'What's it like?'

'Good.'

Scott opened the door and a thin shaft of light sliced through the darkness. I couldn't help feeling that the fuck room was like something you might find in Auschwitz. There was a horrible, seeping coldness in there. It seemed to penetrate deep into my bones.

'What,' I continued, ' . . . you just all pile in here and fuck?'

'Or work each other off, you know.'

'Jesus. How many of you?'

'Loads.'

'What do you mean, "loads"?'

'It gets packed out. I don't know how many, that's the idea. You don't know how many.'

I began to feel very cold. So much so, I began to shiver. 'Do you still go to places like this?' I asked Scott. He turned his pale, gaunt face towards me. Again, I was disturbed by an unwanted resonance. An unwelcome mental impression that suggested concentration camps and emaciated figures.

'Yeah,' Scott replied, 'though not so often these days. When I was really young I used to go a lot, but I don't go so much now. I'm getting old maybe.'

I began to feel uneasy. Scott seemed so fragile, so delicate. I couldn't imagine him surviving the powerful crush of sweating, heaving bodies. The invasion of flesh and the pressure of muscle.

For some peculiar reason I was overcome with emotion. I reached out and touched Scott's arm. Contact was something of a taboo for us. Scott and I rarely touched. It was one of those stupid tacit rules of behaviour that had developed to keep the nature of our relationship absolutely clear. Like people in a lift, who always make a show of looking away from each other, Scott and I were always careful to compensate for our mutual affection by outlawing any physical contact. Yet in that moment my feelings were so strong, I was prepared to break the rules if it meant I could get through to him. 'Scott, if you use one of these places again, you'll be careful, yeah?'

Scott paused for a moment, perhaps embarrassed. I let my hand fall. 'What are you on about?' he replied, almost amused by my concern. I realized he was completely unaware of the intensity of my experience; however, I was unable to articulate my feelings. I didn't know what I was trying to say. I just felt that I had to say something, and that it was important that I should do so. 'You'll . . . I don't know . . . Look after yourself, that's all.'

'What, use a condom?'

'No. You do that already. I know that! I mean, just, look after yourself.' There was only coldness, and a terrible sense of foreboding.

Scott shook his head and stepped out of the fuck room. 'Come on!'

I could see that he was thinking: *What the fuck's got into him!* I was too confused to attempt an explanation and followed him out, feeling stupid and self-conscious. Scott was keen to finish setting up the gear and wanted to chat about a few technical things, so I was soon relieved of any obligation to explain my behaviour; however, the atmosphere of the fuck room clung to me, like a tenacious, cloying odour. And the chill remained, that terrible seeping coldness, a reminder of an unspeakable horror that had little to do with sex, and carried with it a memory of the charnel-house.

Scott and I trudged upstairs to the Prince Albert club, where Andy and Phil were stacking cabinets. 'Oh, *come on*, you two,' said Phil, 'for fuck's sake!'

We both said sorry and busied ourselves with our respective instruments, pedals and leads. I looked around the Prince Albert, which wasn't so much a club as a large room with blacked-out windows. Presumably, before the collapse of civilized life in King's Cross, this room must have been for private functions. The good people of Pentonville, Camden, and Somerstown must have gathered here to celebrate births, weddings and departures. And, as though to mark the demise of this proletarian *noblesse*, the cornicing had been painted black, as had the enormous moulded ceiling rose, from which, no doubt, an enormous chandelier had once hung. This black ornamentation gave the room a grim, bleak atmosphere that served only to worsen my disturbed mood.

Once we had set up the gear, we played through a couple of numbers to get the sound right. The room had a respectable acoustic, which is often the case in old buildings. Then we went downstairs to the pub. Andy and I sat on our own and pretended to be having a deep, intimate conversation. That way, no one would hassle us. Phil and Scott sat at the bar talking to Pete and, ever so slowly, the Eddie began to fill up. Someone fed the jukebox and very soon the atmosphere was quite normal. Pleasant even.

I wondered what on earth had got into me earlier. It occurred to me that I might have suffered a side-effect from the Naloxyl. Coldness? Nervousness? It was possible, although I had never experienced such side-effects before. But then, why should I have? That was the whole point of the trial, wasn't it? To track the development of side-effects over a lengthy period of time. Perhaps I would mention it to Dr McDougall. I took out my blister pack and suddenly noticed I had forgotten to take yesterday's pill. I popped out two and swallowed them.

'Give us one,' said Andy.

'I can't. They're for my drug trial.'

'Can I join the trial, just for tonight?'

'No. Anyway, they don't do anything. Apart from give you a headache when you start.'

He wasn't convinced.

I scanned the pub. Most of the people coming in were obviously gay – a muster of screamers and a sprinkling of eighties-throwback clones – but there were a significant percentage who wouldn't have looked out of place in a bank, just ordinary-looking blokes. As Andy and I chatted, we noticed that a number of men were coming in the pub entrance and going straight upstairs.

'They don't look that weird,' said Andy.

'No, they don't,' I responded, 'that's what I was thinking.'

A little while later Scott and Phil came over and said that we were going on stage in half an hour. We checked the set order for one last time.

'Look,' said Phil, 'in the break, you two had better come down. You might be uncomfortable up there.'

'We'll be fine,' said Andy, angle-poising his hand at the wrist and adopting the tones of a New York drag queen. 'Don't worry already!'

In response, Phil gave him a look that was almost – but not quite – lethal.

When we finally stood up, I must say, I felt a little unsteady. We really had been drinking too much while hanging around. Ascending the stairs, the pulse of a sound system drowned out the jukebox below. We had to wait behind a few of the punters who were queuing on the stairs. There wasn't enough room to get by.

At the top of the stairs was a corridor, in which a small kitchen table had been set up. People were handing over cash and, in return, heir hands were stamped with three green inky letters – 'PAC' – enclosed in a ring logo.

The guy taking the cash was unremarkable, a pretty standard eighties clone, although he lacked the air-brush finish. Age had overtaken the image and he clearly hadn't seen the inside of a gym for years. A fairly big bloke was sitting behind him.

Scott nodded at the big guy, who seemed to know him, while saying to the clone, 'We're the band.'

The clone looked around, and the big guy nodded. Then we all got stamped with our PAC pass.

'Make it a good one,' said the clone.

Just before we got to the club door, which was open, I noticed that people were going down an adjoining corridor to a place signed '*the cloakroom*'. Obviously, people were dressing for action but, even so, I really wasn't prepared for what I saw when we stepped into the PAC.

I hate to admit it, but I was shocked. The guys who were dancing and talking were mostly dressed in leathers, rubbers or PVC. Many had the arse or crotch areas cut out of their 'trousers'. Their cocks were dangling, and most were pierced – not once, but several times. Other guys were bare-chested, exhibiting rings through belly buttons and nipples. As I walked toward the stage, a guy leaning up against the wall poked his tongue out at me; a *come on*. His tongue was like a pincushion. A beam of light arced across his face and, for a moment, his mouth looked as though it were full of stars. I increased my speed.

Tattoos were also pretty much par for the course; blue and green stains mottled naked flesh, like some disfiguring skin disease. Some of the guys were wearing leather or PVC hoods over their heads. Most of these had mouth-zips; however, the remainder had nothing at all where their mouths should have been, their lips were sealed. Mutes.

The place was really buzzing. It was amazing. Although comparatively early, the PAC was very nearly full, and the smoke, and the noise, and the gyrating bodies gave the impression of an event running with the throttle fully open. Moreover, the room was still being fed by a parade of characters who would not have looked out of place in a medieval dungeon.

When we reached the stage, Andy took me by the arm and said, 'Fucking 'ell. What is this?'

I could see that the PAC had fazed him, too.

The DJ was an extraordinary creature, somewhat overweight and dressed up in leathers and rhinestones, giving the appearance of a kind of post-apocalyptic late Elvis. He had a quick word with Scott. Then Scott signed for us to get up on stage. When I say 'stage', it was a small wooden elevation that took us to no more than six inches higher than the floor. Nevertheless, it defined the band's area. We were all too close together to move around much, so the show was going to have to be somewhat static. That didn't bother me. Being a keyboard player, I'm always static anyway.

We pissed about with our amps and things, and Scott and Andy attempted a last-minute tune-up, bending down with their ears pressed against the cabinet stacks. I gave them an 'E', just to make sure they hadn't drifted. When the techno stopped, the DJ jumped on to the stage, sending a perceptible tremor through the building, and grabbed the mike. 'All right!' he called.

A terrible wave of feedback came out of the loudspeakers and almost deafened the audience, who started groaning. Scott fiddled with the amp and nodded back at the DJ. 'All right!' he called again, although perhaps a little more subdued. 'We've got some live music for you. Rockin' on down at the old PAC. Soon to be released on the Retro label, and all the way from Essex. Let's give them a throbbing welcome, the *Free Radicals*!'

There was the usual half-hearted round of applause before Scott and Andy launched into the funky opening of 'Coke Party', and we were off. It didn't take long for the audience to get going. They were out to have a good time and, even if we had played badly, that wouldn't have stopped them. They were bopping around and engaging in full-contact, amphetamine-powered dance routines.

Some of their steps and Cuban moves would make it impossible for me to hear the term 'Come Dancing' again without automatically ducking.

'Coke Party' went down well and, without pause, we gave them 'Pocket Patrol', 'Smart Peroxide' and 'Zoo People'. I produced a few suspect chord changes in 'Coke Party'; however, the guys didn't seem to notice. I made a mental note: *no more drinking before gigs*. Even though I was pretty keyed up, the alcohol seemed to be slowing me down. I began to feel distant. I could play, but I felt as though a few of the wires connecting my fingers to my brain had been cut. It was like working on a back-up system that wasn't quite up to the job.

This club was, without doubt, a very 'heavy' scene. I couldn't help thinking of Eric: *Bad vibes, bad vibes, man.*

There was some serious shit going on in the far corner. A group of men were huddled together, watching something I, thankfully, couldn't see. Nearer the stage, spectral shapes, tightly bound in studded straps, were coasting through waves of smoke, like fiends in a horror pic. I kept on getting distracted by the sight of mutilated cocks, swinging under the weight of thick, brassy rings.

After a while I began to get quite annoyed with myself. The PAC was getting to me. What was my problem? What right had I got to pass any kind of judgement on these guys? If they wanted to turn their cocks into mincemeat, that was their business. They were keeping themselves to themselves, and they were obviously all consenting adults. So what was the problem? Although I couldn't think of any rational objection, the atmosphere continued to bother me. It was as though there was some dark undercurrent. Something wasn't right.

In spite of all this thinking, and my brain-wrist malfunction, I was still able to play, although my performance was quite mechanical. By the time we were half-way through 'Cherie Blair', I was aware that Scott was really enjoying himself. He was far too much of a performer to forgo the opportunity of making a spectacle of himself. He had started to milk the front row of the audience, wiggling his hips and striking the odd rock' n' roll pose.

Even Andy seemed to be getting into it. Yet I couldn't lose my feeling of discomfort.

I shook my head and focused on the chord changes. I even took a solo, which was actually quite good – so good that a few of the creatures standing next to me started to put their hands together in appreciation. As I looked up, to acknowledge their gesture, I couldn't help catching a glimpse of someone – a shadowy figure – out of the corner of my eye, although to say that I caught a glimpse of him isn't really true. He was standing too far back to be seen properly. Yet I knew he was there; a ghost, at the edge of awareness. He was standing directly behind me, looking at me. I was getting a wave, but a wave unlike any I had ever experienced. It was confusing. This wave was cold. I was getting coldness, mixed with desire. *And hunger?* Yes, hunger.

I turned to bring him into view, and there he was. A really big guy, wearing a leather hood, a hood with a small mouth-zip. He wasn't dancing, or moving, he was just standing still, looking at me.

I hit the wrong chord and quickly had to change. Scott glanced over, and I mouthed 'Sorry'. It was really weird, I wanted to move away. His closeness was unsettling me. It felt like if I let go and closed my eyes I would be drawn into a dark, frozen vortex. I fought against it and made another mistake. *Shit!* I was beginning to panic. *Pull yourself together! For fuck's sake!*

I lost it completely. I stopped playing and felt like I was falling backwards. Andy and Scott were looking over at me and clearly wondering what the fuck was happening. They kind of saved me. Their eyes seemed to hook my mind and yank me forward again. *Pull yourself together!*

I raised a hand to show Scott and Andy that I was OK and played a few block chords before recovering my part.

Slowly, I was able to shut him out, but it was so hard. It was like trying to climb a steep hill against the pull of a huge elastic band. And, all the time, I could feel him there, watching, ready to snap me back.

We ended the first half of our set with a standard, 'Foxy Lady', which really got the crowd going. And when we finished by turning the last chord into a wall of noise – with Phil going absolutely spare before a final cymbal crash – the crowd seemed to be very much won over. Scott shouted into the mike, 'Back in 45', and undid his guitar strap.

I left the stage really quickly. I wanted to get away, fast. Glancing over my shoulder, I saw he was still there, his head rotating in my direction. It was like being in a gun sight. As I trotted toward the door, it was as though my back were being stroked by a finger of ice.

Andy caught up with me and slapped me on the shoulder. 'All right?'

'Yeah.'

'That wasn't too bad. Not bad at all.'

We made our way downstairs and had a few pints. In spite of my earlier resolution I decided that I really needed a drink. Scott, Phil and Andy were quite high (as they always were while gigging). They were sweating profusely and had all acquired that glazed, slightly manic look. To talk, they had to shout over the jukebox, and they couldn't prevent themselves from spitting. Every utterance came through a spray of water droplets. I apologised for fucking up but they were too into it all to make a fuss.

Unfortunately, the interval soon passed. I didn't really want to go back up but forced myself. As I walked across the dance floor, I saw two guys wheeling some timber stocks away. Some serious shit had been going on in the interval.

'Well,' said the DJ. 'What a night! A new PAC record!'

There was a cheer from the audience.

'And thank you, Master Lash. An excellent performance. I'll be needing your services later in the Red Room so, please, keep your pleasure-string supple and swift!'

A few laughs and handclaps.

The DJ beckoned us back up on stage. 'You loved them before and you'll love them again. The delightfully pretty *Free Radicals*!'

The cheer from the audience was enthusiastic as we launched

into 'Trade' but, as soon as my hands made contact with the keyboard, I knew that he was there again. And as I felt the wave of coldness sweep over me, I seemed to get an image in my mind, an image that I couldn't understand: *darkness, movement . . . blood?* I moved forward in my seat, and looked down at the keys, blocking every damn thing out of my head. The second half of the set seemed to last for ever.

When I got home, which must have been at about two or three in the morning, Eric still wasn't back. I figured that he had opted for a night on the tiles. God knows where he might be. Our original discussion about a two-week review had long since been forgotten. I wished he was around. I wanted to talk about the evening.

I was dead tired but too psyched-up and disturbed to sleep. My head was full of images of dangling, ringed cocks and the fuck room. I was trying to keep the hooded figure who had been staring at me out of my head.

I'm not homophobic, by any means, but there was something about hanging out in a gay environment for that long that made me feel homesick. I wanted breasts, and smooth skin, the smell of fanny, and a well-upholstered arse. I wanted to be on familiar territory again.

I slipped Joni into the CD and pulled the cans on. I lit a cigarette and thought of Cairo. I was so tempted to give her a call. *So* tempted. But I didn't; I knew she wouldn't appreciate it.

Cairo was such a part of my life now, it was near impossible to imagine life without her.

I thought of her eyes, her hair and the contours of her body. I immersed myself in images of Cairo. A mental purification ritual. I imagined kissing her neck and inhaling the scent of patchouli. Her long, delicate fingers, manipulating and teasing my flesh.

She said it was *fated*, our first meeting. *We meet the people we need to meet, to learn the lessons we need to learn.* That's what she had said. I could almost hear her voice. Sweet and husky. Words from a different time. *Moksha, Marrakesh, Samadhi . . .*

from Bindu to Ojas, Chelsea to Carnaby Street, here to there,
without moving . . .

We met in Highgate Wood. I was still at school, preparing for my
A-levels. I remember it was late afternoon. I was strolling along,
humming to myself, and in the distance I could see this woman,
reaching up into a tree. As I approached, I saw that she was
talking, too. At first, I thought she was just crazy, talking to the
birds. She was wearing a long coat, a big hat and loads of scarves.
As I walked by, she called out, 'Excuse me!'

I went over.

'I'm sorry to trouble you, but there's a cat up this tree. I think
it's stuck.'

'Oh,' I replied.

I peered up and, there, sitting on the first branch, was a smallish
black cat, almost a kitten, but not quite. It started to mew.

The woman smiled at me. 'Poor thing. Would you mind giving
me a leg-up?'

'No,' I said. I joined my hands together and bent down to make
a step.

The woman looked at my hands for a moment and then said,
'But my boots are muddy.'

'That's OK,' I said, trying to oblige.

'No, I don't think so.'

She slipped one of her boots off and placed a warm nylon-
covered foot in my hand. 'OK,' she said, 'lift.'

She wasn't that heavy. I lifted her up, and she reached out to get
the cat. The cat mewed and moved along a little, so as to be just
out of her reach. 'Here, puss-puss,' she said. 'Here, puss-puss.'
Then she added, 'Can you give me some more lift?' I heaved her
up, as high as I could get, and my arms began to tremble with the
effort. 'Just a bit more,' she said.

I moved a little closer to the tree, and tried to keep a discreet
distance from her buttocks; however, I couldn't help feeling the
curve underneath her coat, against my face. It didn't seem to
bother her. I don't know what happened then, but I guess I must

109

have lost my footing or something. Anyway, I slipped, and we both came down, into the mud. The woman landed heavily on top of me.

'I'm really sorry,' I said, winded.

'No, no, it's my fault entirely.'

We both got up and she put a muddy foot back into her boot. The back of my jumper and my jeans were soaked.

'Oh, dear, look at you,' she said.

'Oh, don't worry. Shall we have another go?'

'If you don't mind.'

And so, this is what we did for about half an hour, as the sun began to set. I repeatedly lifted Cairo up, and then dropped her. During the course of this exercise, the normal boundaries that exclude certain types of physical contact were completely dissolved. I held her round the waist and enjoyed the sensation of her warm, large breasts under her jumper. The scent of patchouli. She had a few attempts at lifting me, too, but they were completely unsuccessful. They ended up with us both rolling around in the mud.

The situation was finally resolved when the cat saw a squirrel, suddenly became animated, and scrambled down the trunk before taking off into the dusk.

We both looked at each other, feeling pretty stupid. Cairo's face was spotted with mud, and her lipstick was all smudged. Although she was old – by my standards – she had a kind, pretty face. I could tell that she must have been staggeringly attractive – before I was born.

I don't know what I looked like – with leaves stuck to my jumper and leaves in my hair, patches of brown rainwater covering my clothes. I learned much later that Cairo had thought I looked 'vulnerable and sexy'.

She introduced herself, and I can remember asking if Cairo was her real name. She laughed, 'It is now.' From which I guessed it had been assumed. Then we walked off toward the park entrance. We got chatting and, when she found out I was into music, she began to tell me a little about herself.

She had had a lot to do with the music industry; she had been a model in the sixties, her first job had been as a house model for Dickens & Jones. Apparently, she earned £8 a week and thought herself well-off at the time. During the morning she did boring chores but at lunchtime she would put something groovy on and walk around the restaurant tables. Eventually, she was spotted by Jean Muir. I didn't know who Jean Muir was, but I sort of nodded, recognizing that it was appropriate to look impressed. I had heard of some of the photographers though, Lichfield, Bailey. But when she talked about Donavon, I thought she meant the singer.

It was nice. She was, I guessed, nearly – although not quite – as old as my mother, but nowhere near as uptight. And I liked her scarves and boots – my mum would never be seen in such clothes. So we strolled on, talking about this and that. Then, out of the blue, while I was listening to the stream of talk about London in the 1960s, the cost of living, and so on, I heard her say, '. . . and Jimi Hendrix came to that one.' My heart stopped.

'You met Hendrix?'

'Sure.'

I was walking with history. 'Wow!'

'I only met him once.'

'Wow!'

Cairo laughed. 'It was just after he came over to England. He had an amazing flat in Soho. He had blacked out all of the windows, and everything was black. Even the bedsheets . . .'

I hung on to the implication. Jesus, I thought. I'm walking in Highgate Wood with a woman who has slept with Jimi Hendrix. 'What was he like?' I asked, unable to disguise the tremor of veneration in my voice.

'Oooh . . . it was so long ago now. He was . . .' she paused, and looked out into the shadowed wood in a kind of sad way. 'He was young. Very full of himself . . . He dressed in this really flamboyant way. And back then, of course, it was even more arresting. And . . . he grinned a lot.'

111

'What did he say?'

'God, I can't remember what he said.'

'What, nothing?'

'Not really. I wasn't really listening.'

'You weren't listening!' I couldn't believe it.

'He was just this . . . guy around town. You know?'

I wanted to find out more and wasn't prepared to give up. 'But what was he like? Hendrix. Was he . . . good company . . .' when I said those words I almost died. What a dick-brained thing to say. As if that would have been important; however, Cairo just took the question straight.

'As I said, I can't really remember the detail. To be honest, we were both totally out of our heads. Apparently he was always out of his head then. And . . . he was quite short . . .'

'Short? I thought he was huge.'

'God, no, he was really short . . . but he had . . .' She suddenly cut herself off before saying, 'Look, I can only remember one or two things, it really was a long time ago.'

When we got to the park gate, I was getting ready to go off to the bus stop, but Cairo said, 'No, you can't. You're soaked. Come home with me, I only live over the road. Dry out, and then I'll call you a cab, OK? It's all my fault.'

'It's OK, really,' I replied.

'No, I insist.'

So we walked out of Highgate Wood, as one of those fantastic, North London autumn mists settled in. It was worthy of Keats. We crossed the road and walked up Highgate Avenue. As we did so, Cairo linked her arm with mine . . .

Remembering my first meeting with Cairo had helped keep the images of the Prince Albert gig out of my head. By the time Joni was singing the last track, I was well on the way to oblivion – but I was snatched from the edge of sleep by the sound of a bottle smashing outside. I took off the cans. My heart was suddenly loud in my ears. I listened. The tenant upstairs stirred and walked slowly across the ceiling. I expected to hear Eric come in; however, nothing happened. Again I heard footsteps upstairs, then silence. Gradually, my heart slowed down. It must have been another hour or so before I finally started to drift off again.

code 10

'Look, hope you don't mind,' said Eric – which suggested very strongly that I might – 'See, I've got a bloke turning up this afternoon.'

'Here?' I asked.

'Yeah.'

'Who?'

'A comrade.'

I guessed that he was referring to another GLF man.

'You don't mind, do you, Nick, old son?'

'Err . . .'

'Not a problem, is it?'

I thought for a moment. 'No, I suppose not.'

I lit a Benson and Eric began rolling an unusually spartan joint, a tiny cylinder that enclosed a miser's pinch of tobacco and dope. It could barely sustain two draws. I assumed that he wanted to keep his head in order. As I watched Eric, it suddenly occurred to me that, what he described as 'a bloke turning up' might mean virtually anything, so I considered it prudent to ask further questions.

'Will he be staying long, your man?'

'No. About half an hour maybe. That's all.'

'Are you allowed to tell me his name?'

''Course I am, his name's Code.'

Eric took a drag, and approximately a third of his roll-up

vanished, the glowing red terminus crackling toward his lips. He showed no sign of having said anything suspect.

'Code,' I repeated. 'As in codename?'

'Yeah, that's right.'

' . . . And that's his real name? Code?'

'Yeah. It's short for Cody. His name's Nigel Cody. But he hates being called Nige or Nigel, so he calls himself Code. Sounds cool, eh?'

It certainly did.

'So what does Code do for the GLF?'

'He advises.'

'About what?'

'Oh, you know. This and that . . .'

Eric drew on his joint again, reducing it to a minuscule stub. He then held the stub between thumb and forefinger and took a final drag. For a moment I thought he was going to smoke it all and that the denouement of this procedure would be to let a fragment of ash fall from his lips (without burning them), while rubbing his thumb and forefinger together like a stage magician, to show that the joint had vanished; however, instead, he simply plucked a sodden flake of paper and tobacco from his mouth and flicked it into the ashtray.

I said, 'And . . .', to urge him on.

Eric realized that he had lost the plot, and continued, 'Sorry, yeah. He advises on animal welfare.'

'Animal welfare?'

'Yeah.'

'What is he, some kind of . . .' I couldn't think of anything other than animal-welfare expert, which didn't seem to help clarify matters. Fortunately, Eric finished the sentence for me.

'Vet. He's a vet.'

'A veterinary surgeon.'

I used the full job title just to confirm that Eric and I were sharing the same waveband.

'Yeah, that's right. He works in a group practice out Queens Park way. Clever blokes, vets.' Eric was suddenly moved to praise the profession. 'When you think about it, a doctor has only got to understand the human body. One species. But vets, well, they've got to understand everything. Budgies, cows, cats, snakes . . . Apparently, it's really difficult to become a vet. Only the stupid ones become doctors. So they say.'

I made some approving noises before asking, 'So when's he coming, Code?'

'This afternoon.'

'Right.'

I dropped the subject of the GLF man. Eric and I let an hour or so slip by; our brains functioning on a low wattage. He rolled another modest joint, from which I took a toke or two. No more than that. For the most part, I stuck to my Bensons. Eric seemed pretty relaxed. He even put on some music. Joni Mitchell's much neglected *Mingus* album, which contains some truly startling bass lines, courtesy of the late Jaco Pastorius.

'He was fuckin A, wasn't he?' said Eric.

'Who, Jaco?'

'Yeah.'

'He certainly was,' I agreed.

'They used to call him the Hendrix of the electric bass. Fucking tragedy. That they should both go out. Like they did.'

Jaco was snapping and popping those strings. Bending notes and punctuating chords with a bass line that bounced your musical intelligence on to a different plane.

'Bar fight, wasn't it?' I said. 'The sleeve notes on my Weather Report compilation say he copped it in a brawl or something.'

'Sort of,' said Eric. 'He got ill. Became manic, I think, started getting irritable and aggressive. Usual shit. Anyway, he'd been barred from this club in Florida and wouldn't take no for an answer. And the bouncer was pretty evil. Put Jaco in intensive care. Within a couple of weeks he was dead. Still. Lasted ten years longer than Hendrix.'

'Did you ever meet him? Jaco?'

'No, after my time, mate. But I knew a bloke who did. A yank

called Trent Kazsniak . . . said that Jaco was really cool.
Funny, kind, gentle – crazy that he should have gone out in
a fight.'

'What happened, then? Had he done too much speed, or what?'

'No. I don't think he did very much at all. Just one of those
things . . .' Eric looked at me. One of his knowing looks.

We both sat and respectfully waited for the tape to finish. I
could see Eric's lips moving. Ever so slightly. He was obviously
saying some sort of prayer. It was kind of moving. The atmosphere
gradually lifted.

Eventually, Eric looked up and smiled. 'I heard an interesting
fact the other day, Nick, old son.'

My expectation was that he would now treat me to some high-
grade rock trivia. He was obviously feeling relaxed enough to
talk about music and the past. 'Oh yeah?' I said, eagerly.

'Concerning English usage.' My heart sank. Eric had a real flare
for unpredictability. I would never have anticipated that the
subject of English usage would arise in our conversation at that
point. 'What was that then, Eric?'

Pause. 'Did you know that the word "puss", or "pussy", was
a seventeenth-century term for "cunt"?'

'As in vagina, rather than an undesirable person?'

'Yeah. But that isn't the interesting bit.'

'Right.'

'The interesting bit is that the word "pussy" had nothing to do
with cats. It was only in the nineteenth century that pussy came
to mean cat. Apparently, children started using the term "pussy"
as a pet name for cats, and it just kind of caught on.'

'So?'

'Well, that's totally mind-blowing. I mean, can you imagine if
all the kids now suddenly started calling their cats "cunts".'

'I see your point.'

'First you've got to ask yourself, why? Why was it that all these
Victorian kids suddenly started calling their pets the equivalent
of our word for cunt and, secondly, you've got to ask yourself how
they got away with it! How come it caught on . . .'

'Well, Eric,' I ventured, 'language is a funny thing. Think of words like "bad" or "wicked". They're getting to mean "good" and "jolly good". Yeah?'

'No, mate,' Eric replied, 'not the same thing. Not the same thing at all. There are precedents in African-American culture. You know, when jazzers played a really "hot" set, it was "cool". It's a black rap, you know? But kids suddenly calling cats "cunts" and getting away with it, among tight-arsed Victorian families – no, man, something weird was happening there.'

'Like what?'

'I don't know. Interference from other universes maybe . . .'

I let the cosmic implications of the word "pussy" hang in the atmosphere for a while, before saying, 'I've got an interesting fact, too.'

'Oh yeah?'

'How long can a cockroach live after it's been beheaded?'

'About seven days.'

I was deeply upset. 'How did you know that?'

Eric laughed a wheezy, crackling laugh and looked smug. I realized I wasn't going to get an answer. 'Here, guess what?' Eric continued, apropos of nothing.

'I don't know. What?'

'I might be going into business.'

'You! Business!'

'Yeah.'

'But you hate business, you hate everything to do with business.'

'Well, it's not a *straight* business, of course. More a way of raising capital for the cause.'

'But I thought you didn't like handling money.'

'I don't, but we live in desperate times, Nick, old son. And desperate times means desperate measures. We had a convocation of the Supreme Council, and it was decided that I should go ahead.'

'With what?'

'I'm going to act as consultant to a green-friendly software house. They want to market a new computer game called

118

Eco-Crash, it's a sort of *Civilization*, but in reverse. And very educational. I have to help think up the crash menu. The story lines. You know, there's obvious ones, like Meltdown, polar caps and all that. But there's plenty of less obvious ones too, like Heat and Dust.'

'What's that then?'

'You know, Mexico, but on a global scale.'

'What about Mexico?'

'It's a desert, right?'

'Yeah?'

'Never used to be. That was the Spaniards. After kicking the shit out of the Aztecs they tore up the trees and put too many animals out to graze. The same thing's going on now. Deserts are growing by about 20 million acres a year.'

'Fuck.'

'So this game will educate kids and help the cause. Good, eh?'

'Yeah. Sounds all right. Hang about.' I thought that I might make a modest contribution to this project. 'What about this . . . It's called Pink Planet. There are too many non-degradable oestrogens in the water. Yeah? These start to affect the male nervous system. Blokes start fancying blokes. The sperm count goes down, but men become better and more enthusiastic dancers. Everyone now feels comfortable doing a crotch frame. Gym membership soars, as do sales of designer jeans and old ABBA albums. This destabilizes the economy and, hey presto, *Eco-Crash!*'

Eric tugged on his beard for a few moments. 'You know, Nick, old son, the basic idea isn't that bad.'

'Ten per cent?'

'Fuck off.'

We carried on thinking of *Eco-Crash* story lines for a while – some of which became quite complex (and silly) – but had to stop when Code arrived. In my imagination, I had constructed a mental picture of some kind of renegade. A typical, aging GLF militant, with dreadlocks and combat fatigues. But, instead, I opened the door to a youngish, clean-shaven man in a tweed jacket, tie and corduroys. His one concession to fashion was a pair of groovy-looking oblong glasses.

'I've come to see Mr Wright?' He was well spoken. Not what I expected at all.

'You're Code?' I asked. I guess I must have been wearing an expression of sheer disbelief because he replied, almost indignantly, 'Yes! To see Mr Wright.'

'Sure, come in. Come in.'

Eric greeted the young man with a firm and vigorous handshake. 'Good to see you, Code, old son.'

Code, old son! It sounded ridiculous. 'Do you want a coffee?' I asked.

'I don't drink coffee I'm afraid,' replied Code. 'Do you have a herb tea?'

'No. I'm out of herb teas.'

'Then a mug of hot spring water will be fine.'

'Hot water?'

'Spring water. Yes, please.'

'Coffee, Eric?'

'No thanks, old son.'

I boiled a mug of hot spring water for Code and left the GLF conspirators to talk in the front room, but not before removing a large glass from the kitchen cupboard which would serve as a makeshift hearing-aid when placed against the bedroom wall. At first I couldn't hear much. They were talking too quietly, and Eric had turned the blaster up a little; however, as they became more relaxed, their talking became more natural, and I was able to catch the odd fragment: *That bastard . . . let us down again . . . said he was behind it 100 per cent.* I was intrigued . . . *a very healthy young chimpanzee.* What? *Mill Hill . . . Mill Hill? . . . reliable source. Very reliable.* And so on.

I didn't know what the fuck they were on about. Fascinating though these fragments were, it was like listening to a play by Harold Pinter. You know the sort: *My mother died today. Did she? Yes. Oh, the goats, they frighten me.*

Sadly, I returned the glass to the kitchen cupboard, none the wiser. Whatever Eric was up to would remain a mystery. I lay on my bed, put the cans on and listened to Zappa doing some guitar-hero stuff on *St Etienne*. Track seven. 'Jazz From Hell'.

At the next rehearsal, Scott handed me a copy of *Gay London*. 'Read this. It's terrible.'

At first, I thought he was showing me a bad review of our gig at the Prince Albert club. I only registered the letters – PAC – in bold type but, as I read down the column of text, I became quite cold, a familiar coldness that made my bones and my veins ache.

'It happened the same night,' he continued, 'in the fuck room.'

'Oh my God!' was all that I could say. I looked at the small, grainy photograph of the Edward II and shuddered.

'Here, let me have a look,' said Andy, leaning over my shoulder. I let him take the paper.

'It's really weird,' said Scott. 'I'd taken Nick to see the fuck room before the gig and . . .' He trailed off, perhaps remembering my reaction, perhaps unsure of what to make of it. Our eyes met, but I looked away.

'Jesus,' said Andy, 'and it's happened before?'

'Not there, not at the PAC,' said Scott, 'but at another club. A place called the Departure Lounge, up west.'

'Fuck. What a way to go' was Andy's only further contribution. I could see that he was shifting his hips from side to side as he read the final paragraphs, in sympathetic agony. He tossed the paper aside and went out to the van.

'I'm surprised the national press hasn't made more of this,' said Phil.

'I'm not,' replied Scott. 'Why should they? As far as they're concerned it's just another dead bender.'

'I wonder if the police will try to contact us?' I asked.

'Maybe,' said Phil. 'Maybe.'

The victim, named as Jeffrey Dowd (a twenty-six-year-old nurse employed by Riverside Health Authority), had died of internal bleeding. His iliac vessel had been severed, resulting in a catastrophic haemorrhage. While fisting Dowd, the murderer had apparently released a handful of four-inch razors (and several tabs of acid) into his rectum. The Met had logged a similar murder three months earlier at the Departure Lounge (a club not too dissimilar to the PAC). On that occasion, the murderer had released a quantity of disinfectant containing isopropanolol into the victim's rectum, a substance that stops the heart. There were no suspects.

I shook my head. I remembered the creeping cold in the fuck room. I also remembered the tall hooded figure standing behind me. His stare. His chilling presence.

'Are you all right?' asked Scott.

'Yeah.' I got up and poured myself a drink from Vince's bar. 'I'm all right.'

Scott came up to me and said, quietly, 'You felt something. Didn't you? In that fuck room?'

'It was cold. And it freaked me out a bit. That's all.'

'Are you sure? Just that. And nothing else?'

'I don't know. It felt weird. And . . . I was worried. You know? About you and Phil?'

'What was that?' Phil came over, having heard his name being mentioned. 'What's up?'

'Nick's worried about us!' said Scott.

'Why?'

I looked Phil in the eye. 'I think you two should stay away from fuck rooms and all that shit, OK?'

'We do,' said Phil.

'Really?'

'Sort of. We're not serious players any more. Not really. We're really boring now.' He kissed Scott on the cheek. Scott shrugged.

'You will be careful, won't you? At least while this crazy fuck's around,' I said.

'Sure we will.' Scott reached out and squeezed my arm. I was glad we were putting that taboo to bed. It felt OK; I didn't tense up or anything.

'Good.' I said. 'Good.'

'Come on,' said Scott. 'We should set up.'

I left the bar area and helped Andy lug his old H&H out of the van. The ritual of shifting the amps, untangling the leads, juggling with plugs and avoiding accidental electrocution diverted my thoughts for a while.

After tuning up, we were ready, and played through the set order prepared for the Cranbrook gig. But I was playing on autopilot. I couldn't help thinking about Dowd's ignoble demise. In the darkness of the fuck room, offering his arse to the greased-up fist of an anonymous partner, his temporary lover. The slow penetration. The movement. Pushing down, and releasing. Pushing down, and releasing. And then his sudden awareness that something was very wrong. The pain. The blood, seeping out of his anus. A slick, sticky pool on that ice-cold floor. I felt sick. *Darkness, movement . . . blood? Darkness, movement, blood!* These were sensations that were, in some curious way, familiar. I stopped playing.

Scott, Phil and Andy were all looking at me. However, they carried on playing, as though we were doing a live performance. I lifted my hand up, as if to say: *Go ahead. It's OK.* I fiddled about with my amp, pretending that I had a problem, and then dropped back in at the chorus. I wanted to get the rehearsal over with. I wanted to get back home as soon as possible.

nine inches

We made love that first evening. Cairo and I. She told me that she would dry my clothes while we had coffee. She encouraged me to have a bath and gave me a silk dressing-gown. A black Chinese number, with a dragon emblazoned on the back in fluorescing reds, golds and greens. We sat by the fire drinking from heavy earthenware mugs, talking about music and art, my aspirations and hers. The cats came in and joined us, stretching and arching their backs before collapsing sideways on to the carpet – purring, like motorbikes. Their decadence was infectious.

Cairo lit night-light candles under tiny ceramic bowls containing scented oil. The room filled with the fragrance of rose blossom, heavy and soporific. Then she produced some dope, and we smoked and relaxed. Outside, the mist was damp and cold. Inside, was warmth and the gentle lambency of firelight and candles. She was wearing a thick red-towelling bathrobe with a hood, which made her look like a priestess from some obscure sect. She had put some Japanese bamboo-flute music on, very quietly, in the background. It evoked a sense of stillness and meditative calm.

I can remember how Cairo invited me to rest my head in her lap. She was sitting cross-legged and placed a small pillow in the dip between her thighs. She stroked my hair and massaged my temples. It seemed to last for ever. I was so stoned and chilled out, it was like a dream. I had inadvertently passed from one world into another, moved between universes. My life receded, A-levels, school, even the piano. It's really curious how fragile reality is, how unreliable it can be. Load up your brain with THC and even the bedrock of your life begins to crumble.

I can remember thinking how subtle the bamboo flute sounded. I can remember listening to how the player let his melody rise and fall in quarter-tones. He was one with his instrument, his breath – his life-breath – vibrating in the bamboo. In comparison, the piano seemed absurd, a wardrobe full of metal and string, felt hammers and matchsticks; the pianist entirely divorced from the music he produces. In that weird, dreamlike state, I began to wonder whether I had made some dreadful mistake. Whether I had in fact imagined an instrument called a piano because, in reality, such a ludicrous mechanical device could never be taken seriously as a musical instrument.

My centre shifted; the usual landmarks were no longer visible. So it seemed perfectly natural when Cairo loosened her bathrobe and let it fall down to her waist. That kind of thing could – indeed would – happen here.

I opened my eyes and looked up at her breasts. Two substantial fruits, ripe to the point of bursting. The nipples, pink and erect. She slipped her hands inside my dressing-gown and rubbed my chest. Then she pulled the dressing-gown open. I lay there, exposed, breathing heavily, my cock, sticking out, so still I could feel it jerking with every heartbeat. I was desperate for her to touch it. Desperate. I moved my hips upward and groaned. 'Hush now,' she said. 'Be still.' Cairo stroked my hair and passed her fingers down over my eyelids. 'Close your eyes,' she whispered.

I hadn't seen a bottle of oil; however, when her hands touched my chest again, they were viscous and slick. She massaged my forehead. She massaged my temples. She massaged my neck. And all the time, my cock ached for contact. I tried to give it a squeeze myself, to release the tension, but Cairo laughed and pushed my hand back.

'Patience,' she said. 'It'll be so much more enjoyable, if you wait.'

'But it's almost painful. It's so . . . tense.'

'Patience, Nick. Patience.'

She continued to massage my chest with warm oil while my cock jerked, marking time, like the second hand of a weird biological clock. The need for contact was intolerable. I couldn't stop pushing my hips forward. It was automatic, a hard-wired response. My nervous system was forcing my cock to search the empty space around it for a surface, anything that would resist, anything that could be pushed up against.

'Oh, please.' I had never been reduced to begging before. 'Please . . .'

Cairo reached down and stroked the underside of my cock. As she did so her breasts settled on my face. I was surrounded by their warmth and softness. My mouth opened, and filled with musk-scented flesh. I raised my hands, eager to grab, and squeeze, to feel ridges of dough rise between my closing fingers.

'No.' Cairo guided my hands back.

I looked into her eyes. They were blue and grey at the same time. A beautiful, watery colour. Both pools were momentarily concealed, as her heavy lids descended. She inhaled, and as her lungs filled with the opiate, ambrosial air her breasts slowly lifted, recalling the majestic buoyancy of whales rising from the ocean.

She sucked her fingers and moistened her lips with saliva so that they glistened in the firelight. She then reached forward again and drew wet circles of pleasure on my restless and sensitive skin. Her touch was infuriating, more absent than present, exposing my utter need to penetrate.

'Oh, Christ,' I said.

'What?'

'I think I'm going to come.'

Cairo reached down, expertly squeezing the helmet between thumb and fingers, just at the right place. She then, very gently, almost like a doctor caring for a patient, began pushing my balls down inside the scrotal sack. The tension went.

'Is that better?' she asked.

'Much better, thanks.'

'You're so horny,' she said, like a compliment, like you're *so beautiful*. And as she said those words, in such a husky sexy voice, I felt the pre-come tingle, again, vibrating through my genitals like a mild electric current.

'Oh, Christ!' I said again.

Cairo slipped my head off the cushion, and accomplished a 69 in a single, graceful movement. Her thighs were hot against my cheeks. I felt her breasts on my torso and her mouth close around my cock. The pleasure was so intense, I groaned out loud. 'Oh fuck . . .'

It was hopeless trying to control myself, so I let go. I came immediately and Cairo sucked on each pulse, drawing me into her mouth. She sucked the marrow from my cock, while every sinew in my body was pulled taut and tight. It was exquisite, by far the most extraordinary, explosive orgasm I have ever experienced. I cried out as though I were being tortured, a long, agonized moan. Curiously, I can still remember how my moan seemed to precipitate a good deal of ground-level action. Several cats rocketed out the room, shocked by the sudden onset of my climax. A kind of whoosh, skid – plonk.

Cairo didn't let my cock slip from her mouth. She just kept it there. Locked into place, vacuum-sealed. Cairo then eased her thighs apart and let her cunt smother my mouth. It was like being kissed, by huge, moist lips. They parted, and I pushed my tongue deep inside of her; and then it was my turn to suck and draw her essence out. Threads of sticky fluid, released from some internal spindle, passed though my lips and slipped down my throat. The atmosphere was narcotic. The dope, the rose blossom and her cunt juice combined, a heady cocktail so powerful, it almost made me lose consciousness. Cairo began to moan and move backwards and forwards. As the pitch of her moaning rose, waves of sympathetic vibration revived my cock. I began to stiffen again.

As soon as I was full, and hard in her mouth, she released me. She turned her body around and squatted above me, her elbows resting on her thighs. She then descended, down on to my cock, impaling herself on my stiffness. A sudden furious descent, like a fist crashing down on to a tabletop in anger. There was no fumbling, or groping, redirecting or pointing, only swift descent and a glorious running through.

Then Cairo fucked me. Pounding, repeatedly falling on to my cock, again and again and again. Her breasts bouncing and sweaty. I reached up to feel their weight and let them slap heavily into my upturned hands. Then she fell forward and pushed her tongue into my mouth. Our eyes were wide open, staring at each other, almost appalled at what we were doing, almost appalled by the intensity of our pleasure. And then I came, another wild explosion of sensation. Cairo could feel me releasing, inside of her, and began to grind her hips down. I reached out and pulled her hips lower. Grabbed the fleshy handles of her hips and pulled her down further, and further still, until it hurt. Then I let go, and we both became limp and lifeless, our breathing, synchronized.

The fire hissed and crackled, and the cats gradually returned. Soon I could feel soft fur against my feet. I curled my toes into the living warmth.

After coming, reality pulls you back on board with astonishing speed. Although I wanted to hold the moment for ever, I couldn't help saying 'I've got to call my mother. She'll be worried. Do you mind?'

'Of course not,' said Cairo.

She slid off, and we both wrapped ourselves up in our previously discarded clothes. We spoke quietly to each other, politely, almost over-politely, as though we had both been guilty of committing an act of great violence and we wanted to show each other that it was all right, really.

I called my mother and explained to her that I had met an old friend and that we had been for a drink together. Mum said that she had been worried about me, and I said I had figured she would be worried, which is why I had rung. And she said, 'Good boy.' *Good boy!*

Cairo insisted that I got a cab home, and insisted that she pay for it. She gave me a ten-pound note (which was way over the top). Some people might have felt bad about that, accepting money. Accepting pay? But I didn't. I merely felt that she wanted me to get home quickly and safely.

I called around to see Cairo quite often, that autumn. I suppose I was in love with her. Well, how could I not be. Of course I was in love with her. I was seventeen, read a little poetry, and Cairo had opened up whole realms of sensory experience that were previously unknown to me. I had had sex before. Lots of it, in fact. I've always been able to score. But, before Cairo, sex had always been so rushed, so amateur. And the girls who I had had sex with were so inept. Prior to having my cock sucked by Cairo, fellatio was always such a . . . *dental* experience, a kind of 'wait for it', followed by *ouch, ouch, ouch*. And being touched was so wooden, contact without sensation, contact without warmth. Cairo was entirely different: of course I fell in love with her.

And, looking back now, I can see that Cairo was so good with me. The way she guided me through my hopeless crush: 'Nick, you don't love me. Well, at least not in the way you think you do. You really don't. You're seventeen.'

Just saying my age seemed to confirm and reinforce her views. If I felt that I loved her, she suggested I should wank twice and review the situation.

Although I took some persuading at first I now recognize that she was right. As my passion subsided, the true nature of our relationship became clearer: we were friends who fucked – and Cairo had quite a few friends who she fucked. By the time I was nineteen, my other sexual partners were beginning to pick up a few tricks of their own. They were younger and firmer, and I began to see Cairo differently: not so beautiful as I had originally thought, not quite as sexy . . . and so on. I never had to say to Cairo: *I don't love you any more*. And because I never had to say that, we remained friends, good friends.

Cairo hasn't had to work since the 1960s. She calls her art her work, but she hasn't really sold that many canvasses. In the late sixties she was part of an 'in crowd' who seemed to live within, and off, a social stratum divorced from economic pressures. Once you had penetrated it you could live between its floor and ceiling, travelling from party to party (and country to country), at the expense of various minor royals, film celebrities and pop stars. Of course, for some (like Cairo), passage was only secured on the basis of a fundamental expectation; that a time-honoured exchange would eventually take place. Cairo was a stunner in the 1960s, a real stunner. No one that good-looking had to do a stroke of work between 1966 and 1969.

I guess she must have sensed that the seventies were going to be a bit more grim, and in 1971 she married the American concert promoter, Hayden Hughes. He was pretty successful and handled a number of the big prog-rock bands of the early seventies. It was during this period that Cairo came into contact with the Turtle Tree for the first time and, of course, the young and very talented, Eric Wright. Cairo's marriage to Hayden didn't work out. He didn't adapt when punk happened, and when the big prog-rock bands became extinct, Hayden's year planner was empty. He had grown out of touch. His solution to the problem was drink and, subsequently, things went from bad to worse. He got to smack Cairo once, and once only, before she stormed out of their place in Miami, leaving him to top up his bourbon with tears. Unfortunately, he had squandered most of his assets, and the divorce settlement was virtually nothing; however, Cairo was still resourceful. Although somewhat older, she was still very good-looking. She exhumed her address books and made it to the right parties. Within a year, she had married Tom Clark of Trooper, a heavy-metal band who enjoyed moderate success in the States all the way through the seventies – although God only knows why; they were appalling.

Again, the relationship didn't work, although the reason why it didn't work was the best one: they just didn't love each other. Tom and Cairo had come together, still hurting, on the rebound, and desperate to prove that they could love and be loved, desperate to prove that they could find happiness in the world. After eighteen months they stopped living together, an amicable recognition that they had both made a serious mistake.

Tom and Cairo always meant to sort out the divorce, but they never got around to it. When Tom's body was found in a Chicago hotel room in 1980, Mrs Cairo Clark immediately came into a considerable sum of money.

The verdict was accidental death. Tom had become quite fond of autoerotic asphyxiation. His preferred method was to lower concrete paving-slabs on his chest while jerking off. Unfortunately, the Heath-Robinson apparatus that lowered the paving stones broke, and Tom crushed his ribcage and several crucial internal organs. Cairo learned about his death two weeks after the funeral.

When the settlement came through, Cairo was given some good investment advice, so by the time Trooper's album sales had dwindled to a trickle and nothing more Cairo had secured a modest but reliable income. This was now largely enjoyed by her cats and would in due course be enjoyed by a nominated cat charity.

It was Cairo who introduced me to Eric. I had heard of the Turtle Tree. The name was usually linked with disparaging remarks about prog-rock dinosaurs and pretentious concept albums; however, Cairo had a copy of *Eugene's Moment of Truth*, which, when I heard Eric was coming to town, I listened to as a token gesture of respect. There was something quite haunting about Eric's guitar work – first thrashy, then long, sustained notes, carrying the principal melody but embellished with complicated quick licks and, underneath, Veale's big mellotron chords (and wailing VCS3 synth). It was pompous and overblown, but I was somehow drawn into it. I had just joined the band (who had advertised for a new keyboard player in the music press). Their old keyboard player had left the band to get married. I was the only person to reply to the advert.

'What's he like,' Scott had asked, 'this Eric bloke?'

'All right, bit of a nutter, but all right,' I had replied. But I remember, that day, I wasn't really thinking about music, Eric's guitar sound or in which direction we should take the band.

Cairo had decided to give me and Eric a treat. She had booked a table in a very respectable vegetarian restaurant in Finchley. She had warned me not to talk too much about music, but I couldn't help it. Nevertheless, Eric was cool. I guess it wasn't that long ago now, but Eric was definitely less intense and more 'with it' then. I hesitate to use the word, but he was more 'normal', I suppose.

After the meal we went back to Cairo's, and I watched Eric construct his prodigious joint. We sat and got really, really stoned. At about one or two in the morning Cairo said, 'Goodnight, boys' and went to bed. But me and Eric just stayed up together, talking.

I can remember that Eric spoke a lot about the GLF, but eventually he lost altitude, stopped preaching and began to reminisce a bit, something he hardly ever does now, and it was then that he told me about giving Hendrix his spare E strings before Jimi went on stage at the Hillside Social Club in Folkestone. I couldn't believe it. Upstairs was a woman who had – in all probability – slept with Hendrix. And here I was, sitting with a man who had given the legend a packet of high Es. Extraordinary.

I don't know why, but as so often happens when two guys sit talking into the night, our conversation drifted towards sex. We had already covered drugs and rock 'n' roll. I found myself asking Eric if the stories about Hendrix's cock were true.

'What, the size?'

'Yeah.'

'Sure it was true, old son.'

'How do you know though?'

'You must have heard about those two chicks, yeah?'

I thought for a moment, but my mind was extremely sluggish. 'What two chicks?'

'There were these two chicks. Artists, I suppose, and they had this idea of taking casts of famous tackle. Anyway, I think it was about sixty-eight . . .' Eric took a toke and did some mental operations (which I took to be date confirmation). 'Yeah . . . sixty-eight. After a gig – Stateside – these two birds came up to Jimi and said they wanted to do a cast. So Jimi says OK, and they went back to his hotel room. Well, in the version I know – which I got from Pat Costello' – (whoever he was) – 'these birds got Jimi stiff, filled a vase with mix and shoved his cock in. Well, normally, under such conditions, your average rig shrivels up. Stands to reason, I suppose. But he was such a horny bastard, Jimi, he stood proud. So proud, in fact, they couldn't get the fucking vase off his cock. Anyway, eventually the thing came off . . .'

I nodded, my heart sinking.

Eric continued. 'Well, after these birds had done the mould, there was this sort of exhibition, party, what have you. They got all their moulds together and put them on show. Well, as you might imagine, the exhibits, they were all pretty much small and shrivelled – except for Jimi's. Jimi's cast was about nine inches long and apparently really fat.'

I felt, somehow, diminished – winded almost.

'So it's true then?' I asked, senselessly hoping that there was an outside chance of Eric suddenly stopping to shout, 'April fool'.

'Oh, yes, my son. Very true.'

I was still getting 'love-type' feelings for Cairo then and, I must say, perhaps as a result, I found Eric's tale curiously affecting. Maybe Eric noticed.

'Thinking of Cairo, Nick, old son?'

We looked at each other, and what passed between us redefined the meaning of a knowing glance. I nodded assent.

'Yeah,' said Eric. 'I felt the same way too . . .'

We looked at each other again. My heart was beating faster. I was almost, although not quite, out of my depth. Although it was difficult, I could tease out the principal themes from the background noise.

We carried on smoking and gradually retained only the most modest link with reality. A thin, attenuated thread of consciousness, linking an inner darkness with the greater universe.

'Is Cairo expecting one of us to follow her up?' I asked Eric.

'Don't know, Nick, old son,' replied Eric.

The rest of the night melted, like candle wax. Time slowed down and, eventually, seized up completely, congealed.

When I woke the following morning Eric's head was on my stomach, using it like a pillow. And Cairo, in her red bathrobe, was squatting next to me, with a tray of coffee.

12

the cranbrook

When Jarl came to the Cranbrook, he was accompanied by two guys from Retro, one old, one young. The old guy looked fairly standard: longish hair, trainers, 501s, short biker-jacket and black T-shirt. The young guy looked more contemporary (although a bit of a nerd). The old guy was called Gunter and the young guy Weibo. They were both German, although they spoke much better English than Scott, Phil or Andy. I felt that I could give them a better run for their money and subsequently made an effort to use the odd obscure word, just so they wouldn't get too confident; however, when Weibo referred to the big multinational music companies as procrustean I gave up.

The Cranbrook was a shitty little gig in Ilford. Nevertheless, its size was an advantage; it began to look full even if there weren't that many people in, which was good from our point of view. We had managed to get the gig mentioned in one of the big listings magazines and, less auspiciously, the *Ilford Gazette*. It was possible that a little advertising might swell the crowd, but our feeling was that the audience would comprise mostly of the usual Cranbrook Saturday-night regulars – which proved to be the case.

We knew what to expect: a largely disinterested audience for the first half of the set; then, on our return, a few people standing around the stage, wanting to dance, but not daring to. Finally, in

135

the last half-hour, people would forget their inhibitions and bop. In spite of the fact that we were on show, and quite nervous, we played well. Doing the Prince Albert gig had been a good idea after all. Concentrating on our playing under those testing conditions had been really difficult, whereas playing to a straight Essex audience in a pub we were familiar with was, by comparison, a doddle. If anything, we were too laid back; it was all too easy. If I wanted to be critical, I would say that we lacked energy. It was too slick.

Fortunately, we *had* attracted a small group of Free Radicals fans. As usual, they were not in the least distinctive or tribal. Just a group of youngish people who lifted our spirits near the end by calling out ' "Forever Young" '.

'That's a bit slow, for this bit, isn't it?' said Scott, engaging his audience.

'Play it!' they called out.

'Are you sure you want that one?'

'Yes.'

I could see that getting a request would go down well with Jarl and the Retro boys; but 'Forever Young' was a bit of a downer. Scott looked over at me. I shrugged my shoulders, which he took to be a consent.

'All right,' Scott announced, ' "Forever Young".'

A modest, half-hearted cheer came from our small huddle of fans. We did a competent, straightforward rendition and then thought we had better compensate for the slightly subdued atmosphere the song had created. We had intended to end our set with 'Trade' but Scott, quite rightly, brought it forward. He turned away from the mike and called out to us, ' "Trade"?' We all nodded.

He turned, swung his arm around, and crashed out a lovely, scrunchy, in-your-face chord, and yelled, 'I'm, I'm, I'm, I'm . . .', extending the last cry to introduce a load of sexy blue-notes ' . . . going down!'

Having had to show restraint on 'Forever Young' Phil really gave 'Trade' some stick. We steamed through it and went straight into the last four numbers, finishing with a very tight 'Smart Peroxide'.

The playing was good, no doubt about it, but I didn't feel that we had given the audience a performance. We had simply played through the set, nothing more than that.

When we got to the bar, Jarl had lined up four pints.

'Where are Gunter and Weibo?' asked Scott.

'They had to get away quickly.'

'Oh . . .' We looked at each other, the fear of having blown it quite palpable in the air between us.

'Well?' I asked Jarl, 'what did they think?'

Jarl took a sip of his lager and we braced ourselves for the bad news. 'Congratulations,' he said, 'they liked you very much.'

'Yeah?'

'Oh, yes.'

The tension evaporated.

'Look, let's sit down.'

The pub was beginning to empty, so it was easy to find a table. The thuggish barman had already begun to intimidate the punters. As he thundered around the pub, a tyre of fat pulsated around his torso, giving the impression that another person was trying to escape the confines of his orange nylon shirt. When he came to our table he was completely oblivious to the fact that we were the band, and said, 'Ain't choo got 'omes t'go to?' He left us in a cloud of body odour. We ignored him.

'Now, listen,' said Jarl, 'I think that the plan is this. We would like you to go into the studio again. We would like you to cut three singles, "Smart Peroxide", "Trade" and "Forever Young".'

' "Forever Young",' said Scott, rather surprised.

'Yes, it's a good song. It will show that you are a versatile band. You know that you can carry off a ballad. And additional tracks we will take from your Watford demo. OK?'

We made various noises of consent.

'I had hoped,' Jarl continued, 'that we could make use of the version of "Smart Peroxide" straight from the Watford master. But Weibo felt that there is a bit of a tempo change . . . you know?

It kind of gets faster. To tell the truth, I didn't even notice, but it bothered Weibo. OK?'

'Fair enough,' said Andy.

'OK,' Jarl continued. 'So you just have to do those three: "Smart Peroxide", "Trade" and "Forever Young". There's a studio I'd like you to use out in Letchworth. It's nothing fancy and will suit your sound. No computers or hi-tech paraphernalia, just a solid old sixteen-track console. A musician's studio. The sound will be very authentic, let me tell you. If I can book you in for a couple of days – maybe the week after next – will that be enough time, do you think?'

'Yeah, I suppose so,' replied Scott.

'Look, I don't want anything special. I just want you to go in and play the right notes. And keep the beat solid. You can play around a little in the studio if you want, but I don't want you to fuss over the production too much, OK?'

A second barman passed, shouting 'Time, gentleman, please.'

'So, you'll give us a call?' asked Scott.

'Sure,' replied Jarl, 'as soon as I get confirmation that the studio is free.'

'What's the studio called?'

'The Limits of Influence. It's a small place, but I've used them before and they have good engineers. I'll drop in, of course, for the mix. Bo – you remember Bo? – he might come, too.'

'Fine.'

The lights in the pub came up bright. Suddenly the place looked very tired and tawdry. The stains on the carpet, the ashtrays piled high and the sticky sediment of spilt beer coating every available surface.

Jarl drained his glass and placed it on the table. He then peered into the distance. 'Looks like my chauffeur has arrived.'

We followed his gaze to the door, where Emma was standing. She looked a little like a child prostitute. Needless to say, she almost immediately started to get attention from the Cranbrook punters.

'I had better be off,' said Jarl. 'I'll be in touch.' He got up, took a wide birth of some boisterous stragglers, collected Emma at the door and left.

'Fuck. She didn't even say hello,' said Andy. He was clearly disappointed.

There was a moment's silence.

'Well, what do you think?' asked Scott.

'Fucking rude,' replied Andy. 'I mean, we've . . .'

'No, not her!'

'Oh . . .'

I ventured, tentatively, 'Seems all right.'

'I would have preferred it if Gunter and Weibo had hung around,' said Scott. 'You know, to talk about things . . . the gig and that.'

'Yes,' I agreed.

The manager of the Cranbrook suddenly materialized. 'Come on, you lot, ain't it 'bout time you started shifting your gear, then?'

'All right,' said Phil, 'we're on to it.'

''Bout fucking time!'

The bastard was about to have another go, but Phil stood up and gave him one of his *are you absolutely sure you want to start something with me?* looks, which helped move him on.

'Cunt!' said Andy – but quietly.

'Come on, then,' said Phil, 'we'd better get on with it.'

We all got up.

By the main door, the thuggish bar-man was shouting at a few people standing in a corner. 'Come on you lot, piss off 'ome!'

Before setting about dismantling the Rhodes I nipped into the toilet. I looked at myself in the mirror. I looked exhausted and sweaty. My hair was sticking up as though I had just got out of bed. Under the bright strip-lighting I looked much older. It was like peering into the future, seeing another version of myself – Nick at thirty, or thirty-three, even. My eyes were dull; there seemed to be too much flesh hanging off my face. I looked like I had been leaking life-force. Soon I would have to break into the reserve supply.

Something didn't feel right. It was disappointing not to talk to

Gunter and Weibo about the gig but, somehow, that didn't explain how I felt.

I walked over to the urinal and began to piss. We had been playing pretty loud. I had been standing right next to our largest amp, and my ears were whistling like a badly tuned radio, an irritating, high-pitched wail.

It was then that I felt it; it was as if the blood in my veins were being replaced with embalming fluid; a cold wave. Someone, someone I had felt before, was watching me. I turned around quickly, just fast enough to see the door closing, the hint of a figure. For a few moments I was unable to move. I was shocked, rooted to the spot. *Shit!* I came to my senses and ran for the door. I looked around the pub but it was almost empty. I was dimly aware of the band packing away the gear and a sense of exposure as I walked across the brightly lit floor. Out on the street, I looked around but couldn't see anyone.

Scott came out after me. 'Where are you going?'

'Did you see anyone?'

'What?'

'Did you see a big bloke, really tall, leave just then?'

'I've seen lots of big blokes. Enormous, in fact.'

'No, don't fuck about. I'm serious. Just then.'

Scott looked at me as though I was off my head. 'Are you all right, Nick? What's up?'

'Nothing. I thought . . .'

'What?'

I didn't know how to explain, so I made something up. 'I just thought I'd spotted someone I knew.'

'Oh yeah?'

'Julian. A bloke I used to know called Julian.'

'Right.'

I noticed that Scott was looking at my crotch.

I looked down and saw a large, circular urine stain. 'Oh fuck!' I said.

Scott shrugged his shoulders and went back inside the Cranbrook.

xenoquon

I hadn't seen Eric for four days. I was beginning to think that he was wasn't going to come back. Then, on Saturday night, the phone rang. I didn't pick it up (in case it was my mother). So I just let the answerphone take the call.

'Nick? Pick up the phone, Nick, old son.'

I picked up. 'Eric?'

'Nick. Terrific. Thank fuck you're home.' He sounded out of breath. 'Listen, I need your help, mate.'

My first thought was that he'd been done for possession and wanted a solicitor. 'What, is something wrong, Eric?'

'Could say that, yeah.'

'What?'

'Nick, could you get to Stanmore Tube in about an hour?'

'What?'

'Could you get to Stanmore? It's only a few stops from Kilburn.'

'What for?'

'I need your help.'

'But what kind of help?'

'Just help.'

'Eric. It's ten-thirty. I'm not travelling out to Stanmore unless you tell me why.'

'Don't be like that, Nick.'

'Like what?'

'Difficult.'

'Then tell me what it's about.'

'I can't.'

'Then I won't come.'

There was a silence – a long one. I could hear Eric breathing heavily. Finally, he said, 'Fair enough . . . See you around, old son.' He was about to hang up.

'Hold it!'

Eric was definitely becoming more cranky. 'Sorry. No time, babe. If you can't help, you can't help.'

'No, listen. Don't hang up, for fuck's sake. Tell me what you want me for.'

'Help, that's all.'

'But what kind of help?'

Again there was silence. Maybe I could hear Eric talking to someone, very faintly, his hand must have been clasped over the receiver. When he spoke again I recognized the peculiar, artificial use of language employed to communicate subtext. Eric was speaking slowly, and ordinary words were being given unusual emphasis. It was the kind of conversation you have with a dealer. 'Listen, Nick. The motor . . . the motor's broken down. I'd appreciate your help. I'm going to be seriously – stuck – without your help. It'll be a piece of piss, once you get here.'

'The motor?'

'Look, Nick. I really haven't got the time to talk. Are you available?' He sounded desperate, in trouble.

'OK, OK. I'll be there in an hour!'

'One day. One day, Nick, old son, I'll make it up to you. You'll see. You're a fucking star, mate.' The line went dead.

I went to get some cash out of a drawer in the kitchen while saying to myself: *Why did you pick up the phone? Why?* Of course, I was certain that this escapade was going to have bugger-all to do with motors.

I arrived at Stanmore station too early. It was a cold night, and it had begun to rain again. By the time the small Ford van pulled up I was absolutely frozen. Code was driving. 'Round the back,' he said.

The back door opened and Eric hauled me in. He threw his arms around me. 'Nick, old son!'

'All right, Eric!' I wasn't in an effusive mood.

'Here, sit down.' Eric gestured toward a pile of cushions and straw.

I sort of fell down as the van pulled off.

'Thanks for coming. I really appreciate it.'

'I hope so.'

'Oh, I do, mate.'

'So, what the fuck's going on, Eric? The motor seems OK!'

'Yeah, sorry about all that, but you know the score. See, right now, like this moment, we're on a job.'

'A GLF job?'

'Sure.'

'Off to fuck over some plant?'

'No, not exactly.'

I suddenly remembered the Fall-out Express. 'Look, I'm not getting involved with that fucking train. That's way – '

Eric cut in. 'It's nothing to do with that.'

'So, what then?'

'Let me give you the low-down.'

I lit a cigarette.

'A little way past Mill Hill there are these laboratories. They're owned by one of the big drug companies . . .' Eric paused for a moment. 'Can I have one?'

'Oh, sorry.' I gave him a Benson. He must have been more tense than usual to smoke a regular.

'Thanks.' He lit it with his flame thrower and took a long drag. 'They're not big, these labs. They're in this building. Looks like a bunker. It's out of the way . . . do you know Arrendene?'

'No.'

'Highwood Hill?'

'No.'

'Well, anyway. There's quite a lot of open space out that way. Fields and that, off the main road. Most of the work they do in this lab is on rats. But very occasionally they get a primate.'

'What, an archbishop?'

'Do I look like I wanted to hear a crap joke like that?'

'Sorry.'

The van suddenly stopped abruptly and threw us both forward. I banged my head hard against the partition. 'Oh, shit!'

'It's all right,' I heard Code call out from the front, his voice muffled. 'A piss artist pulled out!'

'No prob. We're OK,' Eric shouted.

'I'm not,' I said, rubbing my head.

'You'll live.'

I had dropped my cigarette. As I was on – as it were – a bit of a roll, I wondered whether the straw would suddenly ignite and turn the van into a mobile crematorium but, fortunately, nothing happened.

'So,' Eric continued, 'we know that they've got a primate in there now – a chimpanzee – and we're gonna heist him.'

I rubbed my head. 'Eric, are you telling me that we're going to lift a chimpanzee from a research lab?'

'Yeah.'

'Then I reckon I'm in deep here.'

'No. Not at all. All I want you to do is keep a look-out. There's no risk. Really.'

'No risk.'

'Not at all, mate.'

My head had begun to throb. 'So this is what you're in London for? This is the business?'

'Yep.'

'I see.'

Eric smiled. A sort of retiring, bashful smile. 'I really didn't want to get you involved in all this. Really.'

I signed. 'Yeah, I know.'

'But, now that you are, you'll be needing this.' Eric handed me a mobile phone, and continued, 'If you see any pigs or security, press that button there. When you hear me say *Hello*, just say the password. Then switch it off.'

'What password?'

'The one we agree on, now. So what's it going to be?'

'Err . . . anything?'

'Yes.'

'For some reason I can only think of "cocktease".'

'All right. "Cocktease" it is. Any trouble, press the button, wait for me to answer, say "cocktease", then switch it off. All right?'

'Look, if security's a serious issue here, shouldn't you have special walkie-talkies or something?'

'No. A mobile's fine. If they show, give us the word and just walk off down the road. Got it?'

I was feeling quite sick. The van was rocking around like a boat. 'So why *did* you have to drag me into this?'

'Look, I'm really sorry, Nick, I really am but I had no choice. We've been working with this bloke from Greenpeace. Seemed to have balls. Said he wanted to be more radical, join GLF and all that. Anyway, he started wobbling a few weeks back, and then, right at the last fucking minute, he pulled out, said he couldn't go ahead with it. And this is our last chance, see? It's got to be done tonight.'

'Why?'

'The autopsy's tomorrow morning.'

'What, they're going to kill it?'

'Him.'

'All right, *him.*'

'Yeah. He's for the slab. Once they've fucked up an animal brain, they like to slice it up and bung it under a microscope. See?'

The journey to Mill Hill didn't take that long. By the time the van ground to a halt I felt like I had been at sea for a week. I guess it must have been about midnight. 'How are you going to get in, Eric?' I asked.

'Don't you worry about that, Nick, old son. You just keep your eyes peeled.'

When we got out of the van it was still drizzling. We were parked on a largish road overlooking what seemed to be parkland. There were some neon lights in the distance; however, where we were

145

situated, it was dark. The place felt remote but, even so, the odd vehicle still came by. Most were big articulated lorries, rumbling through and creating a cloud of haze in their wake.

Eric instructed me to go and stand behind a tree on the other side of the road. 'OK. Don't come out until we reach the van. When we reach the van, come straight down, and jump into the back with Code.'

'OK.'

'You see anyone stop near the van, anyone, give us a call. If you see the pigs, like I said, give us a call and scarper. Don't hang about. All right?'

'All right.'

Eric looked at Code. 'You cool?'

'I'm quite ready, yes,' replied Code. I could see a muscle twitching next to his tight-lipped mouth.

'Right then,' said Eric. They turned and began walking.

By the time I got to my tree on the other side of the road there was nothing to be seen. A smallish Ford van, parked by a hedge, and darkness beyond it.

I waited and tried to reflect on my circumstances, but I was kind of numb. I couldn't come to terms with what was happening. Another lorry rumbled past. Rain was still dripping from the leaves and branches above me. My hair was beginning to get wet, and I could feel water trickling down my back.

I stood under that tree for a long time. I looked at my watch: 12.48. Then, out of nowhere, a car pulled up. About fifty yards in front of the van. *Fuck, fuck, fuck.* I peered out. My face was pressed up against the cold, rough bark. What was I to do? Eric had said call if *anybody* turned up but surely he didn't mean that literally. I took out the mobile and was about to press the redial button, but decided not to. I would give it a few more seconds. A light went on in the car. I waited. The light went off again. Then the indicator light blinked and the car pulled away. I watched as its tail lights disappeared into the night. *Thank Christ for that.*

I continued my vigil, quite proud of myself for having shown some initiative in the field. Then I detected movement. Shadow against shadow. It was them. They were amazingly quick. They just darted out of the hedge, Eric and Code, carrying a large – an awfully large – 'thing'. Fortunately, there were no vehicles around, so I just walked across the road and hopped into the back of the van.

'Pull the door to,' said Code.

I was stunned.

'For God's sake!' he called.

I slammed the van door shut and Eric took off at speed. I fell back and hit my head for the second time. It was a good thing really, because it helped bring me to my senses. I had slipped into a curious trance-state, stupefied by the creature in front of me.

It was big. I didn't realize chimpanzees came that big; it was more like I imagined a gorilla to be. And, the fact was, I was scared shitless.

When you think of chimpanzees, you think of old Tarzan films, or adverts, where they are used to raise a laugh. Chimpanzees are cute and funny; they are not heaving barrels of muscle covered in coarse black hair with lips that part to reveal evil, pointed, yellow teeth. When you think of a chimpanzee, you rarely think of its smell, the rattle in its throat, or the veil of saliva that cascades over its slack lower jaw.

As I stared at this awesome creature, I noticed that its head had been shaved. The bristles had started to grow back a little, but its scalp was cratered with scabs. Large, crusty scabs which, on closer inspection, were exuding a thick, gummy fluid.

The chimpanzee was propped up against the cab-partition. Code was seated next to it, his arm around its shoulder. He was looking at its tormented face with an expression of pure compassion. It was extraordinary. It was like a perverse *take* on one of those old masterpieces, that stock image of Jesus having been removed from the cross, being held in the loving arms of his disciples.

As I watched, the van stopped (at a junction maybe), and a beam of neon light shone through the tiny, frosted roof window.

It gave the chimpanzee a dirty orange halo. A tear trickled down Code's cheek. 'Bastards,' he said. Not to me, but to himself.

'What have they done to it?' I asked.

Code didn't reply. He simply continued to look at the chimp, like it was his lover, or his child.

Clearly the chimp had been drugged. Either by the scientists in the lab or by Code. I assumed both; however, suddenly it started shifting around. It started to grunt. Disturbingly human grunts.

'Easy, boy,' said Code, but the chimp was not responsive to Code's solicitous murmurings. It continued to twist and started to kick. Only feebly, but its legs looked pretty strong. Then something very freaky happened: it started to move its hands – but not just random movements – curious controlled, repetitive movements.

'Oh, Christ, no!' said Code.

'What's happening?'

'He's signing.'

'Signing?'

'Sign language. BSL.'

My nightmare was becoming more disturbing. 'I don't understand. How? I mean . . .'

'Sometimes they teach them rudimentary signs.'

'Why?'

Again, Code didn't reply. I was bewildered by the bizarre, repetitive movements. 'What the fuck's he saying?' I asked.

'I don't know . . . I don't know BSL.'

The chimp began to kick again.

Code looked over to me. 'Hold his legs.'

'Fuck off!'

'Nick. Hold his legs, I've got to sedate him.'

'No way!'

'Hold his legs, for God's sake. If he regains consciousness fully he'll go ape.'

Well, at that point I reached my limit. Maybe I was just so jittery and freaked out, something had to give. Some kind of release had become a necessity. I started laughing. I had to. And,

148

with Code's ludicrous words echoing in my mind, I reached forward and held the chimp's legs together. They yielded with little effort. Code took a small syringe from his pocket, flicked off the protective cap and stuck it into the chimp's thigh like a dart. The legs twitched as Code pressured the plunger down. The chimp relaxed and became still again.

'Thank you,' said Code.

'That's all right. Any time.'

I was still laughing, under my breath. I was finding it difficult to control myself and began to think that maybe I had had too much for one night. Perhaps I had started to lose it and I had better get Code to sedate me, too. Maybe it would be better for all of us.

'All right,' said Code, looking up (and aware of my shaking shoulders), 'It was a bad choice of words.'

I burst out laughing again. An explosive, hysterical roar, which really worried me. Then I got even more worried by Code, who started laughing, too. An equally explosive detonation. Eric tapped the partition and called out. 'What the fuck's going on in there?'

Neither of us could reply, we were both laughing so much. I've seen more sanity in a Marx Brothers' film.

As my laughter trailed off I noticed a file on the floor. A large ring-bound file. The cardboard covers were laminated and caught the light. I was able to read 'DEMA'. I picked up the file and looked at the cover closely. It read DEMA-Pharm and, in smaller writing underneath 'Innovation, Commitment & Care'.

'Code, did you get this from the lab?'

'Yes.' He was surprised by my interest.

I flicked through the folder. I could hardly read any of the text. It was too dark. However, I could read some of the larger headings: 'Pelozide', 'Lozaril', 'Perotin', 'Octan'. And then, almost inevitably, 'Naloxyl'. I started to tear out the page.

'Stop that at once!'

I looked up. 'I want this page. Just this one.'

'What do you want it for?'

'I just want it, OK?'

'Well, you can't have it!'

149

'Fuck off. I'm having it. Call it payment. Jesus Christ, I think I've earned it!'

Code sighed. 'I'm sorry, Nick. You're quite right. Take it if you want.'

'Thank you.'

We didn't say anything else to each other. I sat, looking at Code, looking at the chimpanzee and, for the first time, began to wonder where we were going; however, I didn't get the chance to contemplate our destination for very long. The van stopped, and Eric banged on the partition. 'Nick, get out.'

I didn't ask any questions. I got out the back and walked to the front of the van. We were parked in a sideroad. I didn't have a clue where we were. Eric wound his window down.

'Where are we?'

'Stanmore. The Tube's that way,' Eric gestured vaguely to the right. 'Not far.'

'OK.'

'Look, Nick, old son. I can't give you a lift back to Kilburn. I don't want you to get into trouble, all right? We could get stopped.'

'Sure.'

'So, we'll be off.'

'Sure. When will you be back?'

'Back?'

'In Kilburn. Back at the flat.'

Eric paused for a moment. 'No, Nick. No, my son. That's it. I'm done now.'

'What, you're off? Really off?'

'Yeah, I'm splitting.'

In spite of everything, my heart sank. 'Where?'

'Don't know yet. Look, I've really got to go, all right?'

I didn't want him to leave. 'Where are you taking the cargo?'

'Southampton.'

'Southampton?'

'Yeah, he's going home.'

'What, Africa?'

'Yeah.'

'Fuck . . .'

'He'll do some rehab, then he's back to basics, man.' Eric gave the accelerator a touch and revved. 'Nick. Listen. What you've done tonight is . . . is . . . fucking ace, man. I tell you, you've earned some seriously high-octane karma. Mark my words, Nick, old son. You won't regret it . . .' The van started to move.

'Hang on.' My hand was clutching the mobile in my pocket. 'Here.' I handed it through the window.

'Cheers, Nick.'

Eric smiled, and the van pulled away. He did a U-turn and sped off down the road. The street seemed unnaturally silent after the sound of the van had died away.

I got out of the cab at about two forty-five. I let myself into the flat and went straight to the bedroom, where I collapsed on the duvet. The flat seemed really empty now there was no prospect of Eric turning up. I felt lonely and cold; my T-shirt was soaked. After a few minutes I got up and went into the front room.

I slumped down on the sofa and ran a hand through my damp hair. It had been quite a night. Upstairs, the floorboards creaked. I could hear a slow, measured pace, moving from one corner of the ceiling to its opposite. Curiously, I had never seen the single occupant of the flat upstairs although I had often heard him (or her), particularly late at night. There were never any voices, only movements.

I was suddenly revisited by a mental image. I remembered the night Eric and I walked to West End Sidings. I remembered that solitary figure staring at the wall. It still disturbed me, that intense expression, those penetrating eyes. So many people, I thought, in little, isolated boxes, so many people living dangerously close to the edge.

I jumped. There had been a loud thud. Whoever it was upstairs had dropped something on to the floor. There was some creaking and then the footsteps resumed. *Another insomniac*. I felt no sympathy. No connection. The regular tread from above just made me feel more lonely.

I got up and made myself a cup of tea. My nose had started to run, and I put my hand in my pocket to pull out a tissue. Instead, I pulled out a crumpled sheet of paper. At the top was printed 'Naloxyl'. After this, in brackets, 'a Xenoquon derivative'. Xenoquon. It sounded like a crappy nightclub in Romford.

The text began with a reference to the purchase of the Xenoquon patent from ZRB-(Bio)Tech (a name that sounded vaguely familiar, but I couldn't quite place it). The rest of the text was almost indecipherable. It was all chemical names: 5-hydroxy-triptamine, Hg, Pb, dopamine, noradrenaline, and so on. Then it got really complex: cell bodies located in various raphe nuclei . . . ligands . . . affecting receptor sub family 5-HT(1D) [5-HT(1B), 5-HT(1D alpha)]. I couldn't understand a word. However, there was a footnote that I really didn't like the sound of: * See IntMem D 73.79 para 32. Santa Maria Hospital Pilot Study (Cusco). Terminated prior to completion. v. (data sets) S 6, S 28, S 34.

'Dr McDougall?'

He had been scribbling a few notes in my file and, when he looked up, he seemed somewhat disorientated. 'Yes?' His eyes became more focused.

'Dr McDougall . . . you know the company who make Naloxyl?'

'DEMA, yes?'

'Well, have they tested Naloxyl before?'

'How do you mean exactly?'

'You know, have they run any other studies, like this one?'

McDougall leaned back in his chair and stifled a yawn. 'No. Although there are two other trials – identical to ours – being run simultaneously. In France and America.'

'How are they going?'

'I don't really know.'

'Don't you talk to each other?'

'No.'

'Compare notes?'

'Well, yes, we do compare notes; but only when the trial is finished.'

'So Naloxyl has never been tried by anyone before?'

McDougall thought about my question carefully. 'No, that's not quite right. Many people would have taken Naloxyl before. The process of developing a new drug is very involved, laddie.'

'DEMA would have run . . . pilot studies?'

'Yes, that's right. Pilot studies.'

' . . . And what happened? To the people who took part in them?'

'What happened?'

'Yes. What happened to them?'

'Nothing. Nothing happened to them.'

Dr McDougall frowned, clearly perplexed (and a little irritated) by my questions. He looked at me for a while, before his features softened and his irritation turned to concern. 'Nick. You seem to be a wee bit worried.'

I wasn't sure how to answer. 'Yes, I suppose I am.'

He turned on his chair and flicked through his notes. 'That's right,' he said, more to himself than to me. 'I remember.' He swivelled his chair round again. 'The last time you were here, you expressed some concern, didn't you?'

'Did I?'

'Yes, you did. So what's up?'

There was an uncomfortable silence.

'Nothing really, I just . . .' I had a question to ask, but I wasn't sure how to ask it. Subsequently, I decided to employ a modest fiction. 'I just got bothered by something I read. It was in a magazine article. A women's magazine actually.'

McDougall smiled and began to nod his head. He didn't have to say very much, you could simply read the expression off his face, as if the creases and convolutions were suddenly text: *I might have known!* they read.

'And,' I continued, undaunted, 'it mentioned this drug study. A pilot study that had to be stopped. And, I got thinking. It wasn't a very detailed article, but it left me with a lot of questions. I mean, something pretty bad would have had to have happened to bin a drug study. Wouldn't it?'

Dr McDougall had stopped listening to me. He knew exactly what he needed to say as soon as I had used the words 'magazine' and 'women's' in the same sentence. 'Now listen here, laddie,' he said, in a confidential, avuncular way, as though he were about to let me into an old family secret. 'The fact of the matter is, with respect to medical matters, at least, these women's magazine's are an absolute menace. Believe me, I know all about this.'

I had obviously pressed a significant button.

'You get some young slip-of-a-thing journalist telephoning and asking you to comment on this problem or that problem – premenstrual tension, seasonal depression, CJD, what have you – and after you've been good enough to take thirty minutes out of a busy afternoon to give them a professional opinion they reward you by publishing a totally vacuous and misleading article in which virtually everything you said is trivialized or distorted. I don't know why they bother. Really. They may as well just make something up. Never' – he gripped my arm – 'but never take a blind bit of notice of anything you read in a women's magazine!' He released me, and leaned back.

'Sure,' I said. 'A lot of it is probably utter rubbish. But what I read *did* get me thinking. Why are some drug trials stopped?'

McDougall laughed out loud. 'A drug trial can be terminated for all sorts of reasons. Funding might dry up. The drug under investigation might be superceded by a clearly superior product. Too many people might drop out of the trial so there aren't enough subjects. There are numerous reasons why a drug trial might be stopped, and none of them worth a moment's vexation.'

'But presumably some must be stopped because of problems. People getting ill? Whatever.'

'Very, very rarely. By the time a drug has got to the trial stage, Nick, you can be pretty sure that all the preliminary investigations have proved successful, and the manufacturers are very confident. These trials cost a lot of money. The manufacturers wouldn't embark upon such a major undertaking if they felt that a trial would have to be abandoned because of illness! Good God, it's out of the question.'

It seemed to make sense.

'What magazine was this article in anyway?' asked McDougall.

I thought I would improvise. '*One Won't Do.*'

He laughed out loud again. 'For heaven's sake, man! What are you doing taking any notice of an article written in a magazine called *One Won't Do*?'

I nodded. 'Yes, I suppose you're right.' And to tell the truth, I did feel reassured. McDougall was very convincing.

After he had stopped laughing he said, 'Nevertheless, the fact that this silly article bothered you suggests to me that maybe you're worrying more than usual? Would that be true?'

'No. Not really.'

'You haven't been more nervous, more jittery than usual? Think about it.'

We had already been through the checklist.

'No. Absolutely not.'

'Very well.'

After our small talk I got up to leave. But again I couldn't get out of the office without asking another question.

'Dr McDougall? Naloxyl. Would it have been tested on animals first?'

Without pausing he said, 'I imagine so. Why do you ask?'

'Oh, it doesn't matter. Be seeing you.'

I closed the door, clutching my sealed DEMA-Pharm envelope, listening for the chink-chink-chink of thirty pieces of silver. I had been so distracted by everything, I hadn't even mentioned that I had smoked more dope since the last blood test. *Oh fuck it!* I thought. If the tests prove positive then . . . they prove positive. There's nothing I can do about it now.

By the time I got to the Tube, I was drenched. It was pissing down. I was getting fed up with this. It hadn't stopped raining all year. As I stepped beneath the station canopy, I had to stop to buy the *Evening Standard*. The headline read SINATRA IS DEAD. So, Ol' Blue Eyes is gone.

Although I realize Sinatra is pretty hip, I've never been a great fan. And he said some very dodgy things about rock 'n' roll (which I can't quite forgive him for). Nevertheless, I recognized that his passing was of momentous importance. Something seemingly permanent was now – to the disbelief of the general public – gone. I loved the Gore Vidal quote: 'Half the population of the United States over the age of forty were conceived while their parents were listening to his records.' That *is* an achievement, if it's true. I wondered what music I had been conceived to . . . but I didn't pursue it.

Apparently, outside the site of the house where Sinatra was raised – now a derelict lot – devotees had begun leaving flowers and CDs. I liked the idea of a compact disc being used as a kind of digital wreath. A star which marked the birthplace of Francis Albert Sinatra, 'The Voice', was surrounded by mementoes and relics.

I looked at the air-pollution chart. Nitrogen oxide, low. Ozone, low. Sulphur dioxide, low. It was OK to breathe in London today. Great news.

There must have been a time when the evening papers reported only the weather. It is surely a sign of the times that we now have updates on how likely it is that breathing will kill us. I mean, it's hardly an incentive to give up smoking, is it?

As the Tube bounced me along, I couldn't get 'My Way' out of my mind. The words struck me as particularly ominous – all those references to the end coming nearer and facing the final curtain.

I imagined the decaying, gangrenous corpse of Sinatra, dressed for Vegas, providing the backing track for the ultimate demise. The ice-caps melting, flooding, famine, refugees, disease, political unrest, panic. A finger poised over a button. Nuclear winter . . . 'My Way'.

I close my eyes and begin to drift off. I am hurtling through tunnels and passages, a dark labyrinth, cut into London's sacred soil. I am hammered insensible by the clatter of metal and steel. The big rattler, seals *the hushed casket of my soul*. And there are thoughts in my mind:

– God bless him. He was the greatest.

– But there was that scene in *The Godfather* . . .

– (A snatch of song) 'Fly me to the moon and . . .' (which fades to)

157

– Shagged Mia Farrow, Marilyn Monroe . . . shagged 'em all . . .

And in my half-awake, half-asleep state, I think to myself, are these my thoughts?

– Francis Albert Sinatra

– (Fading in) 'Strangers in the night' . . . (and fading out to) . . . and she looked so beautiful. It must have been what? Fifty-six? Or was it fifty-seven? I still remember the cover, *Songs for Swinging Lovers*.

But I don't remember the cover. And who looked beautiful?

And, suddenly, I am standing on Hampstead Heath. In the distance is the Millennium Dome, and next to it, the tower – Canary Wharf. Both are completely wrecked. I look at the moon, and realize it's the sun. There's something wrong with the sun. Fuck! There's something wrong with the sun!

I wake up, sweating.

Next to me, a drunk is singing at the top of his voice: 'My Way'.

His smell makes me retch.

15
letchworth

I missed having Eric around far more than I thought I would. Originally, I had imagined that I would be relieved when he went. I was looking forward to getting back into a routine of practising and writing. But I wasn't relieved at all. I listened to 'Vigil', from the Tree's *Tortoise* album, then the whole of *Eugene's Moment of Truth*. I wanted to reconnect with Eric. And it struck me, for the first time ever, that I wasn't listening to music but to captured moments – real moments.

It's curious but once a recording has been made, it becomes a product, a thing. We listen to *records*, and we think of it like that. We listen to the purchased article; we don't think that we're *replaying* moments in time – which is what we're really doing.

I sat listening to Eric in his twenties. Playing riffs with young, supple fingers, ripping melodies out of his Fender Strat, years before I was born.

The *Moment* came to a close. Eric's final chord began to fade over David Veale's floating mellotron. A collage of sound evoked a pastoral scene, a running stream, a bee buzzing from the left speaker into the right, and a church bell tolling in the distance. *Slow fade.*

Was there more to Eric's concept album than at first met the eye? *Eugene's Moment of Truth.* An album about moments, comprised of moments, which could be replayed, over other moments . . . I wanted to ask Eric; but of course, he wasn't there.

I got up and went for a piss. When I saw the mould colony growing on the wall I knew I had to get out.

I drove up to Hampstead and parked on the heath, then I walked into the village for my ritual visit to Our Price. I couldn't resist buying the new Massive Attack album. Then I went into Waterstone's. Upstairs, I started flicking through the popular-science books again. I found myself drawn to those that dealt with environmental themes. Among them was Lovelock's classic, *Gaia*. I doubted that Lovelock – a scientist – would ever have anticipated (in his wildest dreams) that this book would be the principal inspiration for the GLF.

Eric had told me quite a lot about the Gaia hypothesis. Lovelock's idea was that the earth could be viewed as a single living organism. His idea, and its implications, seemed to correspond with a load of old hippie nonsense about earth power and the Great Mother. Lovelock was subsequently adopted as a father figure, a prophet. I doubt whether the old man welcomed the attention. He was, after all, a proper scientist. Although, it has to be said, he was asking for trouble by calling his book *Gaia* (which, apparently, is hippie-speak for Mother Earth).

I had never read *Gaia*, so thought that I should, just for Eric. I also saw the book on physics I had seen before, *Many Worlds*. So I thought *Fuck it*, I'll have that, too. If Eric ever turned up again, I intended to have a proper conversation with him. Instead of always thinking of things from my point of view – the Turtle Tree, Hendrix, the music business – I would try to see things from his. The sun was shining, and I was feeling selfless and full of virtue.

I walked down the hill and turned left. On the way to the heath I passed Keats's house. I stopped, looked over the fence and thanked him for the sonnet about sleep. I then thought about Peter Pears and Benjamin Britten having sex, then about Scott and Phil having sex, 'the stream of consciousness', James Joyce, my English A-level and my first sex with Cairo – in that order.

I walked back up on to the heath. The sky was blue and clear and, I must say, my spirits lifted a little. I didn't feel quite so maudlin. Eventually, I found a bench, quite high up, and looked out over London. A tower of glass and steel caught the sun's rays, and for a moment I had to turn away. I wished I had brought my shades. A plane was leaving a trail of white cloud across the azure, producing an effect similar to a painting by Cairo. I imagined what she might call it. *White on Blue*. Or maybe just *Blue*. I lit a Benson and had a think about the imminent studio session in Letchworth.

After a while I got my books out and read through a few pages of each. *Gaia* was OK, but not mind-blowing. The *Many Worlds* book, on the other hand, really was mind-blowing. The author – a physicist from Cambridge – seemed absolutely sure that what we call reality represents only a tiny slice of what is going on. The 'real' universe is absolutely vast and contains an unimaginable number of versions of itself. As Eric had said, the main evidence for this was from the two-slits experiment.

It all looked very genuine and serious. The reviews on the back were all favourable and written by industrial-gauge academics, from Oxford, Harvard and MIT. There wasn't an old hippie in sight.

Maybe Eric was right. Maybe there are millions of universes and, in each one, there is a different version of ourselves and each one of those different versions thinks: *I'm the original. I am the real one.* A million, million demonstrations of human egocentricity.

As I sat contemplating London I imagined all the other 'Londons'. All parallel, occupying roughly the same space, all oblivious of each other. And I imagined some of those other 'mes', sharing the same bench, sharing similar thoughts. I found the idea vaguely disturbing.

I made my way back to the car and drove home to Kilburn. There was a message on the answering-machine from Andy confirming the arrangements for Letchworth. After his message there were three silent messages: beep-pause; beep-pause; beep-pause. They were left within a minute of each other. I keyed in

1471 to find out who the last call had been from, but the number had been withheld.

We spent Thursday morning getting the basic sounds right. The engineer was really good and managed to get a lovely smack on Phil's less than concert standard bass-drum. In the afternoon we got the backing tracks down, although there were a few problems. Phil and Andy were a bit tetchy. I guess it's because they have to listen so carefully to each other; they start hearing *things.*

I must have been about half-way through the fifth shot at 'Trade' when Andy pulled off his cans and shouted at Phil. 'Look, you're coming in too early. You should be holding back with the bass.'

Phil shook his head. 'No, no, no . . . if anything's wrong, it's you mate. You're coming in too late.'

'Oh, fuck off!' Andy was beginning to lose it. 'You must be joking.'

'I'm telling you,' continued Phil, 'it's you. You're late.'

Andy turned around, extended his hands and looked at me and Scott as if to say: *I hope you two are going to back me up on this?* Interestingly, during musical arguments, Scott was never biased. He never favoured Phil's point of view. If anything, he went the other way. I didn't want to get involved.

Scott asked the engineer to play back the last take. While we were listening to the rewind, Andy and Phil were still arguing. I played a few random chords.

'Leave it out a minute,' said Andy, waving at me.

I looked at Scott and raised my eyes to the ceiling. He smiled back. We were used to this routine and knew exactly how it would end.

We heard Phil counting: *One and two and three and four.* Then the first few bars. We all listened carefully, up to the point where Andy had interrupted the take. None of us could hear anything wrong.

'Shall we just get on with it now?' asked Scott.

Andy and Phil were still giving each other dirty looks when we finished the sixth take.

After we had got all the rhythm tracks down, Scott overdubbed just one or two guitar lines (fairly late in the day). On Friday morning Scott recorded the vocals, and I put a tiny bit of synth on the chorus of 'Forever Young'. Just a subtle, repeating figure, in a high register. I used the Odyssey: the notes sticky, with a hint of portamento. By midday on Friday we were ready to mix.

Jarl turned up at about five to 'help' with the production, but he did fuck-all really. He just sat there talking crap and smoking dope with the grim-faced Bo. I had to do the whole thing myself, which was OK really. In fact, I preferred it that way. Although Jarl was the official producer, I was glad that he didn't interfere. I had some very clear ideas about how the final mix should sound.

By ten o'clock we had our three singles in the can. The engineer made us all cassette copies, and Jarl took the master. Outside the studio, he shook our hands, and said, 'Well done.'

'So what's the next stage?' I asked.

'Well, it's out of my hands for a while. The Retro boys take over from here. They'll keep me posted, and as soon as I hear anything I'll give you a call. OK?'

Scott looked puzzled. 'But what about the publicity shots? Haven't we got to do some promotional stuff?'

Jarl laughed. 'Not yet, no. It's far too early. But when we get nearer to a release date I'll give you a call. And then, Scott, you can get dressed up, I promise you.'

Jarl turned to Bo and said something in German. Bo sneered and gave Scott a look which I can only described as contemptuous.

'So I'll be in touch,' said Jarl.

The four of us said nothing. We just watched Jarl and Bo walk across the car park. Bo took out a keyring and aimed it at a big blue beamer. The car made a *whoop* noise, and the lights flashed on and off. Jarl was laughing.

When they pulled away he didn't even bother to wave. None of us said anything, but there was a definite atmosphere.

brain damage

Although initially I had been far from happy about going to the Brunelleschi exhibition, when the time came I was quite keen. To tell the truth, I was bored. Eric had gone, leaving something of a vacuum in my life. There wasn't much happening with the band, as we were waiting to hear from Jarl. I seemed to spend most of my time lifting chord sequences from Bach and attempting to turn them into songs. It was all very dull.

The Brunelleschi exhibition was not an exhibition as such, but rather an installation. I had heard Cairo talking about installations before. The term was not one that I associated with art. The word 'installation' was more closely associated in my mind with boilers and cookers. Nevertheless, Cairo assured me that what we were about to see was art, and I was happy to go along with it.

She surprised me, that day. Surprised me by demonstrating how, with a little effort, she could recapture something of her past beauty. She had obviously decided to go the whole way with respect to the pose. She was wearing black boots, tight black jeans and a black blouse. On top of this she wore a long black trench-coat with wide lapels which flapped like crow's wings. My impression was that she had powdered her face to look somewhat paler than she actually was. Her copious blonde hair was pulled back in the most severe fashion and tied at the back of her head in a retentive bun. The finishing touch was a pair of very classy hi-tech shades. There wasn't a flowing scarf or tie-dye design in sight.

Her dress, that day, was very untypical. Usually, Cairo was completely disinterested in dressing up. The amazing thing was that she carried it off; heads turned. She looked seriously chic. A cross between a fifties film star and one of those women who can sit for a whole afternoon outside a café in Soho reading Sartre.

Cairo still has the most amazing posture and carriage. If she wants to, she can do that model walk, that curious glide that shocks the observer, the improbable result of being able simultaneously to cross one's legs and sustain locomotion. I have tried to copy it at home, but have only succeeded in falling over and head-butting the skirting-board.

Cairo was attracting *so much* attention. I got wave after wave. There was a lot of rear action going on. I kept on wanting to turn around and had to make a conscious effort to resist.

The installation was in a large warehouse in East London, a little way past Whitechapel. It was quite difficult to find. It was situated in the middle of a fairly run-down area, not too dissimilar to Kilburn. The warehouse was attached to an old factory (with an imposing chimney) and must have been hired out by the organizers just for the Brunelleschi exhibition.

Cairo parked her Saab and looked around apprehensively as she tested the locked doors. 'Do you think it'll be safe here?' she asked.

'Probably not.'

'Oh, well,' she shrugged, 'I'll just have to risk it now.'

When we got to the warehouse there was a large queue, an astonishingly long one – the kind of queue you associate with gigs not art exhibitions. I was very surprised, having never heard of Brunelleschi or his work. The people who were queuing up looked very peculiar. Most were very thin and anaemic-looking. (Andy wouldn't have looked out of place.) In addition, most were dressed in what was clearly some kind of mandatory black strip. Trendy glasses and shades were also very much in evidence.

The reason for the queue was that the installation had a limited access-time. You could visit the installation for only about twenty minutes. So about forty people would disappear inside the building and then the queue wouldn't move for a while. We waited outside for a full hour. Even Cairo got pissed off.

When we were finally ushered into the building, Cairo paid for both our tickets. These came with a programme; however, the programme consisted only of a folded sheet of paper with a detailed article on it by an art critic called Douglas de Jong.

We all walked down a corridor and into a huge open, empty space. It was like stepping into a massive box. The walls were high and largely windowless; however, a gloomy light seeped in through a small line of windows that went the whole way around the building near the ceiling.

There was a row of chairs lined up against one of the walls, so we all sat down. In front of us, about twenty yards ahead, was what looked like a large abstract sculpture. But the more you looked at it, the more you began to see that it resembled a crossbow. For the first time I began to wonder whether it had been sensible to come to the installation after all. An attendant – the only attendant – closed the door.

There was a soft hum of conversation. Reverential, intense whispers. Cairo leaned toward me. 'Astonishing, isn't it?'

'Absolutely,' I said.

'The intensity of the atmosphere.'

'Absolutely.'

I hadn't noticed at first, but at the far end of the warehouse was a steel arch made from girders. Underneath it was a small pile of smashed glass. 'What's that?' I asked Cairo.

She handed me the programme. 'Here,' she said. 'Read about it.'

I began to read a paragraph:

Brunelleschi invites us to explore the ambiguities of the moment. A central theme of the realismo school. In *Brain Damage*, we are forced to confront what we are, and what we might be. The 'I' is suspended, and the potential transience of identity exposed without compromise or concession. When Diaghilev said: '*Étonne-moi, Jean!*' Cocteau did his very best to oblige . . .

My tolerance of Douglas de Jong's pretention reached an early limit, and I started to scan down the page:

When I experienced *Brain Damage* for the first time in Paris last year, Brunelleschi revealed to me – yet again – the precarious multiplicity of worlds that crowd each second. I was ravished. Totally undone. My companion, made painfully aware of the insubstantiality of his own selfhood, caught the last plane to Nepal that very evening, and has never been seen since. Such is Brunelleschi's muscular grip on the sensibilities . . .

Yet more wank. I handed the programme back to Cairo. 'Very interesting,' I said.

'It is, isn't it?'

'Absolutely.'

I guess we must have all been sitting there for about ten minutes when suddenly there was an electrical buzz. There was movement along the arch in the distance, but it was too far away to see what was happening. Then the 'sculpture' in front of us began to move. The main section tilted upwards.

There was absolute silence. We all sat perfectly still.

Just as I was thinking to myself: *Maybe that's it*, there was a loud bang, followed by the sound of shattering glass. The sculpture had apparently discharged a projectile to the far end of the warehouse. The arch was a kind of machine that lowered panes of glass down from the ceiling. You only knew that one was there, at the far end, when it shattered.

As the 'cannon' detonated the highly strung audience screamed. I quite enjoyed that. To tell the truth, I jumped, too, but I didn't scream.

Cairo turned towards me. 'Astonishing.'

'Truly,' I replied.

The audience became more animated, and there was a burble

167

of excited chatter; however, the chatter began to subside as the sculpture began to turn. Slowly, the cannon revolved all the way around. The barrel lowered such that a further projectile would impact at the head-height of a seated adult human. We all tensed. You could feel a Mexican wave of anxiety making its way down the line. Every single member of the audience had the opportunity to look down the muzzle. When it came to my turn, I knew exactly what Mr de Jong meant: 'In *Brain Damage*, we are forced to confront what we are, and what we might be.'

Yes, I could now see that I might very easily become a red stain on a warehouse wall, just beyond Whitechapel.

I relaxed as the sculpture released me from its grim single eye and felt Cairo bristle (for a few moments). When she relaxed I knew that it was someone else's turn to sweat. When the sculpture had turned through 360°, the electrical humming stopped. A door opened on the other side of the warehouse, opposite the entrance, and an attendant stepped in. The audience, humbled, were invited to leave, with a bow and a subtle gesture.

When we got outside, I must say, I felt that the world *was* different. I had had a very interesting experience.

'Well, what did you think?' asked Cairo.

'Really cool.'

'I knew you would like it.'

'I did. I thought it was really, really cool.' Unfortunately, I couldn't think of another way of expressing my appreciation.

'It was vintage Brunelleschi. The man is a genius.'

When we got back to the car, no one had attempted to break into it or steal it; however, we didn't comment on this, because Cairo was still high and buzzing.

'What was it about Nick? For you?'

'Life, death . . .'

'And . . .'

'And . . . parallel universes.'

'How do you mean?'

I knew I could really impress Cairo. 'There's a theory . . . a genuine, scientific theory . . . that our universe is one of many.

And whenever it's possible for something to happen or not to happen, the universe splits. Every possible combination of eventualities exists . . . in a greater reality. So, in that moment, when I looked into the Brunelleschi cannon . . .'

'The ballista.'

'Sorry?'

'It's in the programme. He calls it the ballista.'

'Oh right. In that moment, when I looked into the ballista, I was also, in a very real sense, looking at my own death.'

'My God, that's so profound.' She looked over to me and smiled. 'I knew that you would appreciate Brunelleschi. I just knew it.'

I wanted to impress Cairo because I wanted her to be in a good mood. And I wanted her to be in a good mood because I wanted to have sex with her. She was looking that good.

When we got back to Highgate we sat in the kitchen, talking. Cairo poured my third coffee. She then sat down and let one of the cats jump on to her lap. When it got off, I knew it would leave a mat of hair on her chic costume. But she wasn't bothered; as always, the cats came before any other consideration.

'So you haven't heard anything?' she asked.

'From Eric?'

She nodded.

'No. Not a thing.'

'That was such a crazy thing to do.'

'Sure was.'

I shook my head. It was still difficult to believe what had happened up in Stanmore.

' . . . But,' continued Cairo, 'you have to admire him. You have to admire his sincerity, his conviction.' She looked over at me. 'It's certainly a rare commodity now, conviction. People just don't believe in things any more, do they?'

'How do you mean?' I asked.

'Well, back in the sixties . . . and seventies – let's say the early seventies anyway – people believed in things. Passionately. They would go off and follow gurus to find enlightenment. They would protest. On the news there was always footage of students, putting up barricades and occupying buildings. Marching . . .'

I obviously looked puzzled.

'They had beliefs then,' Cairo went on. 'Now nobody believes in anything. I mean, what does the government believe in? Their selling point seems to be that they *don't believe* in anything.'

'Yeah, but isn't that a good thing? In some ways?' I said.

'No, not really. Because you need people who believe strongly in what's right to stand up to people who believe strongly in what's wrong.'

'But who's to say what's right and wrong?'

'Everybody. That's what I'm saying. When I think back, everybody seemed to have an opinion then. Now, people just don't seem that bothered.'

The cat on Cairo's lap lifted its head, stood up, arched its back, tore a few threads out of Cairo's jeans and leapt on to the table. I scratched it under its chin. It permitted me to do this for a few seconds before walking off.

'You know,' said Cairo, 'what really worries me is that now I'm just the same. When I think about Eric – and everything he does, I feel quite ashamed. I do so little. So little of any consequence.'

'You've got your art.'

Cairo waved her hand, dismissing my statement.

' . . . And there's the cats,' I continued, 'and, eventually, your cat charity.'

Cairo sighed. 'But maybe I should be doing more now. Something of consequence.'

'Like what?'

'I don't know.'

'Well, you can't do what Eric does.'

'No, I realize that. I'm hardly GLF material. But maybe I should get involved in some other way. Join a local pressure group. Go to the bottle bank more. The trouble is, there's always something else to do, isn't there? Something else that seems more important!'

'Yeah, like doing the laundry or going to Tesco's.'

Cairo smiled. 'Yes, exactly!'

I took a sip of coffee. Another cat jumped on to Cairo's lap, tore at her jeans and then collapsed, purring. 'Oohh,' said Cairo to the cat, 'what a lovely, lovely, girl.'

'What's she called?'

'Oh, this is Madame Blavatsky – although she answers to Zatsky.'

I reached over and scratched the cat's cute, chocolate-coloured head. 'Eric told me that you can find traces of pesticide – you know, DDT – in the body fat of every animal on the earth now. I'm carrying it, you're carrying it, the cat's carrying it. Poison. They've even found it in penguins. It's everywhere.'

Cairo winced. The thought of her beloved cats suffering – even a little – was all too much. She abruptly changed the subject. 'So what's happening with the band? You haven't said a word about the band in ages.'

'Well, quite a lot's happened. Where were you up to?'

'You told me that there was a producer who was interested, and some guys from an independent label were going to one of your gigs.'

'God, it was that long ago?'

'It must have been.'

'Yeah, well. We did the gig. They decided that we should go into a studio in Letchworth and record three singles, which we did.'

'Oh, I'd like to hear them.'

'They're not new. Just old ones off the Watford demo.'

'Which?'

' "Smart Peroxide", "Trade" and "Forever Young".'

'Oh, yes, I liked "Forever Young". Was that one of yours?'

'Yeah, but it's a bit slow for a single.' Unfortunately, I couldn't resist adding: 'I also wrote "Smart Peroxide".' It sounded like a boast – which of course it was. I really didn't like myself when I did things like that.

'You must be very happy.'

'I am,' I said, although Cairo perceived the lack of enthusiasm. 'But . . .'

171

I shrugged. 'I don't know.'

'For the past two years you've been trying to get a record deal, and now that you've got one, you don't seem that pleased.'

'I am pleased.'

'You don't look it.'

I took another swig of coffee, lit a Benson and thought for a few moments. 'I guess it's an anticlimax. You try and try and try. All those rehearsals, all those gigs, all those wanky A&R men telling you that you're crap. You stick it out, you see it through, and then . . .'

'You get a contract!'

'Sure. But . . . it doesn't feel like it. It doesn't feel any different.'

'I'm sure it will. When you've got the CD in your hand. Or when you walk into Our Price in Hampstead and see your single advertised. Or see that it's made the charts! Then you'll feel different.'

'I guess so. But at the moment it doesn't seem real. It doesn't feel like it's going to happen.'

Cairo lifted Madame Blavatsky on to the table, got up, came to my side and lifted my head up. She bent down and kissed me on the lips – not a lingering kiss, just a small, dry kiss. She then kissed my forehead. 'Are you all right, Nick?'

I raised a half-smile. 'I have been feeling down, not depressed or anything – just down. We've been waiting a while to hear from the guys at Retro, the label. But nothing much is happening. And I'm bored . . . and, after all the excitement of having Eric around . . . Eric leaving has . . . produced a space on the floor.'

'Maybe you're lonely. You should get yourself a girlfriend.'

I laughed. 'Perhaps.'

Cairo took my hand in hers, stroked my fingers, then walked me to the front room. She sat down on the sofa, and let me lay down with my head resting on her lap. I guessed she was in one of her maternal moods. This was OK, up to a point. But I didn't want her to get too maternal.

'Cairo?'

'Yes.'

'What happened to Eric?'

'What, in '73?'

'Yeah.'

'I don't know. You know that.'

'But is there anybody who does?'

'Eric, of course.'

'No. Someone else. Was anyone with him . . . when he . . . changed?'

Cairo pulled a face.

'Nick, it was all such a long time ago. I honestly can't remember . . . I think, there were a few people out there with him.'

'In the Middle East?'

'The Middle East, Morocco . . . and all that. Yes.'

'Who?'

'God, I don't know.'

'Could you find out?'

'No. I haven't spoken to any of *those* people in' – she affected a theatrical gulp – 'in over twenty years.'

'So, what do you think happened to him? Really.'

Cairo locked her fingers in my hair. 'Look. I really don't know. Believe me, this conversation is one that I've had many, many times before. I was having this conversation before you were born, Nick.'

'Yeah, but' – I tilted my head back to catch her eyes – 'I really like Eric, and I want to understand him.'

'That's lovely, but, Eric doesn't want to be understood – clearly. Otherwise he would have been more forthcoming over the last twenty-five years!'

'Yeah. I guess you're right.'

The conversation subsequently fizzled out. So we just passed the afternoon, talking in a noncommittal way about whatever happened to enter our minds. Eventually, I excused myself.

I went to the bathroom and washed my cock; a single gesture that combined compassion with optimism. I was getting the feeling that we were definitely *on for it*. While I was in the bathroom, I remembered my Naloxyl. I hadn't taken one for three days. I had just forgotten. I popped two out of the blister pack and swallowed them. Then I thought, bugger it, and popped a third. I didn't really get any side-effects. The worse I would have to put up with would be a headache.

When I went back down to the front room Cairo had gone. By the sofa was a pile of women's magazines. I flicked through some of the titles. *G* and *The Curse* were aimed at a slightly older – and single – readership, professional women who had opted for a womb bypass and had become preoccupied with young men, health, income, art exhibitions and the modern novel. *Gagging For It* was far more interesting. An enterprising publisher had obviously realized that 'laddism' was an ideology shared by a considerable number of women. All of these 'new men' were *doing it* with 'new women'. Clearly there was a market. *Gagging For It* contained a number of semi-pornographic shots of famous pop stars. The lighting was always designed to enhance crotch-geography: page after page of undulating denim or lycra; folds and crevices, bulges and ravines.

The articles were fabulous. A feature called 'Cock Collector' consisted of a submission by two readers (Karen B. and Karen C.). It described a *girls' night out*, in which the Woodbridge Road Posse sought to break a previous penetration record. It was compelling stuff. One column, 'Slag', was written by a doctor and contained a guide to venereal diseases and their treatment.

Cairo came back into the room. She had shed her chic clothes and replaced them with a dressing-gown. She was now looking more like her normal self, her hair free and unconstrained. 'Ahhh,' she said, 'you've found my copy of the *Gagg*!'

'I have.'

'Give us it.' She snatched it from my hands and placed it on her lap. She then took out some dope and rolled herself a joint, using the mag as a work surface.

'I didn't think it was your kind of thing.'

'It isn't!'

'Then why have you got it?'

'A friend of mine is the editor. She sent me a copy. It's new . . .

issue one, see.' She pointed to the issue number. Then she added as an afterthought ' . . . Although, some of the young boys are real peaches.' Cairo lit her joint and offered me a toke.

'No, thanks.'

'Still on the trial?'

'Yeah. But I haven't been very good . . . It's difficult not to smoke with Eric. He sort of encourages you.'

'Well, you had better be good now then.'

I sighed. 'I suppose so.'

'I bet you'll be glad when it comes to an end.'

'Yes and no. I still need the cash.'

'Are you allowed to give me a blowback?'

I considered the proposition. 'Err . . . I guess so. Providing I don't inhale.'

'Then don't inhale.'

She handed me the joint. I took a toke and held the opiate cloud in my mouth before releasing it into Cairo's. She exhaled out of her nose and let her tongue explore my mouth. 'And another . . .' she said.

We repeated the manoeuvre.

I could tell what she wanted. She let the dressing-gown fall open and parted her legs. Her body was white and marred only by little wrinkles around her nipples and a certain papery texture on her abdomen. I knelt on the floor, between her legs, and tongued her open vagina. Her clit soon became swollen and I sucked it into my mouth as though it were a micro-prick – sucked it in, then pushed it out with the tip of my tongue, making sure to scrape it gently between my teeth. She inhaled, and relaxed. Inhaled, and relaxed, until her body convulsed with pleasure. When I drew away and wiped my mouth, she said, 'Come on, let's go upstairs.'

Cairo's bedroom was like a fantasy brothel. The stripped floorboards had been stained black and polished so they looked like ebony, and a number of Turkish rugs, of different sizes, made a haphazard patchwork carpet. Large cushions were casually strewn around the room, and an enormous four-poster was shrouded with semi-transparent veils of crimson and purple silk.

175

Cairo drew the curtains and lit a candle while I stripped. She then got on to the bed and stretched her arms out. I crawled on top of her and entered her on the first push.

It was a nice, lazy fuck. I moved up and down, setting a gentle, easy rhythm. Withdrawing fully, and re-entering, to get the most from her well-lubricated ginch. We had been making love like this for, I don't know, maybe twenty minutes – it was quite hypnotic – when, suddenly, I began to feel odd. My eyes were closed, and I began to experience what seemed like a wave. But it wasn't, it was different. And then, all of a sudden, I was in Cairo's head.

I was lying, gripping black silk sheets, and above me was Jimi Hendrix. He was sweating slightly, and his generous lips were parted beneath his sparse, drooping moustache. His lids were closing, but I could still see his dark, dark eyes. I could feel his enormous cock inside me.

– *Here ah come, baby, ahhm commin to gitch'ya* . . .

It was monstrous. I gasped.

– *Ah'll take you home, baby* . . .

No you fucking won't.

– *Ah'll take you home* . . .

'Fuck off!'

As he bore down on me I passed out.

When I opened my eyes Cairo was standing next to the bed with her dressing-gown on, looking alarmed.

'Nick, are you OK?'

'Yeah, I think so.' Although, as I said these words, I became aware of a throbbing headache.

She asked, 'What happened?'

'I don't know, I just . . .'

'Fainted?'

'Yeah.'

'Shall I call a doctor?'

'No. No. I think I'm OK now.'

I started rubbing my forehead.

'Wow, this hurts!'

176

'Can I get you anything?'

'A glass of water. My mouth's gone really dry.'

Cairo left the room, looking back over her shoulder at me as she opened the door. A cat jumped on to the bed and sat beside me. A large, long-haired cat, with a flat black face. I sat up and pushed it away – a rare opportunity, while Cairo wasn't there. The cat looked truly startled.

Cairo came back. 'Here, take this.'

'Thanks.'

I drank the water and began to feel a little better. 'Wow, that was really weird. I've never passed out before.'

'You just slumped. You told me to fuck off and then passed out.'

'Jesus. Did I? I'm really sorry. I'm really, really sorry . . .'

'Don't be silly.'

'I didn't mean to . . .'

'I realize that.'

'I think it must have been the drug, the Naloxyl. I was really stupid. I took three earlier.'

'Why?'

'I'd forgotten to take my daily dose. So I thought, what the hell, I'll take three.'

'That wasn't very clever.'

'No, obviously not.' I shook my head. 'Christ, this really hurts.'

Cairo brushed the hair off my forehead. 'Are you sure I shouldn't call a doctor?'

'No, I'll be fine. Give me a few minutes.' The throbbing gradually subsided. 'Cairo?'

She sat next to me, and held my hand. 'Yes.'

'When we were . . . fucking just then. Were you, fantasizing . . .'

She tilted her head to one side before saying, 'That's a peculiar question to ask right now.'

'Seriously. What were you thinking?'

'Look, I think you're still a bit dazed. You don't look well at all. Lie back.'

'No. I'm OK. Cairo? What were you thinking?'

'Nothing important. Now lie back will you?'

She eased my head back down on to a pillow.

I wanted to say: *You were remembering Hendrix, weren't you? You were remembering being fucked by Hendrix!* But how could I? If I was wrong, I'd sound crazy. I closed my eyes and tried to forget about it.

Cairo fussed around me for the rest of the day. She cooked me an evening meal and told me to get some sleep. It was surprisingly easy to accomplish, as though I'd been smoking dope or something. When I woke the following morning it was late and Cairo had been up for hours. I found her in her studio working on a uniform orange canvas which she told me she intended to call *Orange*.

'No, I think you should call it *Green*.'

'Why?'

'To demonstrate that, essentially, language is an arbitrary system of sounds, having no intrinsic meaning.'

I was trying to parody the Brunelleschi programme, as a joke, but Cairo bit her lower lip and said, 'Yes, yes. What an interesting idea. An allusion to deconstructionism.'

I didn't have the heart to say *only joking*.

After breakfast I was ready to go home.

'How do you feel?' asked Cairo.

'OK.'

'Sure?'

'Absolutely.'

'Well, take care.'

She kissed me, gave me a hug, and a tiny push to help me on my way.

When I got home I listened to my messages. The first was from my mother: 'Hello, Nick, Mum calling. I haven't heard from you for a while now, and I'm just calling to see how you are.' There was a long pause. 'Do give me call . . . if you get the time. Bye-bye.' There was then a beep and another, silent message. I could hear the sound of traffic. Then Andy: 'Nick . . . are you there? No. OK. Just calling for a chat. I still haven't heard anything from anyone. Have you? Give us a call if you hear anything. Cheers.'

There were then three more silent messages: beep-pause; beep-pause; beep-pause; then beep, followed by a long pause. I could hear traffic again, then a voice, a man's voice: '*We were meant for each other . . . We were meant for each other, me and you . . .*' Then silence.

OK. Now I was really worried.

I felt uneasy, and I had too much time on my hands – a disconcerting combination – so I resolved to occupy myself by messing about with sequences on the Rhodes. Curiously enough, I didn't need the assistance of Bach. The basic progressions came together pretty quickly. I hummed a few experimental tunes over the top and, eventually, a song began to take shape, the melody nice and spacey. It asked for a slow, thumping single-note bass and a really solid drumbeat. I stuffed a cassette into the blaster and taped a few versions. There was a time when I would have taken out some manuscript and jotted down some dots, but not any more.

When I found that I couldn't get a chorus to go with my verse, I left the keys alone and lay on my bed, smoking and listening to music. I started off with some Portishead and then felt a curious urge to play some Hendrix. I fingered the line of 'H' CDs until I found them, a quite comprehensive collection, including some extremely dodgy bootlegs. I flicked a few out and looked at the cover photos.

James Marshall Hendrix, *the flower generation's Electric Nigger Dandy – its king and golden calf.* Those descriptions are still lodged in my mind, outmoded, yet curiously appropriate. I was a little apprehensive. Would listening to Hendrix trigger another weird vision?

I looked into his eyes, *the king of psychedelic vaudeville,* and

James Marshall Hendrix looked back at me. *Ahhm commin to gitch'ya!* It was time to reflect. Time to think things through.

What happened with Cairo hadn't been a hallucination. No way. I had simply dropped into her head. That was the only explanation. Such an explanation also made appalling sense of the experience I had had at the PAC. I had been in *his* head, too. Just remembering the touch of his mind made my stomach turn. It was the mental equivalent of having to handle excrement. I felt quite sick and suppressed the image.

Clearly, I had started to gatecrash other people's heads. Naloxyl was starting to make my mind pervious to other people's memories. First it had made me sensitive to the presence of other minds, but now the channel was opening up. When people were looking at me I could access their memories – either that or I was losing the plot. And I wasn't losing the plot.

So I figured that nothing untoward could happen while I was on my own; listening to Hendrix would be safe.

I slipped on the cans, lit a Benson, crossed my fingers and listened to Jimi go.

Music for the machine age. The crash of sheet metal and the throb of engines. Heavy-duty electric cables, waving, crackling and sparking together. The scream of a chainsaw and a 747 falling out of the sky. I listened to him squeeze the roar of traffic and the rumble of the Underground out of his Strat. Fragmenting each note into quarter tones and overtones, tearing the fabric of music apart with his teeth. Even notes weren't safe in the hands of James Marshall Hendrix. Here was a proper anthem for doomed youth, a score to accompany colliding chrome and aluminium skidding along scorched Tarmac, music for the fast lane. Here was the violence, the reality. Splintering glass, helicopter blades and napalm. I listened to him relentlessly punching the nails into the coffin of complacency.

And for all that, I didn't see him once. He didn't materialize on the back of my eyelids, and I didn't feel him inside me. In one specific way, my very own *Jimi Hendrix Experience* had proved every bit as disturbing as my Prince Albert experience. Merely remembering *that* feeling almost made me lose my grip. Jesus, it was so, so, unnatural. I just couldn't hack being a woman. I really couldn't. Christ, it was like being pinned to the mattress with a truncheon. And, hey, am I *glad to be straight*. Very glad. Very glad indeed.

I think the experience left me with a fear of penetration. Any kind of penetration. Afterwards, even cleaning my teeth was difficult. I wanted everything to just back off – way off.

The days passed uneventfully. Andy arranged a rehearsal at Vince's, and we dutifully played through the set. But we all knew that we were just biding our time, waiting for news. Unfortunately, Andy was finding it hard to cope and had rung up Jarl once too often. Apparently, Jarl's response had been rather curt.

We decided to give it a rest, take a break. Phil and Scott went off for a week in Brighton (to stay with friends), and Andy resolved to go on a ten-day bender with some mates of his Dad's. I was at a seriously loose end; then, I got an idea . . .

I had been listening to *Eugene's Moment of Truth*. When it had finished I just sat on my bed, turning the cover around in my hands. There was the usual list of people thanked in small print on the back of the sleeve: Caz, Len Smart, Mahatma Guru Charnanandji, Zoob, Deepti Hopkins and Tantra Jack, Jim Goggins, Sid, Linda Makepiece (and all at Moonchild), Sooki and Blow, J R R Tolkien, Larry (just guess it) Weiskrantz, Friedrich Caspar, and so on. It was a long shot, but I got out the telephone book and started to look up some of the names – well, all of them – starting off with the band members.

None of the band was in the phone book. I then looked up the engineer: Aloysius Jakoby. I found three Mr A. Jakobys in West London.

The first one was a guy who put the phone down when I mentioned the Turtle Tree; however, the second call was answered by a woman.

'Could I speak to Mr Jakoby please?'

'No, he's at work.'

'Look, I'm sorry, but I don't know whether I've got the right number, is that Aloysius Jakoby's number?'

At first she seemed uncertain, then said, 'Oh, you mean Al. Yeah?'

'The recording engineer?'

'No, mate. Not any more, he ain't.' She coughed, a heavy phlegmy cough.

'But he used to be?'

'You're not from the council, are you?'

'No. I'm a friend of Eric Wright's?'

'Who?'

'A musician. He used to work with Aloysius . . .'

'Oh look, why don't you call him yourself, he's down the workshop.' She gave me the number of Jakoby Coachworks, in Queens Park.

I didn't call. I found the address in the Yellow Pages and decided I should drive over. I wanted something to do, and impersonating a private detective was giving me a real buzz.

The works were situated on a pretty grubby-looking industrial estate, a completely anonymous complex of modern boxes which had fallen into disrepair. There is something extremely disconcerting about new derelict buildings: *Les Slums nouveaux*. Their accelerated rate of decay is unnerving. What must have been – only recently – brightly coloured warehouses and offices were now streaked with filth and grime. Some of the windows had been smashed; no one had bothered to board them up. The place was like a ghost town.

Jakoby's works were difficult to find in the maze of characterless sideroads. But, eventually, I was able to locate it on the corner of a small square called Prosperity Place. I got out of the Honda and looked around. There were no signs of life. I headed for the Coachworks sign. The garage doors were closed, but the padlock was open. I pulled the door and stepped inside, letting it close itself behind me. I could hear the sound of a radio playing, very quietly. An old blue Triumph Dolomite was parked in the middle of the floor. It was in a pretty bad way. The rear lights were smashed and the chrome bumper was hanging off, and the boot had been scrunched up like a concertina.

I called out, 'Hello.' But no one answered. There was an open door at the back, from where the music was coming.

As I approached, I saw a man in overalls sitting in a tiny office, reading a newspaper. Two empty cans of Tennents were lying on their side, one discharging a small pool, which was being absorbed by the paper. The man looked up. 'Yeah?'

'Are you Aloysius Jakoby?'

'Yeah.'

'I'm a friend of Eric Wright's?'

He looked blank. His face was dirty, and he wore his hair in a long, greasy pony-tail. 'Eric who?'

'Eric Wright. He used to play lead in the Turtle Tree?' For a moment, the merest fraction of a second, his eyes became bright. I continued, 'You engineered on *Eugene's Moment of Truth*?' I extended my hand. Jakoby wiped his hands on his overalls before shaking mine, still without saying anything. 'I wondered, could we have a chat?'

'What about?'

'I've got some questions. I thought you might be able to answer them.'

He looked at me as though I were an apparition. Suddenly his face changed. 'You're from the Revenue!'

I laughed. 'No. I'm a mate of Eric's. Really.'

'Eric Wright?'

'Yeah.'

'Fuck me.'

He stood up. His overalls were baggy. I got the impression that they concealed a withered, wasted frame. 'Here, take a seat.'

I looked at the dirty old office chair. 'Maybe we should talk somewhere else. Do you feel like a pint?'

He paused. 'I've got this job to do.' He gestured toward the Dolomite. But he hadn't said no. He continued, 'I should make a start. It's been sitting there all day.'

'We won't be long. Just a swift half then?'

'Fuck it, why not.' He unzipped his overalls.

It was difficult to believe that Aloysius Jakoby had been one of
the most talented engineers of his day. This emaciated wreck of a
human being was a pitiful sight, a kind of wraith, a sort of after-
image rather than a real person. At first he was quite wary. I
suspected he was still entertaining the possibility of my being
some kind of spy from the Inland Revenue. His response to even
small talk was guarded, and he had the habit of suddenly looking
around as though he were expecting to be ambushed. It took
him some time to settle and, eventually, when I told him about
Eric crashing out at my place only a few weeks earlier, he became
visibly more relaxed. Mentioning Eric's ability to construct
unfeasibly large joints seemed to be the final assurance he
required.

In the mid-seventies he had got seriously into smack. He
subsequently became unreliable, and the demand for his services
fell dramatically. By 1978 he was on his way out; he engineered
his last recording session in 1979; the guy who owned the studio
where he was chief engineer asked him to leave. By 1980 he had
blown all his money, and by 1981 he had turned to crime to support
his habit.

He spent three years in prison, and then seven years in and out
of drug-dependency units. After rehabilitation he got a job in a
garage through a fellow patient. He eventually drifted into panel-
beating and bodywork. He had only just started his own business;
it wasn't doing very well.

We talked a little about his work with the Tree, but he didn't
have much to say. I told him about the band and our contract
with Retro, but it didn't mean anything to him. He seemed to get
bored very quickly.

After I had bought him his second pint, I asked *the* question:
'So what happened to Eric?'

'How do you mean?'

'Why did he give it all up?'

'Why don't you ask him?'

'I have.'

'And what did he say?'

'Nothing. He just . . . says a load of stuff. Rubbish, really.'

Jakoby nodded sagely and took a sip of his pint. 'So what's new?'

I offered him a Benson.

'Thanks.'

I lit it for him and waited for him to stop coughing. 'I just thought you might know something. You were around at the time. The Tree had just finished *Eugene* and . . .' I trailed off. He was staring blankly at the bar.

He turned to look at me. 'It was a fuck of a long time ago.'

I tried again. 'I heard that Eric went abroad. And he came back changed.'

Jakoby nodded and took another drag.

I continued prompting, 'He did Morocco . . . and the Middle East?'

'That's right.'

'You remember then?'

'Yeah . . .'

'So?'

'He was out there with Vealy.'

'David Veale. The keyboard player?'

'That's right.'

'Where?'

'The Middle East. I spoke to Vealy when he got back. He was really pissed off with Eric. For dropping out and that.'

'But what happened?'

'I'm not sure really.' I was beginning to think that I was wasting my time when Jakoby said, almost as an afterthought, 'I know where it happened, though.'

I waited but he didn't elaborate, so I gave him a prompt. '*It?* What do you mean? *It?*'

'Where it happened. Where Eric lost it.'

'Where did he lose it?'

'On the road . . .'

'The road?'

'Yeah. The road to Damascus.'

18
waiting for something terrible to happen

Jakoby wasn't able to say much more. After his revelation he became taciturn and morose. I tried to press him for some more details, but he soon became irritable. 'Fuckin' 'ell man, what is this?'

I backed off and tried to make some more small talk to defuse the uncomfortable atmosphere, but it didn't really work. It was as though, having recounted his history to a stranger, he was now having doubts about whether this had been such a good idea. Either that or our conversation had brought his terrible decline into sharp focus. Whatever, he remained glum and withdrawn. Clearly it was time to go.

I shook his hand, thanked him and walked to the door. Before leaving, I couldn't resist looking back. There he was, the most talented recording engineer of his generation, resigned to a life of emptiness and misery. His blank expression caught the yellow light filtering through a stained-glass window, giving him the appearance of a zombie or a man on the brink of physical decay. In the row of empty pint glasses in front of him, the residue had collected at the bottom of each like stagnant marsh-water. He stared at the brown liquid as though some strange augury were about to visit him and grant him a glimpse of his ultimate fate. It was obvious he would not return to the workshop for some time. The smashed-up Dolomite would remain untouched for days, maybe even weeks. When I closed the door, I felt like I was sealing a burial chamber.

I left the empty pub and walked back to the car. I wasn't sure what it all meant. Damascus. The road to Damascus.

Although my knowledge of the Bible is virtually non-existent, I knew enough to recognize Damascus as the celebrated location of another famous conversion; but this didn't get me very much further. I tried to trawl through my memory for the remnants of my religious-education classes in primary school where we would sit cross-legged on the floor while the teacher, Mrs Fielding, told us stories from the Bible, the Koran and other holy books. Yes, Damascus – Saint Paul was converted to Christianity on the road to Damascus – but I just couldn't remember anything else. I could only remember the colour of the classroom floor and my grey socks encased in brown sandals. I would have to get hold of a Bible. Cairo might have one. Or if not I could always drop in to the Catholic shop.

I drove home with mixed feelings. On the one hand I was glad that my half-arsed detective work had proved successful but, on the other hand, my encounter with the cadaverous Jakoby had left me feeling desolate and hollow. His hopelessness was like a vacuum, drawing in any stray motes of optimism and happiness. My drink with him had deadened my spirit.

When I got home the light on my answering-machine was flashing. It had acquired the urgency of a warning signal, a beacon communicating the presence of danger. It was difficult to discipline my body to approach it and press the Play button. I lit a Benson and stood beside the machine, transfixed by its ominous wink.

I hit Play. The effect was now familiar: beep-pause; beep-pause; beep-pause; beep-pause. It went on for a while, each tone followed by silence. Then, the message, the same voice: 'Soon. Very soon now . . .' Then nothing.

This wasn't a joke; this was serious. The telephone had become an object of menace, a machine that allowed *him* to invade my life, that let *him* into my head. Suddenly, the flat felt exposed. I became acutely aware of my own vulnerability. I even felt uncomfortable about walking down the hall to the kitchen. I listened, and the usual house sounds – the background noise of the fridge, the plumbing, the creaking floorboards above – became suspicious. What could I do?

I began to work through my options. I could inform the police that I was getting nuisance calls, but that would get me nowhere. If I told them that I thought it was *him* calling, then they would inevitably ask me how I knew. And then what would I say? Well, Constable, I'm on a drug trial, and I believe that Naloxyl has made me psychic. I recently played a gay S&M gig and received some disturbing mental impressions. I also experienced something similar in a pub toilet in Essex. It is my belief that the source of these impressions was a man described in the gay press as the *fist-fuck fiend*. I have come to the conclusion that these nuisance calls represent his increasing interest in me as a prospective victim. *Yes, sir, we understand the situation entirely.* I was in deep shit.

I listened to the message again. Should I save it? As evidence? What was the point?

In the kitchen I made myself a coffee and smoked another Benson, then another, then another. I began to pace up and down the hall, trying to figure out what to do, trying to get a handle on what was happening. There was a lot to think about. Somehow, while I had been trying to get on with my life, things had become very complicated.

First of all, there was Naloxyl. What was it doing to me? I had come to believe that it was making me sensitive to the gaze of others. But what if I was wrong? Maybe I was just suffering from bad side-effects? Side-effects that were making me lose my grip, making me believe I had strange powers. If so, then I should either stop fucking about and tell Dr McDougall or, alternatively, flush the remaining Naloxyl down the toilet and simply drop out of the trial. The first would probably involve being institutionalized, while the second would most probably result in starvation. Neither seemed attractive.

But it just didn't make sense to conclude that I was losing it! I didn't feel like I was losing it at all; I seemed to be functioning OK. Besides, was it really that weird, what I thought was happening? Most people have experienced the feeling of being stared at. It's a feeling everyone gets now and again. Maybe Naloxyl was enhancing that sense. It wasn't so weird. I could think of precedents. Ravers – high on Ecstasy – say that they can sense other people's minds. Feel their presence . . .

Pace, pace, turn.

But what about the dropping into other people's heads? Information transfer, was that for real? Why not? If I accepted being sensitive to being stared at, then why not head-dropping? Maybe a high dose of Naloxyl knocked the dial up a notch, giving me access to other people's memories while they stared at me. Although somehow – on reflection – head-dropping seemed less easy to accept, less plausible.

Was there a middle ground? I wondered. Maybe I *could* sense people staring at me, maybe I could do that, but maybe I couldn't head-drop. The business at the PAC could have been just . . . impressions which I later interpreted as fist-fuck homicide (but only after I had read about the killer). And maybe what happened while I was screwing Cairo was just . . . suggestibility. Jesus, I'd thought about the Hendrix cock-thing enough!

Pace, pace, turn.

In that case, there wasn't that much to worry about. I had simply put together a scary story that was nothing more than an attempt to make sense of a load of weird shit happening in my life.

I stopped pacing and tried to summarize my thinking, take stock of where I'd got to: Maybe Naloxyl did enhance my sense of being stared at. Maybe that was true. And maybe some nutter had picked my name out of the telephone directory at random. And maybe that was true. But nothing more than that was happening.

I began pacing again. I had had nuisance calls before. Once I kept on being called by an old woman who was convinced that I was her dead sister, Tess. These things do happen.

So what action should I take? Keep taking the tablets and simply ignore the calls.

I felt mildly reassured and sat down, but then a little voice inside my head said: *But what if you're wrong? What if you're just trying to put a positive spin on things?*

I got up and started to pace again. Maybe Naloxyl had given me strange powers. Maybe I had head-dropped a serial killer. And maybe I was being targeted as the next victim, maybe I was next in line. And, if so, what could I do about it? What could I do?

I was back to square one, back to where I started. My head hurt, and all the thinking had got me nowhere. I lit another Benson and collapsed on my bed. Remarkably, I fell asleep.

On waking, the first thing I did was panic. I scanned the sheets for my smouldering Benson, frantically turning over the pillows and the duvet, but I couldn't see it anywhere. Eventually, I found the elusive dog-end in the ashtray, although I had no recollection of putting it there. My heart began to slow down. The digital display told me that I had been asleep for just over an hour. Amazing. I had obviously let my ruminations churn my brain matter into a curdled pulp.

As I lay, waiting for my mind to become fully engaged, I remembered Jakoby:

    ' – *On the road . . .*'

    ' – *The road?*'

    ' – *Yeah. The road to Damascus.*'

Recollections of my visit to Queens Park meant that I still felt as though I had only recently quitted the grave. I felt dirty, and the corners of my mouth were caked with solidified spit. I dragged myself off the bed and lurched into the shower.

I began to feel better immediately. The water seemed to wash away my malaise. I shifted my upturned face from side to side in the spray and decided that I should get out of the flat for a while. It felt claustrophobic. I turned off the water and, using a towel to make an improvised toga, went straight to the telephone to call Andy.

Mr Cash answered. 'Hello, Nicky, how are you?'

'Fine. Is Andy there, Mr Cash?'

'No, I haven't seen him for days. He's been out with some friends of mine.'

'Yeah, he mentioned it.'

'They are all good boys.'

I wasn't sure how to handle the reply. 'For sure. But, have you any idea where I can catch up with them?'

'Who knows, eh?'

'Is he expected back soon?'

'I really can't say.'

'I see.'

He suddenly shouted, 'Put that down, you stupid bitch! I put it there for a good reason!' There was a hysterical scream, which I took to be Mrs Cash's reply. The old boy had been drinking. He continued as though nothing irregular had happened, 'So when are we going to see you again, Nicky? We haven't seen you for months, no?'

For a moment I thought of offering to go up to the pub there and then, just to get out of the flat. But an evening with Mr Cash was hardly an incentive. 'Yeah, it's been a long time. I'll have to try to get up to see you soon.'

'Yes, you do that. I suppose you will be a big star soon, from what I hear. Then you mustn't forget your old comrades. No?'

'No. I certainly won't. If Andy gets back tonight, will you ask him to give me a call?'

'Yes, yes. Of course.'

'Be seeing you, then?'

'Goodbye, my friend.'

Looking at the replaced receiver, I couldn't help feeling deflated. I didn't really want to bother Cairo again, and I certainly couldn't visit my mother, so I flicked through my old address book. Most of the people in there I hadn't contacted for ages. Mates from school, one or two girlfriends (although to call them girlfriends was rather overstating the case. Actually, they were simply women I had slept with more than once). I realized that I had let my circle of friends and acquaintances gradually shrink, to the extent that I had become socially isolated. For the past year, my life had been the band. There wasn't any room for anything else. Songs, rehearsals, gigs and chasing record deals. I had let things slip.

I suddenly became aware of myself. I was standing in the middle of the room, address book in hand, staring at the wall. I felt my hair. It was sticking up with sweat. My face was rough with stubble. I was just like that guy, the guy I saw when I went for my late-night wander with Eric. I was just another headcase, waiting for something terrible to happen. The memory felt strange, not like a memory at all, but as if I had caught a glimpse of myself in the future. Jesus H Christ! If the band didn't work out, I might end up like that one day. I should watch myself. Too much rock 'n' roll makes Jack a dull boy. I didn't have the heart to call anyone up. I felt wasted.

The next few days weren't so bad. I calmed down and began to realize that my visit to Jakoby's had probably rattled me. It wasn't a cool thing to have done, and I kind of regretted it. It was OK to talk to Eric directly about his 'conversion' – or to Cairo for that matter – but snooping really wasn't on. I had got what I deserved.

Andy returned my call and was disappointed to hear that I had only phoned to arrange a drink. He was really annoyed that we still hadn't heard any news from Jarl. I said we should be patient, which was somewhat dishonest. My own supply of patience had ebbed away and I too was desperate for something to happen. I drove out to Essex to meet Andy. We spent an afternoon in a quiet country pub called the Plough. Andy was drinking only mineral water. He was feeling ill after his recent excesses, the circumstances of which he could barely recall.

'No, I can't remember that much to be honest. And there are other bits, which I think I can remember, but I don't want to.'

'What do you mean?'

'Well' – Andy shook his head from side to side like a horse trying to get rid of a tick – 'I can trust you, can't I, Nick?'

'Sure.'

'Me and me dad's mates went up West, right?'

'Right.'

'And we were rat-arsed by the time we got up there anyway.'

'Of course.'

'Well, you know the score.'

I nodded.

'Well,' continued Andy, 'we got some more in when we got there, and then did a few clubs. Bobo – he's a . . . a sort of . . .' Andy thought for a few moments.

'Criminal?' I ventured.

'Yeah, you know, mate of me dad's . . . He was flush. And he was flashing the plastic and giving it some with a wad of tenners. So we did a load of the clubs – Starburst, Sirocco, Chantal . . . nothing up-market. Just the usual rip-off joints and slag markets. Anyway, there was this gorgeous Chinky bird . . .'

'Don't you mean Thai or Malaysian?'

'What are you on about?'

'Never mind,' I said.

'I won't. So, she was coming on really strong, and I think – '

'Hold it!' I said. 'I know where this is going. You were snogging, you got your hands down her knickers, and she had a hard-on!'

'Fucking hell!' said Andy. 'That's amazing! How did you know that?'

'I must be psychic,' I replied.

'Come on, Nick, how did you know? Has it happened to you, too?'

'Let me think about it . . .' I pretended to be thinking really hard, and then said, 'Mmmm . . . no.'

Andy lit a cigarette and started to cough violently. His eyes began to water, and he finally had to relieve his attack by gobbing a gelatinous, semi-transparent mass at the pub wall. It splattered like something in a cartoon.

'Oh, for Christ's sake, Andy!'

'Sorry, sorry,' he mumbled. He looked really bad.

'For fuck's sake, stop smoking. Your lungs can't handle it! They're on the brink of collapse.'

'Yeah, maybe you're right.' He stubbed out the cigarette, and wiped his nose on the back of his hand. 'You should come out with us, Nick, you really should,' he said.

I looked at him as though he were deranged. 'Yeah,' I said. 'Sure . . .'

'Don't be like that. You'd have a good time, believe me. You know your trouble, Nick?'

'What?'

'You're out of practice. I don't think you get out enough. We could team up. Really. It'd be really great. I know you get your oats from that old hippie bird you knock off but, I tell you, there's some quality skirt around. And they're up for anything now . . . anything, if you know what I mean. Toys, group, the lot.' He winked, and said, 'I could do with a proper pulling partner.'

'I'll think about it,' I said.

He meant well. In his terms, he was trying to do me a favour. 'Yeah, you do that,' he added, 'and you won't be sorry, mate.'

The weather kept on changing, so we couldn't stay outside for very long. After a few minutes of bright summer sunshine clouds would race across the sky. A brief thunderstorm would then make way for more sunshine, and so on.

Eventually, out of sheer boredom, I spontaneously decided to reverse my previous position and used the public telephone to call Jarl. Given the prevailing atmosphere, I had assumed that he wouldn't be there, so I was quite surprised when he answered the phone.

'Hi, Jarl, it's Nick.' He paused, almost as though he didn't recognize the name. So I added, perhaps irritably – 'From the Free Radicals.'

'Hello, Nick, good to hear from you.'

'I was just wondering if you had heard anything?'

There was a momentary pause before Jarl answered. It was really weird, like talking to him on a satellite link. Every response seemed to take a fraction longer than was necessary.

'Well, you see, it's like this. Retro are having some distribution problems at the moment. They're a little unhappy with the current distributor and want to change. So, negotiations are in progress and that's caused a hold-up. I know it's frustrating, but there's really nothing I can do. It's out of my hands.' He paused, and I didn't say anything. He went on, 'But the thing is, when it is all sorted out, it will be better for you. Better for the band.'

'What kind of problems are they having?'

'Nick, it's a side of the business I have little to do with. I'm just a talent-spotter. They have explained some of the problems but, well, it goes in one ear and out the other.'

'So, when do you think you'll hear?'

Pause. 'I would very much like to give you an answer, but, I can't. I really don't know.'

There was an uncomfortable silence. 'Look, it will go ahead, won't it? This isn't going to stop our release, is it?'

'No. Not at all. There'll be a delay, that's all. Nick, you must forgive me, I have a meeting right now.'

'OK. Let us know when something happens.'

Jarl replaced the receiver and I listened to the crackling, empty line.

Andy read my morose expression before I got to the table. 'No news, eh?'

'No. He said that there were distribution problems. Nothing to worry about, but there will be a delay.'

'Was he bullshitting?'

'I don't know. Maybe. He sounded . . . shifty.'

We talked about what might be going on but didn't reach any conclusions, so we sat and waited for the evening to draw in. At about seven I gave Andy a lift back to the Mitre, then drove back to Kilburn.

That evening I sat at the Rhodes and worked on the new number, but I didn't get very far. I felt depleted and uninspired. I couldn't even be bothered to pick up my copy of the 48, let alone open it. What I really wanted, what I really, really wanted, was a joint. I wanted to just shut down operations for a while, get out of my head and wake up feeling that a significant amount of time had elapsed.

Outside, it had begun to rain again, and the black sheets of my window-panes were streaked with tiny rivulets that caught the street light. They were like tree roots of liquid metal.

I gave up on the new song and lay on the floor reading *Many Worlds*. Maybe doing something completely different would help. And, besides, I really wanted to get my head around this book. It was a challenge.

Again I started reading about slits and light. This time I felt confident. This time I would really come to grips with it. Having familiarized myself with the vocabulary, it was easier to understand.

In the two-slits experiment, the trajectory of a single photon is influenced by something that – apparently – isn't there. Under these experimental conditions a single photon behaves as though it's been whacked off course by another, invisible, photon, a counterpart. The effect is really reliable. And the reason why we can't see the invisible photon is because it's not in our universe. The guy who wrote the book suggested that these findings could only be explained by accepting the existence of photons in parallel universes. All the universes are completely sealed off from each other – completely sealed off but for the weak influence of their light on ours; their photons on ours.

I imagined myself again, in my various forms, lying on the floor, reading my book, or in versions more removed. The kind of me that my mother would approve of, a graduate of the Royal Academy of Music, perhaps, or a version of me who had never even taken up the piano, me as a physics student or an assistant in a coachworks. Maybe they all existed – somewhere.

Without warning, out of nowhere, I felt a wave. My heart began to pound. This wasn't possible: *There's no one here*. My hand was shaking. *I'm alone. This isn't possible.*

I kept looking down at the page: Words on paper; an illustration – a torch shining at a panel with two slits in it and on the other side of the panel, a zebra-crossing pattern. Light and shade.

The book seemed to fluoresce. My heart was beating so loudly the whole of my visual field seemed to pulse. Everything was expanding and contracting. *You've got to look up.* I gave myself the same instruction. *You've got to look up.* The temperature was plummeting. Intense cold. Desire. Hunger. *You've got to look.*

I slowly lifted my head and stared at the window. Behind the black reflective surface of the window-pane, veiled by the rivulets of rain, was a face, a human face, the features blurred. I felt a sensation like ice spreading through my limbs. Then I screamed.

acts 19

I screamed, a loud, guttural yell. The face retreated slowly backwards and vanished; a shrinking oval that suddenly disappeared.

I was trembling. I immediately grabbed the phone and called Cairo.

'What is it, Nick?'

'Look, I'm in trouble. Can I come over, right now?'

'What sort of trouble?'

'Please, Cairo. I'll explain when I arrive. This is very serious.'

'OK, but – '

'See you in a few minutes. And thanks.'

I ran into the kitchen and grabbed a cab card from my noticeboard. I wasn't prepared to risk going outside alone. Not even for the few seconds it would take me to get to the Honda. I called the cab company and told them to come as quickly as possible. Before putting the phone down, I said, 'Tell your man to knock five times. OK? Five times, or I won't open the door.'

'Yeah, all right,' said the controller, seemingly accustomed to hysterical callers.

I stuffed a few essentials into a carrier bag and then went back into the front room. For the next fifteen minutes I smoked continuously. I sat at the Rhodes, staring at the window, while my nerves fizzed and jangled. When I heard steps on the concrete stairs outside I tensed until I heard the knocker slam five times.

Walking to the cab felt like a journey across no-man's land. Even though I knew I was now relatively safe, I still felt exposed. The cab driver hunched his bomber jacket over his head to avoid getting wet. I followed him, jerking my head around, staring into shadowy corners, like the victim of some dreadful nervous disease. I jumped into the back of the cab.

'Highgate, was it?' asked the driver.

'Yeah. Highgate Avenue.'

He pulled off at speed, shaking his head at the weather. 'Fuckin' . . .' he whispered quietly, too demoralized or tired to add 'hell' or 'bastard'. In the mirror his two black eyes, nesting under heavy eyebrows, looked intensely at the road. As an afterthought, he managed to summon the energy to say, 'Diabolical'. Fortunately, he was too angry with the sky to bother with conversation; the last thing I wanted at that moment was to make small talk. I rested my head against the window and watched my breath mist its surface. Kilburn flashed past. *Kilburn Meadows*.

Suddenly, the driver slammed his foot down. The car skidded and screeched to an abrupt halt. There was no safety-belt in the back so I was thrown off the seat. I could just about see – between the two front seats – that another car had pulled out into the middle of the road ahead. The rain was pouring down the windscreen so heavily the wipers were having a negligible effect.

'Fuckin' cunt!' cried the driver, 'Would you fuckin' believe it?'

He opened the car door and leaped out but, as he did so, the other vehicle pulled away at speed. I could hear him shouting as the sound of its engine faded. Rain was coming through the door and splashing my face. I clambered back on to the seat.

The driver got back in and slammed the door. 'Where was it we were going?' he asked, in a tone of voice that suggested I was responsible for our near-miss.

'Highgate Avenue.'

'Oh yeah.'

When Kilburn gave way to West Hampstead, he was still swearing under his breath. We headed north, north, to the uplands of London. The salubrious, smug rise of Hampstead, and then Highgate, and sanctuary. As the car stopped I sighed with relief.

When I gave the driver his money, he showed no signs of eagerness or interest. I didn't give him a tip, and he didn't notice. He was too far gone.

Cairo threw her arms around me as I came through the door. I was in a bad way. 'Nick, darling, you look terrible. What's happened?'

'You wouldn't believe it!'

'Well, try me.'

'I think someone wants to kill me.'

She released me from her embrace and looked at me very carefully. 'Have you been dealing?'

'Shit, no.'

'Then . . .' Her voice trailed off as she struggled to understand the situation.

'Cairo, can I have a drink?'

'Of course.'

She closed the door and ushered me in. I dropped my carrier bag in the hall. When I entered Cairo's lounge I was welcomed by the scent of burning rose-oil. I inhaled and tried to slough off the tension, the night and its violence. By the fire the cats were sprawled in a heap, vibrating with pleasure. And on the B&O, Ravi Shankar was wending his way through a magical evening raga against the shimmer of his sitar's sympathetic strings. I looked at Cairo and said, 'God, I'm glad to be here.'

She poured me a whiskey and said, 'Sit down'.

I slumped back on the luxurious sofa, and she handed me the glass. Cairo knelt beside me and rubbed my leg. 'You poor thing.'

I took a sip of whiskey and felt it warm my throat. It took me a few moments to compose myself. Then I turned to look at Cairo. 'This is going to take some explaining. I think I should tell you everything.'

'Everything?'

'Yeah. A lot's been going on. I don't know where to start.'

It was going to be very hard to summarize. Nevertheless, I gave

it a go: the trial, Naloxyl, the feeling of being stared at, the Prince
Albert, the murders, the Cranbrook, the phone calls and, finally,
the face at the window. It took me about an hour to tell the
whole story. I told her everything – everything but the Hendrix
business. I still didn't have the balls for that.

Cairo listened carefully throughout. When I had finished she
said nothing for a while. It was difficult to read her. Ravi Shankar
had long since finished, and now there was only the crackling of
a few dying embers in her fire. She looked concerned, but not in
the way that I had expected.

'I don't know what to say.'

I shrugged.

Then she said, 'Can you do it now? Get inside my head?'

'No. I can't do it to order. It just happens, especially when I've
taken more than one Naloxyl.'

'Well, how about the sense of being stared at? Can you do that
now?'

I tried to understand her expression. Then the penny dropped.
'You don't believe me, do you?'

'No, no, I do. This is your experience, I can see that.'

'But you don't think it's real.'

She paused. 'I'd like to see you do it.'

I sighed. 'Cairo, it doesn't work like that. It kind of just happens.
Although, on a good day, it's pretty reliable.'

'And today's not a good day?'

'Of course it's not a fucking good day. I'm completely fucked!'
I had raised my voice. I shook my head and reached out to touch
her. I thought I saw her flinch. 'Oh, God, Cairo, I'm so sorry. I
really am.'

She sighed and held my hand. 'Nick, I think you had better talk
to your doctor. The one you've been seeing at the Maudsley.'

'McDougall?'

'Yes.'

'Why? Do you think I'm crazy?' My voice climbed up a few
registers.

'No, but something strange is going on, isn't it?'

I had not heard such an understatement in many years. 'But I can't tell McDougall, for Christ's sake, he'll lock me away.'

Cairo got up, walked over to her dope box, opened the lid, then stopped. She shut it again and said, 'On second thoughts, I think I'd prefer one of your cigarettes.'

'Sure.'

She took one and lit it. 'What are you going to do, Nick?'

'I don't want to go back home.'

'You don't have to go back home.'

'Thanks. I really appreciate it. I was so scared. When I saw that face at the window I was . . .' Cairo's eyes were widening, so I thought I'd better shut up.

There was an awful, uncomfortable silence. Of course, I had anticipated this outcome all along. I had known from the very beginning that my experiences wouldn't translate well, wouldn't be squeezed into language without losing something, plausibility, for example. That was why I had never said anything in the first place. So I didn't blame Cairo for giving my disclosures a cool reception but, nevertheless, I still felt disappointed, let down.

'So,' said Cairo, 'you think the drug makes you sense others?'

'Not all the time, but a lot of the time.'

'OK. Well, if it does, then that's pretty important, isn't it?'

'How do you mean?'

'It would be something of a scientific breakthrough. A drug that makes you . . . psychic?'

'Sure.'

'So, you should tell Dr McDougall.'

'But he won't believe me, just like you don't.'

'Well, you can prove it to him. And if you prove it, scientists will want to study you. It's so important you shouldn't keep it to yourself.'

I thought about what Cairo was saying but, for some reason, I couldn't answer. My batteries were really low, my charge-light dim. I suddenly felt drained of energy. 'Cairo, I'm really sorry but I'm exhausted. Can we go to bed?'

'Sure. I'll prepare the spare room.' She got up and left, almost on tiptoes, a quiet, self-conscious retreat. *Spare room?*

That was really too much. She didn't even want to sleep in the same bed with me. I felt like getting up and running after her. Running after her and shouting: *For fuck's sake, Cairo, it's me! Nick!* But my anger was like a flare. It burned intensely and then exhausted itself, becoming a thin thread of pique, dissipating in a big black sky. My anger was snuffed out and replaced by resignation.

I had almost certainly freaked Cairo. Maybe she would see things differently in the morning. Maybe I would see things differently in the morning.

'Nick, it's ready.'

I raised my tired body from the sofa and trudged up the stairs. In the *spare room*, Cairo was plumping up the pillows. I walked in and she gestured toward the bed.

'There . . .'

'Thanks. It looks nice.'

Cairo gave me a hug and said, 'See you in the morning. Sleep well.'

As the door began to close I reached out and stopped it. 'Cairo?'

'Yes?'

'I really, really appreciate this.'

She smiled and closed the door quietly. But her smile could not conceal a sudden flash of anguish that distorted her features. I sat on the bed for a few moments, with my head in my hands. Then I stripped and lay on top of the duvet. My body felt hot and sticky, but I just couldn't be bothered to wash. I reached out and switched off the bedside lamp. I could hear Cairo washing in the bathroom and, some time later, her bedroom door closing. Then, there was silence, apart from the gentle rumble of traffic on the Archway road.

I waited, waited for the *soft embalmer* to come, but he didn't show. Even though I was tired, I knew that sleep just wasn't going to happen, so I settled for resting. I sighed and looked at a patch of grey light on the ceiling, my companion for the night. Perhaps at four (or maybe even five in the morning), I drifted off. Only for a couple of hours, but it was a welcome release.

I got up before Cairo and made myself a coffee in the kitchen. Although I hadn't slept that much, I was feeling a lot better. My mind seemed less confused, more able to get things into some kind of perspective. I hadn't handled the previous evening very well. That much was obvious. I couldn't help regretting how much I'd said. I had really been very careless.

Away from my hovel in Kilburn, life seemed to be operating on a different plane. It was a bright, clear morning, and Cairo's kitchen was filled with light. After drinking the coffee I was at a loose end, so I went into Cairo's study and looked along her bookshelf. I found the bible, next to the *Bhagavadgita*. I had no idea where the Damascus bit was, so I flicked through looking for a section titled 'Paul'. But there was no Paul. I then looked for Damascus, but there wasn't a section titled Damascus either. Eventually, after a good deal of pissing around, I found the passage. Acts IX: 'Now as he journeyed he approached Damascus, and suddenly a light from heaven flashed about him. And he fell to the ground and heard a voice.'

I had never given the conversion of Paul much thought before, but it was a damned good story. The light and the voice; Saul getting up after being floored by God, blind. Three days without sight, food or drink, and then turning into God's *instrument*. I thought of Eric, trudging along some dusty Syrian highway in his flared denims and headband . . .

Cairo popped her head around the door. 'Good morning.'

'Hi.'

'How are you feeling?'

'OK, really. Thanks for letting me stay.'

'No problem. Do you want a coffee?'

'I've already had one.'

'Then do you want another?'

'Yeah, OK.'

'See you downstairs.'

Cairo smiled and left. I replaced the bible on the shelf and went down to the kitchen. Cairo filled a large earthenware bowl with some chunky-looking muesli from a glass jar. She then added some dried figs and soaked the whole lot in fresh apple juice. After her first mouthful of muesli she asked, 'Why were you reading the bible, Nick?'

'Because I'm gradually turning into one of those religious maniacs you see in horror films. I mean, if I'm going to do this properly, I need to brush up on my bible. No self-respecting lunatic would go into free fall without a few soundbites from the big one.'

She looked at me without smiling.

'OK,' I said. 'Bad joke.'

'Why were you reading the bible, Nick?' she repeated.

I hadn't told her about Jakoby and figured that this wasn't the time either so I didn't really have a very good excuse. I inadvertently made things worse by suddenly becoming very embarrassed. 'I don't know. One of those books I never got around to . . . reading?' This wasn't a good start.

Cairo changed the subject. 'Shall we go for a walk? In the woods?'

'Sure.'

'I think it'll help. And I think we need to talk some more.'

'OK.'

'Have you eaten anything?'

'No.'

'Then maybe you should.'

'I'm not that hungry.'

'Eat. It'll do you good.'

She handed me the jar, and I poured a small pile of nuts, raisin, and grains into a breakfast bowl. There was a sudden noise. I jumped, startled. A cat had shot through the cat flap and was skidding across the tiles. My hands had started to shake. When I looked at Cairo, she had stopped eating and was just staring at me. I said, 'Still a bit jittery, I guess.' But Cairo didn't reply.

Our subsequent conversation was fragmented. So much so that

I asked her if I could switch the radio on. It was tuned to Radio 4. Two people with plummy voices were arguing about the concept of Englishness. I could only take about two minutes of that before it was necessary to retune the radio to Jazz FM, whereupon I was rewarded with Jaco Pastorius's 'Portrait of Tracey', a bass solo of such subtlety, such beauty – harmonics and unexpected chord sequences – that I said out loud, 'God bless you, Jaco, wherever you are . . .'

'What?' asked Cairo.

'Oh, nothing,' I replied. It was a private moment.

We were sitting on a bench in Highgate wood.

'Look, Cairo, it's unreliable. It's something that you have to practise. And, to tell the truth, I haven't been practising as much as I used to. At first, when I realized what was going on, I used to spend time down the Tube. Quite a lot of time, refining the skill.'

'The Tube?'

'Yeah. It's a good place to practise. People are always copping a stare on the Tube. And the more I did it, the better it got. But, recently, I haven't been practising at all. There's been a lot going on. What with Eric, the band . . . and this freak following me and leaving messages on the answering-machine.'

Cairo looked far from convinced, so I persevered.

'If we were to sit here all afternoon, there would be a good chance that I would improve. Then you'd see.'

'Nick, I'm not waiting here all afternoon.'

'Sure. Maybe that's a bad idea. But I could. I could practise this afternoon, and you could come back in a couple of hours, and you would be able to see the difference. I bet.'

Cairo sighed. 'I don't think so.' She put her arm around me and pulled me toward her. It was a sign of affection that I really needed. Something gave inside, and I began to cry. Not a great explosion of blubbering and gasping, far from it. A few tears simply welled up and spilt over the lip of my eyes. They ran down my cheek and I had to wipe my nose on the back of my hand. I was in worse shape than Andy.

'What's the matter, Nick?' Cairo's eyes were caring and compassionate.

'I'm just grateful. Grateful that you held me just then.'

'Oh, Nick!' She threw her arms around me and cuddled me, pulling me so close that I could hardly breathe. I buried my head in her breasts and enjoyed the soft, fragrant warmth. I inhaled her distinctive, patchouli smell and felt less distressed, relieved in some way.

'Look, Cairo, I'm sorry. I've been a complete pain.'

'No, you haven't.'

'And I'm really grateful. Grateful that you put me up. Grateful that I could tell you all this . . . stuff. Because, there's no one else, no one else who I can tell.'

'What about Dr McDougall?'

'You know I can't.'

'I really think you should.'

Perhaps she was right. Perhaps I should get to the bottom of what was going on. But I felt weak and exhausted. I didn't want to think about it. Cairo got up, and raised me with a linked arm. We walked around the woods, arm in arm, talking about art and music, but we always returned to the main topic of conversation: Naloxyl.

'Nick, do you think the wave – this feeling you get – is more reliable if you're being stared at by women, rather than men?'

'Yeah. I do actually.'

She didn't say anything else, so I said, 'And?'

But she replied, 'Oh, nothing.'

I knew that something was going on in her head, but I wasn't sure what.

'What are you doing tonight, Nick?'

'Cairo, I don't feel ready to go home. I'm still pretty scared.'

'OK.'

'I'm really not ready.'

'OK. Don't worry. You don't have to leave.' Her voice was steady, and reassuring. 'Nick, when is your next check-up. At the hospital?'

'In a couple of days. Why?'

'I think you should tell Dr McDougall.'

'I can't.'

'So, what have you got in mind? What's the plan? Are you just going to move in with me until . . .'

I stopped and sighed. 'Until I'm feeling more confident. Until I've got my head together.' I gripped her arm, 'Please Cairo. Let me stay with you. I'm too scared to go back home.'

Cairo kissed me on my forehead as I bowed my head. 'Sure you can stay,' she said. 'You can stay as long as you like. I won't chuck you out. I promise.'

I kissed her on the lips, and she opened her mouth. But when I withdrew she looked strange. I saw compassion but also uncertainty, and I didn't understand it.

20

the representative from dema

Two days later I went to the Maudsley. Cairo had insisted that I say something to Dr McDougall. Although I had promised to tell him what was happening, my resolve was beginning to weaken the nearer I got to the hospital. By the time I walked into Out-patients, I really wasn't sure I was up to it.

I let the receptionist know that I had arrived, and then took a seat. Once again, I had the opportunity to examine humanity on the edge: neurotics, wringing their white-knuckled hands; depressives, more dead than alive, their flat, inexpressive faces staring blankly into space; and psychotics in various stages of mental disintegration. There were also one or two people like me, normal-looking, but obviously disconcerted by the company. I just couldn't risk telling McDougall the truth. Nobody was taking any notice of the 'No Smoking' sign. So, I picked up a copy of *Hello*, lit a Benson and buried my head in the magazine's inane pages.

After a short space of time a little guy wearing a dirty old anorak with tin foil covering its raised hood came and sat next to me. 'Good afternoon,' he said, in a surprisingly posh voice.

'Hi,' I replied, and looked back at my copy of *Hello*, with its full complement of biro-written millennial prophecies and biblical proclamations. I felt a sharp tap on my shoulder. I had to look up.

'Could I possibly trouble you for a cigarette?' He was quite old, and his unkempt beard was streaked with yellow.

'Sure.' I gave him a Benson.

'Most kind,' he replied.

I nodded, and returned my attention to a minor celebrity's puja room, dedicated to the memory of Frank Sinatra, and complete with a 'shrine', on which rested a serviette used by the legendary songster in 1972 to mop up some dilatory pasta sauce from his lips. Unfortunately, there was another tap on my shoulder. I looked up again.

'You think it wise, to venture out without protection?'

I looked up. At first I thought he was talking about condoms; however, he resolved any ambiguity by tapping the tin foil around his head with a nicotine-stained forefinger. 'Err . . . I guess so,' I said.

He was wearing glasses that were absolutely filthy. A greasy film covered both lenses, so that when he tilted his head to a certain angle, his eyes vanished behind two windows of reflected light. It was very disconcerting and made him appear like an alien or a science-fiction character – a man from the future, perhaps. The effect was spoilt, however, by his amateur repair work, which had necessitated the use of what appeared to be a whole roll of Sellotape – wound again and again – around the right arm of his glasses. This large yellow mass was colour coordinated with his beard.

'No. No, no,' he said, shaking his head from side to side, 'Most unwise. They'll steal your thoughts . . .'

'Who will?'

'The military.'

'The military?'

'Psicorps.'

'Who?'

'The Psicorps.'

'Well, I'll try to remember that.'

'Yes, do.'

212

That clinched it. There was little doubt in my own mind now. I would be saying nothing to Dr McDougall. Nothing at all.

'If I may,' said my companion, extending his hand. 'I am Dr Edwin Rosenthal.'

'Pleased to meet you, Dr Rosenthal.' We shook. His hand was sticky.

'Edwin, please. And you are . . .'

'George Michael. But you can call me George.'

'Pleased to meet you, George. Terrible weather we're having, don't you think?'

'Yes. Worst summer I can remember. Rain, rain, rain.'

Dr Rosenthal agreed. 'It hasn't stopped, has it? There's clearly something very much amiss.'

'Global warming, I imagine.'

'Indeed. Global warming. Make no mistake.'

'I have a friend,' I said, 'who's part of a group called the Gaia Liberation Front. They're a sort of, ecology group and – '

'The Gaia Liberation Front?' Dr Rosenthal cut in.

'Yeah.'

'They sound like a fringe organization to me. I have very little to do with fringe organizations.' Dr Rosenthal clearly disapproved. He sniffed and looked away.

Having been put in my place, I thought it wise to immerse myself in *Hello* again; however, Dr Rosenthal almost immediately resumed our conversation, as I lowered my head. 'Another good reason for protection, of course.'

I looked up again. 'I beg your pardon.'

Dr Rosenthal tapped the tin foil again. 'The greenhouse gases,' he continued, 'the CFC group. Potent destroyers of ozone. Without the ozone layer, our brains will be bathed in ultraviolet radiation.'

'I see.'

Dr Rosenthal suddenly sat up straight and assumed a posture that I can only describe as proud. He pushed out his little chest and raised his chin.

'You know, one day, George, I *will* be recognized.'

'Yeah?'

'One day, they'll be begging me for my data. Begging me for the Rosenthal preparation – the formulae – the shielding device. Begging me.'

He took a drag from his Benson and flicked the ash into a polystyrene cup, his fingers tapping the cigarette repeatedly, swift, nervous twitches that continued unnecessarily. He looked across the waiting area, but his eyes were focused many miles beyond the wall.

'Are you a scientist then?' He didn't reply, so I repeated the question. 'Are you a scientist?'

'I'm sorry?'

'Are you a scientist?'

'Yes,' he smiled, but it was a weak, wistful smile, 'I am a scientist. Although I doubt that my old colleagues would describe me in that way. Not now. Even though most of them have made fine careers for themselves, exploiting my generosity. Exploiting my willingness to discuss ideas over lunch. They stole all my ideas. All of them!'

He stubbed the cigarette out in the cup and let it roll off the table and on to the floor. It made a surprisingly loud noise. The receptionist looked up but didn't say anything.

'If only I had stayed,' he said. I really didn't want to hear his life story, but I had a terrible feeling that this is what he had in mind. 'I should never have gone to America,' he said firmly.

'No?'

'No. I should never have got involved.'

'With what?'

'The CIA, the military. They wanted supermen, enhanced bodies, enhanced minds . . . It was a terrible error of judgement, George. The money just dried up. They expected too much from us. They expected too much from me.' He looked upset. For a moment I thought that he was going to cry. 'Enemy location, remote viewing . . . they made me a laughing stock. Unemployable . . . a disgrace to the profession, eh? Well, we'll see about that! We'll see about that!'

His fists were clenched tightly. Slowly, they opened, and he turned to face me. Again the light caught the grease on his lenses and I was presented with an unfathomable, alien expression. 'I . . .' He suddenly started looking around wildly. 'I'm sorry. Forgive me, I . . . George Michael . . . that name, that sounds strangely familiar.'

He suddenly got up, tightened his hood and stormed over to the other side of the waiting area, where he stood in a corner, occasionally looking over his shoulder at me. I felt ashamed of myself. And there was something else – I felt uneasy, very uneasy, but I wasn't sure why. I wanted to be called in quickly. Dr Rosenthal's agitated presence was getting to me.

Finally, the receptionist called my name – my real name – and I made my way up the stairs to Dr McDougall's office. I knocked on the door and from inside came a familiar Caledonian bellow. 'Enter.' Inside, Dr McDougall swivelled around in his chair and rose to greet me. 'Nick, laddie.' He shook my hand with characteristic violence. 'Good to see you. Take a seat.'

I sat down. Dr McDougall had my file lying open on his desk. He quickly glanced at a page covered with his indecipherable, spidery scrawl. 'Well, how have you been?'

'Fine,' I lied.

'Fine?'

'Yep, fine.'

His expression was somewhat quizzical. He seemed fazed for a moment and actually said, 'Errr . . .', before swinging around and taking some forms out of my file. He seemed to get back on track and said, with more confidence, 'Right then, let's do the checklist.'

We went through the list as usual, and everything seemed to be going well. Then McDougall said to me, 'Last time you were here you seemed a little worried. About being on the trial. Do you remember that?'

'Yes, I do,' I replied. 'But you were very reassuring. I haven't been worried at all since.'

'Not at all?' he asked, as though wanting to make absolutely sure that he was understanding me correctly.

'No. Not at all,' I repeated.

There was a pause, during which McDougall looked at me and began to scratch his head. 'And you haven't been taking any more cannabis?'

It was just possible the blood tests hadn't come through. Why else would he be asking? 'No.'

'And no other drugs? E, acid, speed?'

'No chance!'

'Good lad,' said Dr McDougall, still scratching his head.

We had reached the point where Dr McDougall and I usually indulged in a little small talk. But he was strangely quiet. There was a sense of inconclusion, unfinished business. Dr McDougall turned back a few pages of my file and pulled a face. He then sighed.

'Well,' I said, thinking this an appropriate juncture to get up and leave. McDougall raised his hand and waved it from side to side, indicating that he was not happy to finish the session. He raised his head and turned to face me.

'Nick,' he said. He leaned forward and looked over his half-moon spectacles. His slightly bloodshot eyes held me for quite some time, as though, if he looked hard enough, he would see what I was thinking.

'Nick. I want to be honest with you. I'm a little concerned. I think something's bothering you.'

He didn't say anything else, just let the silence pressure me. Eventually, I coughed (perhaps nervously). The cough became a gravelly reply.

'No. You answered all my questions in the previous session.'

'So everything's fine?'

'Yes.'

For a brief moment, McDougall looked irritated. This was very peculiar. I began to feel unhappy with the way things were going. 'Now that's not right, is it?' said McDougall.

'What do you mean?'

'Nick. Things haven't been fine. Have they?'

216

'Fine enough.'

McDougall sighed. 'I hoped that it wouldn't come to this, Nick, but I'm afraid you leave me with no choice. I received a call yesterday from Mrs Clark. A friend of yours, I believe.'

'What!' I felt winded. As though the air had been forced out of my lungs by a powerful blow.

McDougall saw that I was speechless and continued. 'She is very worried about you, and has explained that you have been experiencing certain . . . symptoms . . . for many months now.'

My heart sank. I was stunned. *How could she do this? How could she do this? To me!*

McDougall leaned even closer. There was a faint, ever so faint, smell of whiskey on his breath. 'Now, as I've said to you many times before, we are undertaking important work here. This is medical research, important research. We expect our subjects to tell the truth.'

Again, he let the silence pressure me into speech.

'What did Cair – Mrs Clark – what did Mrs Clark say?'

'Why don't you just tell me what's been going on?'

'Dr McDougall. With respect, I have a right to know what Mrs Clark told you!'

'You do, indeed, Nick. And I'm happy to tell you, so that you can give me your side of the story. But I had hoped that you would let me know, voluntarily. I had hoped that you would just tell me what you were experiencing.'

I wasn't prepared to say anything. I shook my head. There was still a remote possibility that Cairo had not discussed details, specific symptoms. Again, the uncomfortable silence demanded that I speak, but this time I didn't cave in.

'Very well,' said Dr McDougall. He reached over to my file and took out a red sheet of paper, one that I hadn't seen before. He pinned it to a clipboard, crossed his legs, and asked, 'When did you first realize you could tell when people were staring at you?'

She had told him everything. Absolutely everything.

McDougall's interrogation lasted for about an hour. When he had finished I got up, ready to leave.

'No, Nick. You can't leave.'

'Yes I can.'

'Please, Nick, sit down. I'm afraid this is very serious. Very serious indeed. We need more information.'

'But you know everything now. There's nothing else to say.'

McDougall leaned forward again. 'I would like you to wait downstairs. Don't leave the hospital, OK?'

'But . . .'

'Nick, I am very worried about you, and I would be most grateful if you would wait downstairs for a wee while.'

I assented with some reluctance. A grudging half-nod, before saying, 'All right.'

McDougall looked sad. He shook his head. 'Why didn't you tell me about all this, Nick? Why?'

I felt ashamed.

'Because . . . it sounds crazy.'

'You've been worried about this for some time. I went over your notes before you came to refresh my memory. This has been on your mind for months. Hasn't it? All those questions . . .'

I felt defeated. 'Yeah. It has.'

'I do wish you had said something. It must have been terribly distressing for you.'

'It was.'

'Well, now you've told us about it, everything is going to be fine. OK? Really fine.'

In a peculiar way I felt relieved. I no longer had to worry about the Naloxyl and its effects. It was all out of my hands now. I would almost certainly be thrown off the trial. I wondered what would happen next? And what kind of job I might get if I went to the job centre?

Dr McDougall accompanied me down to the waiting area and had a brief word with the receptionist before disappearing. Presumably he had told her to keep an eye on me, but it was unnecessary. I didn't feel like legging it, I just wanted to get everything sorted. I wondered what was going to happen next. McDougall said he wanted more information. From my point of view, there wasn't much else to say, but I could see that maybe from his point of view, more questions needed to be answered. And things weren't so bad. Towards the end McDougall had been very sympathetic. I guess things could have turned out a lot worse. He could have had me banged up, for example.

But as I sat there, with time on my hands, I began to worry. Would there be some official reprimand for bad behaviour? Would the drug company want their money back? How would I pay? And there was Cairo . . . I couldn't possibly go back to her place. I thought for a second that I should call her on the pay phone, but then bottled out. What was the point? What would I say?

Time passed, and I was getting really bored, so I bought myself a cup of tea and a Kit-Kat. As I got up to go to the kiosk, I noticed that the receptionist was watching me like a hawk. I waved, just to let her know that I was cool, but she didn't smile back. I returned to my seat, and stewed in my own emotional cocktail of shame and anger.

After maybe an hour and a half Dr McDougall appeared. 'I'm sorry that you've had to wait so long.'

'That's OK.'

'We're going up to my room again.'

As we walked up the stairs he said, 'You're to be interviewed by a representative from DEMA. The drug company . . .'

Shit! They were going to want their money back!

'A representative?'

'Yes. He's a psychiatrist. Like myself, but more of a specialist. There's nothing to worry about.'

I wasn't reassured, mostly because I could see that McDougall was nervous.

We went into his office. Seated in his chair was a short, thin man, with cropped silvery hair. He was wearing a rather sharp black suit. He was very still and looked composed, as though posing for a photograph.

'Nick, this is Dr Stengle from DEMA.'

'Hi,' I said. Stengle nodded, and stood. We shook hands. It was the total opposite of McDougall's enthusiastic arm-wrench, a momentary coupling; I felt that he wanted to keep physical contact to an absolute minimum. And when he sat down he kept his right hand away from his trousers, as though it might dirty the material. McDougall sat next to Stengle on a plastic chair which he had obviously taken from another room. He then nodded to Stengle.

I had expected a foreign accent but, instead, Stengle spoke the Queen's English in a thin, quiet, reedy voice.

'Mr Farrell,' he began. 'I am sorry to hear that you have been experiencing problems on Naloxyl. Obviously we are very concerned.'

I looked at McDougall. He smiled at me. But he smiled with his mouth, not with his eyes. I could see that he was sweating. He shifted uncomfortably.

Stengle continued. I am going to have to ask you a number of questions. And, although I understand that you may be reluctant to answer them, I promise you, in the long term, it will be to your advantage if you answer them as honestly and as comprehensively as you can.'

I rocked my head backwards and forward. I didn't reply, because my mouth had gone dry. There was something unnerving about his composure, his lack of movement.

Stengle had been well briefed by McDougall. He asked me about everything. The feeling of being stared at, the telephone messages, my belief that I was being stalked by a serial killer – everything, even what seemed to me to be trivial details.

'You claim to have read an article in a woman's magazine called' – he gingerly flicked through my file before looking up – '*One Won't Do?*'

'Yes.'

'There isn't a women's magazine called *One Won't Do*.'

'No?'

'No.'

'Oh. I must have got it wrong then.'

'Yes' – and so on.

After another hour Stengle had completed the interview and went outside with McDougall. Their conversation was quite brief. McDougall came in alone and sat down heavily.

'Can I go now, Dr McDougall?'

'No, Nick. I think it's best that you stay with us for a while.'

'Stay?'

'Yes. I'd like to admit you for a few days. Just for observation.'

'But . . .'

'I think it's for the best. We need to take you off the Naloxyl as soon as we can.'

'But . . .'

There was very little to say. As the panic subsided I began to consider my predicament. If I refused to be admitted, then I guessed they could lock me up anyway, section me, so maybe it would be sensible to cooperate, go down gently. But there was another reason, too, a more compelling reason for acquiescence. It occurred to me that, now, I couldn't go back to Cairo's place. Clearly, she thought that I was out of my tree. So, if McDougall said, you're free to go, I would have to get on the Tube and go back to Kilburn, and I really wasn't ready for that. The image of the face at the window was still impressed on my memory. The darkness, and my animal scream. Even if everyone else thought I was a raving lunatic, I was far from convinced. Dr McDougall was still looking at me.

'If you think it's for the best . . .'

'I do,' he said. 'Really.'

I was interviewed by yet another psychiatrist, a Dr Angst. He asked me a load of questions about my background, next of kin, that sort of thing. When he had finished, he called Dr McDougall on the phone.

McDougall appeared within minutes and escorted me through the long, dimly lit corridors of the Maudsley to the Aubrey Lewis ward. I noticed that the door was locked. I said to Dr McDougall, 'I thought this was a voluntary admission?'

'I'm sorry Nick,' he said, resting a hand on my shoulder. 'I'm afraid not.'

'You've sectioned me?'

'You'll be out again soon enough' was his sanguine reply.

21
aubrey lewis

The idea of admission into a mental hospital had always filled me with fear. Perhaps I had watched too many films about misunderstood creative types, cruelly incarcerated. In actuality, life on Aubrey Lewis turned out to be quite comfortable, at first, anyway.

I was given a private room, away from the dormitory area. It didn't have much in it, a bed, a bedside cabinet and a grey plastic chair. The floors and walls were clean and a sort of off-white colour. The window didn't offer much of a prospect (concrete blocks, Portakabins, and a car park in the distance) but, really, I was grateful for any window at all. My worst fantasies about being admitted into a mental hospital involved being locked in a padded cell under the constant glare of a merciless strip-light. My view – however grim – was an unexpected luxury. It was clear that I was something of a VIP, a special patient, one of Dr McDougall's guests.

Aubrey Lewis also had a leisure or recreation area, where I was at liberty to mix with the other patients and watch television. I was given a guided tour by a nurse called Mick. He was dressed in civilian clothes, as were all the nursing staff. Again, my preconceptions were horribly wrong. There were no starched white outfits. Mick wore jeans and a checked shirt. His hair was long, and he sported a little goatee beard.

I soon realized that the nursing staff had been instructed to keep me on thirty-minute observation. Every half-hour someone would open the door and say, 'All right Nick?' To which I would respond, 'Yep.' And our conversation wouldn't proceed beyond this point. Mick was kind enough to get me a radio and even nipped out to get me twenty B&H. So I sat in my room smoking and listening to Jazz FM.

The ward had a pay phone, and I was allowed to call whoever I wanted. I was going to call my mother, but Dr McDougall said that he would notify her if I wanted, which I agreed to. I didn't feel up to calling her. I had finally managed to disappoint her in the most extreme fashion. It would be hard for her, finding out that her son – the son who she imagined might do justice to his early creative promise – was now languishing in a loony-bin. I felt very guilty.

McDougall had already informed Cairo of my admission. He suggested that I should give her a call. 'Your friend, she's very concerned about you,' he had said.

'Yeah,' I had replied. 'I'll call her later.' But I had no intention of doing so.

In the evening I had dinner in my room, a truly magnificent egg mornay, two rubbery eggs floating in a wash of melted cheese and grease. Followed by a sponge pudding splashed with thin custard the colour and consistency of ejaculate. Institutional cuisine at its best. When Mick came to my room to collect the tray I said, 'My compliments to the chef.' He didn't laugh. I think he thought I meant it.

I lay on my bed and watched the sky dim, listening to *Dinner Jazz*. At ten o'clock a nurse came in and offered me a sleeping pill. I took it, but it was still difficult to get to sleep.

The next day my mother arrived. I didn't think that she would want to see me locked up, and it came as something of a surprise. One of the nurses knocked on the door and said, 'You've got a visitor.'

I was just lying on the bed smoking and looking at the ceiling. I sat bolt upright when I heard her say, 'Nicholas?'

The nurse said, 'I'll leave you two alone,' and closed the door, quietly.

I stubbed out my cigarette on a little disposable ashtray. The ward was littered with them. My stubbing out was a reflex action because I knew that Mum didn't like me smoking. Indeed, she had never actually seen me smoke, because on my rare visits home I always refrained. 'Mum.'

She didn't say anything for a moment. She just looked at me as though I were a cripple or had lost an arm. Although my hospital admission was entirely legitimate, I felt something of a fraud. I didn't deserve pity. I didn't feel that bad. Moreover, I was still enjoying the relative safety of being on a secure ward. In a curious way I wanted to be in hospital. Mum seemed deeply hurt.

I moved to get up, and she said, 'No, don't.'

'It's OK,' I said, 'there's nothing wrong with me. I haven't broken a leg or anything.' I hopped off the bed and pulled the grey plastic chair over. 'There, have a seat.'

My mother sat down on the chair, and I sat on the side of the bed. It was quite high, and I could swing my legs underneath it.

'Here,' said Mum, handing me a holdall. I was so distracted by her expression that I hadn't noticed that she had my red Wilson tennis bag.

'What's this?'

'It's your things. Clothes, underwear . . . I managed to contact your landlord. He let me into your flat.'

'Oh,' I said, embarrassed, at the state she would have found it in – and embarrassed at the thought of her stumbling across my modest collection of porn mags. 'Thanks,' I added.

'I'm not sure it's what you would have chosen yourself.'

I unzipped the holdall and looked inside: T-shirts, pants, socks. 'No, this looks fine.'

She then handed me a plastic carrier bag. 'And I brought you some fruit.'

I looked inside that, too: there were some grapes, apples, oranges and plums. 'Looks like you busted the local greengrocer.' I reached over and put the carrier bag on top of my bedside cabinet. 'Thanks.'

'That's all right.'

We sat looking at each other, I, slightly elevated, looking down at her, a rather frumpy woman in late-middle years, with a furrowed brow. The silence was so uncomfortable I could barely tolerate it. Her universe and mine occupied the same space but were virtually incapable of contact. Even our photons couldn't touch.

'So how are you, Nick?' she asked.

'Fine. Really I am. Have you spoken to Dr McDougall today?'

'No. I spoke to him yesterday on the telephone.'

'What did he say?'

'He said that he was worried about you.'

'Because of the Naloxyl.'

'I'm sorry?'

'Because of the drug he gave me. He told you about the trial, yeah? The medical research I was doing?'

'Yes. He did.'

'And they're upset about how Naloxyl has affected me?'

'Yes. That's right.'

'So what did he say?'

She shifted uncomfortably. 'Not very much.'

'Sure, but what did he say exactly?'

'I can't remember, not . . .' She trailed off, clearly uneasy.

'Mum! I know that he thinks I'm crazy, OK. I kind of picked that much up when he put me in here. He sort of gave himself away by doing that. So what did he say?'

She sighed before saying, 'He believes that you're mentally ill. Yes.'

'I guess he told you why?'

'Yes. He gave me some reasons why he and his colleagues think that.'

'Right.'

I couldn't imagine how McDougall had negotiated the difficult task of telling my mother about my fear of being pursued by a gay serial killer. Somehow I didn't really want to hear the details and felt satisfied to assume the conversation must have been both guarded and euphemistic.

'I don't think I'm crazy,' I said.

'No.'

'But I guess they all say that.'

'Quite' Her last word was terse and bitter. She suddenly reflected on her response, and said, 'I'm sorry. I didn't – '

I waved my hand. 'No problem. Really. It's a fact. The vast majority in here think they're fine. And so do I. What does that prove?'

I wished she hadn't come; I wished that she had just stayed at home. I couldn't think of anything more to say now. Nevertheless, I persevered. The sense of duty was as strong in me as it was in her, I suppose. When separated, we were partially free of the obligation. But when together, we were compelled to try.

'Thanks for coming, anyway. And thanks for the fruit.'

Mum nodded. 'That's all right. I don't suppose the food in here is very good.'

'No, it's not.'

There was a long silence. Outside, someone called out, 'Cunt!' Mum shook her head. I could hear nurses congregating beyond the door. A brief scuffle, then soothing voices.

'Have you spoken to the other patients?' asked my mother.

'One or two.'

'What are they like?'

'Mad.' I laughed. But my mother didn't find it funny. Again, silence.

'When I come again do you want me to bring you anything?'

God. The thought of more visits was too much.

I said, 'Look, don't bother coming again. Really. I'll be out in no time. It's a long way, and there isn't anything you can do. There's just no point. Once they've washed the Naloxyl out of my bloodstream they'll let me out. And that'll be that.'

She didn't seemed convinced. It's really weird. When people think you're crazy, even fairly innocuous statements start sounding completely nuts. *I think I'll have a cocoa* starts to sound like: *Pass me that axe, Brother Iglesias.*

'It's no trouble coming,' Mum repeated.

'No. It is.'

'It isn't.'

'It is.' *Stand-off.* She didn't reply. I fell back on a strategy that had proved quite helpful in the past.

'How is Aunty Maureen?' I hadn't asked that question in a long time.

'She's dead!' My mother looked at me, aghast.

'Dead?'

'She died last year. I know you didn't go to the funeral but surely you – ' She stopped herself.

That was my last attempt. I was happy to let things roll toward a cold, uncomfortable parting, which was as painful as it was emotionally spastic.

The day after I was visited by a new psychiatrist, Dr Shaw. He introduced himself as the senior registrar, which didn't mean that much to me, although I got the impression that he had a respectable position in the pecking order. Not so exalted as Dr McDougall's but well on the way. He was quite young, in his late twenties or early thirties. Although his general dress was sombre, he was wearing a bright red and green tie. The kind of tie that says: *Although I may look boring, there's a very interesting, wacky individual hiding inside.*

'So how do you feel today?' he asked.

'Fine'.

He nodded, slowly. *Pause.* 'I understand you're a musician?'

'Yeah.'

'What do you play?'

'Keyboards.'

'In a band . . .'

'Yeah.'

'What sort of music do you play?'

'That's a difficult one.'

'Why?'

'Because we sound sort of . . . seventies-ish. We use old equipment, fuzz-boxes, wah-wah pedals, and I play a Fender Rhodes. That's an electric piano. But we're definitely a modern band. Our ballads sound a bit like . . . Portishead.'

'Portishead?' He repeated, as though I had unexpectedly referred to a new form of oral sex.

'Yeah. They use a lot of Rhodes . . .'

'I see.'

But I could see that he didn't. 'So tell me about yourself,' he said, in a friendly, casual manner.

I gave him a potted history of the band and our involvement with Jarl, the fact that we were waiting to hear from Retro. He seemed quite interested. We then talked about my dire financial circumstances, and Dr Shaw instantly saw a good opportunity to raise the main issue.

'So you joined the Naloxyl trial for the cash?'

'Yeah. You don't make much dosh gigging in Essex.'

'I suppose not.' He opened his file and started to make a few notes. 'I spoke to a friend of yours on the telephone this morning.'

'Mrs Clark?'

'Yes, that's right.'

'She thinks I've gone crazy.'

He scratched his head. Then his cheek ballooned out as it strained to contain his tongue. 'Do you mind if we talk about some of the things we discussed?'

'Not at all.'

'OK. She told me that you thought you could tell when people were staring at you.'

'That's right.'

'Can you remember the first time it happened?'

'The very first time?'

'Yes.'

'Well, the first strong impression was about two weeks after I had started taking the Naloxyl.'

'And why didn't you mention it to Dr McDougall?'

229

'Because he would have thought I was crazy. And I didn't want to be thrown off the trial.'

'I see. Had you ever experienced anything similar before?'

'How do you mean?'

'The feeling of being stared at. Had it happened prior to starting the Naloxyl?'

'Err . . . yes. A few times. Don't we all get that? Every now and again?'

Dr Shaw made a few more notes before saying, ' . . . and how do you feel about it now? Do you still think you can tell when people are staring at you?'

'Not like I used to. I haven't taken any Naloxyl for two days.'

'But if I gave you some Naloxyl now. Do you think you could still do it?'

'I suppose so.'

'Right.'

Again I found myself talking like a platinum-grade lunatic, so I thought I had better say something to Dr Shaw to indicate that I was aware of this.

'Listen, Dr Shaw. I know it sounds crazy, I really see that, but . . . it's true. That's what happened.'

'OK. So tell me. What evidence do you have? What made you think that it was happening?'

'I would feel a sensation – a kind of odd sensation. Then I would turn around, and people would be looking at me. I wasn't able to do it all the time, and it didn't always work. But, on the whole, if I thought that someone was looking at me, when I turned around, they *were* looking at me.'

'Maybe people look at you a lot anyway?'

'Why should they?'

'Well, can you think of any reasons?'

'No. I only have one head and the usual complement of limbs.'

Dr Shaw laughed. 'Sure, but . . . do you think you might be conspicuous in some other way? An ordinary way?'

I assumed a suitably modest expression and said, 'I've been told that I'm quite good-looking.'

' . . . And what happens to good looking people?'

'All right, I can see what you're getting at. But that still doesn't explain why I got that weird sensation.'

'A side-effect?'

'But it only happened when other people were around.'

'Maybe you only noticed it when other people were around?'

'I don't think so.'

'Why not?'

'It was just too distinctive.'

'OK. But sometimes we only notice things when we're looking for them. Even when *they are* distinctive.'

I paused and thought, before saying, 'Such as?'

'All right. What does the back of your left knee feel like right now?'

'Nothing.'

'Concentrate on it, the area behind your left knee. What can you feel?'

I focused my attention as directed. 'Well, it's warmish . . . and . . . I can feel my jeans.'

'Right. And you weren't aware of those sensations until you looked for them.'

He had a point. 'OK, I see what you mean. But this . . . sensation, was a lot more distinctive than what I can feel here.' I touched the back of my left knee.

'Fine. All I want you to do is think about it.'

Shaw looked down at my file before continuing. 'I notice in your records that you suffer from insomnia.'

'That's right.'

'Before taking the Naloxyl, had it got worse at all? Did you find sleeping was getting more difficult?'

'Not really. I've always had problems sleeping.'

'Were you getting up early as well?'

'No. I just found it hard to get to sleep, and I tended to lie in.'

'So what time do you get up usually?'

'I don't know. Late morning, early afternoon . . .'

'OK.'

He scribbled for a while, then said, 'Mrs Clark told me you said that you were being followed. And you thought that the guy following you was a serial killer.'

'Yeah. That's right. Sounds really mad, doesn't it?'

'I don't know. Tell me about it.'

I had nothing to lose, they knew everything anyway. So I told him about the PAC gig, the article in *Gay London*, the Cranbrook, the phone calls and the face at the window. Shaw listened and made notes. When I finished he said, 'And how do you feel about all that now?'

'How do you think I feel?'

'I don't know, that's why I asked.'

'I feel . . . scared. It was very, very frightening.'

'I'm sure it was.'

'But you don't believe me.'

Shaw paused. I could see that he was trying to think of something to say but, eventually, he just gave up. His expression changed. He shrugged, and said, 'OK. I really think it would be a good idea if we put you on some medication. How do you feel about that?'

'Not too happy.'

'I really think it would help. You'll feel more relaxed.'

'But I'm not so agitated now.'

'Sure. But I still think it'd be a good idea.'

'Do I have a choice? Really?'

Shaw paused. 'Would you take some if it was offered?'

I sighed. There was no point arguing.

My first few days on Aubrey Lewis passed quickly, but then time began to slow down. There was bugger-all to do. I wasn't allowed to go out so I spent a good deal of time just looking out of the window in my room. When the sun came out between cloudbursts I began to regret my acquiescence. I really wanted to walk on the heath or nip down to Our Price in Hampstead to buy a CD. I began to feel like a prisoner; however, I kept on reminding myself that I was safe. Whenever I thought of the phone calls or the face at the window, my regret vanished.

I would sometimes watch the television in the recreation area. I would sit there, smoking with a few of the other patients. Chris was a guy of about my age. He had been in for some time. Apparently, he had taken a serious amount of amphetamines while clubbing, and this had triggered a kind of breakdown. He had started to believe that he was being controlled by 'a boss man' and that he might be forced to kill his brother. In order to prevent this, he had thrown himself in front of a car just outside Oval Tube. He had been rushed to King's to be patched up (luckily he had only sustained a few minor injuries) before being transferred to Aubrey Lewis. Chris was over the worst of his problems and was reasonable company. He wasn't terribly bright, though, and preferred football to music so our conversations were strictly limited. He didn't seem that interested in sex either, which puzzled me.

Another one of my smoking partners was Lucus. His full name was Herbert James Lucus, but everyone knew him as Lucus. Not Mr Lucus, just Lucus.

One night Mick was doing a late shift. He was on with an agency nurse who was so unpleasant and uptight, he was dead eager to get out of the nursing station. I had asked for a sleeping pill. Mick gave me a Temazepam but then used his visit as an excuse to hang out for a while in my room. We had a few smokes and talked a bit about some trip-hop bands and clubs he was into. Then we got around to talking about some of the other patients, most notably Lucus. I don't suppose it was right for Mick to disclose the details of Lucus's case, but I was grateful for his indiscretion.

Lucus was about sixty-four. He had once been a moderately successful novelist. He wrote adventure stories with occult themes which had achieved modest popularity in the 1960s. They had interesting titles like *He Walks in Darkness*, *The Pentacle* and *Professor Gregory's Grimoire*. Unfortunately, he had had something of a creative crisis in 1970 and came to the conclusion that everything he had written was utter rubbish. He decided to write a great novel, a kind of *À la Recherche du Temps Perdu*, set in (of all places) Penge. His publishers wanted another occult thriller and told him that if he wasn't prepared to write another, then he could consider his contract terminated. His agent attempted to persuade him to abandon his chosen course but failed. After five years Lucus realized that his great novel was nothing more than a stream of unrelated recollections from his childhood put together with idiosyncratic punctuation and non-standard use of capitals. He burned the manuscript and then drank so much his brain started to rot. He began to hallucinate. Every evening he was visited by Marcel Proust, who would come into the bedroom and shout '*Vous êtes merde*' before legging it. Lucus took to following Proust down the street. One fateful winter the police picked him up outside a local branch of Sainsbury's, in his pyjamas, at two in the morning. He was taken into care and never returned to civilian life.

Dr McDougall had been a fan of Lucus's books in the sixties and subsequently had a soft spot for him. He should have been on another ward, really, or in a home or something, but McDougall was reluctant to discharge him.

Lucus wasn't so much a conversationalist but rather an entertainment. You could sit next to him, and he wouldn't turn to look at you. He would just say something like, 'Daphne du Maurier. Fine woman, I once saw her *nudam*, bathing by moonlight in the creek' or 'W. Somerset Maugham, no friend of mine, sir. A little too fond of ringlets and fancies for my liking'; however, my absolute favourite was, 'Dennis Wheatley! Take your hand out of my pocket before I count to twelve or I'll thrash you to within an inch of your life!'

Ah, happy days.

The Naloxyl took a week to wash out of my system properly. After giving me a blood test, they considered it appropriate to put me on medication. I asked them what it was, but they just said it was something to calm me down, a tranquillizer. At several points in the day a sour-faced nurse – her hair tied back to emphasize her pointed features – would arrive and give me a small off-white tablet impressed on one side with the letters 'LG', and '10' beneath them. I had been taking the tablets for a few days and really wanted to know what I was taking.

'What's this?' I asked.

'A tranquillizer.'

'But which one?'

'It's a neuroleptic. It's to make you settle.'

'But what's its name? What's it called?'

Eventually, she sighed, as though I was being an absolute pain, 'Chlorpromazine, OK?'

'OK.'

I was none the wiser. It was, however, one hell of a sedative. It made me feel really dopey and, I have to admit, I did start sleeping better. In fact, I could hardly stay awake.

22

The following week I had a visit from Andy and Scott. They were shown into my room by Mick, who I understand showed uncharacteristic deference when they introduced themselves as 'the band'.

When the door closed there was an uncomfortable silence. They stood with their backs to the wall, looking at me, unsure of what to say.

'At last, you have come to take me back to the mother ship,' I said, in a steady, neutral voice.

They looked at each other, then back at me. 'Nick?' said Scott.

'I am impressed by your disguise, Glartak. I am sure the humans suspect nothing.' Andy and Scott were speechless. I looked at Andy, and continued, 'Greetings, Gluton,' and raised my hands, making a hexing sign with my fingers.

Andy silently mouthed the word 'Fuck'.

My stomach convulsed, until suppressing the laughter became a physical impossibility. I was almost incontinent. While I was trying to regain my self-control, Scott and Andy began to show signs of alarm. 'I think we'd better call a nurse,' said Scott.

I shook my head while I struggled for air. Between gasps I managed to say, 'No, no . . .'

'Nick, are you all right?' asked Scott.

'Of course I am, you twat! You should have seen your faces!'

'What, you're only pissing about?' he asked, still very uncertain.

'No, I'm deadly serious. Take me back to the mother ship!'

I started laughing again, and this time Andy and Scott joined in. 'You cunt!' said Andy. 'You scared me shitless!'

'And me,' added Scott.

'I'm sorry. I really couldn't resist it. I've never seen you two looking so worried before.'

Eventually we settled down, although every now and again someone would make a reference to the mother ship, and we would all collapse again.

'Phil says get well soon,' said Scott. 'He said he was sorry he couldn't make it. He's had to go to work today.'

'Work?'

'Yeah. He's helping a mate of ours – a builder – to do a decorating job in Gants Hill.'

Scott reached into a carrier bag he was holding, and said, 'I thought you might want to borrow this.' He gave me his Walkman and a large packet of spare batteries.

'Oh, fucking brilliant, but – '

Scott raised his finger before I could continue and reached into the bag again. He pulled out about five or six cassettes, which he dumped on the bed. 'I made you some compilation tapes . . . Some jazz, seventies prog rock and some new stuff.'

I was genuinely moved. It was a very considerate gesture. 'Thanks! I've been bored to fucking tears in here.'

'And I got you this,' said Andy. 'I found it in a sale.'

He produced a cassette of Donald Fagan's *Kamakiriad* out of his pocket and handed it to me, adding, 'It's a concept album.'

'Far out,' I replied.

'Take a look at the sleeve notes.'

I opened the cassette box and flipped out the blurb. The album was about a guy who embarks on a journey in a Kamakiri – a futuristic car – in radio contact with a routing satellite called Tripstar. The car was also supposed to have a built-in vegetable garden. *Nice one.*

'You'll really like it,' said Andy. 'The horn section is as tight as a cat's arse.'

We sat and discussed Scott's compilation tapes for a while and
then disputed the relative merits of the diverse performers
represented in his selection. Gradually, the mood became more
serious.

'So what's happening here? What's going on?' asked Scott.

'Do you mean, why have I been locked up?'

'Yeah. We were told you were ill.'

'Crazy, you mean.'

'Yeah, I guess.'

'Well, I'm not.'

'No, you don't seem to be.'

'So why are you here then?' asked Andy.

I didn't really want to discuss what had happened to me in any
depth, so I provided them with a largely faithful account of
events, although larded with small fictions and minor inaccuracies.

'You remember that drug trial I was on?'

'Yeah,' they nodded together.

'Well, it sort of went wrong. I started to get some odd
experiences.'

'Sounds good,' said Andy.

'No way,' I replied. 'It was a lot of weird shit. Headaches,
dizziness, not being able to think straight. I started getting a bit
confused. Maybe I said some stupid things, I don't know, I'm not
sure really. My feeling is, I probably did. Anyway, the doctors took
me off the trial and brought me in here to monitor my condition.
And since I stopped taking the drug I've felt a lot better, so it
must have been fucking me up.'

'Jesus,' said Andy, 'sounds like it could have been serious.'

'I'm sure it could have been. If I'd kept taking it.'

'So when will you be out?' asked Scott.

'Fuck knows. They want to do tests. Loads more tests. I guess
it's quite important for them to find out what went wrong.'

'They've got no idea then?'

'Not really.'

A little while after, the sour-faced nurse came in to give me my
pill.

'Can I have one, too?' said Andy.

The nurse turned on him like a Rottweiler. 'I beg your pardon?'

'Can I have one, too?'

'Look, if you can't behave responsibly, then I am afraid you'll have to leave.'

'So what time do you knock off this afternoon?'

'Right. That's it. Out.' She pointed at the door.

'I thought you might like a quick one, before you go home.'

Her mouth fell open. Recognizing a fatally inappropriate choice of wording, Andy attempted to recover some ground. 'No, no, sorry . . . I meant a drink. That's all.'

She just glared and said, 'Out.'

'What?'

'Out. Now.'

Andy shrugged. Not wishing to cause a scene, he left without protest, saying to Scott, 'I suppose I'll wait outside.'

The nurse followed him. We couldn't stop laughing as we listened to the nurse give Andy a total bollocking when the door closed. 'Any news from Jarl?' I asked.

Scott shook his head, 'No, nothing.'

'Has anybody given him a call?'

'Yeah. Phil gave him a call at the office. He spoke to some woman called Ute, or Utt, or something like that. She said that he was out of the country. On business.'

'So when will he he back?'

'Fuck knows.'

This wasn't good news. I asked Scott if he was getting up to anything. He mentioned that a friend of his and Phil's – some old queen – was treating them both to a holiday in Berlin, a threesome. I said, 'I didn't know there was a gay scene in Berlin?'

'There's a gay scene everywhere. Fuck, there's probably a gay scene in here, if you could be bothered to look.'

I didn't think much of it at the time, Scott and Phil going off to Berlin – but their jaunt would prove to be very significant.

Time went by, more time than I cared to consider. Dr Shaw visited me most days, and McDougall about once a week. McDougall would ask me about how I felt, and I gave him the same answers to the same questions. He had raised my dosage of Chlorpromazine twice, and I now took tablets with '50' impressed on them. I wasn't happy about the side-effects: I now felt very tired, very tired indeed; my nose started to feel stuffed up and my mouth went dry; I had to keep on drinking water to ease the discomfort.

McDougall sat staring at me.

'Dr McDougall, I think I'd like to go home now.'

'But what about being followed? Are you not worried about being followed?'

'Sure I am. But I'm really bored now. I really would like to be discharged.'

'Isn't that a bit risky? Given that you feel that someone might be waiting for you?'

I yawned and must have drifted off.

'Nick?' McDougall reached over and shook me a little. I opened my eyes.

'What?'

'I was asking, is it sensible to go home? When you're still worried about someone waiting for you?'

'No, I guess not.' My head felt full of shit.

'I think we should keep you in for a few more weeks and review the situation then.'

'Sure.'

I didn't have the energy to argue. When McDougall left, I got into bed and slept. Chlorpromazine was equivalent to about five joints.

By the time Cairo visited me I was just too tired to be angry. She came in, hugged me and sat next to me, on the grey plastic chair. I can't remember what she was wearing. In fact, I'm sure whole chunks of our conversation never registered at all. I can remember how apologetic she was, though.

'I'm so sorry, Nick, I had to say something. You do understand, don't you?' I nodded, and she continued, 'I felt so bad about it, after, but it was the right thing, it had to be done. I was so worried, so very worried about you.'

I was kind of listening and not listening. I reached out for a glass of water on the bedside cabinet but somehow miscalculated and almost knocked it over.

'Here, let me.' Cairo picked it up and handed it to me. The water was warm and thousands of tiny bubbles had collected in it, but it still helped to unstick my tongue from the roof of my mouth. My lips felt cracked and dry. Cairo took the glass and put it down for me. 'You do forgive me, don't you, Nick?'

'Yeah, sure.'

'I couldn't bear it if you . . .'

'It's . . . no problem. Really . . . you did . . . you did what you had to do.'

'I'm so glad you understand. You know, I was expecting that you would be angry with me. That you would shout at me, or . . .'

I waved my hand. 'It's cool. Really.' I just couldn't be bothered.

Cairo had brought me a huge hamper of fruit. She asked me if I wanted some grapes and I said, 'OK'. And I sat there, popping grapes into my mouth, trying to maintain moistness.

Cairo attempted to keep the conversation going, but she could see that I wasn't really with it. I listened to her pleasant, husky voice, coming and going, while I faded in and out. Eventually, she said, 'I think I had better go now. I'll come back and see you soon. When you're feeling a bit better, eh?'

She put the grapes on my bedside cabinet, kissed my forehead and left. When I woke two hours later, her visit had the quality of a dream. I had to ask Mick if it had really happened.

I suppose my body must have taken about a week to adjust to the higher dosage of medication. Whatever, one morning I woke up and achieved just enough lucidity to make a decision: I was going to get discharged. This just wasn't on, I felt like a zombie; it was time to make a recovery. As for the risks I would face on discharge,

I would cross that bridge when I came to it. The pressing need was to engineer my discharge before my brain turned into tinned soup.

When Dr Shaw came for his chat, I was able to put on a reasonable performance. 'So how do you feel today?'

'Tired. But less tired than I have been feeling.'

'There, you see. You're tolerating the higher dose now.'

'Definitely. I can tell there's a difference.'

'Good.'

We chatted about a few irrelevant things before he finally steered the conversation back – as he always did – to Naloxyl. This time I was prepared. 'You know, Dr Shaw, I'm a little confused.'

'Oh, what about?'

'About me.'

'Go on . . .'

'I just feel less certain about things . . . about what happened.'

'Go on . . .'

'How long have I been in now?'

'Six weeks.'

'Jesus . . .'

Shaw leaned forward. 'Forgive me, Nick, but I'm unclear about what you're saying here. What are you confused about?'

'My memories, I guess.'

'What about them?'

'Well, I can remember doing things before being admitted. You know, feeling people staring at me . . . all that. But, it just seems very distant now . . . and . . .'

'And?'

'Stupid.'

'You don't think it happened?'

'No. Of course it happened. That's what I felt at the time. But now, looking back on it, I must have been wrong.'

Shaw made some notes, scribbling quickly. 'So what's made you change your mind? Why do you think you . . . got it wrong, or were mistaken?'

I sighed. 'That's really difficult to answer and I'm not sure that

I *can* answer it. It's just that, over the past few days, my mind seems to have changed gear. I look back on what I said, and it seems . . . I don't know, unrealistic.'

Shaw nodded.

I guess what I said was true. I had started to question a lot of things, and it felt good. It was a relief, a relief to accept that maybe I had got it wrong. Maybe there was nothing to worry about. Maybe I could go home, play the Rhodes, rehearse with the band and nothing, absolutely nothing, would happen. There would be no face at the window, no calls.

I had been thinking about that guy – the guy who I had seen while walking the streets with Eric, that guy, all alone, staring at the wall. Maybe that's what I had been on my way to becoming. Maybe my hospitalization had been – as my mother would say – a blessing in disguise.

Shaw closed his file. 'Good,' he said. 'I think the medication is finally beginning to have an effect.'

'Yes,' I replied. 'I still feel tired. But I do feel better.'

Mick looked in, and said, 'Is everything all right?'

'Oh yes,' replied Cairo,' and thank you so much.'

I could see that she had gained a fan. He looked at me, smiled and reluctantly closed the door. 'Go on,' said Cairo, 'You were saying?'

'I still feel very tired,' I said, 'but I do feel better, too.'

'You are looking better. God, you were looking so rough a few weeks back.'

'I know, I felt rough.'

Cairo hugged me. 'You know I spoke to Dr Shaw. He said that Dr McDougall is very pleased with your progress. He's thinking about discharging you.'

'When?'

'Oh, he couldn't say exactly, but soon.'

'That's great news.'

Cairo looked out of the window, and the sun caught her face. The creases and folds seemed deeper than ever, and I noticed two small bulges, just below her mouth, on either side of her chin; two new convexities, swollen with excess tissue and drawn down her face by gravity. She looked dignified, – but she also looked old; old in the same way that my mother looked old.

'Cairo?'

'Yes, Nick.' She turned to face me. 'Look. I don't know how to say this. But . . . I'm grateful for what you did.'

'Oh, Nick. Thank you so much.' She took a pink tissue out of a pocket in her voluminous dress and dried a tear from her cheek. 'You know, that's the most wonderful thing I've ever heard.'

'I'm sure that can't be true.'

'No, it is. It's absolutely wonderful.'

She sat on the side of the bed and kissed me, on the lips. A friendly, hard kiss. 'I don't suppose I should do that in a hospital, should I?'

'I'm sure it's OK.'

She reached out and rested her hand lightly on my cheek. 'I've had enough of seeing all the people I love and care about change . . .'

Cairo had seen many people come and go. Two husbands, her lovers and friends. Even Eric was still coming and going, an irregular emanation from the past, who might one day vanish without trace. I suddenly realized why she was so fond of her cats; they were always the same, they never changed and they always came back.

'I didn't want to lose you, too, Nick,' she added. She hugged me again, 'It's good to have you back.'

I smiled.

'Do you want to stay with me for a few days. After you're discharged?'

'No,' I said. 'That won't be necessary. I think I should get back home.' And, strangely enough, I meant it.

My Chlorpromazine was reduced to what was called a 'maintenance' dose and, although I felt tired and dopey, I *was* feeling a lot better. My dry mouth had improved, and my lips were looking normal. The Chlorpromazine had certainly done something to my head. I found that I could reflect on my experiences without my mind racing. I didn't feel the urge to get up and pace. More importantly, I was prepared to accept that I could have been wrong and everybody else right. I didn't think that I had gone crazy, not like Chris or Lucus were crazy; I had just become a bit, unstuck, maybe. Perhaps I *had* read too much into things. As Dr Shaw had suggested, perhaps I had misinterpreted things.

I must have been in hospital another two weeks when Dr McDougall paid me a visit with Dr Stengle. They sat in front of me and, again, I couldn't help noticing that McDougall looked uneasy.

Stengle was – as before – inscrutable. 'I hear that you are much improved,' he said.

'Yes. I think so' I replied.

'Good. I have a few questions to ask, if you wouldn't mind?'

'No. I don't mind at all.'

'I understand that you now no longer believe that you can sense other people's minds. Why do you think it happened? Why do you think you suddenly felt that you could tell when people were looking at you?'

McDougall tensed up.

'I'm not sure.'

'Do you accept that you have had an illness? A mental illness?'

'I guess so. It's a difficult thing to accept, but . . . I suppose that's the simplest explanation.'

'Indeed.'

His face showed no emotion. No feeling. 'If we accept, then, that you have been unwell, do you believe that participating in the Naloxyl trial precipitated your illness?'

I could feel McDougall tensing again.

'Well, Dr McDougall has told me that the Naloxyl had nothing to do with it – that I would have become ill anyway.'

'And do you accept that?'

'I'm not a doctor, I wouldn't know, so I guess . . . yes. If that's what you think.'

'Yes.'

For a moment Stengle and McDougall looked at each other. I could sense that the glance was very meaningful, but whatever meaning was there eluded me.

'I would like to be frank with you, if I may.' Stengle paused, before continuing, 'It would seem that you have suffered a brief psychotic episode, characterized by paranoid beliefs. Such episodes are extremely common, particularly in people of your age. Most individuals who suffer from such an episode never experience another again, so you needn't be overly anxious.'

'That's good.'

'It is, indeed; however, I note from your records that have you have a history of cannabis abuse . . .'

'I smoke a little, yes.'

'Well, could I strongly advise you to avoid taking cannabis in the future. It is associated with psychotic illness, in those who have a predisposition. In fact, the term "cannabis psychosis" is one that has gained considerable currency in recent years.'

'But I wasn't smoking much dope when this happened.'

He looked at me as though I were lying.

'Really I wasn't,' I added.

Stengle looked at McDougall again and McDougall cut in. 'Nicky. You didn't smoke that much cannabis during the trial, over all . . . but the most recent blood tests were far from clear. Now you must know that.' He paused before continuing, 'Anyway, that's not important, not really. I think what Dr Stengle is getting at here is that you, maybe, overdid it a little?'

I nodded. I didn't want to get into an argument at this stage.

'So,' continued Stengle, 'it would be very much in your interests if, in future, you abstained from cannabis altogether.'

'Yes. I suppose that's sensible.'

'Oh, yes, very sensible.' I couldn't help thinking that the conversation was going somewhere, but I couldn't for the life of me work out where.

'Of course,' continued Stengle, 'you are no longer eligible to participate in the Naloxyl trial.'

'No, I guessed that.'

'And I dare say you will miss our financial incentive?'

'The £200 a week? Sure I will.'

Dr McDougall began to smile. Whatever was supposed to have happened had obviously happened.

'Dr McDougall tells me that you are a struggling musician.'

'Err . . . yeah. I suppose I am.'

'Well, as a goodwill gesture, DEMA has decided to make you a discretionary award.'

'Award?'

'Yes. We have decided to award you the outstanding remittance, in a lump sum.'

'Outstanding what?'

McDougall cut in again, 'The amount of money you would have got had you stayed with the trial to completion. It's about £2,500.'

'But why?'

'A goodwill gesture,' said Stengle.

I laughed out loud. 'Thanks.'

Dr Stengle smiled, ever so briefly, and inclined his head a little, a tiny mannerism that recognized the generosity of his gift rather than my appreciation. 'Before I leave,' he said, 'do you have anything you would like to ask me?'

'No,' I said.

A deal had been done. I took his limp hand in mine, and we shook on it. I wasn't up to causing them any problems anyway. I wanted to get on with my life.

23

rückblick

I had been an in-patient on Aubrey Lewis for two months, two whole months – consequently, I was eager to leave. Cairo had offered to collect me in her car, but I refused; I only had one sportsbag full of clothes so it wasn't as if I needed practical assistance. Besides, I really wanted to do it on my own. I was sick of being an invalid.

When I let myself into the flat, I was greeted by an overwhelming stench of damp and fungus. I was expecting to see the walls peppered with spores and a small colony of mushrooms growing out of the sofa. As it happened, the stale air that assaulted my nasal passages promised a more serious fungoid invasion than proved to be the case. Apart from a few new islands on the toilet-wall archipelago, there were no other significant changes. I opened a few windows to allow some ventilation.

The flat felt very still. I hadn't been back since seeing the face at the window and, in spite of my earlier confidence, I did feel nervous. Nevertheless, it was daytime, and the light (although weak) was reassuring. I felt compelled to check out the answer-machine first. In two months I had collected only ten messages. Two were from Andy (and clearly left prior to being informed of my admission); another was from a one-night stand who – seven months earlier – I had gone home with after a gig in Walthamstow. I could remember her name, Bianca, but I couldn't remember her

face. She wanted to go out for a drink. A further message
provoked a sad smile.

'You there, Nick, old son?' *Pause*. 'No. Oh, well. Stay cool, eh?
See you soon, maybe. Cheers.'

It was strangely satisfying to know that he was still out there,
somewhere. The telephone line was clear, so he must have been
close. For a few moments, I allowed myself to believe that he just
might drop in again. *See you soon, maybe*: it sounded promising
but of course, with Eric, you never could tell.

The rest of the messages consisted of long silences, beep-pauses.
Most of them were consecutive and gathered together at the
beginning of the tape. I found the absence of any spoken messages
mildly reassuring: perhaps he – whoever he was – had simply
got bored. I hoped so.

On leaving the Maudsley, I was instructed to continue my
maintenance dose of Chlorpromazine and to attend out-patient
appointments once a week. When I found out that Chlorpromazine
was – in fact – Largactyl (one of the major tranx), I took to
throwing two tablets a day down the lavatory instead of down my
throat, and I didn't feel any the worse for it; in fact, I started to
feel even better.

I did, however, choose to attend the out-patient appointments
at the Maudsley. These were mostly with Dr Shaw. We would sit
and chat for twenty minutes, mostly about my appetite, sleep and
practical things like diet, and then I would get up to leave. Now
that I was better he seemed more relaxed, and he was determined
to show me that he was still young and groovy. He seemed to be
trying to compensate for having never heard of Portishead when
we first spoke. When we got to the point where some small talk
was necessary, he would say something like: 'So what do you think
of the Verve then?'

'They're OK.'

' "The Drugs Don't Work", great track, don't you think?'
(Ironic or what?)

'It's all right, yeah.'

But he could never follow through with anything else. I always got the impression that just before my arrival, he religiously called a thirteen-year-old nephew up to find out what was 'happening'.

I guess it must have been about two weeks after I had been discharged that Andy gave me a call to tell me that a band meeting had been arranged at Vince's the following Friday. He was quite cryptic about it. At first I thought, *Shit, maybe they want to throw me out or something*. But I soon realized that my dismissal wasn't what was on the agenda, it was the Jarl situation. We needed to discuss things properly.

So, the following Friday afternoon I drove out to Essex to meet the boys. No rehearsal, just a meeting. Given that it was the first time we had all been together in a long time the atmosphere was surprisingly subdued. I realized that something was very, very wrong but kind of thought that I shouldn't get too agitated. I didn't want them to think that I was unstable or anything like that.

We sat around Vince's bar, consuming his dry-roasted peanuts and damp cheese-and-onion crisps. Phil performed the honours, and we sat in our preferred places either side of the tiger-skin rug.

'So,' I said, 'what's all this about? I'd really like to know.'

The three of them looked at each other. Phil shrugged, Scott scratched his head, and Andy grimaced.

'Well?' I asked.

Scott started to say something, then stopped, and said to Andy, 'You tell him.'

Andy sighed.

'For fuck's sake, will somebody tell me!'

'OK, sorry,' said Andy, before continuing, 'Look, Nick. We've got some news about Jarl. We didn't want to tell you while you were in hospital because we didn't think it was fair. You had enough to deal with without . . . so don't get pissed off with us, OK?'

'Fine, just *tell me*, will you?'

Scott finally summoned enough courage to come clean. 'You remember about a month ago we went to Berlin? Our friend Harold took me and Phil, yeah?'

'Yes. I remember. You mentioned it when you came to see me.'

'Well, anyway, we were in a club, Der Jäger. It's a gay club in the centre. Anyway, we were dancing when – guess what?'

I shook my head: 'I don't know.'

'The DJ put on "Smart Peroxide".'

'What? Our "Smart Peroxide"?'

'Yep.'

'By a band called Rückblick! It means "looking back" in German.'

'I don't understand, they've recorded it?'

'No. It's us playing. It's our single. But it's marketed as Rückblick.'

'Shit!'

'And over the last month, it's done really well.'

'It's selling?'

' . . . In Germany, yeah. A friend of Harold is keeping his eye on it for us. We don't know but it might have been released elsewhere in Europe, too.'

'Is it on the Retro label?'

'Yeah.'

'Did you contact Jarl? What has he got to say about this?'

'We can't get hold of him.'

'What about the office?'

Phil answered, 'I've been down a few times. There's this bird there called Ute. She claims to have no idea where he is and to be worried about him, said that he left on a business trip weeks ago . . .'

'But I don't understand. What's going on?'

Phil topped up my scotch, 'We've been fucked over.'

'So what are we going to do?'

'We're going to talk to Vince tonight. He said he'd help us out.'

'Jesus . . .'

We sat, silently, none of us saying anything. I couldn't quite believe it. Rather foolishly I said, 'Are you sure about this? I mean, maybe Rückblick are us. The Free Radicals is a pretty stupid name for a German band, so maybe they decided to call us Rückblick.'

Andy shook his head. 'We didn't want to show you this but . . .' He reached into his pocket and handed me a CD. The cover design showed a black woman with peroxide blonde hair posing on the bonnet of a Rolls-Royce. The lettering was in a mock seventies font: Smart Peroxide, Rückblick. I opened the little plastic case and looked at the track list: 'Smart Peroxide', 'Pocket Patrol' and 'Zoo People'; one from Letchworth, the other two from Watford. The musicians were Hans Beagle, Franz Hoop, Leo Rückert and Mo Herring. It was produced in Dortmund by Jarl Haarle and Bo Legge for Retro records.

'Fuck,' I said.

'What a cunt!' was Andy's response. 'You hear about this sort of shit but you never think it'll happen to you.'

I sat staring at the cover. The CD held a curious fascination for me. I took the disc out and let it catch the light. Then I put it back in its case and handed it back to Andy.

'Sickening, isn't it?' said Scott.

I was speechless.

The rest of the evening we sat, saying little and drinking a great deal. We tried to play some pool upstairs but lost interest pretty quickly. At about nine we heard Vince's Merc pulling up outside. He came though the door, followed by a young lady from Essex who – although almost an exact clone of Deb – was unexpectedly distinguished by having the name Madonna. Vince was in his customary frantic state.

'Hey, boys. Good to see you.' He shook our hands. 'Come through to the office. And Madonna, be a good girl, will you, fix us some drinks.'

Vince took us to his office and slumped down in his big leather chair. 'So Andy and Nicky – what do you think? Will she go, or will she go?'

Andy asked, 'Is Madonna her real name?'

'What the fuck sort of question is that?'

'Bet it's not.'

'Hey, do you think I'm going to be giving a fucking monkey's bollock about that when her face is against the mattress? Do you?' Vince slapped his thigh and laughed out loud. 'Shit, I can't wait.' He then did his routine of looking at Scott and Phil and shaking his head. 'OK, what you do is your business. Your own business. But, boys! Hey! Can't you see what you're missing? Can't you?'

Scott and Phil looked at him blankly.

Vince continued shaking his head before suddenly saying, 'Hey Nick – I hear you had to go into hospital recently. Sorry to hear that.'

'Thanks.'

'You went nuts or something.'

'That's right. Some medical research I volunteered for went wrong. The doctors got a bit worried . . .' This was the story I was sticking to. With the band at least.

'Are you suing?'

'No.'

'Well you should. OK?'

'They gave me some money, as a goodwill gesture.'

'Aaachhh! Goodwill? Goodwill! What a schmooze for the schmuck! They gave you some money to keep you sweet. If you change your mind, let me know.'

It was a thought.

Madonna came in with the drinks.

'Hey, thanks, baby.' As she leaned over Vince's desk he rubbed his hands together and held them a few inches away from her arse as though it were radiating heat. She looked around, gave him a curiously enigmatic smile and removed herself without saying a word. 'Beautiful, beautiful,' mumbled Vince. He took a swig of his scotch and then smacked both hands flat on the desktop. 'OK! Business.'

The boys had had a meeting with him two weeks earlier, so he was well informed.

'Right. It seems to me that you four cunts have been totally roasted. Fucked over big-time. This Jarl character has released your single in Germany and has subsequently pissed off. And, if your sources are correct, it's beginning to sell. You stand to lose a fair whack, but we're not sure how much yet.'

We all nodded, and Vince added, 'OK. That's where we are now. Agreed?'

We replied, 'Yeah,' in a glum chorus.

Vince took another swig.

'I don't understand,' I said. 'I don't understand why he would do that. Surely he can't get away with it?'

'My guess is that he can, and he does. You tell me, what's number 29 in the Italian charts right now? Or number 12 in France? Or this year's summer hit in Belgium? If you go around getting little-known bands to record their best numbers and release them abroad, you can probably make a few bob. The investment is negligible, and I imagine the return quite good. It's smash and grab. As long as no one finds out what you're up to, you can keep a scam like this going for years. Let's say this Jarl character signs twenty bands a year, and even a small number produce singles that have modest success abroad – he's laughing. He puts together a promo-package for, say, Spain, takes the money, and then moves on to the next group of hopefuls.'

'But what if they find out?' I asked. 'Isn't it a risk?'

'Maybe they'll get themselves together and do something about it. Legally. Or, more likely, they'll be a bunch of dopehead musicians like yourselves who couldn't get it together to piss straight, let alone start an intellectual property action.' He paused. 'And besides . . . Getting the money off a guy like Jarl is going to be difficult.'

'Why?'

'Two reasons. One is that the legal system favours the defendant, particularly an elusive defendant who does his shit out of jurisdiction. A case like this can be spun out for years, and years – to no good end. And secondly, I fucked up reading your contract.'

'I'm sorry?' said Andy.

'You ain't got a leg to stand on,' said Vince. 'When you showed me your contract, I had other things on my mind. I didn't give it proper attention. I looked at it again this week and . . . I fucked up. It's worthless. So, I guess I should say, sorry, boys.'

'Vince!' Andy was looking very pissed off.

'Cool down. Don't get your truss in a twist, eh, Andy? I had a lot on my mind that night. I was thinking about my guests. What did you think they were, fucking meter-thieves or something? You remember my guests? And who was it, that night . . . used to work in the office? Deb, that's it. Deb.'

We all looked at Vince, like he was the biggest arsehole the world had ever produced.

'OK,' he said, 'like you're all thinking, Vince, he's the biggest arsehole the world has ever produced. But, hold it. Just hold it for a while. I know I fucked up. And, yeah, I feel bad about it. Sure I do. I like you boys. So, leave it with Uncle Vincent.'

'You think you can help?' said Scott.

'Now I'm not making any promises. But leave it with your Uncle Vincent, eh?'

'Are you going to sue?' I asked.

'Come on!' he said. 'I'm a lawyer! I haven't got time to fuck around with the law!'

We left shortly after, feeling sick and angry. Vince was obviously keen to slam Madonna's face against the mattress, and we didn't want to take up any more of his valuable time. Outside the east wing, we commiserated with each other. Things didn't look good. It seemed extremely doubtful that Vince would be able to catch up with Jarl. What could he do? Jarl was obviously a professional ball-squeezer. A slick operator. And it was all very well to throw us that *leave it to Uncle Vincent* line, but Vince had let us down badly. Very badly.

Nevertheless, we arranged to convene for a rehearsal early the following week. It had been a long time since we had played together.

The rehearsal proved to be a bad idea. It was raining, and the sky was the colour of lead, the kind of ill-intentioned sky that makes you want to just draw the curtains and pretend that it's not there. On the radio, an expert announced that if the weather didn't change, 1998 would qualify as the warmest and wettest year on record. By the time I got to Essex I was feeling quite low.

We played through the set, and it was OK, I guess, but for some reason I felt dead inside. The music wasn't the same. And it wasn't just the disappointment of having been fucked over by Jarl. I felt, in some odd way, different. I lacked enthusiasm. I also instinctively felt that Scott was feeling the same way. He was singing and playing, but his performance was empty.

When we took a break, I asked him if he'd written any new material.

'No,' he said. 'Not really.'

Life was kind of dull in general. Whatever had happened to me while taking the Naloxyl had stopped. Just out of curiosity I thought I would spend some time Underground, to see if I could get a wave, like I used to. But nothing happened; I couldn't do it any more. I didn't even *think* I could do it any more. Although the kind of deadness that I experienced on Largactyl had gone, it had been replaced by another kind of deadness, in a way, a more profound deadness.

Maybe I had gone crazy. Maybe I had wandered too close to the edge. But if I had, then I sort of missed it. Life had been more interesting. It had been fun checking out if people were staring at me. Maybe I needed a holiday. I hadn't been away for years. And now, I had some cash in the bank – from DEMA. Perhaps I should just take off, back-pack or something.

I closed my eyes and let the Tube rock me. I listened to the screeching brakes as the train came into Paddington and tried to get a riff in my head, a riff that would be the basis of a new song, but no riff came, absolutely nothing.

I did a circuit of the Circle line and became bored, so I took out *Many Worlds*. It had been a long time since I had read any of it and I had forgotten most of the main arguments. I had to flick through the previous chapters to get a handle on it. The end wasn't as interesting as the beginning. It sort of fizzled out.

By the time I got to Baker Street I had finished it. *Zillions of universes*. Even if there was scientific evidence for the multiverse, it still seemed difficult to believe. And, anyway, what did it really matter? What did I care?

I changed trains and took the Jubilee line up to Kilburn; an uneventful and tedious journey.

When I surfaced, the front page of the *Evening Standard* curled around my legs, carried on a gust of wind, like a wounded bird. The headline announced that a recent government report had uncovered links between high-ranking members of the Met. and the League of St George. After a string of suspected racist murders in Stoke Newington and Hackney, new evidence suggested wilful suppression of key evidence, from above. A spokesman for the black community expressed profound disappointment at the Home Secretary's failure to publicly support demands for the Commissioner's immediate resignation.

What was it Cairo had said? It was months ago now, but I could still remember it clearly. *You need people who believe strongly in what's right, to stand up to people who believe strongly in what's wrong.* Where were the people who believed strongly in what's right? What were the government going to do? More focus groups, no doubt.

I screwed up the *Standard* and threw it in a bin. I looked up and down Kilburn High Road. For the first time, the first time ever, I began to think to myself: *I don't want to live here any more. This isn't the country it used to be.*

A plane was making its way across the sky. An omen, I thought.

24
'unravish'd bride of quietness'

In spite of my initial misgivings I had harboured the hope
– against my better judgement – that we would get some news
from Uncle Vincent, even if it was just bad news, but we didn't
hear anything. After two more rehearsals, we kind of stopped. Phil
was finding it difficult to get us a new gig, and we knew the old
set backwards. Without any new material to rehearse there was
no point.

Dr Shaw said that he thought I could reduce my number of out-
patient visits to once a month, which was cool. I had resolved to
stop traipsing down to the Maudsley as soon as I could. Dr Shaw
said that this would be possible, soon, although he wasn't
prepared to say how soon.

I had started to see more of Cairo. One of the benefits of being
off the trial was that I could get back to smoking dope. I knew
that Stengle was talking crap. It wasn't the dope that had fucked
up my mind, it was the Naloxyl. So it was nice to hang out with
Cairo again, smoking, and relaxing. We even started having sex
again. Although, as with most things, it didn't seem quite as
much fun as it did before.

One afternoon we went for a walk on the Heath and happened
to stroll near Keats's house. I suggested that we drop in. We
walked past the wasted, stunted old tree under which he had
written his 'Ode to a Nightingale', and I pointed it out to Cairo.

'You're really into Keats, aren't you?' she said.

'Yeah,' I replied. 'I suppose I am.'

'Why's that?'

'When I was a kid, my mother played me a piece by Benjamin Britten. It was a setting of Keats's "Ode to Sleep". He wrote a lot about sleep. I always used to have difficulty sleeping, and . . . I don't know. It just appealed to me. Then we did some Keats at school . . . I don't know what the fuck he's on about half the time. But other bits are . . . really cool. You know, like the "Grecian Urn" one?'

'I don't know any Keats, I'm afraid.'

'Oh, you do. It's the one that starts "Thou still, unravish'd bride of quietness, Thou foster-child of silence and slow time"?'

'Oh, yes,' she said, her expression lighting up with recognition.

' . . . And there are loads of other famous bits in it. "Beauty is truth, Truth beauty" . . . and "for ever young".'

'That's one of your songs.'

'Yeah. Well, there you go, I nicked it.' Cairo smiled. 'He used to go walking in Kilburn,' I added.

'Oh?'

'It was rural then. He used to go walking in *Kilburn Meadows*.'

'I can't imagine rural Kilburn.'

'No, it's difficult, isn't it.'

We went inside the house and looked around. In the front room was a bust of Keats, raised on a pedestal to the poet's actual height.

'Wasn't he small?' said Cairo.

'Yeah, a real midget.'

I suddenly remembered what Cairo had said all those years ago, about Hendrix being short. It hadn't occurred to me before, but they had a lot in common, Hendrix and Keats, romantic figures, dying young. Perhaps it was some curious sexual connection that made me say, 'He had the clap, you know. Keats.'

'Did he?'

'Yeah. They used to treat it with mercury then. They used to swallow it or rub it into the skin. They even thought that dripping mercury into the cock-hole wasn't a bad idea either.'

'But it's poisonous.'

'Yeah, fucks the brain up.'

'Did it fuck his brain up?'

'A bit. He used to get depressed or overexcited at times.'

'When I hear things like that, I really wonder whether I should stop seeing my GP. I mean, he's a darling, but at the end of the day . . . medical opinion is so fickle.'

'He hasn't advised you to take mercury, has he?'

'No, but . . . I'm sure you know what I mean.'

'Keats was a doctor.'

'Really?'

'Well, a sort of doctor. Did some surgery, too. Never really practised though, not properly. Just wrote his poems.'

'You know, I didn't realize you were so knowledgeable, Nick,' said Cairo, squeezing my hand. I think all this scholarship was turning her on.

'Not really. I read a book, that's all. A huge thing. Boring, but very informative.'

We walked through the various rooms, until we came to one full of display cabinets. They contained letters and drafts of poems – virtually illegible; Keats's handwriting was appalling. While Cairo was looking at some of the artwork – a sort of Pre-Raphaelite number – I tried to decipher a letter. It was to one of his mates, a bloke called Woodhouse. It was all pretty routine stuff, until I came across a line that said: *When I am in a room with People* . . . then some illegible scrawl . . . *the identity of everyone in the room begins to press upon me*. I didn't want to think about it. I just walked away.

'Let's have some tea,' I said.

'OK,' replied Cairo.

We went downstairs to the kitchen. The place was still relatively empty. A couple of rich old women and a lone Japanese tourist.

'Have you heard from Eric?' Cairo asked.

'No, I haven't.' The last time I had heard from him was the message on my answering-machine (left while I was in hospital). 'Do you still miss him?' she asked.

'Yes. I do.'

She smiled.

'Cairo?'

'Yes.'

'I have a confession to make.'

'Oh.'

'Before I went into hospital, I traced Aloysius Jakoby. Do you remember him?'

'No. Who is he?'

'He was the engineer who worked with the Tree . . . on *Eugene*.'

She couldn't remember him. Although, thinking about it, there was no reason why they should have run into each other.

'I traced him to see if he knew what had happened to Eric. He – Jakoby – is in a bit of state now. He owns a small coachworks business, out Queens Park way.'

'How do you mean, bit of a state?'

'He got into smack.'

Cairo shook her head. 'Another casualty . . .'

'Yeah. I guess so.' I paused before continuing. 'I wanted to know more. You know? About Eric's change. He said that Eric changed on the road to Damascus.'

'Did he? And how did he know that?'

'David Veale told him. He was out there with Eric at the time.'

Cairo grinned. A curious, twisted grin. 'And what do you think that means?'

'Fuck knows.'

She nodded. As if to say: *What's the bloody point then?*

'Do you want some more cake, Nick?'

'Yeah, OK.'

I guess she had been right all along. It was a long time ago and, really, nothing to do with me. Eric's past was his own. I thought to myself: *You really should drop this now.* And I did – well, almost.

After having tea we drove back to Highgate. We smoked some dope and played with the cats. We were both quite hungry then, so Cairo made a bulgur-wheat bake. After dinner, we listened to some music together, then she said she was tired. She sounded genuine: she was tired and wanted to sleep.

'Do you want to crash out here?' she said.

'No, it's OK. Thanks for the meal.'

She gave me a hug at the door and I made my way to the Tube.

It was late when I got back home. The nearest street-light had stopped working, and it emitted only a dim, irregular flicker; each flash like the valedictory beating of a moth's wing in a candle flame. The stairs were submerged in darkness and I made an unsteady descent to the basement door, using the wall to guide me. Although the evening had been quite warm, it had suddenly turned cold, and a freak gust of wind sent a shiver down my spine. Standing in the concrete pit, I reached into my pocket and pulled out my keys. I searched the plane of the door with my fingertips, felt the sharp edges of peeling paint, and finally located the cold, raised disc of the lock. I turned the key and rested my shoulder on the door. It gave easily and I was welcomed by the familiar, vegetable fragrance of home. In spite of the crappy smell, it was good to be back inside. The walk from the station had been oppressive. I had had to step over at least three drunks, one of whom I had left lying in the road, his cheek resting on the pavement as though it were a soft, downy pillow.

I switched on the light and looked down the corridor. The walls looked grimy, and the dark-green carpet (giving way to faded lino in the half-lit kitchen beyond) made me think again about the quality of my life. Cairo's house was so clean. Fresh. Maybe my mother was right after all. Maybe I could do more with myself. I never thought that I would ever get to the point where I could see things from my mother's point of view. But I guess I was reaching it.

The flat had stopped looking like a counter-culture stronghold and just looked like a dirty shit-hole.

I trudged down to the kitchen, pulled the light cord and put the kettle on. I noticed a curious smell, a kind of chemical smell. I didn't think anything of it and assumed that it was filtering down from upstairs. I wondered what the faceless occupant above was up to.

Cairo had given me some dope to be getting on with, and I figured that this would help cancel out the effects of a coffee. So I spooned some granules into a mug and looked in the fridge, only to find that I had enough milk for a coffee or a bowl of cereal the next morning, but not both. I tossed the spoon into the sink and opened the door to my bedroom.

The chemical smell was suddenly very strong. I wondered if maybe the gas fire was fucked. But it didn't really smell like gas, it was too caustic. I hit the light switch, and then became immobilized by fear. The sheets had been stripped from the bed, and on the floor was a blue plastic bottle. The smell was disinfectant. Even before I understood the significance of what I was seeing, my brain had registered danger, imminent danger; electrical signals pulsed through my nervous system, and my blood became thick with adrenalin. My senses sharpened. Before I could scream or turn around, I felt what I thought to be the ceiling crashing down on my head. Then nothing.

I woke up. The first thing I noticed was that my mouth had been stopped with a cloth bung. I was also wearing a gag that covered half of my face. The next thing I noticed was that I was naked. I had been tied, with what looked like tights, face down on the mattress, my arms and legs pulled apart, splayed. I could feel pain around my back and shoulders. There was some kind of binding, ropes, perhaps, holding my trunk hard against the bed. It was cutting into my skin. My wrists had been bound so tightly they were numb. My feet also felt numb, two inert lumps of flesh, fixed to my ankles.

At first I was just sensation, my identity reduced to nothing more than the registration of pain and discomfort. Then, gradually, I became properly self-aware, began to remember what had happened. I suddenly panicked and tried to struggle free, but the bindings were tight and I could hardly move. It was possible, however, to turn my head a little, and when I did, I saw, squatting by the side of the bed, the bulky figure of a man, a large man, wearing a leather jacket and jeans. His head was encased in a black-leather mask. He reached up and slowly pulled at the zip that covered his mouth. I could hear its soft tear distinctly.

I grunted, but when I tried to make the sound I began to choke. He raised a large finger to his mouth. 'Shhh . . .'

I stopped. He was very still. I could see his eyes, peering out through the oval apertures in the mask, dark, brown eyes. He tilted his head to one side. He was thinking, thinking of what to do next. Reaching out, he – ever so gently – touched my lips through the gag. I tried to pull back, but he began to shake his head – a minuscule movement, yet so full of menace my blood ran cold. He wanted me still, absolutely still. I could feel his fingers exploring the shape of my lips, a gentle, circular action, round and round.

He leaned forward so that I could feel his breath on my face. I was expecting it to smell, I was expecting to recoil in disgust, but it was clean and clear: antiseptic, as though he had just gargled with mouthwash.

He leaned further forward and let his lips touch my cheek. I could feel a slight vibration, as though he were sighing, a barely audible hum of satisfaction. Again I tried to shout, but the bung in my mouth slipped backwards. He drew away, his finger, large and bony, vertical against the open zip. 'Shhh . . .'

I'm going to die.

There was a movement upstairs, the creaking of a floorboard and a door shutting. I saw his eyes look upwards and then back down at me. The skin around his eyes creased. He was smiling.

I'm going to die.

He started to move sideways, like a grotesque crab, but he maintained eye contact until he slipped from view. The mattress rocked and the springs sounded. When he touched me it was like a splash of acid. Instinctively, I tried to force myself deeper into the mattress, to get further away from him. It didn't matter that the attempt was an irrational, futile expenditure of energy, it was just something that I had to do.

His hands were large. I felt them gently caressing my buttocks; then his lips, hot breath and tongue. I tensed up. It was repulsive, totally repulsive. He rested a moist finger on my anus and pressed a little. I began to cry.

How curious is the intimacy shared by the murderer and his victim. I could see it now. He had said: *We were meant for each other . . . We were meant for each other, me and you.* And we were – our different, separate lives, leading to this moment, this unique, private moment.

'It's all right,' he said, his voice, calm and soft, like a lover's. He removed his hand from my anus and stood by the bedside. I turned my head to see what he was doing.

He unbuckled his belt and pulled down his jeans to show me his penis. I flinched. At first I thought it was some kind of artificial device, a weapon. Then I realized that I was looking at a penis so shot through with metal, so pierced and studded and clamped, that it had become a near-useless appendage. A piece of raw, elongated meat that swung from side to side under the weight of its appalling decoration. I became aware of a whiff of decay, infection, eating away at what was left of his sexual organ. I felt my stomach convulse. I was about to be sick. But if I was sick, I would almost certainly choke and die.

A curious impression came to mind: Jimi Hendrix, drowning in his own vomit, dying in a girlfriend's flat. His central nervous system so saturated in Vesparax that he had paralysed his gagging reflex. The vomit couldn't be fully expelled. What came up into his mouth, he breathed back into his lungs. His failure to gag killed him, but gagging would kill me; a peculiar reversal. My mind then forged a perverse and irrelevant link. We had both shared Cairo's cunt; we would both of us have died by drowning in our own vomit. I fought the gagging sensation down.

Why was I struggling to survive, knowing the nature of the ordeal that lay ahead? Knowing that I could only buy myself an extra hour or two of absolute terror, before an unspeakable death?

I was trembling. I had begun to shake, violently. Involuntary spasms racked my body. He didn't seem to notice. He had begun to masturbate. His penis wasn't erect; it was clearly far too damaged but, nevertheless, he was becoming aroused. He seemed to be whispering things to himself as he manipulated the flesh and metal in his large, bony hand. I thought I heard him saying: *I'm gonna fuck you, I'm gonna fuck you* – again and again. His breathing was becoming erratic, his hips moved backwards and forwards, then, quite suddenly, he became rigid. He held the position as a few globs of semen fell to the floor. A thin thread of viscous fluid remained, swinging from his penis like a pendulum. He groaned, and his body relaxed.

– *Marche Militaire, Nicholas?*

– *Oooh, yes, Mum.*

– *We're getting so good at this, aren't we?*

Again he squatted beside the bed and looked at me. His big fingers touched my cheeks again. My stomach turned over; they were sticky with semen. He was writing something, but it was impossible to tell what.

Go away now. Please, fuck off now. For God's sake, please fuck off now!

He pulled his jeans up and secured his belt.

'I want to show you something,' he said, still calm, dispassionate, cold.

– *Oh, Nicholas, that was lovely.*

– *Thanks, Mum.*

– *You've been practising, haven't you?*

– *Yes.*

– *For Mummy?*

– *Yes.*

– *I do love you. You know that, don't you? When Mummy's sad, it might seem like she doesn't love you. But she does.*

– *I know that, Mum.*

He raised his right fist and let his fingers open. The palm was scarred, a delicate network of dead white flesh and raised weals. He then rolled up the sleeve of his jacket to reveal a tattoo. It was a tattoo of a ruler, marked in feet and inches, extending from his wrist to his bicep. He waited for me to respond, waited for me to register its meaning, for my eyes to show horrified disbelief.

I won't let you see.

I won't let you have what you want. I closed my eyes.

'Open them,' he said.

I kept them closed.

'Open them.' He stroked the hair from my forehead, a curtain of sticky, sweat-soaked hair. He then grabbed my nose and held it tightly. I couldn't breathe. Within seconds my eyes were open again, wide open.

He extended his right arm. I looked at the tattoo. And as I did so, he let the fingers of his left hand travel its length, from wrist to bicep, start to finish, beginning to end. It seemed a physical impossibility, but his intention was absolutely clear.

– Do you think Dad will ever come back, Mum?

– I don't want to talk about it.

– But . . .

– Nicholas. That's enough!

Suddenly, he stood up, took off his jacket and threw it across the room. He was wearing a black string vest, and lumps of metal poked out of the netting, silver rings and studs, catching the light. Again he showed me the ruler, and let me savour its terrible implication. He walked out of view.

A moment's stillness; then, his hands on my buttocks again stroking, touching, kneading the flesh. Stroking, touching, pulling; pulling apart, pulling wide. Hot breath, like fire, and contact. Contact. His tongue violating me; his tongue inside me, pressing into my sphincter, hard, repetitive stabs. I could feel him forcing saliva into my arse, forcing himself into me.

I'm going to die.

The mattress springs complained as he got off the bed. A moment's reprieve. A moment's release.

I could hear him walking around the room. Unscrewing a bottle-top and pouring a small quantity of liquid. The smell of disinfectant was strong, unmistakable now. He held his breath as he poured, concentrating hard. When he had finished, he began breathing again.

Squatting by the bed, he showed me a large tube of KY and waved it in front of my face. Then, after removing the screwtop, he squeezed the entire contents of the tube on to his right arm. The ruler markings glistened.

Someone help me. Someone help me, please.

He worked the KY around each finger, each knuckle. He did so with terrible efficiency. Swift, concise movements, like a surgeon scrubbing up; workaday efficiency.

Then, when he had finished, he opened his massive fist to show me what was concealed inside. Against the network of scar tissue and weals, he held three razors, two glass ampoules and about five or six tabs of acid. I closed my eyes. This time, he didn't ask me to open them again.

Movement. He sat behind me, and I waited for intolerable, inhuman pain.

Oh my God. Oh my God. Oh my God. The phrase just repeated itself through my head. I felt his knuckles, pressing up against my sphincter.

I screamed but produced only a dull moan and choked immediately.

'Let's go . . .' he said.

There was silence, a kind of deep, almost spiritual silence. And in that stillness, in that absolute quiet, I heard a footstep; then another; then another. At first I thought it was the upstairs tenant again, then I realized someone was walking slowly down the hall. My tormentor remained perfectly motionless.

The bedroom door-handle turned, and Eric stepped in. I began to shake as violently as I could and moaned.

'Oh, man!' said Eric, covering his eyes, 'Oh, shit, man. I'm really sorry. I didn't know you were into this . . . I'm so sorry, man.' I saw his eyes glance in the direction of *him*. Eric looked away again and covered his eyes.

I tried to groan louder, but Eric clearly thought that I was angry.

'OK, OK. All right. I'm really sorry. I'll give you a call. Stay cool, eh?'

He closed the door. I heard his steps recede and the front door close. My heart almost stopped beating. I was stunned, horrified, completely and totally distraught. I could hear the beginnings of laughter from behind, a cruel, glottal laugh. 'Fuck . . .' he whispered. 'Incredible.'

I gave up. At that moment I lost my will to live. I began to moan; I choked; I gagged. I didn't care; I just wanted to die and to die quickly.

'Quiet now,' he said.

I continued to moan.

He grabbed my testicles and squeezed them hard. His voice was suddenly ragged and urgent, triumphal; the calmness had evaporated.

'Shut up, you little shit. Shut up! Keep still!'

I didn't care any more. I groaned.

He yanked my testicles as though he were pulling a rip cord. My abdomen filled with fire. In spite of my desperation, the great, eloquent, universal language of pain was enough to silence me. He stroked around my anus with his hands and then began to ease a single finger in. It hurt – just one finger. It hurt so much I couldn't believe it. The tears rolled down my cheeks, and I lifted my head.

Dear God, I thought. *Dear God. Please don't let this happen.*

I prayed. For the first time in my life, I prayed. I prayed to a God I knew to be impotent, a God who presided over a hopeless, miserable planet, spinning through an empty, meaningless void.

Bang! The door flew open – violently, as though a bomb had exploded behind it. Quick movement, a draught of air.

I could hear a struggle behind me, a scream, of horror and surprise, then two dull thuds followed by a cracking sound almost like bone splintering. Then silence.

Cold air from the hall, chilling my sweat-drenched back. The sound of heavy breathing.

Eric's face appeared in my line of vision. He squatted beside me, a kind of inversion of the evil that had occupied the exact same place moments before. His eyes were alight, alight with victory. He looked at me, his face creased with pity and compassion.

'Did you really think I'd be that stupid? Did you?'

When Eric released me from my bonds I could barely turn around. I was shaking and could not speak. I was entirely mute.

'Here.' Eric wrapped the bedsheet around me.

I turned. Collapsed at the end of the bed was a supine figure. I was suddenly filled with wild anger and rage. I leaped from the bed and began to kick the leather mask, one kick after another. I jumped on his head and stamped my foot down heavily on the neutral, metallic mouth. Eric dived across the room and dragged me away. His strong arms held me still. He looked into my eyes. For a moment I felt as though he were hypnotizing me.

'Easy, old son. Easy. He'll be out for a while. You got nothing to worry about . . . you're safe. All right?'

I swallowed, more absent than present, more animal than human.

Eric guided me around the body and down the hall. I kept looking over my shoulder, terrified of movement. Eric sat me down on the sofa. 'Just stay here. I'll go and tie him up. Don't do anything. Just stay here and breathe. Concentrate on your breathing. Easy . . . that's it, Nick. That's it, my son.'

He backed out of the door, and I sat, concentrating like he told me to. I could hear movement and wished that he would come back soon. There was a sound outside, the sound of a car starting. I screamed, a stupid bark. Eric came running back down the hall and looked in.

'It's all right. I'm sorry.' My voice sounded strange, like someone else's.

'Stay cool,' said Eric, before disappearing again.

I started to cry once more, a mechanical contraction of the

270

muscles in my chest. When Eric came back, he picked up
the telephone and called 999. The police arrived within fifteen
minutes.

25
modern life

I was admitted as an in-patient into the Royal Free Hospital, having been diagnosed as suffering from Acute Stress Disorder. My nervous system was like a network of uninsulated wires. In the wake of my ordeal, my spinal cord felt like a lightning conductor. I was given vast quantities of Valium. Without Valium, I would spontaneously shake and jump at the slightest sound.

It is difficult to describe my mental state. At first I could barely speak. Doctors came to see me whose presence I was able to acknowledge; however, I was disinclined to answer their questions. It was as though I could no longer face the world and was seeking refuge in my own skull. There was also a curious yearning for numbness, non-existence; if I had been able to lay my hands on some dope I would have escaped into oblivion without a moment's consideration.

I didn't sleep for two days, in spite of having been given a powerful sedative. On the third night I accomplished sleep and sank into a nightmare world of terror and obscene carnage, though my way back into this world was through a familiar set of images and impressions.

I was in a room, standing behind a guy with sweaty hair. He was staring at a wall. 'They're coming,' he said.

'Who's coming?'

'Them.'

'But what do they want?'

'You.'

'Me?'

'Yes, you. Your thoughts.'

The wall began to crack and the plaster to fall away. I turned to run out of the door but my feet were stuck to the floor. A thick dark liquid was oozing up through the carpet – blood. 'I can't move!'

He turned and smiled. His right arm was lined with a tattoo, a ruler, from his wrist to his bicep. 'No, you can't. You'll never leave this room: *We were meant for each other, me and you.*'

I screamed. Then, quite suddenly, the floor beneath me opened and I fell downwards. I found myself lying on a hospital bed, breathing heavily.

I turned my head to see a masked face, next to my bedside cabinet. *A thing of beauty is a joy for ever,* he said. Keats – I recognized the line. My limbs were paralysed. I screamed and woke again. 'Please stop this . . .' I said into my pillow. 'Please stop this.' I raised my head slowly and stared into the shadowy corners of the room. The sheets were drenched, soaked through with perspiration. I could hear brisk footsteps outside. The door opened, and a nurse came in.

'Are you all right?' she asked.

'No, I'm not all right,' I replied.

'Nightmare?'

'Yeah, a bad one.'

'Do you want to talk about it?'

'No.' I shook my head, and said again, 'No.'

She switched on the bedside lamp and looked at me. It felt uncomfortable. Not because she was staring at me in a funny way but because I felt ashamed. I knew that she would know what had happened to me. 'Do you want me to change the sheets?' She could see that they were soaked.

'No, it's OK, really.'

'Then, would you like some more medication, to help you sleep?'

I thought about this for a moment. What if the drugs kept me asleep in a nightmare world of torment and pain. Sleep was my enemy, the dark portal through which he could still reach me. 'No. No medication, thanks.'

She waited, for a moment, looking at me. I could see that she was thinking about calling a doctor. 'Lean forward,' she said, and reached down to plump up my pillow.

'There,' she added, 'that'll be more comfortable.'

Although moved by her kind ministrations, it was still beyond me to open up. So, when she switched off the light and closed the door, I was curiously relieved. I curled up into a ball and listened to my breathing. *In and out, in and out. In and out*, until morning.

Eventually, my physical symptoms diminished in intensity, and I began to receive daily visits from a clinical psychologist. Her name was Dr Roberts, but she insisted on being called Katie. I liked her; however, her sessions were long and exhausting. She said that my initial reaction was actually normal given what I had been through. Most people subjected to such a traumatic experience would suffer the same kind of problems. The important thing was to make sure that my symptoms resolved as soon as possible.

At first I was a bit worried about the treatment. She wanted to go over the trauma again and again. What had happened? How did I feel? What was going through my mind at the time? I was quite resistant to the idea. But, gradually, the more we spoke about it, the less distressing I found the mental images. She used a term, 'emotional processing', to describe the gradual adjustment to traumatic experiences.

The police wanted to talk to me. At first Katie said I wasn't ready, but after about ten days she thought that I could handle it. Indeed, she said that if I was to make sense of what had happened to me, then talking to the police would be necessary – therapeutic.

I was escorted to an office where I was introduced to Inspector Ross, a middle-aged man in plain clothes. He was accompanied by a WPC who said little but looked on with interest.

Inspector Ross asked me a load of questions about my 'assault'.

Without the preceding weeks of therapy it would have been impossible for me to supply him with answers. I would simply have broken down. Although I became tearful once or twice, I managed to struggle through his sensitive but difficult interrogation. He then asked me if I had any questions.

'Who was he?' I asked. I wanted to know.

'Are you sure you're ready for this?' Inspector Ross asked.

'Yeah. I need to know.'

'Victor Joseph Parish. Aged thirty-eight.' Inspector Ross paused before adding, 'A homosexual. For the past five years he's been living in a small flat in Finsbury Park. There's very little to say about him really. A loner. Kept himself to himself.'

'What did he do?'

'Jobwise?'

'Yeah.'

'He was a laboratory technician in a school – Manor House way. By all accounts he did his job very well.'

'What, and nobody knew that . . .'

Inspector Ross registered my disbelief. 'He never gave anybody reason to complain, not once. Staff or pupils. He turned up, did his job and then went home. The headmaster described him as diligent and hard-working, although quiet.'

'Did he have a criminal record?'

'No, not really. He was almost taken to court during the eighties because he refused to pay his poll tax. He paid though, in the end. Other than that nothing.' Inspector Ross threw a sideways glance at the WPC, then continued, 'However, I expect that, eventually, people will come forward. The ones that escaped. That's always the way. They always come forward, in the end.'

'But he was so crazy. What about a hospital record? Did he have a hospital record?'

'No. I believe he was treated by his GP for depression a few times. Antidepressants. But he was never sent to hospital.'

I looked at Inspector Ross and then at the WPC. It seemed incredible that someone so ordinary, so unremarkable, should be responsible for such terrible crimes. 'Why me? Why did he pick on me?'

'He saw you at the Prince Albert Club. There doesn't seem to be more to it than that. He – as it were – chose you, then.'

I remembered that night. The chill of the fuck room and those dreadful, fleeting impressions.

I shuddered but managed to maintain control. 'But how did he know where I lived?'

'It was very straightforward. You're in the telephone directory. He had a conversation about you – and your pop group – with the manager of the Edward II. Mr Hogan, if my memory serves me correctly, Mr Peter Hogan.'

I nodded. 'So . . . why? I mean, what was the motive?'

'Other than immediate sexual gratification, there was no motive as such.'

'He just got it into his head to – ' I couldn't find the words to describe his predilection, his interest, ' – and just went ahead and did it?'

'Mr Farrell. Since the 1970s there has been a dramatic increase in motiveless crime. Often quite horrible. It's just one of those things. One of the unforeseen costs of modern life, perhaps.'

I shook my head. *Global warming, pit bulls, alienation, junk food, acid rain, road rage. Motiveless murder. Modern life. Modern death.*

'Mr Farrell?'

'I'm sorry?'

'Do you have any more questions?'

'No. None at all.'

Lying on my bed that afternoon, I stared at the ceiling and turned over the facts in my mind. Parish had followed me. He really had. I hadn't been paranoid at all. McDougall, Stengle, Shaw – even Cairo – they had all been wrong.

The following day Katie came to see me. I could see that she was a little apprehensive, concerned that my debriefing session with Inspector Ross had been too much for me.

'So how do you feel about him? Now that you know who he was?'

I thought long and hard. 'Still angry. But . . .'

'Yes?'

'Less scared of him.'

'Why do you think that is?'

'He was only human. He had a name – Victor Parish.'

'That's right.'

I paused before asking the next question. 'Do you believe in evil, Katie?'

'I think it might be more helpful to ask yourself that question?'

'All right' – I was now quite used to the evasive, stock responses of psychotherapists – 'but I'd like you to help me find the answer to that question. You know things that I don't. You've studied psychology, I haven't.'

'OK. What do you want to know?'

'Who we are – what we do – has got a lot to do with our brains, hasn't it?'

'Yes.'

'The brain sort of generates the mind.'

'Yes. Although some people believe there's a lot more to it than that.'

'The soul?'

Katie nodded.

'Well I can't really buy all that. Scientists don't buy it, do they? They've only got time for brains, right?'

'That's right. The soul doesn't seem to show up on MRI scans.' She smiled.

'So if a brain gets fucked up, you'll get a fucked-up person, won't you?'

'Depends. Depends on the extent of the – ' she paused before adding '– the fuck-up.'

'Sure, but in principal. A fucked-up brain will produce a fucked-up person. Won't it?'

'Speaking as a scientist, yes, that's true.'

'Then isn't what we call evil just the product of a seriously fucked-up brain?'

'You could see it like that.'

Katie made a brief note, then asked, 'Do you find that helpful, to think of evil in that way?'

I paused. 'Not so much helpful. More interesting.'

Katie was about to ask me what I meant by that. But being a sharp therapist, she read my expression and moved the conversation on.

I was feeling better. Not great, but a whole lot better. Katie suggested that it might be time to leave. I could start seeing her as an out-patient. I also stopped taking sedatives.

After my second week at the Royal Free, Cairo had visited me nearly every day with Eric (who she was surprisingly happy to put up). When I was discharged I went to stay with them. They were like a New Age Mum and Dad to me. For a short while we formed a kind of post-apocalyptic nuclear family. Insofar as it was possible for me, I was happy.

Eventually, however, Eric had to move on. When he left Cairo's house I gave him a long hug. 'I love you, Eric,' I said. And meant it.

'Well . . . yeah,' came his embarrassed reply. 'Like. That's how it is . . . good vibes, good karma . . . goodbye.'

Cairo and I watched him make his way up the road toward Hampstead. He didn't tell us when he would be back. I cried. When I looked at Cairo I saw that she was crying, too.

While I was staying there I had arranged to move out of the flat in Kilburn. I just couldn't go back. Cairo had been kind enough to arrange a pretty good place for me in West Hampstead, through a friend. The editor of *Gagging For It*, as it happens. There was a sort of self-contained bit to the woman's very large house, which suited me nicely. It was only to be a temporary arrangement, for about eight months, but I wasn't going to complain about that.

In my absence the band had got together to rehearse a little as a three-piece – and they didn't sound too bad without me, quite tight, in fact. They welcomed me back, but still my heart wasn't in it. When we rehearsed my fingers touched the keys, but nothing kicked back. Something in me had gone. The Jarl thing had left us thinking: *What's the fucking point?*

I wanted to get away from it all, from everything, so I booked myself a holiday, just a week in the Algarve. I still had quite a lot of dosh left from the trial. I flew direct to Faro and got a bus into Carvoeiro, a small, touristy village on the coast.

I lay on the beach, reading novels and watching the sun make its way across the sky. Then, in the evenings, I ate swordfish steaks on the beach and drank sangria. The night-clubs were pretty crap, but I was able to spot the odd dealer and managed to get hold of some dope, so my last few days were very relaxing and I didn't have any trouble sleeping. I even managed to get laid. An American girl – Charon, pronounced Sharon, as in Pluto's moon – sat beside me one night and asked if she could share my joint. She was young and pretty, sun-bronzed legs and streaky blonde hair. She was living out there with her 'folks'. 'Pa' was something to do with the sports industry. His company had a contract to build some new golf-courses, and he was out there coordinating things. Charon was about seventeen, and her body had that solid, almost rubbery feel that young girls have. We made love on the beach. It was quick but beautiful; I didn't see her again.

Walking around Carvoeiro, I noticed the price of property in the estate agents' windows. It was really cheap. For the price of a shit-hole in Kilburn you could buy three or four small whitewashed villas overlooking the glittering blue sea. Jesus, I thought. *If only I had just a little cash*. Perhaps he was listening.

The day after I got back I got a call from Andy. He said that Vince wanted to have a word with us. We all went over to Epping, and Vince went through the usual routine: he introduced us to another 'bird' from the office, made some politically incorrect statements about Phil and Scott's sexual orientation, ordered some whiskey and then slapped his hands on the desk.

'Good news,' he said.

He paused to get some sense of drama. To get him to move on I had to say, 'Yeah?'

'Yes. Your man – Jarl – was traced by a friend of mine. Well, a friend of a friend actually. Thinking about it, you might have met him once . . . Bill?'

'That big guy with the gun?' I asked.

'What gun? I never saw no gun.'

'Err . . . You're right. There wasn't one,' I added.

'I never allow shooters in here, Nick. It's a house rule. Surely you know that?'

'Sure, it was stupid of me to forget.'

'That's-a-ma-boy,' he said, in mock Anglo-Italian. He reached over the desk, grabbed my cheek and shook it. He leaned back and continued, 'Anyway. Back to Bill. We're not talking about big Bill here, we're talking about extra-large Bill. He has a brother-in-law called – you'll love this – Nob. I mean, what the fuck is Nob short for, eh?'

'Nobby,' I said.

'No, no, no. That's another abbreviation. I mean, Nob, Nobby . . . what's it short for?' We all looked at each other and said nothing. 'Anyway, so if Bill is extra-large, then Nob is fucking Durex Gold. I mean, this guy is like a house. What's a really big house called?'

'A really big house,' I said.

'OK. So, Nob is the size of a really big house. You're getting the picture here?' We all nodded. 'So anyway, Bill – extra-large Bill – owes me one or two favours, so I asked him if he could put Nob and a few of the boys on the case. They hung about outside Jarl's Notting Hill place for a while and had words with some of the people there. They figured Jarl was still around, so they waited and eventually this BMW turned up, carrying Jarl and a couple of Krauts. So Nob had a word. And, sadly, your Jarl man was rude. Most uncivil. Just didn't want to talk.' This was getting interesting. 'Well, a few days later, guess what? Your Jarl man had a minor accident. Had to get a cast fitted on his leg. Then guess what? Your Jarl man is the most unlucky guy, because a few days later he had another accident and had to get another cast fitted on the other leg. And, you'll never guess what happened next. All this time in the casualty department gave him time to reflect on his life, and he sort of signed a document that I had had prepared. You guys have made quite a lot of money, you know . . .'

Uncle Vince had delivered. Although he took 10 per cent to cover overheads, Vince had retrieved all our royalties for the Retro singles. He had also negotiated a big chunk out of Jarl's cut.

Of the three singles, two had been released and done very well in Germany; 'Forever Young' had made the Top 40 in France, and 'Smart Peroxide' was a hit in Italy; 'Trade' had just been released in Spain, and initial sales figures looked promising. Anyway, by the end of 1998, we each had about £40,000 to spare.

I flew out to Portugal and bought three villas. I rented two out, one at a high rate for German tourists, the other at a lower rate to a local family; the third I lived in.

26
a prophesy and a promise

I spent a lot of time smoking dope and drinking sangria, sleeping with young women with sun-bronzed skin, streaky blonde hair and sweet little snatches that split open with a gentle prod. I watched a lot of satellite TV.

One day I caught this amazing wildlife programme. Some David Attenborough-type guy was investigating a colony of chimpanzees in Africa, who communicated using British Sign Language and had started to use rudimentary tools. A scientist came on as a sort of expert on the paranormal. He said that the spontaneous emergence of signing in a remote colony of chimps was conclusive proof of what he called morphic resonance. The really big chimp – the alpha male – was very familiar to me. I thought of writing in to let them know what the score was. But then I thought, *Fuck it*; life should be full of mystery.

With time on my hands I started composing again. I hate the word – but I started composing *seriously*. Once my Portuguese improved I was thinking of checking out the University of Faro. There was a resident composer there, Martin Cordez, who I thought might look over my first quartet. Maybe, just maybe, I had written something decent. If he thought it was OK, I might even give my mother a call.

I corresponded with Cairo. She was doing well but felt that she really, really needed to do something with her life. Her art was

OK, but it all seemed 'so self-indulgent' to her. After about a year Cairo sold up and moved to Dorset where she opened a cat sanctuary.

It transpired that Dorset council had decided to celebrate the millennium by carving up the countryside with a few more motorways, and the GLF became very active in the area. They used the Cairo Clark Cat Sanctuary as a sort of secret base. Cairo and Eric started to see quite a lot of each other, and they got it together – properly. Then they decided to – and I really didn't believe this when I heard – get married.

They tied the knot in a place called Worth Matravers. After the small church ceremony they went up a cliff somewhere and had some pagan ceremony; then they swam naked.

And what did I feel about this? Happy – really happy for them.

Married life had a calming effect on Eric. Cairo's Cat Sanctuary was a legit operation and, perhaps under her influence, Eric began to turn the GLF into a less militant movement. Negotiations took place with organizations like Greenpeace at the CCC sanctuary. Eventually, they worked out a way of using Eric's GLF expertise to the benefit of all parties. Many environmental groups were getting inquiries from people – ordinary people (not nutters) – who wanted to be more active; however, they didn't have the know-how. I mean, your average retired accountant knows fuck-all about tunnelling or building a network of tree-houses; young mothers have no idea how to decommission a plant vehicle. So Eric was made the commanding officer of the E-brigade, a crack team of environmental activists which trained ordinary folk to do those little, irritating things that could one day save the world. They were a mobile unit and would drive in a huge truck all over the country to get local environmentalists up to speed; however, they also had a small training camp in Dorset, next to the sanctuary, where people could come and learn. So the GLF folded, and its place in the grand scheme of things was taken by a more user-friendly service.

I guess it must have been maybe two years later that Eric and

Cairo came over to Carvoeiro. They looked amazing – radiant – and Eric was more together, much more together.

One evening Cairo was doing some meditation, and Eric and I were down on the beach smoking. 'We can learn a lot from the Tao, Nick, old son,' he said.

'Yeah.'

'I mean, the principle of harmonious action is just so beautiful. Wu Wei . . .'

'Wu what?'

'Wu Wei, the principle. It teaches us to cooperate with nature, natural patterns and cycles. Blending with the energies around us instead of imposing our will on the planet and other life forms.' He took a drag of his joint. Eric was exerting his usual influence on the flow of time; we were definitely flowing backwards. We were approaching the early seventies and heading towards sixty-nine or sixty-eight, maybe. 'I mean, it makes so much sense. Why swim upstream? Against the current? Yeah? When you follow the principle, there's growth. Growth and progress.' He picked up a stone from the beach, a bright orange stone made flat and smooth by the sea. He admired its contours, smiled and then flicked it at an oncoming wave. The stone jumped three or four times before vanishing. 'Without harmonious action, you don't get anywhere. I mean, as a species, we're just treading water, that's all. Everybody thinks they're getting ahead, but they're not. They're getting nowhere, man.'

'I'm not so sure . . .'

Eric was a little surprised. 'What did you say?'

'I said, I'm not so sure . . . There's been progress. B&O decks, midi-systems, modems, CDs, DVDs, autoroutes, the Web. Heat-sensitive polychrome T-shirts . . . Teflon. You know, progress.'

Eric shook his head. 'Most people don't have B & O decks.'

'All right then, Teflon. Most people have Teflon.'

'Listen,' said Eric, with an air of finality, 'the average – not the well-off – I said the average citizen of the Western world spends about a third of his income on food. So let's say that means about a third of his working life is all about getting food. Well, that's exactly how much time our early ancestors spent getting food. It's taken us a couple of million years to go nowhere. THC, my son?'

'Thanks.' I took a toke. Almost immediately my brain shrank to the size of walnut, two tiny crinkled hemispheres clinging together for comfort in the suddenly vast, shadowy hangar of my skull. 'This is fucking strong.'

'It'll help you think straight.'

'Yeah – ' my head began to swim ' – but you see, Teflon . . .'

'Will you just shut up about Teflon?'

I wasn't quite sure what kind of a point I had meant to make, so I took another toke and handed the joint back to Eric.

'Will you just look at this?' said Eric, waving the spliff at the horizon.

I breathed in the salty air. A thin band of cloud obligingly passed across the sun, allowing us to look directly at it. The perfect solar circle descended slowly until its lower extremity touched the sea. A path of shimmering fire burst across the water. It was so staggeringly beautiful that, for a while, we were speechless.

My brain expanded a little, occupying the emptiness. 'How's the game doing Eric?'

'What *Eco-Crash*?'

'Yeah.'

'Very well. Next year we're bringing out EC-II. It's got more complex plots than EC-I. We've got some hot new titles like *Clone City, Underclass Rebellion* and *DDT-Head*. It's good stuff.'

'What about *Pink Planet*?'

'I think we'll save that for EC-III.'

'Fair enough.'

'I'm dead glad I got involved now,' continued Eric. 'EC-I has been really successful. Just as well, because we've got a big job coming up. We're going to need a lot of dosh.'

'What's that then?'

'Oh, you'll see, Nick, old son. In fact everybody'll see,' he chuckled.

'Come on, tell me.'

'Have another toke . . .' Eric still enjoyed his secrets, his conspiracies.

The sun slowly sank and slipped behind the sea. The sky darkened and the stars appeared. The night was so clear you could see the Milky Way, opaque and luminescent, a thing of almost incomprehensible subtlety and beauty.

'Do you think there's life up there, Eric?'

'They say there's got to be.'

'Yeah, but do *you* believe there's life up there?'

'I'm not sure. There might be. But then again, maybe not. In which case, there's only us. All alone.'

'Only the lonely . . .'

'Only the lonely.'

He handed me the joint again. I took a deep, lung-popping inhalation and felt reality shift gear and pull into a lay-by. The world turned slowly on its dark side. I had something to ask Eric, a question that had been on my mind for a very long time. 'Eric?'

'Yeah?'

'Eric. I know you don't like talking about it but, for some reason I just can't leave it alone. It would really mean a lot to me if you could . . .'

'What?'

I took a deep breath and blurted out. 'You saw God, didn't you? On the road to Damascus. In 1973, you saw God. Yeah?'

Eric took a pre-rolled spliff out of his top pocket, torched the end and looked out across the softly murmuring starlit sea. He didn't say anything at first, but then said, 'Funny old world, isn't it, Nick, old son?'

'It certainly is.' He turned to look at me, but still said nothing. 'Eric. What happened? Did you see a light or what? What happened?'

Pause. 'Sure. There was a tremendous light. And He spoke.'

'He spoke?'

'Yeah.'

'. . . And what did He say?'

'Do you really want to know all this?'

'Of course I do.'

'But why?'

'Because it happened to you. And, you're important to me.'

He smiled and punched my arm. 'Silly tosser.' He sat nodding and took a long drag. 'THC?'

I shook my head. I still had the first joint smouldering in my hand. 'So? What did He say?'

'He said that He thought the last album I did was crap. He said that He thought the two earlier albums were more honest, and that *Eugene* was a really pretentious album. He said that I would be better off doing something more useful with my life in future, because I wasn't going to produce any interesting new material . . . besides, punk was about to happen and soon everybody would think my stuff was shit.'

'He said *that*?'

'Yeah?'

'What did He sound like?'

'What do you mean?'

'What kind of a voice did He have?'

'Deep, of course. And with a slight East London accent. Not unlike my own, in fact.'

'East London?'

'Yeah. Weird, eh?'

Behind us some drunk tourists were singing along to the latest Eurohit: 'Situ-Situ'. I scratched my head and grimaced.

'But, Eric, how did you know it was God? I mean, had you done much acid?'

'Loads, man.'

'Then maybe you were just off your head?'

'But how come He knew about punk?'

'Are you sure He said punk?'

'Yeah. I think so . . .' He didn't sound too sure. I didn't know what to say. Eric picked up another stone, and threw it into the sea, adding, 'But it was a long time ago now . . .'

There was silence. I felt curiously dissatisfied. 'Did He say anything else?' I asked.

'Yeah.'

'What?'

'He said that He thought He had got creation wrong. It was a bit of a fuck-up, and He was sorry now He hadn't thought about it more carefully. And, because He hadn't thought things through, creation had some serious problems . . . and, well, He could do sod-all about it. It was out of His hands. He said something about making himself imperfect to allow us choices. Excluding Himself from time . . . Then He said . . . He said He'd appreciate some help. Any help. And that He hoped that I didn't feel He'd let everyone down. Then the light went out.'

'And you really think it was God?'

'I don't know,' said Eric, smiling. 'Might have been.'

'What do you mean? *Might have been!*'

'Maybe it was, maybe it wasn't.'

'But it changed your life. You never went back to the Tree. You went to Scotland . . . the GLF. How can you be so flip about it?'

Eric tugged his beard and thought for a few moments before answering. 'Does it matter that much . . . really? The point is, since then, I've done the right thing. The world's full of people, doing the right thing, for the wrong, or stupid reasons.' He picked up yet another stone, and threw it through the air. It landed with a musical plop and splash. 'But,' he continued. 'if it was God. If *it was* God – I liked Him. He was all right. You know, I've read all the scriptures. The lot. The whole fucking lot. And I've never really warmed to the big G. I mean, take the Old Testament – what a vindictive old bastard He was. And the Eastern scriptures . . . really, they aren't much better. It's true, their God isn't so vindictive, but He's so vague . . . so remote. My God was all right. He was like a mate. Instead of God the father, God the son, or God the holy spirit, it was God the geezer. I could relate to Him. He might have fucked up, but somehow that made Him more approachable. It appealed to me, this . . . partnership. God and His creation. Him and me. Him and us. In it together . . .'

Eric smiled, a broad satisfied smile. 'And what that means,' he went on, 'is that He really needs us. Not in some stupid, abstract way, but in a real, practical way. The world is a fuck-up, plain and simple. You can't put positive top-spin on evil, cancer or pain, Auschwitz or Hiroshima. Anybody can see that. There's no divine master-plan behind it all. It's a cock-up. And it's a sort of relief to know that. You don't have to swallow a load of bullshit any more. It's a cock-up, just like you always thought. But we can help Him to get it sorted . . . It's up to us. It's up to us, now – just us.'

And with these curious words, Eric began to sing, in a coarse, husky voice that was, nevertheless, beautiful. He sang quietly at first but got louder and louder – Lennon and McCartney's 'With a Little Help from My Friends'. And when he got to the middle section – and asked the sea if it needed anybody – I joined in, too, and we sang together, at the tops of our voices. We sang together, at the tops of our voices. We sang together, at the sky, the Milky Way, the universe and everything.

But even before we reached the end of the final verse this perfect moment was interrupted. Eric fell silent and slowly stood up. I was so stoned I just went on singing. Eric reached out and gestured for me to keep quiet. I trailed off . . . and looked up to see Eric staring into the distance. The McBastard's orbital SkyVert had started to poke one of its gaudy arms over the horizon. McBastard's had had their company logo – a large *M* – placed in a non-geostationary orbit around the earth, a massive reflective frame that had been uncoiled and unfurled from the space shuttle with the waking grace of a long-legged but delicate insect emerging from a cocoon. I could still remember the TV pictures, the extension of hinged parts; it was like watching some strange, slow-motion, robotic ballet.

The greatest of ironies was that within a week, the logo had been damaged by space debris. Nuts, bolts, clamps, wires, orbital flotsam from the break-up of rocket parts and exploding satellites, droplets from leaking nuclear reactors; over 5,000 tons of techno-junk had been dumped in space. A tiny piece of this trash, so small as to be undetectable, had hurtled at high speed into the logo. The orbital was now an imperfect *M*, the right arm twisted completely out of shape.

As it rose – a monument to corporate stupidity – its dazzling, reflected sunlight polluted half the sky. Around its misshappen glowing structure, the Milky Way vanished; the most subtle glory of the celestial dome was swamped by razzle and dazzle; stars went out. We watched as the most expensive piece of graffiti ever vandalized the observable universe.

Eric's eyes were shining. I remembered the look I had seen on his face, all those years ago, back in Kilburn – leaning over the bridge at West End Sidings, shaking his fist and shouting at the Fall-out Express. And I saw it again, that same look, although this time his eyes were shining so much more brightly in the unnatural light of the orbital. He raised his hand and his voice, amplified by the rock amphitheatre, sounded high above the waves and sea. 'You cunt!' A voice in the wilderness. A prophesy and promise. *Beauty is truth, truth beauty.*

At once I knew where the money from EC-I and EC-II would go. It was obvious.

27
two years later

I met Julie on Carvoeiro beach one blazing day in the
summer season. The beach had become my stamping ground. I
spotted most of the young women I eventually laid basking on
those sands. Carvoeiro beach is small and situated in a tiny bay
that nestles in the arms of two rocky hills. You can position
yourself, somewhere, on one of these arms, and scan the beach
for talent; and in the summer season, there is no shortage.

Julie was a little older than my usual prey but equally beautiful.
She had small, feline features framed by a mass of thick dark-
brown hair. There was something almost leonine about her
appearance. I had noted that she was a recent arrival. The tubes of
sunblock were lined up on her beach towel and her skin was still
white.

As I looked at her I noticed that she was quite fidgety, constantly
shifting. At one point she flipped over, covered her eyes and
looked in my direction. I thought of waving but then decided it
was a bad idea.

Her body was somewhat thin and, I guess, if I'm honest, she
looked a little scrawny, but maybe I wanted a change. It had been
a good summer.

From my vantage-point I viewed the beach like a predatory bird.
Having fixed my target, I descended. On the way down I passed
a few of the locals. Luis, who owned a boutique in town, was
standing, hands on his hips, surveying the beach behind the

upturned hulk of a blue rowing boat. His nephew José was painting the underside.

'*Bom dia*, Nick,'

'*Bom dia.*'

'*Que lindo dia!*'

'*Sim . . .*'

He slapped me on my back. 'So,' he said, 'where is she? *Mostreme?*'

He knew my routine. 'Over there.' I nodded down the beach.

Luis adjusted his shades and said, 'Ahhh, yes, her. A little thin maybe?'

'Maybe.' I grinned back at him as I made my way across the sand. He retained his statuesque pose and, perhaps, just to underscore the fact that his Mediterranean blood was 90 per cent testosterone, he thrust his hips forward. It was a kind of goodwill gesture.

I sat next to Julie and did the usual stuff. At first she didn't want to know and for one dreadful moment I thought I was going to get told to piss off. I knew that Luis would be monitoring my progress, and I really couldn't face his gibes if I fucked up, so I made a big effort and recovered lost ground – but it was difficult.

Things got better when we realized we had quite a lot in common. She was a freelance music journalist. She'd had articles published in most of the main rags and was very knowledgeable. She had even been to see the Free Radicals at the Brixton Academy earlier in the year. Andy, Phil and Scott were still plugging away – successfully – as a three-piece.

'You were in the Free Radicals?'

'Yeah, I played keyboards with them.'

'So what are you doing out here?'

'It's a long story.' I had aroused her curiosity, and she began to become interested in me.

I asked her if I could buy her a drink at one of the bars and walked her down to a little beach restaurant tucked away behind the oddly sculpted coastal rocks.

I was a regular there, and the waiters knew me very well. As soon as Carlo sussed Julie couldn't speak Portuguese he said to me, 'Very nice. D'you think she'll go?'

'I should think so,' I replied.

'What did he say?' asked Julie.

'He said the swordfish is particularly good.' I handed her a menu.

'Are you eating then?'

'Why not? Are you hungry?'

'A little.'

So we had lunch together. And after lunch we slowly sipped our way through two jugs of sangria, filled with delicious fruit. I guess by early afternoon we were both getting quite drunk. The alcohol made Julie more talkative, and I probably learned more about her than she meant me to.

She had been under a lot of stress at work and had recently broken up with her boyfriend. I listened and ordered another jug of sangria. She had decided to get away from it all, to get away for a couple of weeks so as to get her head together. I told her that she had made a very good decision.

The sea was a deep, deep blue and sparkled between the orange rocks. A warm breeze mussed Julie's hair. She looked very sexy. 'I'm sorry,' she said, 'I didn't mean to bore you with all this.'

'I'm not bored,' I replied.

'You must be. What about you? Tell me your long story . . .'

I gave her an edited account of my involvement with the Free Radicals. I told her about Jarl's attempt to rip us off and how Vince got our money back for us. And how I had got pissed off with life in Kilburn and had come out to Carvoeiro to start again. I didn't mention Eric or Cairo.

'That's not a long story,' she said.

'No, I don't suppose it is,' I replied, thinking to myself, *You wouldn't want to hear the rest!*

That afternoon I walked her back to her hotel, an enormous place called the Almansor. I asked if I could see her again, and she said, 'Yeah, sure.'

We saw quite a lot of each other over the next few days. Eventually, I invited her back to my place, and we talked about this and that, but mostly about the music scene in London. I hadn't realized, but I was really, really out of touch. Most of the bands that she rated I'd never heard of.

Julie inspected my CD collection. Sadly, she didn't approve of my early seventies prog-rock, especially the vinyl. 'What have you got all this stuff for?'

I explained that I was a friend of Eric Wright's and that his music had been a big influence, but she looked at me as though I were speaking in Portuguese.

'You've never heard of Eric Wright?'

'Who?'

'Lead guitar with the Turtle Tree?'

'Who?'

'You've never heard *Eugene's Moment of Truth*?'

'Moment of what?'

It was hopeless.

She did however approve of my Hendrix bootlegs. And when she saw my prized 'out-takes' of the Miles Davis and Jimi Hendrix *Voodoo Blue* collaboration, she was seriously impressed.

'How did you get hold of this?' she said.

'Well, you know,' I said nonchalantly, 'contacts . . .' Eric and Cairo had sent it to me for my birthday.

That evening we had dinner outside on the patio. Afterwards, we got pretty stoned. She didn't go back to the Almonsor. We fucked for hours.

It was, I don't know, about two in the morning. We had been engaging in the usual pillow talk. We had also had a few post-coital joints, so I was well out of it. My mind drifted back to London, and I thought about how my life had changed.

Julie said, 'Did you love Cairo?' in a sleepy, distant voice.

I said, 'I've never been to Cairo.'

And Julie answered, 'I didn't mean . . . Oh, it doesn't matter.'

I was too stoned to continue the conversation.

The next morning I got up before Julie and went into the bathroom. She had left her handbag on the floor. It was open and, inside, I could see a small collection of make-up items: a powder compact, a tube of lipstick and some mascara; however, as I was brushing my teeth, I noticed a small pill container. The label read 'Naloxyl 25 mg. Twice daily.' *Did you love Cairo?* she had asked. I lifted the pill container from the bag and stared at it for some time.

acknowledgements

The Arts Council of Great Britain (20/20)
Patrick Walsh (−1.46)
Hannah Robson (−273.16)

FT

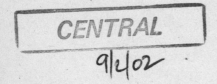